SILVER SCREAMS:

Murder Goes Hollywood

EDITED BY

Cynthia Manson

AND

Adam Stern

LONGMEADOW PRESS
Stamford, Connecticut

We are grateful to the following for permission to reprint their copyrighted material:

DAN FORTUNE AND THE HOLLYWOOD CAPER by Michael Collins, copyright © 1983 by Davis Publications, Inc., reprinted by permission of the author; **FLICKS** by Bill Crenshaw, copyright © 1988 by Davis Publications, Inc., reprinted by permission of the author; **THE MAN WHO LOVED NOIR** by Loren D. Estleman, copyright © 1990 by Davis Publications, Inc., reprinted by permission of the author; all stories have previously appeared in **ALFRED HITCHCOCK MYSTERY MAGAZINE**, published by BANTAM DOUBLEDAY DELL MAGAZINES.

MURDER À LA HOLLYWOOD by Steve Allen, copyright © 1958 by HMH Publishing Co., Inc., reprinted by permission of Meadowlane Enterprises, Inc.; **CLAY LIES STILL** by William Bankier, copyright © 1992 by Bantam Doubleday Dell Magazines, reprinted by permission of Curtis Brown, Ltd.; **UNREASONABLE FACSIMILIE** by George Baxt, copyright © 1990 by Davis Publications, Inc., reprinted by permission of the author; **IS BETSEY BLAKE STILL ALIVE?** by Robert Bloch, copyright © 1958 by Robert Bloch, reprinted by permission of the author; **ONE BIG HAPPY FAMILY** by Lionel Booker, copyright © 1989 by Davis Publications, Inc., reprinted by permission of the Bertha Klausner International Literary Agency; **THE BUM WRAP** by Carleton Carpenter, copyright © 1986 by Davis Publications, Inc., reprinted by permission of the author; **THE CURTAIN** by Raymond Chandler, copyright © 1964 by Helga Greene Literary Agency, reprinted by permission of Ed Victor, Ltd.; **THE TWELFTH STATUE** by Stanley Ellin, copyright © 1967 by Stanley Ellin, reprinted by permission of Curtis Brown, Ltd.; **THE BOOBY TRAP** by Robert L. Fish, copyright © 1980 by Davis Publications, Inc., reprinted by permission of the author; **IF CHRISTMAS COMES** — by Steve Fisher, originally published in *Detective Fiction Weekly* in December 1937, copyright © 1937 by The Red Star News Company, copyright renewed 1964 by Davis Publications, Inc.; **AND THE WINNER IS** — by Ron Goulart, copyright © 1978 by Davis Publications, Inc., reprinted by permission of the author; **CU: MANNIX** by Richard Matheson, copyright © 1991 by Davis Publications, Inc., reprinted by permission of Don Congdon Associates, Inc.; **CLASS ACT** by Jay Speyerer, copyright © 1992 by Bantam Doublday Dell Magazines, reprinted by permission of the author; **HOORAY FOR HOLLYWOOD** by Robert Twohy, copyright © 1989 by Davis Publications, Inc., reprinted by permission of the author; all stories have previously appeared in **ELLERY QUEEN'S MYSTERY MAGAZINES**, published by BANTAM DOUBLEDAY DELL MAGAZINES.

Interior Design by Pamela C. Pia

This Longmeadow Press edition is printed on archival quality paper. It is acid-free and conforms to the guidelines established for permanence and durability by the Council of Library Resources and the American National Standards Institute. ∞™

Library of Congress Cataloging-in-Publication Data
Silver screams, murder goes Hollywood / edited by Cynthia Manson and Adam Stern.
    p. cm.
  ISBN 0-681-00753-2 :
   1. Detective and mystery stories, American—California—Los Angeles. 2. Motion picture industry—California—Los Angeles—Fiction. 3. Hollywood (Los Angeles, Calif.)—Fiction. I. Manson, Cynthia. II. Stern, Adam.
PS648.D4S55 1994
813'.0872083279494—dc20

                                                                94-19561
                                                                  CIP
                                                                   AC

Printed and bound in the United States of America.
First Longmeadow Press edition.
0 9 8 7 6 5 4 3 2 1

Contents

v INTRODUCTION

1 MURDER À LA HOLLYWOOD **Steve Allen**

7 CLAY LIES STILL **William Bankier**

21 THE MAN WHO LOVED *NOIR*
Loren D. Estleman

37 HOORAY FOR HOLLYWOOD **Robert Twohy**

55 CU: MANNIX **Richard Matheson**

67 THE BUM WRAP **Carleton Carpenter**

77 THE BOOBY TRAP **Robert L. Fish**

83 FLICKS **Bill Crenshaw**

105 DAN FORTUNE AND THE HOLLYWOOD
CAPER **Michael Collins**

119 IF CHRISTMAS COMES **Steve Fisher**

133 AND THE WINNER IS — **Ron Goulart**

143 CLASS ACT **Jay Speyerer**

155 THE CURTAIN **Raymond Chandler**

189 ONE BIG HAPPY FAMILY **Lionel Booker**

201 THE TWELFTH STATUE **Stanley Ellin**

243 UNREASONABLE FACSIMILE **George Baxt**

253 IS BETSEY BLAKE STILL ALIVE?
Robert Bloch

Introduction

WE LIVE IN A SOCIETY THAT is obsessed with the glamour of Hollywood and the talent that comprises this community. One needs only to see the vast amount of newspaper and magazine space devoted to filmmakers, dealmakers, and stars to witness the aura of celebrity that surrounds them. Mystery writers find Hollywood an ideal setting for the kind of tale of intrigue, passion and crime so often portrayed successfully in films themselves. SILVER SCREAMS: MURDER GOES HOLLYWOOD brings you a strong lineup of well-known authors and suspenseful stories that have appeared in *Ellery Queen's Mystery Magazine* and *Alfred Hitchcock Mystery Magazine*.

Raymond Chandler captures the essence of film noir in "The Curtain," his brilliant portrayal of an actor on the brink of losing his most precious possession: fame. Robert L. Fish brings us an explosive tale of a Hollywood bombshell who lives up to her drop-dead looks in "The Booby Trap." Steve Allen's "Murder à la Hollywood" examines the power of film as a psychological weapon, while Robert Twohy depicts the creative genius that lies behind the making of an action thriller in "Hooray for Hollywood." Stanley Ellin takes us on location in "The Twelfth Statue" which stars a temperamental director who fails to arrive for the final shoot. In "Is Betsey Blake Still Alive?" Robert Bloch exposes the lengths to which a star will go in order to escape her adoring fans. "The Man Who Loved Noir" by Loren D. Estleman demonstrates that life imitates art when the protagonist acts out the violence he sees on screen.

These are only a few clips from the action that takes place in SILVER SCREAMS: MURDER GOES HOLLYWOOD. You will find the stories of suspense and surprise included in this anthology entertaining and provocative. Get yourself a bag of popcorn, settle into your seat, and enjoy this collection of four-star stories.

— The Editors

SILVER SCREAMS:

Murder Goes Hollywood

Murder à la Hollywood

by Steve Allen

THE POLICE ARE NOT SUR-
prised when, in connection with a highly publicized murder that has
gone unsolved, a number of people come forth to confess to the crime.

It is, on the other hand, unusual if not unknown for a man to
confess to having committed a murder when beyond the shadow of a
doubt a suicide rather than a killing was involved. That is why nobody
paid any attention to Walt Swanson when he said he had murdered
David Starbuck.

Starbuck killed himself in the bathroom of his palatial Palm Springs
home on the night of September 14th. There were at least 30 people
who knew that Swanson had spent that night at the bar of the Villa
Loma, a spaghetti-and-rendezvous joint on the Sunset Strip.

The door of Starbuck's toilet was locked from the inside. He had
slashed his wrists, stretched out on the pink tile floor with a folded
bathmat under his head, and died almost peacefully. As one wag said
when Swanson first confessed that *he* had cut Starbuck's wrists,
although it was clearly established that he had been in Beverly Hills
on the night in question, "Must have had a mighty long razor."

The police spent a little time checking Swanson's story, marked
him as a psycho, and told him to get lost. I guess I'm the only one who
knows that he was telling the truth after all, because I listened to the
whole story.

To say that Starbuck was not widely admired is to win the understatement championship of any year. The movie business is never short of phonies but Dave was the champ. He came out here in the late Thirties with a reputation as a hot-shot salesman and there was always the vague idea that he had *had* to come West, that something he had been involved in in the East had not been strictly on the up and up. The idea was founded on bedrock. Dave had got into the habit of selling things he didn't own. In Hollywood he soon found that this trick could be valuable. First he palmed himself off as a writer, sold a book he hadn't written, stole half the profits from the poor bum who did write it, wangled a share of the production arrangement, and found himself with a smash on his hands. From there on in there was no stopping him.

By 1945 he was second in command at World-American, living in Bel Air with his fourth wife, and climbing fast by reason of his shrewd and ruthless ability to manipulate men with big talent and small guts.

But I am getting ahead of myself, as they say. Let's go back a wife or two. We never knew just who Dave was married to back East. She never made the trip. He stole his second woman from Walt Swanson. Nobody but the old-timers remember much about Walt now, but in his time he was the greatest cameramen of them all. Some of the old stars wouldn't make a picture without him. Eventually he started directing and he would have made a fine director except that he began belting the bottle. Charming as he was sober, he was a mean drunk. They put up with his bats for a couple of years but eventually the word got around that hiring him for a picture meant added costs in lost shooting time. He never had a prayer after that. Well, no, he did have one chance. Dave Starbuck hired him for a picture and made a rather peculiar deal with him.

"Walt," Dave said, "here's the arrangement. Nobody else in town will hire you because you're a stew-bum, right? Here's my offer. I'll give you your regular price for this picture and you get it the day we're through shooting, in one lump. Unless you start drinking. The first day you're drunk on the set the money drops to 50 per cent. If you pull it a second time you get 25 per cent. Take it or leave it."

Walt took it. You have to eat.

The third week of shooting Starbuck hired an out-of-work writer to take Walt to lunch and get him loaded. Then he came around to the set after lunch, walked up to Swanson, smiled broadly, smelled Walt's breath, and said, "Cheer up, baby. At fifty per cent you're still being overpaid." Walt's ego being what it was, he went on a week's bender. Starbuck threatened to throw him off the picture. Eventually he paid him peanuts and kicked him out. In desperation Walt sent his wife around to plead for a break.

"Listen, sweetie," Dave said, "what do you want from me? We made a deal."

"But Dave," Swanson's wife said, "Walt's having a rough time. He did a good job for you, didn't he?"

Dave looked at Swanson's wife. She had good legs and was years younger than Walt.

"Listen, Myrna," he said, "doesn't it make you feel sorta cheap to have to go around town begging for handouts for a has-been like Walt? You deserve better than that. You're a looker. I happen to know you have talent. You should be acting again. Whaddaya say we forget about the deal Walt and I made? It's all over. He made his bed. Let him lie in it. But let's say you have a small part in my next picture, at pretty good money. Now how's that?"

Well, when you're a former call girl, when you'd love to do a little picture work, when you're married to a man 20 years your senior, and when you married him in the first place just because you were tired and he offered some place to rest, a pitch like Starbuck's is pretty hard to resist. To spare the painful details, within six months Myrna had left Walt and moved in with Dave.

That did it. Walt was no good after that. Never directed another picture. It must have been about that time that he first thought of killing Starbuck. He wasn't the first, of course, nor the only one, but he must have been head of the club.

The philosophers tell us that when you lust after a woman in your heart, or long to commit a murder, you're already on record, even if you never get to realize your ambition. On that basis I guess quite a few of us around town are guilty of the murder of David Starbuck. But here's how Walt Swanson did it.

By 1955 he was all washed up as a director, although Alcoholics Anonymous had put him back in one physical piece for the time being. To pay for the booze he had sold everything he had and now to keep eating he had to take any odd job he could get. An old friend eventually landed him a spot with Consolidated Film Service, a subsidiary of the Consolidated Studio, that did film exchange work. For example, when a wealthy producer wanted to go to the movies, well, it didn't work out that way. The movies went to him. His secretary just called the film exchange, ordered a certain picture, or maybe a double feature, and the films were shipped to the producer's home, to be shown in his private projection room, for his private pleasure. Walt Swanson thought it was a pretty grim joke the first time he got an order to ship a can of film to Starbuck's Bel Air pleasure-dome.

Then one day he learned that Starbuck had an ulcer. A snatch of conversation overheard at a restaurant and Walt's own stomach tingled in a momentary frenzy of vengeful glee. So Dave Starbuck could be hurt after all, if only by his conscience, his own fears. At the time that Walt noted this fact he did not file it away with any conscious realization that eventually he would be able to call it out, to employ it. It was just something he heard about and was glad about, and that was that.

The catalyst was dropped into the seething caldron of his mind a year later when he read a story in the *Hollywood Reporter* about subliminal advertising. A theater in New Jersey had cut into a motion picture film some commercial announcements that flashed on the screen too quickly to be seen consciously but, according to the theory, not too quickly to transmit to the eye and the subconscious mind an impression which subsequently would suggest action to the individual. In the test case the action suggested was the purchase of a particular soft drink. Sales of the drink increased markedly on the night of the test.

It was after reading that story that Walt Swanson began to get even with David Starbuck. At first the idea of murder was not actually in his mind. He only wanted to hurt, to lash out, to avenge himself. The first thing he did was to print up two small cards, using white ink on black paper. One card said, *Dave Starbuck, you stink*. The other one said, *Everybody hates David Starbuck*. Then he borrowed a handoperated movie camera from a friend, shot stills of the two cards, clipped out the film frames, put them into his wallet, and waited.

Within a week Starbuck's secretary called to order a picture. When Walt received the shipping slip he got the film out of the vault, set it up on spools, scissored a line, and inserted one of the still frames he had shot at home. Twenty minutes farther along on the reel he slipped in the second insert.

The picture was a comedy, but that night after running it Dave Starbuck didn't feel amused. A certain insensitivity had always been part of his make-up, but faced even subconsciously with the knowledge that he was actively disliked, and being at the same time unable to erect any of his customary defenses, he became vaguely depressed.

Swanson at first, and for a long time afterward, had no sure way of knowing how effective his attack was; but eventually he began to pick up stray bits of information that convinced him that he was striking telling blows. Column items about suddenly planned vacations, rumors about physical checkups, stories about angry blowups in conference rooms. And only Swanson knew the reason. Once a week for a whole year he sent his invisible arrows into Starbuck's hide. *Starbuck, you're no good.*

Dave, you're a heel.

Starbuck, you're sick.

And every Monday when the film would come back to the exchange Walt would scissor out his inserts and patch up the reel, leaving no evidence.

Starbuck, your wife despises you!

David Starbuck is a jerk!

Starbuck, you are the lowest of the low.

Starbuck's irritation increased to the point where he became careless about his attitude toward his superiors, and in Hollywood no matter how high up you are, you have to answer to somebody: chairmen of the board, stockholders' groups. One night at a party he told the head of his studio's New York office to go to hell. From that moment he started to slide downhill, although at first his speed was so slow nobody was quite sure he was moving.

It was about that time that Swanson aimed his *coup de grâce*. The next time Starbuck had a picture run off he received this message: *Dave, why don't you kill yourself?*

The following week it was: *Kill yourself, Dave. It's the only way out.*

Starbuck put up with eight weeks of it. He began to fall apart. Having no friends to sympathize with him, he went from bad to worse fast. Then one day he went to Palm Springs, spent all afternoon lying in the sun by his swimming pool, got drunk, went into the bathroom, locked the door, lay down on the pink tile floor, folded the fluffy lamb's-wool bath mat under his head, slashed his wrists with a single-edged razor, and bled to death, slowly, lying still.

After it happened Walt began drinking again. I wouldn't be telling the story now except that, as some of you may know, poor Walt got careless with a cigarette one night in the lab and burned himself up along with a hell of a lot of film. A few weeks before the end he told me the story one night at the Villa Loma bar.

Good thing Walt didn't work in a TV film lab.

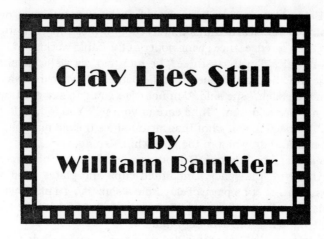

Clay Lies Still

by
William Bankier

THE SHOP WAS CALLED "MUGZ" and it was on the wrong end of Melrose, near La Brea. When Ted Beldon entered through the open doorway, a hidden device went beep. Waiting for someone to respond to the signal, he looked at shelves of ceramic mugs and plates, all brightly painted with vines, wide-eyed faces, and animals.

"How can I help you?" A slender girl with straight dark hair drawn across one shoulder had come in from a back room. She was wiping her hands on a dusty apron.

"I saw your sign in the window." She was not a girl, she was a woman in her forties, probably. But slim and fit. "Help wanted? I'd like to apply."

Her eyes ran him up and down. Beldon believed an interview was over, one way or the other, in this first instant. She was curious. After nearly two months in Los Angeles, he had picked up no protective coloration. He still looked like upstate New York; the bored bank teller fleeing Algonquin Landing while there was still time.

"The job is in two parts," she said. "I can see you'd be okay for the shop." She offered a hand. "I'm Martina Carr." He said who he was. "I need help making cups and plates. Could you work with clay?"

"In nursery school, I majored in mud pies."

"Let me show you what's involved."

So Beldon was suddenly anchored again after weeks of drifting. One thing he had learned was that freedom comes with fear attached. He had been on edge since giving notice at the bank, working at keeping up his morale. "I'm thirty-three," he had told his sister as she fried sausages and he drank a beer from the bottle. "I have to make a move."

"You'll be back," she said. "I'm not even going to say good-bye."

His mother told him, "Take care of yourself. You're just like your father." No need to ask what that meant since the old man had fallen off the pier and drowned in the lake while fishing.

In Martina's back room, Beldon was charmed by the broad work table, the light, the space. Unpainted cups and plates filled several shelves. Martina cut a piece of clay from a slab using a piano wire with a wooden handle at either end. He was reminded of the device used to strangle Luca Brasi in *The Godfather*.

She pressed clay flat with a rolling pin. She cut a circle with what she called a needle-tool, peeling away the excess from the circumference. "We're making a saucer," she explained. "Do what I'm doing. Get your hands dirty."

An hour later, there were two grey saucers in front of the high stool where Beldon was perched. The second was better than the first.

"You can do this," she said. "When can you start?"

Beldon walked back to his upstairs room in the old house on Orange Grove. Purple bougainvillea brushed his head as he ducked in through the front doorway and took the steps two at a time. Inside the tiny room, he was so excited he shadowboxed on the worn carpet, tossing jabs at the pine table, at the floor lamp, at the tall bureau with the framed snapshot of his mother and sister beside the hollyhocks near the kitchen door. Then he fell backwards onto the bed, tingling.

It was happening! Weeks of wandering the streets, eating late in restaurants, drinking alone, had not been wasted. He had been learning the lay of the land. Hollywood was a disappointment. It took about ten minutes to inspect the famous footprints outside the Chinese Theater. Then it was just streets full of drunks and junkies and some truly sick, weird people.

Beldon took pride in staying out of trouble. But he was running out of money. And his dream, that he would get to know famous people, had not come true.

Now, suddenly, he was working for Martina Carr. They had talked for a long time, agreeing schedules and the seven-dollar-an-hour wage. She was the daughter of Jackson Carr, the movie director. Beldon recognized the name. Carr made a lot of B-movies in the forties and fifties and banked plenty of money. When he died ten years ago, he left Martina well fixed with a cottage on King's Road above Sunset Boulevard. Her mother was somewhere in Europe.

Beldon's new employer was quick to see the effect she was having on him and decided to orient him, tactfully, from the start. She said, "You'll be meeting my boyfriend, Skid Wilder. He's a character and a half. Used to be a stunt driver before he racked himself up."

So the relationship was squared away. They could be friends, nothing more. Beldon liked to know where he stood

He slept. It was dark in the room when he awoke. No work tomorrow; he was due to come in at nine on the following day. Beldon got into his other jeans and pulled on the English rugby jersey he had brought with him from back East. Then he left the house and walked flat out along residential streets, making up his mind which bar he would visit first.

When the telephone rang, Beldon was alone in the shop. He picked up the workroom extension and said, "Mugz."

"Is Marty there?" A woman's voice.

"She's out right now. Can I take a message?"

"Who are you?" The rudeness was defused by a tone of childlike curiosity.

"I'm Ted. First day on the job."

"Okay, first-day Ted. I'm Sandy Feldenheimer. Tell your boss I'll be around in a few days to pick up the tiles." Before hanging up, she added, "Please and thank you for a Tootsie Roll."

The name rang a bell. The only Feldenheimer he knew of was the former Olympic swimmer, Larry Feldenheimer, now deceased, who had starred in a series of black-and-white movies as "Zardol, King of the Jungle." Beldon and his friends loved them. Zardol was always swimming to the rescue through crocodile-infested waters. Was it possible the woman was related to the star?

When Martina returned from her errands, she was not alone. Skid Wilder was with her. It was like shaking hands with a tree. Wilder was the size of an offensive tackle. He wore, in fact, a black and silver Raiders T-shirt. The high-domed head was bald on top. Massive forearms gleamed with golden hair.

Beldon gave Martina the message and asked his question.

She said, "Oh sure. Sandy is Larry's widow. She's a lot younger. He left her a real nice piece of property in Coldwater Canyon."

"I must have seen every movie he made."

"Better you than me. My father directed a couple of them. He thought they were squat."

Wilder was taking in the conversation with half a grin on his face, the big head turning back and forth, pale eyes alert as if this was a new game he would have to learn to play. "Tell him about the ditzy daughter. Tell him about Ferris."

"Ferris Feldenheimer," Martina recited, "is nineteen years old, awesomely beautiful, and pure poison. Sandy has already paid twice to have her detoxed at a very expensive clinic."

"The kid snorts more cocaine than a Philly jazz band," Wilder said.

"While Larry was alive," Martina continued, "it was Ferris and him against Sandy. Dad spoiled her, Mom was the cop. Now all Ferris wants from Sandy is money. I've heard her. She'd like her mother to die so she can inherit."

The stunt driver had to go. Watching him out the door and past the window, Beldon got a look at the limp. He swung his left foot forward and the boot hit the pavement as if it were a rock on a rope. Martina said, "They did a lot of work rebuilding one whole side of him."

"Did he crash on a stunt?"

"No. Skid had a perfect record in the industry. Then he goes and totals his car on the freeway. He fell asleep and went over the side."

"Can he drive now?"

"Not and get paid." Martina went into the workroom, then she came out again and stood in the doorway. "Does he spook you?"

Beldon was afraid of Wilder but he was not ready to admit it. "I'll just be careful not to make any sudden moves."

"Skid thinks of me as his personal property. Any other man around, Skid keeps watching him. Some people get freaked."

"Thanks for the warning."

When the shop closed that evening at six, Martina borrowed Beldon to help her transport several cartons of mugs to the cottage on King's Road. She would be delivering them tomorrow morning, early, to a customer in the Valley.

The house was white stucco, wedged into the hillside, mostly concealed by willows and palms. When he was all done carrying, Beldon stood on a concrete patio looking down onto the next level at a circular pool brimming with blue water. "Take a swim!" Martina yelled from an open window.

"I don't have a suit."

"We stock all sizes."

She showed him where to change. The bathing suit was extremely brief. He frowned at his reflection in a full-length mirror; pale body, sunburned forearms, face, and neck.

He was doing slow lengths when he made a turn and saw Skid Wilder standing poolside with a drink in his hand. The lopsided grin revolved as the big man chewed ice. Irrationally, Beldon was afraid Wilder would think he had nothing on. He climbed the chrome ladder, then had to tug the soaked bikini back up across his belly.

"Job has perks," the stuntman said.

"Water feels good."

"One of these days, I'll have to challenge you. When I'm sober."

Martina appeared with a tray of snacks. "That day may never come," she said.

Beldon ate an olive. He swallowed some beer. Wilder was sprawled now in a deckchair, looking nowhere but at him. A chilly breeze flickered down from the hills.

"I have to go," Beldon said.

"Don't run away," Martina said. "We're here for the evening."

He toweled himself off in the bathroom and got into his clothes. They were clammy from the carrying. He came out to say goodbye and Martina said, "Need a lift?"

"I can walk where I'm going."

"You shouldn't let this bastard drive you away."

Skid was watching him with profound amusement, as if Beldon with his anxiety, his confusion, his cowardice, had been hired to entertain him. "I have someplace I have to be," Beldon said.

"And here I thought we were going to get to know each other," Wilder said.

It was days later, in the shop. Skid Wilder cleared his throat and Beldon almost leaped onto a display of plates. He had not noticed the big man in the doorway. "Sorry about that," the stuntman said. He came inside. Large hands adjusted Beldon's position on the floor, like a displaced piece of furniture.

"Martina isn't here."

"I know. I came to see you."

"What about?"

"Let me buy you a drink."

Through his panic, Beldon felt flattered. "I have to work."

Skid frowned at his watch. "It's five-thirty. The store closes at six." Then, after a pause, "I'm not your enemy."

They drove to Westwood in Wilder's shiny Buick, the stuntman taking the Sunset Boulevard curves with ease. "There's the driveway Bill Holden pulled into in the movie."

Beldon was intrigued. It sure looked like the driveway. His chauffeur cut down Hilgard and turned right on Le Conte. They drove past the UCLA Medical Center and parked outside Alice's Restaurant.

The place had a long, wide bar. They climbed onto padded stools with low backs. Wilder ordered bourbon and Beldon asked for a beer.

"One time," Wilder began, "I was working on the 'Hampton' series." He was referring to a long-running TV serial about a detective in a battered car. The stuntman told a story about missing a ramp and plowing into the bus he was supposed to vault at fifty miles an hour. The car was heavily braced and he was securely belted in. Even so, he had to live with two cracked ribs. But the smash was so spectacular, they used it in the episode. "I told the director I figured he hid that ramp on purpose."

The men ate at a table and went on drinking. Wilder got onto the subject of a pro football player, a charismatic giant who had been reduced within months by brain cancer to a big-eyed, hairless talk-show guest. Beldon had witnessed that interview. "I wonder if they've told him he's dying?"

"I think about dying all the time," the stuntman said. "Like any other event that's part of my life."

"Skid, you're morbid."

"No, it's cool. You're only afraid of the unknown. Death is as familiar to me as where I live." Wilder looked thoughtful. "I'll know it when I see it."

As darkness fell, they left Alice's, drove out of Westwood, and headed back to L.A. Wilder drove the straight stretch of Santa Monica Boulevard past the towers of Century City and the lawns of Beverly Hills. In West Hollywood, he parked outside a raucous bar open to the street. The clientele here was all male. Some of them tried to flirt with the giant newcomer.

Focusing on Beldon, Wilder drank doubles and became sour. His mood had gone off. He was bitter and resentful, reciting a litany of injustices. The freeway crash was lousy luck. He would never work again. It was humiliating being supported by Martina. Didn't Beldon realize that? Sure, she kept him for free in the house on King's Road. But she doled out the money. He hated being owned.

Beldon could only listen apprehensively.

It got worse. Wilder went to the bathroom and when he came back to the bar, he was wearing a secret smile. "Can I trust you?"

"Yes."

"The Feldenheimer woman, Sandy. She has more money than she knows what to do with. I been thinking of ripping her off."

"It's getting late, Skid."

"I know her schedule. She and Marty are always telling each other what they're doing."

Beldon did not want to hear this.

"I can get in. Sandy and Martina have keys to each other's homes so they can feed the cats. Some day when Sandy is away, I intend to drop around and help myself to some valuable stuff. On the way out, I can bust a door or a window to show forced entry."

"This is supposed to make you feel better about yourself?" Beldon pretended to scan a headline. "Famous stuntman jailed for burglary."

Wilder's mood was swinging back to joyful. "I have you figured for my partner. You can hold the velvet sack while I grab the jewels."

"Now I know you're kidding."

"It's important to get involved in life, Teddy. Like the poet said, 'Clay lies still, but blood's a rover.' "

Beldon had read A. E. Housman in school and was astonished to hear the lines from the drunken stuntman's lips. "I work with clay," he said.

Wilder winked. "I figured that would grab you."

That evening, while the men were drinking in Westwood, Martina's telephone rang about nine. "Can you talk?" It was Sandy Feldenheimer.

"Sure. What's up?" .

"Do you know where Skid is tonight?"

"He's gone boozing with my new assistant. The guy just blew in from back East. He's terrified of Skid, it's embarrassing. Skid decided to try and cool him out."

"I'm scared stiff about Ferris."

"Ferris will take advantage of you as long as you let her."

"I want you to keep Skid away from her."

"That was all over last year."

"He was here this afternoon. I came home and found him in the house. There was no sign of a car, he must have parked down the hill."

"Did Ferris let him in?"

"She wasn't here. He must have made a copy of the key I gave you."

"But why?"

"At first I thought he was coming on to me. Then I could tell he wasn't interested. So it has to be Ferris. Maybe he called her and she was supposed to meet him. I don't know what those two are up to."

"So then he left?"

"After going around and picking things up and putting them down. Like he was assessing their value. It was spooky."

On the following morning, Beldon walked to work. The marine layer was heavy, it would not burn off before noon. Under the grey overcast, he might have thought he was back in Algonquin Landing.

But not when he looked at the storefronts. They had names like "Wacko!" and "Cool." A hamburger restaurant was shaped like a hamburger, down to the sesame seeds on the round brown roof.

Stopping for a cappuccino at the Continental Bakery, he reflected that he was on a sharp hook. He could only hope that Skid was joking last night, or too drunk to remember. The robbery plan put Beldon in a tight spot. He now knew that Wilder intended to rob Sandy Feldenheimer. Surely he had to tell Martina so she could warn her friend.

But Martina would call in Skid and confront him. With Beldon in the room. Skid would deny everything. Either he never said it, or Beldon was unable to recognize a joke when he heard it. Beldon could not win. He would end up in Skid's bad books. He might get hurt.

Why should he risk himself? Zardol's widow was no friend of his. And what if Wilder did end up robbing the house? She was rich as they come. And the stuff must be insured. Beldon drained the foamy coffee dregs and walked on down the street to "Mugz."

A vintage white Thunderbird was moored at a meter. The girl behind the wheel watched him as he fished out the key entrusted to him by the owner so she could sleep late.

"Where the hell is Martina!" Bracelets jangled as the girl brought a fist down on the steering wheel.

Beldon opened the door and stood in the doorway. The smell from inside was reassuringly familiar. Try as he would to be a rover Ted Beldon seemed destined for stability. "Martina shows around eleven."

"Who are you?" The girl drew herself up from behind the wheel, taking a sitting position on top of the front seat. There were tanned knees and thighs and slender shoulders in a cut-off denim shirt. But it was the bone-hard, wasted face and the emerald eyes widely spaced that put Beldon in mind of a hungry animal. That and something else.

She looked familiar. Even the shoulder-length sun-bleached hair was the same. Here was the daughter of Zardol, King of the Jungle. 'I'm Ted Beldon," he said. "And you must be Ferris."

She was accustomed to being recognized. She kicked off her sandals and braced bare feet against the steering wheel. "I need a couple of hundred dollars," she announced. "Marty is my mother's best friend. She often advances me money and Sandy pays her back."

Beldon said nothing.

"You can give me the money. Marty won't mind."

"I have no such authority." Beldon enjoyed being in a position to turn this kid down.

"Can you give me some cash yourself? I'll pay you back."

"I don't have it." He felt humiliated now, diminished in her eyes "Why don't you get it from your mother?"

Ferris dropped back down behind the wheel. "Because she's a greedy, stingy, vicious, jealous bitch." She turned the key, the engine roared, and the car wheeled away down Melrose.

Martina called at ten-thirty. The buyer from Bullock's wanted to see her so she would not be in until mid-afternoon. Beldon told her about his encounter with Ferris. "You did the right thing," his employer said. "What time did you and Skid finish up last night?"

"I hit the sack around one o'clock."

"Skid didn't show up till four." A pause. "Did Ferris mention his name?"

"She only talked about you. And the money you'd give her if you were here."

"Have you noticed how people lie all the time?"

Beldon made up his mind. "Skid is getting ready to rob Sandy's house," he said. "He told me last night."

"You believed him?"

"He sounded serious. You know him better than I do."

"Skid has a good thing going." Martina sounded confident. "I don't think he'd throw it all away by doing something ridiculous."

It was one o'clock. Beldon had eaten his peanut butter sandwich and swallowed his room temperature Pepsi. He was feeling good because he had sold six mugs and a large platter to a couple from Fresno. But he was still disturbed about Skid Wilder's scheme. Skid had put him in the picture. If the robbery went down, would he qualify as an accessory before the fact? Martina had not taken his warning seriously. Should he think about calling the police? From what Beldon knew, the police were not able to take any action unless and until a crime actually took place.

Now here came Skid Wilder with a rangy, silver-haired woman who had to be Sandy Feldenheimer. Without introductions, she said, "Marty called me. Ferris was here?"

"At nine. She was waiting outside."

"You didn't give her any money?"

"No."

"Don't ever give her any. Not a red cent."

The woman's dictatorial manner disturbed Beldon. He saw Skid observing his reaction with a poker face. "I didn't have any to give her."

The swimmer's widow was not insensitive. "You two can enjoy this all you want. I happen to be the mother."

"If Martina shows up," Skid said, "tell her I'm buying this one lunch."

"Tell her he wants to mend fences," Sandy said. "Marty will understand. I'm accepting because I can use all the help I can get."

Skid straightened the collar of Beldon's shirt and flicked invisible lint from his shoulder. "Thought any more about our project?"

So much for hoping it was only the booze talking last night. Beldon considered warning the woman right now. He could hear himself saying, "Guess what, Skid is getting ready to steal you blind." And the stuntman laughing him off.

"We don't have a project," he said in response to Skid's query.

"Don't be too sure."

"I'm calling the detox center as soon as I get home." Sandy said. "I want them to come and get Ferris."

"She won't go," Skid warned.

"She'll go or I'll get the police to come and drag her."

Martina was walking on air when she showed up at four. The department store had placed a large order. Beldon would be building cups and plates overtime. He told her about Sandy's fence-mending lunch with Skid, and her intention to sock Ferris back inside.

"The tragedy plays itself out." Martina was not focusing on her friend's problem. She was filled to the brim with her own success.

"I have to say this. Skid brought it up again. I think he really intends to rob that house."

"Ted, what am I supposed to do?"

"Talk to him. If he knows you know, maybe he'll forget about it."

"You'd like me to say you told me?" Her smile illuminated his fear of Wilder.

"All right, he scares me. I'd rather he didn't have a reason to be my enemy." Beldon had to retaliate. "You're the reason he wants to steal."

"I'm not his keeper. He's free to go anytime he wants." Martina shook her head to clear it. "I can't believe you're on my case. After a couple of weeks. Los Angeles sure works on people." She headed for the back room. "I want Sandy to pick up the rest of her tiles. We'll need the space."

While the boss was on the telephone, Beldon sold four more cups to a woman whose friend had bought some a week ago.

Martina came back looking peeved. "She doesn't answer the telephone."

"Taking Ferris to the clinic?"

"Whatever. I want you to load the rest of Sandy's tiles into the trunk of my car and deliver them to her house in the Canyon." She gave him a set of keys which included one for the car and one for the Felden-heimer front door, "I'll draw you a map," she said.

In this last hour before sundown, most cars had their lights on. The winding road taking him up into the hills provided an exciting ride. As the car climbed, the air became cooler. His heart was pounding when he saw, finally, the red shingled roof Martina had said would be his signal to wheel in and stop on a narrow gravel forecourt.

The white Thunderbird was tucked in snugly beside the mock-Tudor bungalow. There were no lights on inside the house. When he switched off and got out of the car, Beldon found himself substantially in the dark.

He unlocked the trunk. The tiles were individually wrapped in newspaper and stacked carefully in wicker baskets. They were heavy. One basket was enough to carry.

He took a moment to admire the web of city lights below. The air was cleaner here. The scent of pine put him in mind of Algonquin Landing. He was still calculating the time difference. Three hours later back East. His mother and sister would have watched the late news, eating bridge mix and drinking Mountain Dew. They would be checking the late movies in the guide now, deploring the colorization of *Key Largo*.

Beldon carried a basket of tiles to the broad oak door with its half-moon panel of stained glass. He could not see a bellpush. He knocked and waited. Then he used the key. The door swung open and he walked through into a shadowy interior, feeling his way, searching for a light switch on the wall. He inhaled an unfamiliar scent, something like damp rust.

His hand touched a switch. He flicked it and bright light poured from an overhead fixture. He was in a narrow vestibule leading into a lounge area. The place was in disarray. Cushions had been dragged from an upholstered sofa. A few books remained on shelves, the rest were scattered across the floor. The glass in a mirror above a desk was shattered.

Behind the desk, a swivel chair lay on its side. There was something else; Beldon could see silver hair, a bare shoulder. Breathing hard, he went that way, stood on the other side of the desk, looked down on the body of Sandy Feldenheimer. What he had smelled was fresh blood, lots of it, flooding from a wound in her naked back. She was wearing only a pastel silk robe. Clearly, the woman was dead.

It was time to dial 911. Beldon saw a telephone on a small table near the front door.

"Don't even think about it," Ferris Feldenheimer said.

She was watching him from a dark doorway at the other end of the room. He had not noticed her because she was sitting on the floor, leaning against the doorframe, an automatic pistol held in both hands and balanced across her knees. Her eyes were vacant, like those of a child allowed to stay up much too late.

"Don't you recognize me?" he said. "I'm delivering the rest of your mother's tiles."

"No. You came in here and saw her with nothing on." Said in a dreary monotone. "You got excited, you tried to put your hands on her. She screamed. I ran in and yelled at you but you wouldn't let her loose. I tried to shoot you. You used her as a shield. Then," Ferris cocked the gun, "you came at me so I had to kill you."

Skid Wilder said from the doorway, "If that's what happened, why is the place all torn up?" He came into the room.

"Be careful," Beldon said.

"I came looking for my drinking buddy. Martina said you were on deliveries." Wilder surveyed the room. "Hey, what an opportunity to do what we talked about."

Ferris got to her feet. She was having trouble standing but the gun looked steady as a rock. "I'm not going back to that clinic. She was getting ready to call the police to take me in. We fought and she was winning. So I ran and got Dad's gun."

"Hand it over," the stuntman said.

"Keep back!"

"She means it, Skid!"

"You need help, girl." Wilder made a move in her direction. "Don't make things worse."

Ferris squeezed the trigger, three times, rapidly. The sudden noise shocked Beldon. He saw Wilder break step, then go to his knees. He extended one hand, reaching for the gun. Then he sank forward and lay face down.

Beldon knew he was going to die. The gun swung and pointed at him. The girl's finger squeezed again. The hammer clicked on an empty chamber. Again, click. Children with toy weapons. Beldon went to her and pinned her arms. She put up no resistance. He took hold of the gun. She let it go.

"All you had to do," Ferris moaned, "was give me some money. This is all your fault."

The ambulance drove away. The police, sealing the house, told Beldon he could go. But they would want to interview him further tomorrow. He drove out of the Canyon and took Sunset Boulevard most of the way back to the shop.

It was time to consider what he was going to do. How about getting out of Los Angeles, away from the crazies and the bad air? Skid would have rejected that idea out of hand. You don't go back, you go forward.

He found himself thinking about importing his mother and sister, plucking them out of the path of another approaching winter. They could sell the house in Algonquin Landing. His sister could find a job. The old lady might even buy a fancy track suit and make a nuisance of herself mornings in the mall.

Martina was in the workroom waiting for him. His telephone call had only scratched the surface. He told the whole story now.

"I'll never figure Skid Wilder out," she said when he was finished. "We had a good thing going. But he had to keep messing around with Sandy and that crazy kid. I never thought she'd kill him, though."

Beldon knew how Wilder would want to be remembered. "Skid did what he did because it was something to do. Not because he was a thief or he needed the money. Planning to rip off your friend's house was something to do. So was stepping in front of Ferris's gun. He explained it when we were drinking the other night." The Housman poem was vivid in Beldon's mind. He picked it up now and continued where Skid had left off. Martina listened, trying to comprehend.

"Clay lies still but blood's a rover,
Breath's a ware that will not keep,
Up lad, when the journey's over,
There'll be time enough for sleep."

"I suppose I'll be losing you now," Martina said. "I sent you up there and you nearly got killed."

"No, but maybe you can help me get a car." Beldon could feel Skid's influence speaking out. "This town is a dead end if you don't have a car."

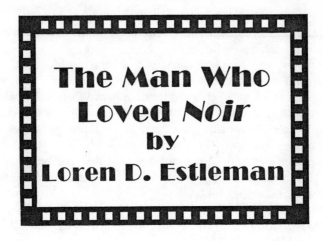

The Man Who Loved *Noir*
by
Loren D. Estleman

HE ADDRESS I'D WRITTEN down belonged to a house in Lathrup Village three miles north of Detroit, the only one in a cul-de-sac that ended in a berry thicket and a cyclone fence. It was a cool, sprawling ranch-style of brick and frame with four great oaks in the yard arranged in such a way that the house would always be in shade. I felt the sweat drying on my body during the short walk from my car to the front door.

A woman in a gray dress and white apron with her hair caught up by combs led me into a sunken living room and went away. She spoke little English.

"Thank you for coming on such short notice, Mr. Walker. I'm Gay Cully."

She'd come in through an open sliding glass door from a patio in back when I was looking in another direction, a small compact redhaired woman with the sun behind her. Assuming she'd planned her entrance, that put her over forty. She had large eyes mascaraed all around, a pixie mouth, and a fly waist in a pale yellow dress tailored to show it off.

"I like your home." I borrowed a warm, slightly moist hand with light calluses and returned it. "They don't design them this way since air conditioning."

"Neil has an eye for that kind of thing. He's a building contractor."

"Neil's your husband?"

"Yes. Can I get you something? I'm afraid Netta has narrow ideas about her housekeeping duties."

"Just water. Anything stronger's wasted on a day like this."

She agreed that it was hot and came back after a few minutes with two glasses and a bowl of crushed ice on a tray. When we were seated on either side of a glass occasional table she said, "Neil's officially missing. Twenty-six hours. I trust the police, but they're outnumbered by their cases. That's why I called you."

"This puts me even up. I take it he isn't in the vanishing habit."

"No. He's never been gone without an explanation except for the time he was in the hospital."

"Accident?"

She drank and set down her glass. "He checked himself into a sanitarium. That was eighteen months ago, when the construction business was in a slump. Our lawyer advised him to declare bankruptcy, but Neil insisted on paying back every creditor in full. It was too much for him, the worrying, the long hours. One day he left for work and never showed up. The police traced him to the hospital after three days."

"I guess you checked there this time."

"I called every hospital in the area, public and private. No one answering his description has been seen in any of them."

"How's he been lately?"

"A little keyed up. We're just now getting back on our feet. I didn't think it was anything serious until his partner called yesterday to ask where he was."

I had some water. I wasn't thirsty any more, I just never liked asking the question. "Any reason to suspect he's involved with another woman?"

"Yes, but I called her and she swears she hasn't seen him in months."

"You know her?" I stroked my Adam's apple. A piece of ice had stalled in my throat during her answer.

"Vesta is her name. Vesta Mainwaring. She was the bookkeeper at the office until I made Neil fire her." She leaned over and touched my wrist. The light found hairline creases in her face. "I should explain something before we go any further. My husband is an obsessive personality, Mr. Walker. He's subject to binges."

"Alcohol?"

"No, but just as intoxicating. Come with me to the basement." She rose.

We went through a stainless steel kitchen and down a flight of clean sawdust-smelling steps into a cellar that had been turned into a den, mahogany paneling and tweed wall to wall. It contained a wet bar, Naugahyde chairs and a sofa, and a television set whose forty-eight-inch screen dwarfed the videocassette recorder perched on top. A set of built-in shelves that looked at first as if they held books was packed with videotapes instead.

"My husband's favorite room," said Mrs. Cully. "He spends most of his time here when he's not working."

I read the labels on the tapes. They were all movies: *The Dark Corner, Night and the City, Criss Cross, Double Indemnity* — not a Technicolor title in the bunch, and none of them made after about 1955. "He likes murder mysteries, I see."

"Not just murder mysteries. Dark films with warped gangsters and troubled heroes and fallen women. There's a name for them; my French isn't very good —"

"*Cinema noir,*" I said. "Black films. I like old movies myself. So far it hasn't landed me in psychiatric."

"You just like them. Neil sucks on them. In the beginning I watched with him. They were interesting, but not as a steady diet. I don't think he even noticed when I stopped watching. Lately he's been spending every spare minute in front of this set, exposing himself to I don't know how many murders, deceits, and depressing situations. It's not healthy."

An empty cassette sleeve lay on an end table. *Pitfall,* starring Dick Powell, Raymond Burr, and Lizabeth Scott. I went to the VCR and punched *Eject.* A tape licked out. *Pitfall.* It hadn't been rewound. "He was watching this one when?"

"Night before last. He disappeared the next day."

"When was the last time he got on this kick?"

"Just before he entered the hospital. About the time I found out he was having an affair with Vesta Mainwaring."

"How'd you find out?"

"The police told me. The little slut caved in pretty quickly when they started asking questions about his disappearance."

I slid the tape into its sleeve. "Where can I find Miss Mainwaring?"

"She's listed. But as I told you, she doesn't know where he is."

"I'd like to hear her say it. What's the name of your husband's firm?"

She'd anticipated that and gave me a business card from the pocket of her dress. CULLY AND WEBB, it read. "Webb is the partner?"

"His first name's Leo. They've been together longer than Neil and I."

"Can I take this with me?" I held up the videotape.

"Of course. You'll need a picture of Neil, too."

Upstairs she took a five by seven out of its frame and handed it to me. Cully was a craggy-looking party in his late forties with sad eyes and dark hair thinning in front. "Any ideas on what he might be up to?" I asked his wife.

She hesitated. "It might sound crazy."

"Try me."

"You have to understand that he might be unbalanced," she said. "I didn't put it together the first time, but I've seen enough of these things now to recognize the plot. I think Neil wants to be one of these *noir* heroes, Mr. Walker. I think he thinks he's in a film."

Cully and Webb had a small suite on the seventeenth floor of the Michigan Consolidated Gas Company Building on Woodward, a furnace-shaped skyscraper with a lobby out of Cecil B. DeMille, complete with sparkling blue lights mounted under the thirty foot ceiling and a bronze ballerina pirouetting among exterior pools. The offices themselves were just offices. A gray-haired woman with reading glasses suspended from a chain around her neck spoke my name into a telephone, and Leo Webb came out to shake my hand. He was a short wiry sixty with white hair slicked back, a power nose, and eyes like glass shards. His suit was tailored snugly, and there was something about the knot of his silk tie that said he'd given it a jerk and a lift just before his entrance.

When I told him my business, he steered me into his office, a square room full of antiques and statuary trembling on the rim of bad taste. I admired the view of downtown Detroit through his window and man-aged to sit down without upsetting a plaster cupid notching an arrow into its bow on a pedestal next to the chair.

"Gay's overreacting," Webb said, settling himself behind a French Empire desk crusted all over with gold inlay. "Cully's just off on a toot. He's that age. He'll be back when he's had enough."

"Vesta Mainwaring told her she hasn't seen him in months."

"This town's full of squirming women. I know. That's why I never bothered to get married."

"How's he been acting lately?"

"Same as anyone in this goddamn business, jumpy. Every time it rains on Wall Street, mortgage rates go up and people stop building houses. If you're looking for security, keep going."

"You wouldn't know that to see this office."

He smiled and ran a finger down the side of a Dresden Marie Antoinette on the desk. "I'm a sucker for nice things. We're into developing in a small way. You get a sixth sense for dying old widows looking to unload their property in order to have something to leave their grandchildren. The bargains would surprise you."

Bet they wouldn't. "Do you know where Miss Mainwaring is working? I can't get an answer from her home phone."

"Her new employer called us for a reference." He slid the pointer down the side of one of those nifty message caddies and punched up the cover. "Ziggy's Chop House on Livernois." He gave me a telephone number.

I wrote it down in my old fashioned notebook. "Do you always hang on to the new numbers of former employees?"

"Everybody has their own records system, and they take it with them when they go. Calling them saves a lot of decoding time."

"Can I see Cully's office?"

"I'll have Frances show you." He picked up his telephone.

"Partners sometimes take out insurance policies on each other," I said when he was through. "Anything like that here?"

"The premiums are too dear for the shoestring we operate on most of the time. His half of the business goes to his wife. Are you suggesting I did something nasty?" A pair of shardlike eyes glittered.

"Just sweeping out all the corners." Someone knocked and the woman I'd spoken to outside stuck her gray head into the office. I stood. "Thanks, Mr. Webb. I'll let you know if he turns up."

He remained seated. "Just tell him to wash off the powder and perfume before he reports to work."

Neil Cully's office was a poor working cousin of his partner's, containing a plain desk and file cabinet and an easel holding a pastel sketch of an embryonic building. The only personal items were a picture of Gay Cully on the desk and a framed movie poster on one wall for *This Gun for Hire*, with Alan Ladd looking sinister in four colors under a fedora. Frances stood in the doorway while I went through the file cabinet and desk. I found files and desk stuff. The message pad by the telephone was blank, but there were indentations in the top page.

"The police called this morning," Frances said. "They said not to disturb anything in the office."

I looked at my watch. "Okay if I call my answering service?"

When she said yes, I lifted the receiver and dialed the number for Cully and Webb. The telephone rang in the reception area. Frances excused herself and withdrew. I laid the receiver on the blotter and tried the trick with the edge of a pencil on the message pad. It made the indentations clearer but not legible. I smoothed out some unedifying crumples in Cully's wastebasket, found a sheet that had been torn off the pad, and got it into my pocket just as Frances returned. I cradled the receiver.

"Odd, there was no one on the other end," she said.

"Kids." I thanked her and left before she could work it out.

In the elevator I looked at the sheet. An unidentified telephone number. I tried it in a booth on the street.

"Musuraca Investigations," wheezed a voice in my ear.

I hung up without saying anything. I knew Phil Musuraca; not personally or even by sight, but the way a hardworking gardener knows a destructive species of beetle. Where he had gone, no honest investigator could follow without risking having a safe drop on him with Musuraca's name on it. What his number was doing in Neil Cully's wastebasket was one for Ellery Queen.

"Hello?"

A low voice for a woman, with fine grit in it, like a cat's lick. Conversations collided in the background with the snarling and cracking of a busy griddle. I could almost smell the carcinogens frying at Ziggy's Chop House. "Vesta Mainwaring?"

"Speaking. Listen, I'm busy, so if this is another obscene call, get to the dirty part quick."

I introduced myself and stated my business. I was looking across my little office at Miss August, kneeling in yellow shorts, high heels, and nothing else behind some convenient shrubbery on the calendar. I wondered if Miss Mainwaring ever trimmed hedges.

"Like I told Mrs. Cully and like I told the police, I haven't seen Neil since last fall."

"Not seeing him doesn't cover telephone calls and letters."

"You forgot telegrams, which I didn't get either. I lost one good job over that crumb, you want me to lose a lousy one, too?"

There was no reason to play the card, just the fact I hadn't any other leads. "What about Fat Phil, heard from him?"

The little silence that followed was like tumblers dropping into place. When she spoke again the background noise was muffled, as if she had inserted her body between it and the telephone. "What do you know about him?"

"Meet me and we'll swap stories."

"Not here," she said quickly. "Do you know the Castinet Lounge on

Grand River? I get off at ten."

"I'll find it." I hung up and checked my watch. Quitting time. Five hours to kill. I had dinner at a steak place on Chene and stopped at a video store on the way home to rent a VCR from a kid I wouldn't have let follow me into an arcade after sunset.

At the ranch I fixed a drink, hooked up the recorder to my TV set with the help of the instructions and a number of venerable Anglo-Saxon words, and fed the tape of *Pitfall* I had borrowed from Gay Cully into the slot. It was a tight black and white crimer the way they made them in 1948, starring Dick Powell as an insurance agent who has an extramarital affair with sultry Lizabeth Scott, only to run afoul of her embezzler boyfriend and a sex-driven insurance investigator played by Raymond Burr at his pre-Perry Mason heaviest. Powell kills the boyfriend and Scott kills Burr, but not before Powell's marriage to Jane Wyatt is threatened, leaving their lives considerably darker than they were when first encountered. There were plenty of tricky camera angles and contrasty lighting and one clever scene involving Powell and Burr with guns in a room full of shadows and reflections.

It was a good movie. It wasn't worth going off the deep end over, but then neither are most of the reasons men and women choose to walk away from a perfectly good relationship. When it was over I caught a rerun of *Green Acres,* which made more sense.

The Castinet Lounge was the latest in a series of attempts to perform shock therapy on Detroit's catatonic night life. A foyer paved with blue and white Mexican tiles opened into a big room covered in fake adobe with a bar and tables, a dance floor, and a mariachi band in sombreros and pink ruffled shirts. At a corner table I ordered scotch and soda from a waitress dressed like Carmen Miranda who wouldn't remember Sonny and Cher.

Ten o'clock came and went, followed by ten thirty. A few couples danced, the band finished its set, rested, and started another. They were playing requests, but everything sounded like the little Spanish flea. I nursed the first drink. What I did with the second and third was more like CPR. I was sure I'd been stood up.

Just before eleven she came in. I knew it was she, although I'd never seen a picture or been given a description, and my opinion of Neil Cully went up a notch. Coming in from the floodlit parking lot she was just a silhouette, square shoulders and a narrow waist and long legs in a blue dress and a bonnetlike hat tied under her chin with a ribbon, but as she stopped under the inside lights to look around, I saw eyes slanted just shy of Oriental, soft, untanned cheeks flushed a little from the last of the day's heat, red lips, a strong round chin. If you were going to kick over the traces, you could wait years for a better reason. When her gaze got to me I rose. She came over.

Seated, she took off her hat, shook loose a fall of glistening blue-black hair, and traded the hat to Carmen Miranda for a whisky sour. When we were alone she said, "You don't look like someone who'd be working with Phil Musuraca."

"Never met him."

"Did Neil tell you he was following me?"

"Who hired him?"

She seemed to realize she'd tipped something. She took a cigarette from her purse and fumbled for a light. I struck a match and leaned over. I didn't smell onions. Whatever she had on made me think of blossoms under a full moon. She blew a plume at the ceiling. "You haven't talked to Neil."

"Me and the rest of the human race," I said. "That part I've been spending time with, anyway. Tell me about Fat Phil."

"First tell me why you're asking."

"I found his number in Cully's wastebasket. Did Cully hire him?"

"I suppose you could find out anyway. Musuraca's working for my ex-husband. His name's Ted Silvera."

"Where did I hear that name?"

"He pushed over a bunch of video stores downriver two years ago. They called him the shotgun bandit."

"I remember the trial," I said. "The prosecution offered him a deal if he agreed to tell them where he'd stashed the money."

"Eighty thousand dollars, can you believe it? I keep telling Ziggy he should sell the griddle and rent out tapes. Anyway, Ted spit in their face and he's doing eight to twelve in Jackson. The police followed me around for a while, but when they got the idea I didn't know what Ted did with the money they laid off."

"But not Musuraca."

"Ted's jealous," she said. "He got wind about Neil somehow and had his lawyer retain Musuraca to tail me. Then Neil's wife found out, and I got fired. Musuraca gave up after that. But a week ago I turned from the counter at Ziggy's, and there he was, looking at me through the front window. He tried to duck, but he wasn't fast enough. I'd know that fat slob in the dark."

"Sure he's working for Silvera?"

"I went to Ted's lawyer and he said no. But you can't trust lawyers.

Who else would care what I do and who I see?"

"Dicks like Fat Phil are simple organisms. They don't give up as easily as the police. Maybe he thinks you'll lead him to that eighty grand."

"If I knew where it was, would I be flipping burgers?"

I lit a cigarette for myself. "It's only been two years. Inflation isn't so bad you couldn't wait a little longer for the coast to clear."

"Thanks for the drink, mister." She stood.

"Sit," I said. "I don't care if you've got the money sewed inside your brassiere. I'm looking for Neil Cully."

"I don't know where he is."

"What was he doing with Musuraca's number?"

She sat. Carmen drifted over and I ordered another round. Our glasses were less than half empty, but it was that kind of night. Vesta said, "I don't know why he'd still have it. I told Neil about Ted and Musuraca — well before. After that I couldn't get rid of him. He thought he was protecting me."

"Did you know he had mental problems?"

"What makes him special? My father died when I was little, and if I didn't marry Ted when I was sixteen to get out of the house, my stepfather would've hung me on his belt with every tramp in Detroit. When Ted got sent up, I saved everything I made waiting tables to pay for my bookkeeping classes. Cully and Webb was my ticket out of places like Ziggy's. Some protection job. Neil cracks up and goes to a cushy sanitarium, and I'm back behind a counter."

"He's got a movie complex, his wife says. Your situation comes right off a Hollywood B lot. If he's gone bugs again, he might look up you or Musuraca to write himself in as the hero."

"I haven't seen him. I haven't heard from him. I don't know how to say it so you'll believe it."

"I believe it. Were you followed here tonight?"

"I wouldn't be surprised. Musuraca doesn't make a lot of mistakes."

"Okay, go home."

"What are you going to do?"

"Get a look at Fat Phil."

"You'll be the first who ever wanted it." She got up. "You know, I usually get taken home from this place."

I held up a fifty dollar bill. "That ought to cover gas."

She didn't take it. "I'm not a whore."

"You're a bookkeeper who waits tables. Put this in your ledger."

She smiled briefly, took the bill, and left, carrying her hat. I crushed out my cigarette, put down money for the drinks, and went out after her. Out front the parking lot attendant held the door of a four-year-old green Fiat for her, and she gave him a dollar and drove away. A moment later a pair of headlamps came on, and a black Olds 98 covered with dings pulled out of the first row in the lot and burbled after her. By that time I was sliding under the wheel of my Mercury eight spaces over. I waited until the Olds turned left on Grand River, then swung out into the aisle behind it. Fat Phil and I had one thing in common: We never used valet parking.

Vesta Mainwaring lived in a house that had been converted to apartments in Harper Woods. She parked in a little lot behind the house and let herself in the back door. After a minute a light went on upstairs. The big Olds coasted to a stop.

I parked around the corner and walked back. The car was still there with its lights off. I got in the passenger's side.

Fat men are often fast. He sprang the gun from its underarm clip with an economy that would have impressed Hickok. But I showed him my Smith & Wesson while he was still drawing and he let his hand fall to his lap with the gun in it.

"You should lock your doors this time of night," I said.

"Who the hell are you?" It was a light voice for so much man. In the glow from the corner he had on a dark suit that could have been used for a dropcloth and a porkpie hat whose small brim made his face seem bloated. Actually it was in proportion with the rest of him. He would run three hundred stripped, a picture I got out of my mind as quickly as it came in. He had one eyebrow straight across and a blue jaw. I smelled peppermint in the car.

"Trade you my name for the cannon." When I had it — one of those Sig-Sauer automatics the cops are so hot on — I put it on the dash out of his reach and lowered the Smittie. "So much gun for such a little girl. The name's Walker. You wouldn't know it."

"Don't count on it. The town ain't that big, and the racket's smaller. What's the play?"

"Who's paying you to tail the Mainwaring woman?"

"Never heard of her. I was getting set to take a leak when you busted in."

"They arrest you for that here. How about Neil Cully, ever hear of him?"

"Uh-uh."

"He had your number written down in his office."

"So what? I ain't so busy I'm unlisted. Listen, I got a sour gut. There's a bag of peppermints in the glove compartment."

I opened it. The second my eyes flicked away his hand went up to his sun visor. I swung the Smith, cracking the barrel against his elbow. He yelped and brought down the arm. With my free hand I reached up and slid a two-shot .22 off the top of the visor. "For a guy that knows nothing from nothing you've got plenty of ordnance," I said. "What's Vesta Mainwaring to you?"

"Eighty grand." He rubbed his elbow. "She's got that dough stashed somewhere. She can't stay away from it forever."

"You gave up on that once. What makes you think she knows where it is now?"

"Just a hunch I got."

"Save it, Phil. There's too much divorce work in this town for you to give up any of it on a hunch. What's your source?"

"I got a note in my inside coat pocket." He didn't move.

"Fish it out. If it's more iron, I'll shoot you in the head. It's not much of a head, but it'd be a shame to spoil that hat."

He took the note out slowly. I pocketed the .22 and took it, a square of coarse Big Chief notepaper with two words printed on it in block ballpoint capitals: VESTA KNOWS. "Who sent it?"

He shook his head. "Came in the mail. No return address and a USPS postmark. Same printing on the envelope."

"You'd drop everything and take off after her on an anonymous note?"

"I'd do it on less than that for eighty thousand."

I put the note in my pocket and showed him Neil Cully's picture. His eyebrow rippled. "Sure, he was sniffing around the Mainwaring broad last year. I ran his license plate through the Secretary of State's office, but he wasn't nobody. I guess Cully could of been the name. I ain't seen him lately."

"Maybe you did and forgot. Like you forgot his name."

"Hey, I hear a lot of names."

I opened the door. "If I find out there's more to it, I'll be back and you and I will go a round."

"What about my guns?"

"Go straight home from here and I'll mail them to your office. Tell anybody you feel like shooting to take a number till then." I left him.

I caught six hours' sleep and was standing in front of the Detroit Public Library when they unlocked the doors. The film section had several picture books on *cinema noir* and one scholarly tract, *Dark*

Dreams: Psychosexual Manifestations of Hollywood Crime Movies Circa 1945-1955, by Ellis Portman, Ph.D. It had been published that year by Wayne State University Press. I lugged the thick volume over to a reading table and waded through a grand's worth of four-dollar words, then turned to the author's biography at the back. Ellis Portman, it said, taught psychology and film courses at Wayne State.

I also found a withdrawal card at the back bearing signatures of those who had checked the book out recently. I took it.

A public telephone on the main floor put me in touch with Dr. Portman and an acquaintance in the Detroit bureau of the FBI who owed me a favor. I made an appointment with Portman and stopped at the Federal Building on the way to give my acquaintance the note Phil Musuraca had given me.

The room number I'd gotten from Portman belonged to a small auditorium lit by only the black and silver images fluttering on a square screen at the far end. I found a seat in time to watch Robert Mitchum and Jane Greer careening down a country road in a big car with bug-eye headlamps toward a roadblock. Spotting the armed men in uniform, Jane Greer said, "Dirty double-crossing —" and shot Mitchum, who sent the car into a spin while the woman traded fire with the officers. After she was killed and the car came to a stop, a cop opened the driver's door and Mitchum flopped out, dead.

The lights came up and a small man with a big head, half the age I associated with a college professor, dismissed the students with a reminder that their papers were due Monday. As they filed out, discussing the movie, I introduced myself and shook Portman's hand. Up close he was older than he looked from the back of the room. I sketched out the case on the way to the projector.

"Just another manifestation of the Don Quixote complex," he said when I'd finished. "How can I help?"

"Most books on *noir* are for buffs. Yours takes on its psychology. I thought you might translate the Latin."

He switched off the projector and removed the take-up reel. "We've always identified with gods and heroes. The appeal of the *noir* protagonist is he's more approachable than Beowulf or Sherlock Holmes. He's an ordinary guy with tall troubles, but he usually comes out on top even if it does kill him sometimes."

"Kind of a complex world to want to be part of."

"Actually, it's simplistic. You've got your good guy, your heavy, your good girl, and your tramp. Upon examination, the *noir* landscape makes more sense than our world. I don't wonder that an obsessive like your client's husband would prefer it to his own tangled affairs. His wife, whom he perceives as the good girl, represents the crushing responsibilities that landed him in therapy the first time. The girlfriend, whose situation might have come out of any crime movie of the forties, promises adventure and uninhibited sex and a respite from his oppressive routine. The whole thing might have been made to order for a man with his fixation."

I watched him place the reel in a flat can labeled OUT OF THE PAST and seal the lid. "What would shake him out of it?"

"Nothing, if he's too far gone. If not, the shock of reality might do it. Our world has more twists than any screenplay. Villains turn out to be just guys trying to get along. Bad girls are just good girls in trouble. Angels become whores in front of your eyes. If that doesn't bring him back, electrodes won't."

Later, in my office transcribing the notes I'd taken in Dr. Portman's classroom to my typewritten report, I took a call from my FBI acquaintance. We spoke for five minutes, after which I hung up and placed two calls. The first was to Gay Cully, who agreed to see me at her place that night.

It was just past dark when Netta, the Cullys' maid, answered the bell and told me her mistress would be with me in a few minutes. I asked her to send Mrs. Cully to the basement when she was ready and went down there.

I slid the videotape I'd brought into Neil Cully's VCR and turned on the giant-screen TV set. As the black and white credits for *Pitfall* came on, I turned down the sound and switched off the lights in the room. Now the only illumination came from the screen. Shadows crawled in the silver glow on the tapes perched on their shelves.

"Mr. Walker, is that you?"

I hadn't heard her coming down the stairs. She was standing on the second step from the bottom, a small trim figure in a fresh-looking pale tailored dress like the one she'd had on when we met. One hand rested at her throat.

"It's not Neil," I said. "Is that what you thought, Mrs. Cully?"

"I — well, yes, for a moment. He used to sit down here with no lights on and a movie on the —"

"Couldn't be him, though. You know that better than anyone."

"I don't — do you have news? Where is he?"

I was standing in shadow beside the TV set. The full light of the screen fell on her, as I'd planned. I said, "You were okay for a novice.

You only made two mistakes. One was natural: Who'd expect Phil Musuraca to show me the note or that it would find its way to the FBI? The other was just plain stupid.

"Printing *Vesta Knows* was good," I went on. "No handwriting expert could pin that small a sample on you. But that coarse paper holds prints like soft wax. When I had a Fed friend check them against yours on file from an old job, it didn't take long."

"What are you implying?"

"Nuts. You've seen enough of these films to recognize the obligatory explanation scene. The note was smart, all right. It got Musuraca back on Vesta Mainwaring's case and made him a prime suspect: Poor crazy Neil got himself involved all over again in Vesta's troubles and stubbed his toe, permanently. Just in case the cops missed it, you hired me, knowing I'd turn Musuraca eventually. The law couldn't convict him without a body, but his interest in eighty thousand dollars stolen by Vesta's ex would divert suspicion from you. You even read up on *cinema noir* to make sure your story about Neil's obsession would hold water. But that was where you made your other mistake, the bonehead one." I took the card out of my pocket and held it up to the light.

"What's that?"

"A withdrawal card from the Detroit Public Library with your name on it, dated a week before you reported your husband missing. You shouldn't have checked out Dr. Portman's book. That was like signing your own name to a murder contract." I put it away. "How much is Neil's half of the contracting firm worth?"

Shadows and light played over her face. "Fifty thousand. More if I liquidate the real property. But that's not evidence. A note, a card with my signature. They won't convict."

"No, but they're enough to obtain a warrant to dig up that berry patch at the end of this street. Before I rang the bell tonight, I poked around with a flashlight. I found a lot of turned earth. With Neil's corpse, the note and the card will convict."

"You don't know what it's like."

I said nothing.

"Listening to him babble about those stupid films," she said. "Even when he had his affair it wasn't with a woman, just a character in a movie. I'd have killed him for that alone; the half-partnership will just be compensation for the past two years I spent living with a zombie."

"How'd you kill him?"

"Guess." She raised a gun in the hand she'd had resting on the banister. I hadn't seen it in the shadows. "I sent Netta out just now," she said. "Call it a feeling I had."

"Drop it, sister."

I almost laughed. It was the one cliche the scene needed, and you could count on Phil Musuraca to deliver it. His bulk filled the upper stairwell. The Sig-Sauer automatic I'd sent to him by messenger after calling him was in his hand. I took advantage of Gay Cully's confusion to remove the Smith & Wesson from my pocket.

"Make that three mistakes," I said. "You're as much a sucker for that *noir* schtick as Neil. Just because a P.I. is greasy enough to hound a woman for eighty grand doesn't mean I can't call on him for help. You've seen the pictures, Mrs. Cully. A staircase is no place to make a successful play."

Her gun dropped, bounced down two steps, and landed on the carpet. Just then Dick Powell shot Byron Barr onscreen.

Fat Phil said, "I didn't care for that *greasy* crack."

I got away from the Lathrup Village cops around midnight. On the way home I stopped at the video store, rented some tapes, and watched Doris Day movies until I fell asleep.

Hooray for Hollywood

by Robert Twohy

WANTING A CHANGE, I FLEW up to San Francisco on Friday night, and on Monday morning when I got on the plane for the return flight I had wobbly disco knees and gongs in my head, which was the whole idea of the weekend.

I cabbed from Burbank to my apartment on Orange Drive, one of Hollywood's classier streets — my lifestyle was good and on the way to getting a lot better. *Catastrophe* was expected to be the big movie of the year, with the great Bora Pelicularu directing — it was his production, the trades said he'd sunk five million of his own in it. And I had the lead role. My first really big one, after 14 years in the vineyards. *Catastrophe* would do for me what the *Falcon* did for Bogart.

As I dropped my bag on the floor, kicked off my Guccis, and fell on the couch, I had yeasty thoughts of the future that lay ahead.

The phone rang.

Half in a doze I reached for it and fell off the couch. Fortunately the rug was thick. I got the phone and, rubbing my ribs, said, "Hello."

A voice with a foreign lilt said, "So finally you are home. This is Bora. I tell Finnegan but for polite, want to give you personal the news . . . *Catastrophe* is *kaputsky*. I return to Rashpudlovik."

I took about eight breaths, finally managed, "Return to where?"

"To family estate, back in homeland. In English mean fertility, fruitfulness, things in blossom. Very poetical name."

"Yeah, really nice . . . *Catastrophe* is *kaputsky?*"

"Not right for today — and I am director for today. Understand?"

"No." All I understood was that suddenly I wasn't going to be the new Bogart. "*Catastrophe* is great! It'd rank right up there with the top detective movies — the ones that are real art. Like the *Falcon, Chinatown* —"

"Fooey on *Falcoon, Chinatown* — only one film from yesterday great for today. You know which one?"

"Which?"

"*Big Schlepp.*"

After a few seconds I figured that one out. ."*Big Sleep.* Yeah, that's another great one."

"You know why great? I tell you why. 'Cause it don't make no sense."

"Huh?"

"No sense. I see it twenty-six time and still not know who do what or why. They just do it. Everything confoozel — and that why it still great movie for today. 'Cause it got right mood for today. And that why *Falcoon* —"

"*Falcon.*"

"Yah, Big Bird — why great film for yesterday but not today. Too much sense — just like *Catastrophe*. Not mood for today. So go back to homeland and get new creative visions. Come up with whole new contraption —"

"Conception."

"Whatever. Work up great new approach so *Catastrophe* be film for today. Call you when get back. Goo'bye."

That seemed to be that. "Thanks for your call. Have fun in Pashrudlovik."

Rashpudlovik. Pashrudlovik means pregnant buzzard."

"Whatever."

We hung up. I needed sleep but thought I needed a drink more. I got a bottle of blackberry brandy, took it to the couch, lay down, and drank from the neck. When it was empty I went to sleep.

The movie life is total unreality but you put eight weeks into a great script, do better than you've ever done in your life, and whamo it's *kaputsky* and you're left with nothing but a big urge to drink enough to take away the taste of crumbled dreams.

But first, before I started on what I intended to rank with the classic drunks of Hollywood legend, I called my agent, Finnegan, at his home. It was about seven P.M.

I went on a while about what a soulless rat Pelicularu was and he made consoling noises, then said, "Geniuses go by their own inner voices. Forget him. Something new has come up."

His voice took on a furtive tone. I got a picture of him crouched behind his phone, shooting furtive glances in various directions. He's basically a very furtive guy. He's repulsive, but not a bad agent as the type goes. "Something very hot. Meet me at Flupo's at eight."

"By eight I'll be a slobbering drunk. Lay it on me now."

"Can't. I had to promise to play clam. Flupo's, eight sharp."

I tried to slam the phone down quicker than he did so he'd get the whack in the ear, but as always he was quicker and I got the whack. You can't beat Finnegan for fast moves with the phone.

I got to Flupo's, took a dinky little table in the bar, looked around, saw no one I recognized, just a few celebrities that weren't very celebrated and the usual mawk of tourists. Suddenly I saw a smile and damned if it didn't belong to a woman with soft reddish hair with lights in it, and green eyes with the same.

She was standing a little away from my table. She wore a glittery maroon dress that above the waist was quality rather than quantity, and her skin was California gold. Around her neck shone a lot of pearls. On her arm she carried a stole that if it wasn't pure mink I'm Laurence of Olivier. This lady was loaded, and in every way spectacularly. She said in a low voice, "May I sit down?"

I half got up, knees rubbery — and not just from the Frisco discos. I looked at my watch. It said 8:10. Finnegan was late. I hoped he'd stay that way.

She sat down. "I was passing, and recognized you. You're Randy Spear."

I'm not, really — I'm Elbert P. Hummell, originally from Sapulpa, Oklahoma. But Finnegan thought Randy Spear had a lot more pizazz, so that's who I've been since coming to Hollywood.

We looked at each other, this woman and I. Finally she murmured, "I didn't stop for an autograph. I recognized you and thought how nice it would be if you bought me a margarita."

I signaled the cocktail girl and gave her an order for a margarita and a refill of my highball. The red-gold goddess smiled at me. "The evening is young, the night is dark and beautiful, the drive to Ojai is a delight that never dulls. Don't you love that drive?"

"With a passion." I'd never driven it but had no doubt it could lead to wondrous places. "Do you live in Ojai?"

"Do I live anywhere?" It was said very low. The brightness of her eyes was dimmed by a sudden shadow.

It wasn't part of the game we'd started, the Hollywood game which I know real good and which she seemed to know too. That shadow over her eyes wasn't Hollywood — it was reality.

Just for a second. Then it was gone and her eyes had the sparkle again. Whatever had brought on the shadow, she wanted to forget it.

Our drinks came. I took a swallow and said, "You know who I am which puts you a square ahead."

"Barbara Bacon." She sipped her margarita, gave me back my gaze. I was wondering — but I'm presumptuous. You were waiting for someone."

"Was I?" I'd forgotten Finnegan. He was always super-punctual — something must have come up. Perhaps an accident. "Maybe I was waiting for you."

She said, in that low voice, "Maybe you were. Maybe some things are destined."

And again her sparkle was darkened — just for a second.

Fifteen minutes later we crossed the parking lot to a blue Cad an open convertible. I thought first it was a beautiful old model, because they haven't made convertibles for years, then saw it was this year's model. For $50,000 or in that neighborhood you can get a standard turned into a convertible, at some specialty shop up near San Jose.

She said, "D'you want to drive?" She didn't wait for the answer — she saw it in my face. She smiled, handed me keys, and got in on the passenger side.

I slid in, turned things on, and reached for the gizmo that works the folding top. She said, "Leave it open."

"It'll get nippy up coast."

"That's why I brought my stole." She'd had me put it over her as we left the restaurant. "I love to drive the coast with the top down."

It was all right by me. Everything was fine. I was driving a beautiful woman in a beautiful car to Ojai — which all I knew about was that it's 80 miles or so from L.A., and a lot of rich people live there.

With that car, the pearls, the stole, she qualified.

We got on the freeway, and it got nippier, but was beautiful — clear dark sky, thin slice of moon, glittering sea. Not many cars on the freeway, easy driving.

I glanced at her, liking the way her red hair flipped around in the breeze. "Tell me about yourself — like what do you do?"

"Not much, when my husband's in town."

Something went *THONNKKK!* in my chest. I should have known. Things don't go on as great as this evening had gone so far. There's always a stray tack somewhere in the stardust, waiting to be stepped on.

But her remark had a reverse twist. I asked, "Is he in town now?"

"No, he's in Rome."

"What's he doing in Rome?"

"Sleeping, probably. That's the most fun he has. But he's in pretty good health for a man in his seventies."

I looked the obvious question at her.

She gave a little shrug, and a crooked smile, and her hand came up and fiddled with the stole, then moved on and up to the necklace.

I drove a while. A few cars passed us, we passed a few — as I said not much traffic. "He's rich, huh?"

"He's a banker."

"But he's in Rome."

"Far as I know."

"So you're on the lonely side."

"Only when he's home. When he's away, I stop being lonely." She looked at me full-face. "Like right now. I'm not lonely now."

I wasn't either.

Then her eyes slid from my face and the look she had been giving me was gone, and now her eyes were two gleaming circles of fear.

She whispered tautly, "Down! Get down!" And that's what she was doing — falling over sideward to the window, arms covering her red head.

She could do that, I couldn't. Not while piloting 6000 pounds of Cad along the freeway.

I looked in the rear-view mirror.

Lights were coming fast in the next lane. It was a greenish sedan. It pulled even. I turned my head, glanced at the dark shape of the driver — dark glasses, sharp profile, eyes straight ahead. He stayed there, keeping the green sedan even with us.

Something bright caught the edge of my glance, and it slid back along the car. I saw bright metal, and it stuck out of a hand that rested on the open rear window. It was a gun, looking at me.

I didn't think, just reacted — hit the brake and rode it, the Cad slewing to the right. Over the skriek of tires I heard a sharp clean pop — and something was happening to the windshield in front of me. It was spider-webbing — and caught in the middle of the sudden web was a hole.

But the skid got my full attention. I eased off the brake, went along with the skid, felt things start back under control, saw I was off the freeway on the shoulder, made a twitch of the wheel here, then there, braking down now firm and steady — and we came to a stop on the far edge of the shoulder.

The green sedan wasn't alongside any more. I looked through the cracked windshield and saw its tail-lights going away very fast down the middle lane.

I took a few deep breaths, then reached out and down and touched the mink.

"You all right?"

The mink moved, came up under my hand. "Yes."

I looked at her tight, white face. She closed her eyes a few seconds, then rubbed her cheeks, and some color came back into them.

She murmured, "Have they gone on?"

"Yes. Who were they?"

"Some of Kay's men."

"Kay?"

"A man I know."

"Kay's a man?"

She looked beyond me. The terror was out of her eyes. The shadow lay over them, but a softness showed through it. She murmured, "Yes. Kay's a man."

I looked at the hole in the windshield. "Why'd he want to kill us?"

"He didn't." She was still looking off. "It was just to — remind me."

"Of what?"

"Things of the past."

This mess I'd got into was getting nothing but thicker. Maybe Kay didn't want to kill us but that was a real hole in the windshield. An inch farther to the right and it would have been in my head, and there'd have been a hell of a car crash, and Barbara would have wound up as dead as me. I said, "Kay seems like a pretty unconventional guy."

Her lips made a slight curve. "Yes. Never dull, never predictable. But believe me — if he'd told them to kill us, we'd be dead. Snecker put the bullet just where he wanted to."

"Snecker? The gunman?"

She seemed to know all the characters involved. I was the new boy in class, knowing no one.

She said, "Can you see to drive?"

"I guess so." It was distorted through the webby windshield, but navigable.

"Then let's get on to Ojai."

I wasn't sold on that notion. The green sedan could be up ahead, pulled over to the shoulder, waiting for us. "We better take the next ramp and get back to L.A."

She said quietly, "No. They've done all they meant to do."

In this deep, I might as well go deeper, try to find out what lay at the bottom. If she was wrong and those guys wanted another try at us, they could do it as well toward L.A. as toward Ojai — so there was no big advantage to turning back. I started the car. "Tell me who Kay is, and what's going on."

"I will. When we get to Ojai."

I looked in the mirror to see if it was clear to turn onto the freeway, then heard a yell up forward, hit the brake, and saw I'd nearly piled into a panel truck pulled in front of me on the shoulder. A guy jacking up for a rear-tire change yelled, "You blind or something?"

"Fogged windshield." I pulled around him, got out on the freeway, leaving him squawking insults.

We passed the Ventura turnoffs and took the turn to Ojai, which the sign said was 13 miles. I drove steady and careful, paying attention now and seeing fairly well through the windshield. I kept checking the mirror, but I saw no green sedan.

We got near the town and she had me take a side road. We climbed a while, and it was low estate homes set in trees — this was the richest part of a rich man's town, high up over it. We came to a long stone fence and approached an open iron gate. Barbara nodded, gestured. I turned in.

We drove on a curving road through trees. There was nothing but trees — no lawn. The trees grew right up to a big two-story adobe, topped with red tile. A wide drive went off around, which would be the garage area. "You want me to put it in there?"

"No, drive on past the house — I feel like walking back."

I did as she said and stopped on the side of the curved road. I gave her the keys and we got out, and walked 200 feet back to the house. She used a key and we went in.

Stylish furnishings, oil paintings, wall hangings, everything old-Spanish style. A wide, low, very expensive and classy main room.

She took off the stole and dropped it in a chair. "It's cool and lovely out. Let's sit by the pool."

I followed her out a big oak door. We were on a patio, where there were a couple of deckchairs. It wasn't nippy like on the coast — Ojai is in a valley, inland. The thin moon was caught in the tops of some tall trees and things were shadowy, the big rectangular pool before us darkly shining.

Barbara went to a switch, flipped it, and lights sprang on from under the house eaves and from the branches of trees near the pool. That wasn't so romantic as moonlight but romance right now wasn't what I was after — that could come later, if it came. Right now I felt better with the lights on because it meant less chance the guy with the gun could come sneaking through the trees. She might be sure that the guys in the green sedan had knocked off work for the night, but I wasn't.

I sat down in one of the chairs. "Tell me about Kay."

"Kay." She stood by me, gazing at the diving tower at the far end of the pool. It was a high tower. "We met in Yugoslavia. That was years ago." The shadow was over her eyes and she had an odd smile. "I look at the diving tower," she said softly, "and I think of then."

I didn't see the connection. Maybe it would become clear. I said, "It's really a high tower." A diving board stuck out from it.

She said, "Twenty feet high."

"Are you a diver?"

"I love to dive. I used to dive off cliffs at Rijeka." So that was the connection. "A lifetime ago . . . so much since then. So very much."

She was looking down at me. Her look was the look you dream a beautiful woman will give you. It got closer. Her face was coming down on mine. Her whole body was coming down on me. Now she was all over me. I had a lapful of California gold, and her mouth had become part of mine or vice-versa. My ears thumped, my hair felt electrified, I was like disappearing under tumbling red hair. Then suddenly her soft weight was off me. I opened my eyes, saw her staring back toward the house. I craned around the back of the chair to see. A mahogany-colored giant in a seedy black suit stood there in the doorway.

"Har-Tai?" Barbara said softly. "You're back?"

The giant made a gurgling noise in his throat.

Barbara murmured to me, "Don't be frightened."

I saw no reason not to be. He was about seven feet tall and had hands in proportion. They twitched. Bright black eyes were fixed on my face.

She said, her voice brisk now, "Bring drinks, Har-Tai. The usual for me, whiskey and water for Mr. Spear."

The giant turned, lumped back in the house.

I let out a few breaths, and said, "Who's he?"

"Har-Tai. From Madagascar. They tore his tongue out."

I blinked at that. She didn't elaborate. "Excuse me, while I slip into something less formal."

As not too much of her was restricted by the maroon dress, I wondered what she had in mind. I watched her move across the patio, through the oak door.

I sat there gazing at the lighted pool and the tall tower at the end, and the trees growing close on the far side. I wondered who had torn Har-Tai's tongue out, and why, and wondered about Kay, who left reminders that ruined windshields. I didn't know how this night was going to wind up. It seemed a night for sudden happenings and odd people — and Barbara was certainly changeable, as to mood and clothes.

A snuffle sounded close behind my head. Something told me it meant trouble — I went to instinct, dived forward out of the chair, and fell flat on the tile.

Pushing up, I threw a look, saw the Madagascan just completing the follow-through of a stiff-finger jab that would have dented my skull as when you squeeze a beer can.

I scrambled to hands and knees. He was coming at me, hands spread. I had no time to ponder things — I rolled on my back, got my feet up, and kicked from the shoulders.

And damned if he didn't slip in a wet place and slide into my kick, I taking it in the belly, and of course continuing his slide and bending my legs back over my head so I rolled on my shoulders all the way over, winding up on my knees with my face in the tile — and wet all over, because he'd gone belly-whacking into the pool.

He made gurgling sounds and beat his arms around. I got up and watched him slap water — he wasn't a swimmer. But he sucked in a suitcase full of air, went under, and I guess crawled along the bottom because his hands shot up and gripped the edge of the pool. I went over to stamp them loose and Barbara's voice sounded sharply, "No!"

She had come out the door, in a frothy green thing that kind of floated around her. She said, "I'll take care of him."

The Madagascan's hands were followed by head, shoulders, and chest, and he was heaving himself out of the pool. I stepped back toward the house.

Barbara stood quiet, and as he got out, shook himself, blew water, and then started for me, she said, low and compelling, "Stop, Har-Tai!"

He blinked, looked at her, stopped.

"Go. Go to trees. Spend night in trees."

His shoulders drooped, so did his head. His mahogany face kind of broke up.

"Go," said Barbara, pointing off.

He spread his hands in an appealing way, then turned, and in draggy fashion walked around the pool, and disappeared into the trees.

She gazed after him. "He'll weep all night, out of shame for losing his cool, but he'll be all right in the morning."

"Why'd he want to attack me?"

She gave me a look that held a lot of meaning, but I wasn't sure what it meant. "It doesn't matter. He won't try it again. Not tonight."

"Nothing seems to matter. Getting shot at didn't matter, now this doesn't matter — "

She said in that low voice, "Things that are over don't matter. All that matters are things still to come."

She was at the edge of the pool, staring in, her attitude one of intensity. She gestured. I came over, looked in the direction she was looking, toward the deep end — and saw a body. Face down, near the bottom. It had a white shirt, dark pants, shoes. Whoever it was hadn't gone in for a swim.

I said, "Time we called the cops."

"Yes." Her look was steady. "Tell them the Bacon place. Don't mention Kay or Har-Tai. While you're phoning, I'll pull the body out."

I was about to tell her that *she* should phone, she was the hostess here — and no need to pull this latest guest out, he could wait where he was for the cops. But she moved fast and there was a puff of filmy green, then a neat splash, and the frothy thing was on the tile and she was in the water, a smooth pink fish in a pearl necklace flashing toward the body.

I watched her go under; then turned and hurried through the oak door, thinking that if I made the call fast and short I could be back in time to help her get the body out.

I looked around the soft-lit living room and spotted the phone on a corner table. I went over, picked it up, and there was a stabby pop and the phone flew out of my hand. I hit the floor as another pop stabbed. A heavy armchair was near and I scooted behind it, staying low. The third pop went through the chair, zizzed past my nose, and thunked into the wall.

Then everything was quiet, except I heard a kind of thumping splash from outside, then quieter slurping sounds. That would be Barbara heaving the corpse out of the pool and dragging it up on the tile.

Some time passed. I got to my hands and knees, went forward a little, and peeked around the chair. Everything stayed quiet, except for the outside slurping. I got my legs under me and came up slowly behind the chair. This time the gunman couldn't have missed — so it was clear he had gone.

I took in air for a while. Then I walked across the room and out the door. Barbara, back in her green froth, was standing near the pool, rubbing her cheeks and gazing down at the body at her feet. It lay on its back and the handle of a dagger stuck out the middle of its chest.

I went over and looked down at the face of a fit-looking old man with a lot of gray hair. "Your husband?"

She nodded.

"I thought he was in Rome."

"No, he's here. Did you get the police?"

"No. The phone was shot out of my hand."

She was quiet, her full lower lip hooked by her teeth, and then she murmured, "So it's all to be settled tonight."

"What is?"

She grabbed my arm, stared up at me, and her eyes were wide and shiny with that fear I'd seen before. "Are you going to help me?"

"What do you want me to do?"

"Drive to Ojai."

"To the cops?"

"Too late for that. Drive down the road we came up till you see a sign that says Munson's Hogs. Take the road there and drive till the road ends in barbed wire. Go through the wire and there's a farmhouse with a well in front. Have you got that?"

"Farmhouse with a well."

"Find a stone, drop it in the well. Wait thirty seconds, then drop two more stones, one after the other. Then wait. Someone will come out."

"Of the well?"

"No, the farmhouse."

"Who?"

"The only one who can help me now."

"Kay?"

Her voice had a ragged undertone of hysteria. "Don't you understand that time is all we have to work with — and it's almost gone?"

Her urgency got me in motion. I went through the door, through the living room, out the front door, and started for the Cad, parked in the drive 200 feet away. The moonlight picked it out brightly. If the sharpshooter was out there in the trees I'd be an easy target. But no pop stabbed the silence.

I knew where I was going to drive. Not to Munson's hog farm — to the Ojai police station, where I'd lay it all out for the cops and they would take it from there. This whole thing had become too sinister and confusing for me to handle by myself.

I ran toward the Cad and when I was 60 feet from it there was a terrific flash, a giant concussion, and I was knocked over on my back. I scrambled up — parts of the Cad were flying around. I ran back to the house, turned, saw pieces and wheels still flying, and where the car had stood, there was only a black patch on the road.

I went through the house and out the door, yelling, "The car blew up!"

But she wasn't there, and neither was the body of her husband. The patio was deserted except for the two deckchairs.

Movement across the pool caught the edge of my glance. I looked fast, saw the giant Madagascan loping away toward the trees. Slung over his shoulder was the body of the dead man.

I shouted, "Where do you think you're going with that?"

He stopped, turned.

"Where's Barbara?" I called.

His teeth flashed at me. Then he turned, and with his soggy burden disappeared into the trees.

I went back in the house. She wasn't in the front room. I started up the stairs. The phone rang.

It had been knocked out of my hand and I hadn't hung it up afterward. But from the stairs I could see it back in its cradle on the corner table, with a bullet hole in the mouthpiece.

I watched it. It kept ringing.

I walked toward it wondering if shots would start popping. But it kept ringing. I picked it up and said, "Hello?"

I heard a whispery laugh.

I said, "Barbara?"

The laugh again.

"Who's laughing?"

A voice whispered, "Too bad for you, Peeper."

It flashed to me — this whole mess could be a mistake in identification — the shots hadn't been meant for me but somebody else. I said, "You got the wrong guy. I'm —" The phone went click.

I hung up. I stood a minute, trying to figure things out.

"Barbara?" I called again. But everything stayed quiet.

The best thing was to get to Ojai, to the cops. I started toward the front door, planning to get out on the road, flag down somebody —

I heard a scream. It came from outside, at the pool. It turned into words: "Help me! For God's sake, help me!"

I ran through the oak door, looked around the patio, saw nothing, heard nothing more.

I stared at the pool, saw something splash into it.

A drop of red.

I looked up. Drops of red were falling from the end of the high diving board, falling into the pool.

The board was bent — it hadn't been bent before.

Bright drops of red, glistening.

"Barbara?"

I couldn't see who or what lay on the diving board. I took various positions on the patio, but couldn't see. If I went in the house, up to the second story, and looked out, maybe I could see.

I stopped. A big dog was in the doorway. Not big, huge. A giant black dog.

He didn't come at me. He just stood there watching. His snout wrinkled, and from deep inside him came an ominous rumbling.

I backed away a little. I held out my hand, palms up, the way you show you're not going to throw anything.

The snarling got higher-pitched. The hairs on his face seemed to get spikier, as if he were charging himself up. More creases showed in his snout. He started to walk, slow and stiff-legged, toward me.

I backed along the side of the pool, toward the deep end. He kept walking toward me. I moved around the corner of the pool, saw his eyes get a sudden crazed look, as if he couldn't stand the anticipation any longer, and was going to make his lunge. I twisted and leaped, a standing broad jump, hoping the ladder to the tower was near enough, and it was — barely. My fingers hooked on a rung, my body swung under, and I pushed up straight and ran up the ladder, running till I was sure I was clear, then looked down. The dog was stretched as far up the ladder as he could go, front paws on the step below me, teeth snapping eight inches below my shoes.

I got a quarter from my pocket and tossed it when his jaws were open at their widest and the coin must have slid down into his throat because he gagged, got a glassy look, and fell backward off the ladder.

He got up all hunched over, choking, shoulders shaking. Finally he gave a low moan, then turned and walked away, not stiff-legged now but shaky and droop-hipped. He got to the patio door, gave me a long look, but the fire was out of him. Then he disappeared inside the house.

I looked in and over the pool. Drops of red, falling in front of me, were splashing into the pool.

"Barbara?"

I didn't want it to be Barbara, but if it was I'd better know now.

I went on up the ladder.

I put my face over the top.

She wasn't there. Nobody was.

I looked along the length of board, and a big flat chunk of iron was out there, making it bend. At the end was a small plastic bag. There were holes in it. Red stuff was leaking out of the holes, puddling around the bag, then slipping, drop by drop, from the end of the board.

I didn't know what to think.

Then I felt something stinging both my palms. It flashed on me that one time when I came home late and turned on a lamp it didn't light. I had reached under to feel if the bulb was loose and found there was no bulb. I stuck my finger in the socket and got bombed across the room. That was what I was getting now — an electric jolt from the ladder rails.

I thought I was. I wasn't. All I was getting was an electric stroke.

Now I got the jolt.

I gave a yell and snatched my hands free, which often you can't do, you just stick to what's jolting you and get cooked. I was lucky. Also I was falling, and I figured I had about 20 feet to wonder about things — then would come crash time.

I waited for the hard tile, trying to tell myself there are worse ways to go. Then I wasn't falling any more. I was lying on something, and it wasn't tile.

Maybe it was a cloud. Maybe you don't remember when you get the fatal knock, maybe your last feeling just fades out, and next thing you know you're lying on a cloud.

That was my first vague thought. Then I came full to reality and knew I wasn't on a cloud. It was something slick and slippery, and soft — I was on something rubbery.

I sat up and looked around. I saw people. They were making noises, they were laughing and whooping.

I heard Barbara's voice — "You okay?" There she was, in her frothy thing, grinning at me.

I started to pick out other faces — there were about 20 people. A foot higher than any other face was Har-Tai's. He gave me a big grin, a wave, called, "Great going!" He must have grown a new tongue.

I saw the gray-haired guy, upright, not wearing the knife in his chest. He had a drink in his hand. Most of the people seemed to have drinks in their hands.

A couple of guys came over, stuck out their hands, took mine and pulled, and I stood up in the rubbery thing, stumbled around on it, and was pulled clear. It was a thick rubber mattress.

A guy handed me a drink. I didn't know if it was bourbon or what, and didn't care. I drank it down. It was bourbon.

Barbara, bright-eyed, said, "I was afraid you'd catch on at the beginning, with the lobster truck in front of us or just behind us all the way from L.A., and pulled up in front of us with the lights out while we were parked off the freeway."

"Yeah," I said. "Lobster truck. Right." I remembered pulling around a panel truck after having the windshield shot up. I hadn't noticed it was a lobster truck Nor had I noticed the truck on the freeway from L.A.

A furtive voice on the other side of me said, "Stroka genius. Like I said — the guy's a genius."

I turned and it was my agent, Finnegan. He was grinning but shifty-eyed as always — he'd look shifty buying cookies from a Girl Scout. "Bora said you had a great build but as an actor you stunk. Said the only way to get life in you was to have you not know you're acting. Then maybe you'd react to things like someone alive, not made of plaster — and all the other actors would go without scripts and react to your reactions. And it would be realism like it's never been done before."

"I was bugged," said Barbara. I blinked at her. "Bugged for sound. From the time we met at Flupo's."

She fingered her pearls, grinned.

"The pearls were bugged?"

She nodded. "Great natural dialogue. It's all on tape, just needs a word change here and there."

"So it all began at Flupo's, huh? With hidden cameras there?"

"Uh huh. Bora arranged it."

"And the dog was a trained dog?"

"Sure," said a guy standing near. "Mitzi wouldn't hurt a flea."

I had the picture now — or at least the general outline. The lobster truck was a film truck, and all around the pool here and in the main room were hidden cameras, as at Flupo's. But some impressions I still had to shake around till they formed up . . . I wanted another drink, and said so. A guy took my glass and scurried away.

Then suddenly across the patio came the genius himself. All five feet four of him. He bounced up to me, jumped, grabbed my neck, pulled himself up, hung on me, and gave me slobbery kisses on the cheeks.

There was cheering and applause. He continued to hang on my neck and slobber. I've had experience with emotional directors, so I put up with it. Finally he unlatched me. I wiped my sleeve over my face. "Thanks. Were the bullets real?"

"Everything real!"

The guy handed me my drink. I swallowed it and handed it back for a refill.

I said to Peliculāru, "So a guy shot an inch from my head, blew a phone out of my hand — weren't you taking a big chance with real bullets?"

"No worry. Great marksman. Retired from Mafia, seek new career in pictures. I give him chance — splendid shooter. Meet Izador."

He beamed at a thin scruffy guy with a bony face who had dead blue eyes.

I said, "Hi, Izador. Good shooting."

He looked at me with his dead eyes. I smiled. He didn't. I doubt he ever had. Peliculāru gave him a pat on the back and he went away.

I drank down my third drink. "The blowup of the Cad — that was real too?"

"Yah. Terrific scene — like whole screen blow up in audience face!"

I was handed a fresh glass. Finnegan said, "Bora told me not to peep — and I was a clam." He grinned, shifting his eyes everywhere.

I said to the genius, "The ladder rails were charged?"

"Yah. Important you reach top of ladder, look over — we have zoomboom on your face — look of fear, then poozlement. Then we give you jolt in the hands." He grinned delightedly. "Make great closing scene."

"That's the end of the picture?"

"Yah."

"I look at a leaky sack of red paint and fall off the ladder?"

"Audience not see sack of paint — just see last look on your phizoozel — the shlock, the shlock!"

"Shock."

"Whatever. Then you drop off ladder. That the end. Audience ask theirself — what he see? What give him such a look? Audience let own sick imagination fill in — so they come up with more sickening finish than even Peliculāru could cook up for them!"

"That's genius," said Finnegan in a reverent voice. And everybody in earshot murmured that was what it was, genius.

Peliculāru didn't argue. He stared into space at private visions — probably a dozen Academy nominations.

I'd finished my drink and stuck out my glass for someone to fill it.

Someone took it. I said, "What's the theme of the picture?"

He came back from space. "I dunno. Don't matter. Up to critics to figger."

Everybody murmured again about genius.

I said, "None of it seems to make any sense."

He leaped, hung on my neck again. "Right! Just like *Big Schlepp!* So is great picture for today and for evermore! Greater and greater as world gradual go *kaputsky!*"

Everybody cheered.

I got my fresh drink and downed it.

The night went on — a party celebrating the quickest filming of a major epic in Hollywood history. Everybody got drunk — me the fastest, because of low resistance due to a pretty harrowing evening. People got loud and started singing. Then some people were saying that the most artistic part of this whole masterpiece was Barbara's informal swim, and would she give a repeat performance? I don't know if she did — just about then I passed out and fell backward onto the rubber mattress.

I spent the rest of the night there, coming to with the sun high. Everybody was gone except one guy staggering around the patio picking up empties, shaking them, then tossing them into the empty pool.

He was the driver of the lobster truck that had done the freeway filming. We walked around to the garage area, got in the truck, and he gave me a ride back to Hollywood.

That was a year ago. I'm still living in the same place on Orange Drive. I've had a few commercials, but not much else since *Catastrophe.*

It got great reviews. Critics said it had real relevance and profound meaning, and was undoubtedly a work of high cinematic art. So nobody came to see it. So they missed the car blowup, the wild dog, that great final shot of my face in shock — and Barbara's swim.

Pelicularu went back to Rashpudlovik, saying America was ten years behind his visions.

I called Barbara a few times, and we made dates, but never seemed to get together. I guess it wasn't our destiny.

Har-Tai and the wild dog, they're pretty busy in horror films.

Izador dropped out of sight.

Hooray for Hollywood.

CU: Mannix
by
Richard Matheson

WHILE MANNIX WAITED FOR the receiver to be lifted on the other end of the line, he gazed at the back of his right hand. It was a trim, powerful hand; the skin darkly tanned, the nails immaculately manicured. He spread the fingers and drew them hard into a fist. A good hand, strong and healthy-looking, not a sign of age.

His legs twitched as the intermittent buzzing in the earpiece broke off with a click. "Good afternoon, Renken-Blasker," said the girl's voice.

"Dale Mannix, dear," he told her. "Burt in?"

"*Yes,* Mr. Mannix—right away." Her tone was properly reverential. Mannix smiled and drew in slowly on his stomach muscles, glancing downward. His chest was spare and nut-brown. Hard, he thought. Who says I'm sixty-two? I'll flatten him.

"What can I do for you, Dale?" Burt Renken's voice inquired.

"Just got a new phone," Mannix told him. "Called to give you the number."

"Shoot," said Renken.

Mannix looked at the receiver. "276-5090," he read.

"Got it," Renken answered. "Old number out the window?"

"No, no—just wanted a second one, exclusively for business." He was briefly, pleasantly conscious of his voice — its warmth and variations.

As he hung up, Mannix stared across the wide expanse of lawn toward the pool. Inger was rubbing tanning lotion over her nude, tawny form. Mannix shivered as she squirted oil drops across her breasts and rubbed them lingeringly into the skin. He thought of going out there in the sun with her. In his imagination, he could feel the soft, hot moistness of her skin.

He made a grumbling sound and picked the script back up. Have to learn these bloody lines, he told himself. He propped the hand-tooled-leather binder on his lap and tried to concentrate. He'd never been too good at reading, though. Not that he didn't have a memory he'd match against the best. No one — but no one — had a better grasp of dialogue than he did. It was the reading itself that bored him. All that damned descriptive garbage.

Mannix crossed his muscular legs and cleared his throat, his eyes on the poolside chaise again. Inger was on her stomach now. She stretched out, resting her head on her arms. What was she thinking of? he wondered. *Who* was she thinking of?

Flexion in his neck again. Trapezius, he thought. He clenched his teeth, visualizing tension spasms in the damaged muscle. He stared out at her naked form. To look inside that golden head, he thought — to see, to *know*.

He glanced at the telephone suddenly, the idea sprung to full bloom in his mind. Smiling, he picked up the receiver and dialed their old number. Fortunately, Maria was out shopping. He started as he heard the jangling of the telephone in the entry hall. To be on both ends of the line at once was an odd sensation. He couldn't hear the poolside telephone.

He smiled as Inger reached out lazily for the receiver. It made him feel godlike to realize that he knew everything and she knew nothing about that ringing telephone beside her.

She lifted the receiver. "Hello?" she said.

That voice — he shivered at the sound of it. Casually, he reached across the table by his leather chair, removed a tissue from its dispenser, folded it in quarters, and held it over the mouthpiece. "Hel*lo*," he replied.

"Who's this?" asked Inger.

"Don't you know?" he asked. His famous blue-grey eyes were crinkling at the corners. He could see them as he had so many times — in closeup, on wide-screen, in Technicolor.

"No," she said. Interest or impatience? Mannix lost his smile. He couldn't tell.

"Let's just say a fond admirer."

Inger murmured. "Oh?"

Ice water running up the backs of his legs. It wasn't impatience. "Come on, you know," he said.

"I don't," she protested — mildly.

Mannix turned his head, releasing shaky breath. She knew, he told himself. She was putting him on, that's all. "Sure you do," he insisted. He felt that internationally famous knot of vein at his right temple starting to pulse. "Take a guess."

"How can I?" she asked.

Mannix fumbled on the chairside table, feeling for his eyeglasses. "Try," he said impulsively. "We've met, you know." He realized abruptly that his voice was that of Gresham, the sly Chicago lawyer in *Point of Order*, Universal, 1958. His agent had told him he was crazy to do that one, that it would hurt his image.

"Met where?" she was asking.

"One of those parties," he answered.

He had the glasses now. He slid them hastily across his ears and nose bridge. Inger sprang into focus. "What do you look like?" she asked him.

You'd better know it's me, he thought. The planes of his face were hardened now — that look of threatening anger movie audiences knew the world over: woe betide his enemies now. He looked out coldly at her, his neck beginning to stiffen. "If I told you what I look like," he said, "you'd know who I am and the game would be over."

He covered the mouthpiece, sucked in breath. Hell, let it go, a voice suggested. *No,* he answered. He'd suspected this for some time now. Let it come out.

"All right," she said, "let's see."

He waited.

"You're — fifty. No, no — sixty," she said.

Mannix grinned. You knew all along, you Köstlich kraut, he thought, delighted. He closed his eyes abruptly, trying not to recognize the surge of gratified relief that filled him. "That old," he heard himself say.

"I'm only teasing," she said.

Mannix opened his eyes.

"You're under forty, I imagine," Inger said.

"That's right." Mannix felt his heartbeat, slow and heavy. "Thirty-eight to be exact." He stared out through the window. Inger had her left arm pressed beneath her breasts, nudging them upward. "That's not old at all," she said.

She *didn't* know. Mannix felt ill. "No, it isn't old," he said with Gresham's voice. "I'm still completely capable of —" (beat): he saw it written on a script page "— quite a bit."

He felt his flesh grow cold as Inger's soft laugh drifted from the earpiece. "I'll *bet* you are," she said.

Mannix blinked. His head felt light. "I *am*," he told her. "Interested?"

He shuddered as she slid her feet back on the chaise, pushing up her knees. Her legs remained together for an instant, then slumped sideways and apart. "Why should I be interested in you?" she asked.

Mannix felt the pulsing at his temple quicken. Her tone, her posture. *She was willing.*

He twitched as Inger sat up, turned around, and looked back toward the study window. She *did* know! Mannix felt his heartbeat jolt. He waited for her smile, her wave, some sign of recognition. He deserved her mockery for this. He'd take it gracefully and —

Mannix felt himself go numb as Inger turned back and reclined once more. "Well?" she asked.

"Well, what?" She had to recognize his voice now — he wasn't even trying. But he had to try! Abruptly, he was back inside the other man. "Why should you be interested in me? Because I'm good in bed. Damn good." Please, he thought. Please tell me that you know it's me.

"Are you really?" Inger said.

Mannix shivered violently. "If I was there I'd show you."

That laugh again. He'd fought the realization for a long time, but he knew it now: it was an obscene laugh. *Inger* was obscene. "If you were here," she said, "you'd *have* to show me because I'm lying in the sun without a stitch on."

He stared out through the window at her. Now her legs were far apart, her left hand was back behind her head. She's ready for you, Mister, Mannix thought.

The swimming pool reflected like a mirror in the moonlight. Mannix stared at it. Bel Air was soundless at this time of night. He heard a bird chirp somewhere in the darkness.

He turned and looked at Inger.

Her body was stretched out on the bed like some sleek, well fed animal. She *is* an animal, he thought. Less than half an hour before she'd straddled him with panting fierceness; *"Kostlich! Kostlich!"* (Delicious! Delicious!) Who had she really straddled in the darkness, though? (She had turned the lamp off, not he.) That man who phoned her this afternoon? He hadn't seen her so excited in a year.

Mannix walked across the carpeting and stood beside the bed, gazed down at the golden flood of hair across the pillow, at her browned, voluptuous figure.

All through dinner he had waited for the laughter. They'd gone over to The Swiss House — she doted on Viennese cooking. They'd gotten one of the tables in back and, as they'd eaten, he'd kept waiting for the laughter to begin — for her to tell him how ridiculous he was. At one point, when he'd seen her smiling to herself, he'd asked her what was funny — felt his hands begin to shake with final, hopeful readiness.

"Nothing," she had said. He'd stared at her and known that everything he'd feared for all these years was true: he was that most despised and ludicrous of men — the cuckold.

Mannix leaned over tremblingly and pulled out the drawer of his bedside table. Reaching in, he drew out his pistol and pointed it at Inger.

No. He shook his head. Ruin his career for her? He smiled contemptuously at her slack, Germanic features. Thirty-seven years he'd been a star. He'd be insane to end that for a moment's dubious revenge. He put the pistol back into the drawer.

He took off his robe and lay down on the bed beside her. Now that he'd made up his mind to divorce her, he was amused at himself for having thought, even for a moment, that she was clever enough to have fooled him.

He clucked. Too bad, he thought. Marriage number four gone down the tube. Amusing that, for the first time, it was not because of *his* unfaithfulness. The public would never believe it, of course. Not that they should — the other enhanced his image better. Mr. Romance. He winced. What idiot columnist had made that up?

It was good all morning. Makeup at six, shooting at seven. The scenes were long and his. There were a lot of takes without excessive waits for setups. With what spare time there was, he entertained the cast with anecdotes about the Golden Years — memories laced with humor, charm, and wit. He did it beautifully. To lure and hold with words — to be "on" before a rapt, attentive audience — there was nothing like it. It was almost sensual.

Then it was over and he was in his dressing room. Lunch was called. He wasn't hungry. He sat inside the lavish trailer, staring at the telephone. How long had she been cheating on him? In the almost three years of their marriage, how many times?

Mannix jerked the telephone receiver off its cradle and dialed his home number. As if it were someone else's hand, he watched it draw the neatly pressed and folded handkerchief from the pocket of his grey slacks and press it down across the mouthpiece. Now what? asked his mind. You're dumping her. Isn't that enough?

It's not, he thought.

"Mannix residence," said Maria.

Mannix cleared his throat. "Mrs. Mannix, please."

"One moment," said Maria.

As he waited, Mannix wondered where she was. She could still be in bed. She liked to sleep late after making love. Love? he thought. He'd never manage to associate that word with her again.

She picked up an extension. "Yes?"

Mannix licked his lips. "Hel-*lo*," he said.

"Who's this?"

"You know who it is," he answered.

"Do I?"

Mannix tensed. "Sleep well?"

"I always sleep well," Inger answered.

Yes, you do, he thought — you aren't bright enough to suffer from anxiety.

She yawned. "Look, I have to go unless —"

Mannix cut her off. "Meet me," he said. He knew it was absurd, and yet he smiled with mirthless pleasure at the thought.

"Oh, I couldn't do that," she protested.

Her coyness made his stomach turn. "Tomorrow," Mannix told her. He could almost see her. She was sprawled across the bed, still naked.

"What makes you think I want to meet you?" she asked.

"Because you'd love it," he answered. His fingers clamped in on the bridge of the receiver. "You and me in bed, like animals."

It was almost anti-climactic when she murmured, "Where?"

The dressing room was blurred around him, swimming. Mannix felt like very heavy, very fragile glass. If he moved, he'd shatter. "Beverly Hills Hotel," he said. It sounded like a first reading. "Three o'clock tomorrow afternoon."

She's going to do it, he thought. He couldn't seem to breathe.

"How will I know you?" Inger asked.

The answer spun immediately to mind. "Just ask for Mr. Smith's room," Mannix said, "Eddie Smith."

"I don't know an Eddie Smith." She sounded suddenly confused.

"Real names tomorrow, baby," Mannix answered.

"Oh, I see," said Inger.

No, you don't, he thought, you don't see anything, you stupid bitch.

"Will it be fun?" she asked. He saw her face quite clearly now. The edges of her teeth were set together, eager and excited.

Mannix answered, "You have no idea."

He'd yet to take the first sip of his Pimm's Cup. He was sitting in a corner of the Polo Lounge, stirring with its slice of cucumber while he stared at the key on the table. The plastic tag was face up: 315. Eddie Smith's room, Mannix thought. A faint smile drew his lips back. Right, he thought.

Some men walked across the lounge and waved to him. He didn't wave back. He had no desire to talk to anyone. He really should have chosen some more remote spot. Everybody knew him here. Still, what difference did it make? He wasn't here to murder her — just to see a look of stupid bafflement across her face.

Mannix had to smile. It was rather funny, actually — the idea of this Eddie Smith. Mannix saw him as a college football player gone to lard, maybe a small-time actor making out with women who set their standards at the minimum level: any stud in a storm.

Smith could resemble that one over there: broad shoulders, curly blond hair, tight clothes — the jacket a shade too loud, the low-grade silk shirt. Sub-par all the way.

He blinked. The blond young man was smiling at him. Mannix tensed, about to cut him off, when the idea came — instantly complete, completely beautiful. Mannix smiled broadly. How much more satisfying than a look of bafflement on Inger's face. He gestured for the young man to come over.

The young man stood with obvious delight and as he crossed the lounge Mannix realized abruptly that he *was* an actor—he had seen him somewhere in somewhere in some distinguished role performed with undistinguished flatness. Mannix almost chuckled. The young man would perform all right, he thought; through any indicated hoop. He'd have to — it was part and parcel of his hunger to succeed. They were all the same.

The young man stopped in front of him. "Good afternoon, Mr. Mannix," he said. His smile was that of all young, struggling actors, Mannix thought, straining for unwonted charm — too bright, too many teeth displayed.

"Sit down," Mannix said.

The young man was unable to restrain a startled grin. "Why, *thank you*," he responded. He sat with lithe dispatch. Lifts weights, thought

Mannix. Studies at some one-horse acting school, played a few supporting roles in non-pay theater groups, has a list of TV credits adding up to zero. "What's your name?" he asked, his voice genial, interested.

The young man swallowed. "Jeff Cornell," he said sincerely. Who made that up? Mannix wondered. Probably some agent. "Cornell," he tasted. "Seems to me I've seen you somewhere."

"I just did a part on *L.A. Law,*" Cornell supplied immediately.

"Of course," said Mannix. He hadn't seen it. "And very good, too," he added, smiling.

"Why, thank you, Mr. Mannix," said Cornell. "That's very kind of you."

Not exactly, Mannix thought. The young man's dazzling smile amused him. Exactly what he needed. "Tell you what I have in mind," he said. "I need a favor."

"I'll do anything I can, Mr. Mannix," Cornell answered gravely.

I know you will, thought Mannix. Anything at all. "I want you to meet my wife at three o'clock," he said. "I want you to seduce her." Not even Olivier could mask a reaction to that, he thought.

It wasn't surprising that Cornell's face went almost completely blank. "Is —?"

"— this a joke?" completed Mannix. "No, it isn't. I have reason to believe that my wife has been unfaithful." With a platoon of different men, the sentence finished in his mind. "I want to divorce her, but I have to have some evidence."

"But —" Cornell looked distressed.

"You have carte blanche," continued Mannix, using the tone of whimsical bittersweetness that had endeared him to a generation of moviegoers. "You can go the distance if you want to. I have every reason to believe she won't object. That part doesn't interest me. My one concern is catching her. You understand?"

He could see that Cornell was trying unsuccessfully to understand.

"Let me give it to you once again," said Mannix. Now his voice had bite. "Number one: I know my wife's been cheating on me. Number two: I need evidence that will stand up in court. Number three: If I can trap her in a compromising state, I'll have that evidence." He leaned back, fingering the key tag, "Not too hard a job," he said. "She won't say no, I guarantee you." He paused for effect. "And, in return," he finished, "you acquire a featured part in my next film which commences shooting this fall in London."

He waited, thinking: I can hear the wheels turn. A featured part in

Dale Mannix's next film? London in autumn? *The big chance?*
Jeff Cornell would draw and quarter his mother for less.

Mannix checked his wristwatch. It was only three-nineteen. Come
on, he thought. He drank some Scotch and sat the glass down irritably. What were they doing now? He winced. His neck was stiffening
again. Disturbances like this were bad for him. He should be home,
relaxing in the sun, not sitting here. *God damn her, anyway!*

He looked at his watch again. Seven minutes more. He drew in
trembling breath. Play it cool, he told himself. He'd have it made in
seven minutes: the delight of seeing Inger's dazed expression and the
evidence he'd need to dump her without cost. As for Cornell — He
smiled. London in the fall would not see Jeff Cornell before any cameras.
Idiot, Mannix thought coldly.

The scene projected on his mind again. Inger entering the hotel at
five to three, heading for the desk. Mannix had been standing where
she couldn't see him and observed her talking to the clerk, then smiling
as she crossed the lobby toward the elevator. Room 315, he thought.
He picked the key from the table and dropped it into his pocket. Cool,
he thought. He pushed away the glass, then eyed his watch again.
Time to go.

Mannix stood. He dropped a five-dollar bill on the table and left the
Polo Lounge. Crossing the side lobby, he ascended a half flight of steps
and entered the men's room. There he scrubbed and rinsed his hands.
I'm washing my hands of her, he thought, the concept pleasing him.

He stared at his reflection as he carefully combed his black and
grey-streaked hair. Sixty-two? he thought. Absurd. He didn't look a
day past forty-five. He was lean and hard. To hell with Inger. Who
needed her? He was Dale Mannix. He didn't need anyone. He
straightened his black knit tie. *Hic jacet,* cunt, he thought, you've had
it. Mannix is about to dump you — right into the garbage can where
you belong.

The elevator was waiting. He stepped inside and pressed the but-
ton. He was Vince DeMaine in *City Heat* going up to kill his faithless
wife. No, that was unreality, he thought. This was happening; he was
merely getting rid of excess baggage. She could play around on someone
else's money. As for him, there were still a lot of numbers in his book.

The doors slid open. Mannix left the elevator, listening to his
footsteps. Room 325. He pressed his shoulders back, visualizing himself as he walked: tall, distinguished, on top of the world. Room 323. If
Academy Awards were given for true-life performances, he'd win one

for the scene he was about to play. 321. He smiled. Let them be naked, he thought. 319. His words were going to hit them with far more impact than bullets. 317. A few more paces.

Mannix stopped outside the room and listened. There was no sound inside. He waited tensely. What were they doing? He reached into his pocket and withdrew the key. Don't let me fumble now! he thought in panic as he almost dropped it. It would be horrible if he unlocked the door so clumsily that she had time to run into the bathroom. They had to be in bed together, naked, staring at him. He would accept no less.

He shoved the key into the lock, twisted it, and pushed the door ajar.

A wave of darkness rushed across him. For a moment, he was certain he was going to faint. His fingers grabbed the doorknob as he wavered.

Jeff Cornell was standing by the window, smoking nervously. Inger was sitting on a chair. Both were dressed. The bed was made.

"*Do* come in," said Inger coldly.

Mannix gaped at her. Her face was pale and rigid, her expression filled with venomous distaste. "Well, are you going to close the door?" she asked. "Or would you rather everyone in the hotel found out about this?"

Mannix pushed the door shut. He felt dazed and numb.

"Disappointed?" Inger asked. "Is your big scene ruined? The out-raged husband telling off the guilty wife? Did you rehearse it for a long time?"

Mannix couldn't speak.

"You must think I'm awfully stupid," Inger said.

It hit him then. "You *knew,*" he said.

"Brilliant!" she exploded.

"But why —?"

"I have to tell you, don't I?" Inger cut him off. "I really have to tell you — it's impossible for you to understand." She stood up, glaring at him. "I've had it, Dale!" she raged. "Is that clear? Do you understand that? I have *had* it! Years and years of living with your damned suspicions! All right for you to have affairs! Oh, yes, of course! *You're* Dale Mannix, you're the big star! Mr. Romance! But *me?* Oh, no, not me! I had to be watched like a criminal! Questioned! Hounded! Con-stantly suspected! *Well, I've had it, Dale!* This is the last damned straw! Trying to trick me into having an affair with a total stranger so you can trap me with him! You're sick, Dale! *You're sick and you're too damned much for me!*"

Mannix reached out feebly. "Inger." He felt cold and sick. "Inger, please." His neck was like a board.

Inger closed the door and locked it, walked across the room, and sat on the bed. Lying down, she gazed up at the ceiling.

That had been the closest one of all. If Cornell hadn't told her what was going on — She shivered, gooseflesh rising on her arms. All that conversation on the phone and she'd never had the least suspicion it was Dale. She groaned. My God, he could have wrapped me up but good, she thought.

She stretched luxuriantly. It was all right now, though. It had worked out perfectly — she might have planned it herself. Dale wouldn't dare suspect her now. Not for a long time, anyway. She laughed softly. It was a riot that the man he'd picked to trap her had gotten her a long reprieve instead.

Inger sighed. And *what* a man, she thought. She was looking forward to spending time with him. She clenched her teeth and murmured, *"Kostlich."*

She turned her head and looked up at the rows of photographs on the wall. Dale Mannix. The big star. Mr. Romance. She snickered. *Old fool,* she thought.

The Bum Wrap

by
Carleton Carpenter

"**N**o, no, dear boy! Not a R-A-P party. I should imagine that would entail a select group of Hollywood wags lounging about an overheated pool, sipping strawberry daiquiries and dishing the latest industry dirt. No, my dear Chester, it's *wrap* with a 'w' — as when an assistant director, with all the pomposity and ill-achieved authority invested in him, calls, upon completion of the final setup for a film, 'That's a wrap.' "

Coolidge Thorpe sipped daintily at his strawberry daiquiri and stirred a slight ripple into the calm of the clear pool with a bare toe — a former dancer's point with the instep gracefully arcing the toes almost back to the heel. His steel-grey bootcamp crewcut belied his somewhat effete mannerisms, still-youthful physique, and uncertain but certainly well advanced years.

Someone once confided to me — overloudly over lunch — that his mother, with whom he shared this sprawling pink-stucco *palais,* was actually his sister. Calling her Mum made him seem younger as he would navigate her, slightly alist and always awash with her ever-present ballast of double bourbons, from the A group to the A-plus group at his frequent parties.

In former days, under long-term studio contract, he had become *the* father figure — practically the American symbol of fertility — and was cast in film after successful film as head of families numbering anywhere from five to a full dozen. Thorpe himself, however, remained a confirmed, devout bachelor.

"Naturally you'll be there. Five p. m. Stage twenty-one. Tomorrow." An edict. Imperiously delivered through thin lips beneath an improbable turned-up nose. A nose to which all odors were obviously semi-suspect.

"Wouldn't miss it." I said, taking another pull at my Amstel light beer. "My regulars will expect a full report when I get back home to my shop next week."

Home is New York City and the shop is Chet's Barber Shop on Eleventh Street in the Village, just off Sixth. It had been more or less innovative, I guess, when I opened for business a few years back. Haircutting for men and women in the same place. Old hat now. There are unisex salons all over the place. Maybe the only unique thing left is that it's really a barber shop — no fancy gimmicks and no fancy prices. I cut hair. And think of myself as an old-fashioned barber. Too much Petersburg, New York — the tiny upstate hamlet I hail from — rubbed off on me to comfortably wear the title Chester Long, Stylist.

How and why I found myself here in Hollywood, being vastly overpaid on this megabucks movie to do hair, is another story. Too long, too convoluted, and has nothing to do with the price of tomatoes.

Maybe I'll tell about that another time.

Anyway, I'm here, winding up my "stint on the flick" — perhaps three months in Always-Always Land has been too long, the local lingo is beginning to creep in — and looking forward to the wrap party tomorrow. With a 'w.'

Parties, I've learned, are the true and foremost Los Angeles product. In the Hollywood horserace, films place a distant second. Parties pop up at the drop of an option. Any excuse will do. "I got the part! Let's party!" "I turned down the part! Let's party!" (No one loses a job or gets fired in Hollywood. One rejects offers and asks to be released from contracts.) "I found the most divine shoulder bag on Rodeo! Let's party!" "It's my Afghan's birthday tomorrow! Let's party!" "I was mugged last night by the hunkiest stuntman! Isn't my shiner gorgeous? Let's party!" And most of the parties seem to be costume affairs. The rent-all establishments, more numerous than banks in L.A., thrive . . .

I was off in a dark corner of Stage twenty-one when the magical long-awaited words broke the silence. "That's a wrap! Let's party!"

The film we'd just finished was an epic — what isn't now? — called *Spartacus III.* I don't remember a II, but no matter. Naturally this called for another costume party. I'd expected total Roman regalia, but discovered otherwise. Tired of togas and other trappings the cast had traipsed around in the last three months, most opted for other party garb. Many of the bit players, however — the beautiful studs and studettes — chose to remain in their scanty wardrobe, which had been carefully designed to display as many muscles and mammillae as good tastelessness allowed. All that bronzing body makeup shouldn't be a total loss.

I watched from my corner as the cameras and cables and lights were hauled away and the set, a Roman public bathhouse, was transformed from reel to real. If you didn't look up toward the catwalks and overhead-light rails, you'd forget you were on a soundstage. The set, incredible in its detailed design, transported you back into ancient raunchy Rome — you could almost smell an oncoming orgy. You could, for real, smell the mountains of delicious food that had been catered and set up as quickly as the camera equipment disappeared.

Already dozens of mini-togaed extras were milling around the groaning tables, looking less like atmosphere than actual publicans, crying out the occasional "Evoe!"

Gradually, the leading players and stars, carefully timing entrances, began to arrive. I knew some slightly more than others, none really well. Hairdressers are only necessary props for most of them. Only Coolidge Thorpe had offered more than token friendship. His initial interest, I suspected, was quasi-amatory, but once he realized my striped barber's pole twirled to a straighter tune we settled into a chummy, comfortable relationship. I liked him. He was an outrageous fraud and poseur but he was a splendid actor and great fun to be around. He took to me, he said, because I was a true New Yorker like himself. Actually, he was from Indiana, I think. However, he'd worked for years on Broadway in a series of smart revues and musicals, and earned his stardom.

Coming West, and going Hollywood at once, he pretended to hate all the glitz while thoroughly embracing it. He would proclaim loudly to everyone within earshot around and in his olympic-sized pool how phony they all were. True actors remained in the East, he'd say. He was here only because Cora, his mum, adored all this tommyrot. Of course, movie money was a pleasant, if insufficient, buffer against all the Hollywood horse manure.

He wouldn't have given it up for the world. Even after the jobs became infrequent and the roles cameo, he hung in there. But pink stucco! Well, at least several thoughtful trees hid his home from Sunset Boulevard. A complete anachronism, Coolidge. This film offered him a meaty role, though not really a comeback, I suppose. More like a last hurrah.

I watched his entrance into the party. White-silk toga (from a Senate scene), flowing phony white beard, bald-cap wig with white fringe, bare-footed and carrying a large scythe. Father Time.

"Stand aside, plebeians! Aside! My tool is lethal," he cried, stroking the twisted handle of the farm implement on his shoulder. Everyone laughed and gave him a wide berth.

By his stately side was young Tony Greeva, one of the new-breed Hollywood brat pack, hunky, horny, and clad only in a designer diaper. His hair was a moptop of sun-bleached yellow curls and he looked as if he'd just stepped out of a Calvin Klein underwear ad. Happy Baby New Year! The applause at their arrival was tremendous.

Greeva's leading lady, Mae Beth Jolson, was dressed in a polka-dotted Shirley Temple thing, ruffled and starched. Hemline way up on the long legs revealing matching polka-dot panties underneath. She, too, sported a mop of blonde curls. Leading lady? She looked more like a leading baby. But I must confess most of the cast seemed practically prepubescent to me. Maybe it's because the big four-o is catching up with me next birthday that I feel ancient. And the fact that everyone out here in California is absolutely beautiful, youthful, and unflawed is a mite depressing. It makes me really miss New York. I long to see a couple of good sallow faces and a blemish or two. And an out-of-condition body. I have the sneaky feeling I'm the only person in all of L.A. with a flat chest. Flat, hell — concave.

None of that at this *Spartacus III* shindig. Even Ethel Teasdale, the spindly character actress who played Thorpe's bitch of a wife and seemed frail enough to tip over if anyone blew a puff of cigarette smoke toward her, held her own in the chest department. Coolidge and Ethel had been paired up often in the past, their mutual loathing increasing with each outing. He claimed she was a bitch off screen as well as on. She claimed the same about him.

I agree with Thorpe. None of the three wigs I did for her, including the curly blonde one she now wore, met with her approval, and her fussing and complaining had been nonstop. However, Jerry Grandig, the young director of the epic, had approved all three and Teasdale was stuck with them. And me. Coolidge chortled with glee one evening when I confided that she was nearly bald. "I knew it!" he had shrieked. "Bliss!"

Grandig, a moody youth, kept mostly to himself during the shooting. From what I saw on the set, he said as little as possible to the actors and seemed to really communicate only with Luke Lassiter, his young cinematographer. Grandig sported a moustache, intense eyes, and skin that, although clear, was untanned. A point in his favor. I'm sure he didn't know me by name. I don't believe he ever looked directly at me during pre-production or the entire shooting. I don't think he ever looked at anyone. His vision seemed centered on some deep inner space far beyond mere mortals.

But not tonight. Although he wasn't wearing a costume — his ever-present cardigan sweater and baggy corduroys are a costume unto themselves — he was being affable. Grinning, backslapping, eyes bright and glistening — mixing and mingling. A whole new persona. All hyped up. Or maybe hopped up. Drugs tended to be pervasive at these parties.

Coolidge once told me over too many drinks, "All of Hollywood is a frigging pharmacy! At a recent party someone asked me if I'd like to do a couple of lines. Flattered, I smiled and recited a favorite bit of Ariel from *The Tempest*. Everyone gave me the oddest stares. Some s.o.b. sniggered, 'He meant coke, you old ham!' My dear, I didn't know where to look I was so embarrassed. My ego and the generation gap joining hands to annihilate me. I wrapped my dignity around me like a feather boa and fled. Not a bad exit. Tallulah would have been green."

I edged into the throng, feeling a bit like an intruder, and managed to gather up a plate, rye bread, lox, cream cheese, a ladle of fresh fruit, and a beer.

I smiled and nodded to one and all as I munched and sipped, juggling plate, bottle, and plastic utensils. No one paid me much attention. The film was finished. I was already a ghost. Disposable goods. Like plastic knives and forks.

I hate parties where I can't sit down, so I avoid most cocktail affairs. Won't even stay in a bar if there's no empty stool. I'm too tall to hover. But here I was, hovering, unnoticed, my stabs at party conversation falling on deaf, perfectly formed ears and my jolly party smile meeting with vacant stares from flawless faces.

I grabbed another beer, deposited my plate, and looked around for Coolidge Thorpe. I knew I could at least make positive contact with him. We could carp together about the caterers, who'd combined fine chinaware with the plastic utensils. But I couldn't find him. He'd vanished into the noisy, self-involved mass of merrymakers.

The music, blasting from overeager speakers, was too loud, too one-note rock, and way too much for me. Way too much to hear someone calling my name. Someone remembering it? No way, José.

I was wrong.

"Chester Long! Chester! Mr. Long!"

I looked around.

"Down here, my darling!"

I looked down into the upturned, actually smiling face of Ethel Teasdale. Had she actually said "darling"?

"Don't stand there like a praying mantis, dear. Get a full beer and let me lead you to a quieter place where we can get off our feet!"

"Miss Teasdale?" I nearly stammered in surprise.

"*Ethel*, my darling. Come along."

My bottle was half full but I reached for another as ordered and carried both as I followed the frail character actress through the maze of dancing, intertwining bodies.

Reaching the outer rim of the main mass of writhing whatevers, she waved her hand at a young couple sitting on a stone bench and coupling at the lips. "Shoo!" she said. "Go cross-pollinate with that nice twosome over there!" She pointed a lacquer-tipped finger and they shooed. Languidly.

We sat. Thankfully.

"Ta for the beer," she said, grabbing the full one. I hadn't realized it was meant for her. She tipped back her curl-topped head and tossed off a man-sized belt. I suddenly realized my jaw was agape. I snapped it shut, hoping she hadn't noticed.

She didn't burp, thank God. Just giggled. "Can't a lady enjoy a beer, my dear?" So she hadn't missed my gape. But she missed the reason for it. It wasn't the beer, it was her whole demeanor. What had happened to her bitchiness? Something else was odd about her. For a moment I couldn't put my finger on it, then it hit me. She'd changed wigs since her arrival. The new curlytop was pinkish instead of blonde.

She looked at me levelly — eye to eye. Another first.

"You were very buddy-buddy with old Coolidge during the shooting, weren't you, Chet?" Chet? I must not have hidden my surprise. "That's what they call you, isn't it?"

I nodded.

"Well, weren't you?"

"Yes," I said, pupil to teacher. "I like him."

"He's an old fraud. Always was." A small smile crept around the almost cupid's-bow lips.

"I know." I smiled. "So does he. It's one of the things I enjoy about him." She reached over and actually patted my knee. Well, the white-duck trouser covering it. That's about as far as my costume went. White ducks, saddle shoes, and blazer.

"I'll tell you a secret," she said, winking. "Me, too. Although God forbid anyone in the industry finds out. Our bitching at each other all these years is the biggest fraud of all." One final squeeze of my knee and her hand withdrew. "Good for business. Which, as you can guess, hasn't been all that terrific lately for Thorpe and me. Our ongoing feud helps. It keeps our fading names bantered about and if a role comes along for me, the producer or casting agent automatically thinks of Thorpe to play opposite, and vice versa. Typecasting is a fact of life out here and might as well be encouraged."

"You could have fooled me," I said

"Could have?" she shot back.

"Did! Did! I thought you hated each other's guts!"

She beamed and gulped down several ounces of beer, like a thirsty lumberjack at Miller Time. "Although we've probably only been fooling ourselves these last few years. It's no doubt a secret the entire industry is in on now, how famously we *really* get along. How we really *like* each other."

As I started to say I hadn't heard any such rumors, a studio guard approached our bench. "You both better come with me," he said in a shaken voice. "Mr. Thorpe has had a terrible accident."

The eeriest thing about the next few moments was the sudden lack of blaring music. And the spaced-out murmur of the crowd — like a giant, simmering teakettle. The Roman orgy had turned Speilberg-spooky.

The L.A.P.D. arrived quickly with ambulance, doctors, photographers, M.E. staff, the works, but they were all too late to help poor Coolidge. He had been found behind one of the portable dressing rooms lined up at the far end of the huge soundstage lying face up, toga bloody where the sharp point of his scythe stuck out from a lethal wound midchest.

The plainclothes cop who seemed to be in charge formulated a bizarre explanation: Thorpe, tired of lugging it around, had dropped his Father Time prop on the floor, blade pointing up, somehow stumbled and fell on it, and then rolled over on his back. The force of his fall would have been great enough for the thin curving blade to penetrate his body. A tragic, clumsy accident.

It sounded like far-fetched hogwash to me.

Accident or not, police had been posted at both exit doors leading from the studio, perhaps until a witness who had seen or heard something (over that ear-splitting din?) came forward to help clarify things. All sorts of rumors and theories began to circulate. Actors acting. Bit players with a chance to take stage.

"Maybe he committed suicide, throwing himself on the blade like a samurai!" "Why was he carrying that real thing instead of a mock-up?" "Thorpe was always a stickler for realism, if you'll excuse my choice of words." "It's to the point. Oops! Sorry!" I couldn't believe what I was hearing. A man was dead, for God's sake! No one seemed to care. They joked and laughed. No one was letting the tragedy affect the party spirit. And no one was suggesting that it might be something other than an accident. Not even the police. They seemed almost as casual about the dead actor as the cast and crew.

Coolidge was quickly covered and carried from the soundstage. Wrapped. Like the film.

Was I the only one there thinking murder? The non-performer being melodramatic while all the theatrical types were underplaying? I couldn't bring myself to think so. Coolidge, jesting when he first arrived at the party, had been right to call the scythe a lethal weapon. When I was a kid back in Petersburg, one of my uncles nearly amputated his left leg with one.

Shortly after the body had been removed, a young policeman found the bloody, wadded-up rag. It had been shoved behind the trailerhitch support for one of the dressing rooms. Only it wasn't a waddedup rag. It was a wadded-up wig. Blood-soaked and curly blonde.

The tight group huddled near me by the portable dressing room went into sudden shock. Ethel Teasdale, Jerry Grandig, Luke Lassiter, the cameraman, a couple of others, and Mae Beth Jolson. Mae Beth went into hysterics, crying uncontrollably, pulling frantically at her short brunette hair with nervous fingers. Shirley Temple had lost her blonde moptop.

Ethel Teasdale was twisting and readjusting her pinkish one. I wondered about her sudden affection for me earlier. And for poor Coolidge. A personality change with a wig change? One thing was fairly evident. I wasn't the only one thinking murder now.

The dressing-room door flew open. "What's all the commotion, chums?" Tony Greeva, diaper slightly askew, hung onto the door frame. He was obviously stoned. Higher than just cocaine. Heroin, too, maybe. And booze. His diction was lazy and slurred, his beach-yellowed curls mussed.

"Oh, Tony!" Mae Beth sobbed.

"Mae Beth Jolson, how could you!" The cold, austere tone had returned to Ethel's voice, her accusation clear and courtroom-loud.

I had examined, without touching it, the bloodied wig. It was not the blonde one I'd styled for Teasdale. It was close, but Ethel's was made from human hair. This was not. It was the one Mae Beth had been wearing when she arrived at the party.

"Oh, God! Oh, God!" she kept saying. "That nice old man."

"Nice try," Ethel told her, "but it won't work — that was your wig."

"I know," Mae Beth said. "But Tony wanted to wear it. He bet no one would notice he was wearing a wig, so I let him put it on." She started crying again. "And he was right — no one could tell it wasn't his own hair."

The detective asked politely, "What are you on, son?"

Tony giggled, then turned sincere-serious. "I did a little coke is all, officer."

"Did you kill Mr. Thorpe?" the detective asked.

"Kill? Are you kidding? Do I look like a killer? I couldn't get cast as a killer if I auditioned with a smoking gun in my hand." He laughed boyishly. "A little accident there with old Thorpie, that's all. A little accident with that nice old man. That nice dirty old man." He giggled again. "Tried to clean him up a little. I mean clean it up a lit — Sorry about ruining your wig, baby. It got itself all messy."

One of the medical examiner's staff helped Greeva to the couch inside the trailer and checked him over. There were no needle marks on his tanned arms or down-covered legs, but high up in the groin area, hidden beneath the diaper, were fresh tracks. The aide reported to the detective, who nodded. "Perversely, it will probably help his defense. The kid was probably too far out of it to know what was going on."

Suddenly, deep in my gut, I knew Tony Greeva was going to get away with Coolidge Thorpe's murder. And no one would ever know for sure exactly what had happened. He was young hot box-office, bankable, a studio saver with millions riding on his future. The industry needed him. And the L.A.P.D. needed the industry. It would end up being a bum rap that would never stick to the brat-star.

Greeva appeared again at the doorway, his smile lopsided. "Send in a female nurse to check me out next time, okay?" He clapped his hands together. "So are we going to party or not? Let's moooove, ole buddies! I'm bored hanging around here! Let's all go somewhere!"

The detective offered a helping hand. "Yes, son, let's go."

"Primo! Primo!" Baby New Year cried. "I'm tired of just hanging out here. Just killing time."

Right, I thought. Father Time.

The Booby Trap

by Robert L. Fish

MARYLYN BURROWS, NÉE
Gorham, was the most beautiful woman in the world. Unfortunately
she was also completely unphotogenic, so a career as a photographic
model or a screen actress seemed ruled out. Producers who saw her
on the streets of Hollywood were inclined to rush her before cameras
for screen tests even before making other proposals, but the tests were
invariably disasters, and so Marylyn ended up a sort of combination
sometimes-receptionist, often coffee-maker, and general message-
carrier at Perplexed Studios because it would have been a shame not
to have someone that lovely around where the producers, directors,
and executives of Perplexed Studios could just look at her.

Marylyn Burrows considered herself one of the unluckiest women
in the world, and not just because her beauty was such that it could
not be translated by a camera lens onto film. Her major complaint
with fate was that when she had first come to work at Perplexed Studios
she had been taken with one Johnny Burrows, a handsome stuntman
on the studio lot. They had been struck with each other's physical
attributes at once and shortly thereafter they married. One month
after the nuptials Johnny had the misfortune of being in a bad accident.

It seems they were filming a sequence in which Johnny was supposed to take a horse at high speed across a railroad crossing inches
ahead of a speeding train. Of course the scene was being filmed at

very slow speed so that when it appeared on the screen it would look as if the narrow escape was much narrower than it actually was; but even so when Johnny's horse — a new addition to the stables at Perplexed Studios and probably not as well trained as it might have been — saw all those succulent daisies on the railroad track between the rails and skidded to a halt to investigate, the charging train knocked both the horse and Johnny a goodly distance.

The worst part was that the horse landed on Johnny and when they had unscrambled him from the horse — whose name is not recorded — the horse was sent to the glue factory and Johnny was permanently crippled. In addition, his face, once so handsome, was now something to frighten Lon Chaney.

At this point Marylyn decided she had married too young, and to the wrong man. Unfortunately for Marylyn, "in sickness and in health" included "in accident" as well; and incompatibility being something that two must agree to, there was nothing Marylyn could do to become free. Johnny would not hear of a divorce.

In addition, Johnny Burrows was a jealous man. He not only wanted to know where Marylyn was at all times when she was not at home, even telephoning the studio during working hours to confirm that she was, indeed, there, but he also had the habit of going through her purse with or without her permission, and opening every package she came home with, searching for evidence that Marylyn was cheating on him. Which she would gladly have done in an instant had she been able to figure out how to do it and get away with it; but she did not want to take the chance that Johnny who, though ugly and crippled, still had hands the size of manhole covers, might do something drastic to that beauty which was the only thing she had left.

Marylyn knew she had a few minor faults: her memory was not too good and she often forgot where she had put things; but basically she considered herself resourceful, so when a certain head technician in the special effects department began giving her long side glances in the studio cafeteria, Marylyn decided to use what she — and she alone — considered her great intelligence to resolve her problem. One day she went to this technician as he sat in the cafeteria, drew up a chair, and sat down, allowing him a goodly glimpse of her cleavage as she did so. She blinked her huge eyes at him a few times and led him skillfully into conversation.

"I saw *Mission Impossible* last night," she began.

"Oh?" said the technician, putting aside his Danish, pleased to have a common interest with this lovely. "So did I."

This confused Marylyn for several moments, because she had invented the scene she was about to describe. But then, after several moments, she saw her way out of her dilemma and was pleased with herself for this confirmation of her brain power.

"Oh," she said, "this wasn't a regular *Mission Impossible*. This was a rerun."

"So was mine."

"I mean," Marylyn said, determined not to give up, "this was a rerun real late at night. Or early in the morning, I don't recall. On an out-of-town station, I don't remember which one."

"Oh," said the technician.

"Anyways," Marylyn went on, relieved at her escape, "in this episode they have a scene where Greg Morris rigs up this gizmo that looks like a woman's purse, only when it is snapped open it blows up in the face of the snapper-opener. Is a gizmo like that possible.?"

"Anything along those lines is possible," the technician said expansively, pleased to be having this unexpected but delightful conversation with the most beautiful woman he had ever seen, and also to be able to demonstrate his expertise. "The only thing with *Mission Impossible* is that when Peter Graves asks Greg Morris for a gizmo that's complicated, like something from a Sci-Fi job — to float a man through prison bars with thought waves or something — Greg Morris rigs it up in a few seconds. If we were doing the same thing in our special-effects department, it would take weeks, if not months."

Marylyn was appalled.

"You mean it would take months to rig up my purse — *a* purse, I mean — to blow up in the face of whoever opened it?"

"Oh, no," the technician said, tolerant of this ignorance. "To rig up a purse is duck soup. You could rig it to give out a loud bang and scare the living — scare the daylights out of him. Or her, or whoever opened the thing. Like those books that have a dirty title and inside there's just a mousetrap —"

"How about something stronger?" Marylyn asked.

"You mean, give out something like a blast of smoke as well as a bang? Scare the clown and make him look like the end man in a minstrel show at the same time? Halloween stuff?" He waved a hand deprecatingly. "Sure. Easy. No problem."

"I mean something to make him look like that car after the viaduct fell on it in *Earthquake*," Marylyn said firmly. "Like the pilot of the plane must have looked after King Kong slapped him from the Empire State Building and he fell a hundred floors to the street. Something like that. Can it be done?"

"Yeah, it could be done," the technician said doubtfully. "But —"

"And how long would it take to rig up my purse — I mean, *a* purse — the way I'm talking about?"

"Time isn't the problem," the technician said in a worried tone. "It's accounting for the dynamite —"

Marylyn gave him her most enticing look; it made the technician dizzy with desire. "I'm sure you could do it," she said in a husky voice. "A man in your position, and with your talent. And I would be most grateful. Most . . ."

The technician swallowed. "You really want me to rig up a purse with dynamite? *Dynamite?*"

"Is there anything stronger?" Marylyn asked.

"Sure, but it would be even harder to get and harder to account for."

Marylyn sighed, making the sacrifice. "Then I guess dynamite will have to do." She thought a moment. "But better make it two sticks, not one."

The technician was staring at her in confused silence, his mind blank to everything except her exceptional beauty. Marylyn ran her fingernail ever so lightly across the back of his hand. He shivered.

"And how long would it take?" she asked softly, caressingly.

"What?"

"I said, how long would it take to rig a purse with a couple of sticks of dynamite?" Marylyn asked, trying to keep the steel out of her voice.

"Oh, I'm sorry. I was thinking about something else," the technician said, coming down to earth. "About an hour is all. Once I get hold of a purse, that is."

"Why don't you use mine?" Marylyn suggested helpfully. "And I'll see you in an hour or so." She came to her feet, gave him a most promising smile, and walked from the cafeteria with the proper sway of her lovely hips.

There were many things for Marylyn Burrows, née Gorham, to think about on her way home that evening. Her purse, heavier than usual by the addition of two sticks of dynamite and a detonator attached to the clasp, lay on the seat beside her as she drove.

First she would resume her maiden name, Gorham; change jobs and probably never tell anyone she was ever married to Johnny Burrows. With her memory being what it was, she was sure that she herself would forget the ill-fated marriage in a short time, especially when she wasn't being reminded of it every day by the poor crippled creature who had once been Johnny Burrows.

Without Johnny, life would be a ball! There would be other men, many men, successful, handsome men she could marry. With Johnny out of the picture she could use her beauty and her brains in a way a younger, more wide-eyed, less experienced and less resourceful Marylyn had never been able to do.

She sighed and pulled the car into the darkened driveway. There was a light in the living room; through the curtains that covered the wide window she could see the shadow of Johnny sitting in a chair with the lamp lit behind him. Poor Johnny, she suddenly thought. We had some good times before the accident, although I can't say I remember any of them in detail. But if Johnny only looked like his shadow, instead of the way he really looks with his torn body and gruesome face! At least, she thought with a sudden rush of tenderness, let him see me for the last time as beautiful as I am! I shall make an entrance!

And she reached for her purse and her house-key —

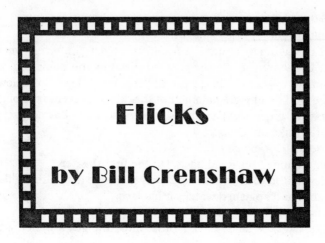

Flicks

by Bill Crenshaw

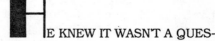E KNEW IT WASN'T A QUES-
TION of if his beeper would go off.

This time Devin Corley was home, his apartment, had just opened
a beer, turned on the TV, stretched out on the couch. He phoned in.
Dispatcher said Majestic Theater, across town. He started the VCR,
took a last pull at the beer, gave the cat fresh water, got a quick shower.
Then he left. Speed was not of the essence.

He knew what he'd find. A body; Ray Tasco, his partner, taking
statements, popping his gum, looking amused and surprised at once;
Maggie Epps with her wedge face and her black forensic kit, diagram-
ming the scene, scooping nameless little forensic glops into baggies;
Joe Franks in a safari shirt, slung with cameras, smiling like always,
always smiling, always angry. He'd give Corley grief about being away
from his desk again, or being late. Corley had been away from his desk
a lot. He was always late.

At the Majestic there were two uniforms in the men's john. The
room was done in men's room tile, blue and white, smelled of urine,
wet tobacco, stale drains, pine. Trash can on side, brown paper towels
spilling out, balled up, dark with water, some with red smears. Floor
around sinks wet, scattered splashes and small pools. Hints of blood
in wet footprints running back and forth across the tile. In near stall
somebody retching. The uniform watching the somebody was pointedly

not looking at him.

"What we got?" Corley asked the uniforms.

"Got a slashing, lieutenant," said the older uniform, twenty-six maybe, Lopez maybe. Corley glanced down at the name tag. Lopez. The younger uniform looked green at the gills. Corley didn't know him, knew he wouldn't be green long, not this kind of green. Lots of greens in Homicide, green like Greengills, green like a two-day corpse, green like Corley, like old copper.

"In here?" Corley asked.

Lopez snapped his head back. "In the first theater."

Corley moved to the stall. Lopez moved beside him. Greengills went to the sink and splashed water on his face.

"Who we got?" said Corley.

"Pickpocket, he says. Says he just lifted the guy's wallet. Says he didn't know he was dead."

The pickpocket turned around, face pasty, hair matted. "I didn't know, man," he said, whiney, rocking. "Jesus, I didn't know. That was blood, oh god, that was blood, man, and I didn't even feel it. My hands . . ." He grabbed for the john again. Corley turned away.

"Any of that blood his?" he asked.

"Don't think so."

The wallet was on the stainless steel shelf over the sinks. It was smeared with bloody fingerprints. Corley took out a silver pen and flipped the wallet open. "Find it in the trash can?"

"Yessir," said the younger uniform, wiping the water from his face, looking at Corley in the mirror.

"Money still in it? Credit cards?"

"Yessir."

The driver's license showed a fifty-five-year-old business type, droopy eyes, saggy chin, looking above the camera, trying to decide if he should smile for this official picture. Bussey, Tyrone Otis. Toccoa Falls, Georgia.

The pickpocket told Corley that he'd like seen this chubby dude asleep at the end of his row, which he'd seen him before with a big wad of cash in his wallet at the candy counter and seen him put the wallet inside his coat and not in his pants. Near the end of the flick when he got to the guy he kind of tripped and caught himself on the guy's seat and said sorry, excuse me, while lifting his wallet real neat, and he dropped the wallet into his popcorn box and headed right for the john to ditch the wallet and just stroll out with the plastic and the cash, but in the john his hands were bloody and the guy's wallet and his shoes, and then he heard screaming in the lobby and he ditched the wallet and tried to wash the blood off but there was too much, the more he looked, the more he saw, and somebody came in and went out, so he tried to hide. He didn't know what was happening, but he knew it was real bad.

There was a spritzing noise and thin, piney mist settled into the stall and spotted Corley's glasses. Corley tore off a little square of toilet paper and smeared the spots around on the lenses. He had the pick-pocket arrested on robbery and on suspicion of murder, but he knew he wasn't the killer.

"Victim here alone?" asked Corley.

"As far as we know," said Lopez.

"Convention, maybe. Is Tasco here? Do you know Sergeant Tasco?"

Joe Franks leaned into the restroom, cameras swinging at his neck. "Hey, Corley, you in on this or not? The meat wagon's waiting. Come show me what you want."

Corley smiled. "You know what I want."

"Yeah, show me anyway so if you don't get it all, you don't blame me. Where've you been?"

"You shoot in here?"

"Yeah, I shot in here." He sounded impatient.

"You get the footprints?"

"Yeah, I got the footprints."

"Get the towels and the sink?"

"Yeah, the towels, the sink, and the stall, and the punk, and I even got a closeup of his puke, okay?"

"See, Joe," said Corley, smiling again, "you know exactly what I want."

"I hate working with you, Corley," said Franks as Corley pushed past him.

In the theater Maggie Epps was sitting on the aisle across from the body, sketchpad on her knees. "Glad you could make it, Devin," she said.

Corley fished for a snappy comeback, couldn't hook anything he hadn't said a hundred times before, said hello.

Franks showed Corley the angles he had shot. Corley asked for a couple more. The flashes illuminated the body like lightning, burned distorted images into Corley's retina.

Tasco came in, talking to somebody, squinting over his notebook. "Ray, you got the manager there?" Corley called.

"I'm the owner," the man said.

"Think you could give us some more light?"

"This is as bright as it gets, officer. This is a movie theater."

Corley turned back around. Franks snorted.

Mr. T. O. Bussey sat on the aisle in the high-backed chair, sagging left, head forward, eyes opened. Blood covered everything from his tie on down, had run under the seats toward the screen. People had tracked it back toward the lobby, footprints growing fainter up the aisle.

"You shoot that?" asked Corley.

Franks nodded. "Probably thought they were walking through cola."

Corley bent over Mr. Bussey. He put a hand on the forehead and raised the head an inch or two so that he could see the wound. "You see this?"

"Yeah. Want a shot?"

"Can I lift his head, Maggie?"

"Just watch where you plant your big feet," she said.

Corley stood behind Mr. Bussey, put his hands above the ears, and raised the head face forward, chin up. He turned his eyes away from the flashes.

"What did he get?" said Corley.

"Everything," said Maggie. "Jugular, carotid, trachea, carotid, jugular. Something real sharp. This guy never made a sound, never felt a thing. Maybe a hand in his hair jerking his head back. Nothing after that."

"From behind?" Corley lowered the head back to where he had found it.

"Left to right, curving up. You got your man in the john?"

"Don't think so. Too much blood on his shoes. He walked out in front, not behind."

"So what have you got?"

'Headache."

Maggie smiled. "It's going to get worse."

Corley smiled back. "It always does."

Corley made Greengills help bag the body. He could say that he was helping the kid get used to it, that it didn't get any better, that as bodies went this one wasn't bad, but he wasn't sure he had done it as a favor. He was afraid he'd done it to be mean.

They spent half an hour looking for the weapon. Corley didn't expect to find anything. They didn't.

He had a videotape unit brought over and sent Lopez and Greengills into the other theaters to block the parking lot exits and send the audiences through the lobby.

The owner pulled him aside and protested. Corley told him that the killer might be in another theater. The owner said something about losing the last *Deathdancer* audience and not needing any publicity hurting ticket sales and being as much a victim as that poor man. "I own nine screens in this town," he said, dragging his hand over his jaw. "I'm not responsible for this. Let's keep the profile low, okay?" There was nothing Corley could say, so he said nothing, and the owner bristled and said he had friends in this town. "I'll speak to your superior about this, Officer . . . ?"

"Corley," he said, walking away. "That's l-e-y."

The other movies ended and the audiences pushed into the lobby. Corley had them videotaped as they bunched and swayed toward the street. Two more uniforms arrived and he started them searching the other theaters for the weapon.

He left Tasco in charge and went to the station and hung around the darkroom while Franks did his printing and bitched about wasting his talent on corpses and about Corley's always wanting more shots and more prints than anybody else. Corley didn't bother to tell Franks again that it was his own fault, that Franks was the one who always waxed eloquent over his third beer and said that the camera always lied, that the image distorted as much as it revealed, that photographs were fictions. He had convinced Corley, so Corley always wanted more and more pictures, each to balance others, to offer new angles, so that reality became a sort of compromise, an average. Corley didn't say any of that again. He made the right noises at the right times, like he did when Franks said how he was going to quit as soon as he finished putting his portfolio together, as soon as he got a show somewhere.

Maybe Franks really was working on a project. Maybe he should be a real photographer. Corley didn't know. He knew Franks about as well as he could, down to a certain level, no further. He imagined that Franks knew him in about the same way. It wasn't the kind of thing they talked about.

Corley lifted a dripping print out of the fixer. "Why'd you become a cop anyway?" he said.

Franks took the print from him and put it back. It was hard to read Franks' eyes in the red light. "You're asking that like you thought there were real answers," Franks said.

Corley took the prints to his desk and did what paperwork he could. He worked until the sky got gray. By the time he stopped for doughnuts on the way home, the first edition of the *News* was in the stands. It didn't have the murder.

He thought sometimes there were real answers instead of just the same patterns and ways to deal with patterns and levels beyond which you couldn't go. He thought sometimes that there was a way to get to the next level. He thought sometimes he'd quit, do insurance fraud, something. He thought maybe he hated his job, but he didn't know that either. He had thought there was something essential about working Homicide, essential in the sense of dealing with the essences of things, a job that butted as close to the raw edge of reality as he was likely to get, and how would he do insurance after that? But whatever kind of, essence he was seeing, it was mute, images beyond articulation. None of it made any sense, and he was bone marrow tired.

The landing at his apartment was dim, and as he slid his key into the second lock, he could see the peephole darken in the apartment next door. Half past five in the morning and Gianelli was already up and prowling. Corley stood an extra second in the rectangle of light from his apartment so that Gianelli could see who he was, whoever the hell Gianelli was besides a name on a mailbox downstairs, an eye at the peephole, the sounds of pacing footsteps, of a TV. Corley's cat sniffed at the flecks of dried blood on his shoes.

Corley tossed the paper and Franks' pictures on the desk, opened a can of smelly catfood, had a couple of doughnuts and some milk. Then he rewound the tape in the VCR and stretched out on the couch to watch the program that the call to the theater had interrupted. It was a cop show. At the station they laughed at cop shows. Things made sense in cop shows. He fell asleep before the first commercial.

Corley woke up with the cat in his face again. He got a hand under its middle and flicked it away, watched it twist in the air, land on all fours, sit and stretch, lick its paws. It wasn't even his cat. The apartment had come with the cat and a wall of corky tile covered with pictures of the previous occupant. The super hadn't bothered to take them down. "Throw 'em away if you want," he'd said. "What do I care?" She was pale and blonde. An actress who never made it, maybe. A model. A photographer. Corley wondered what kind of person would leave a cat and a wall covered with her own image. He still had the pictures in a box somewhere. He used the cork as a dart board, to pin up grocery lists and phone numbers. After eight months he was getting used to the cat, except when it tried to lie in his face, which it always did when he fell asleep on the couch. One of these times he was going to toss it out of the window, down to the street. Four floors down, it didn't matter if it landed on its feet or not.

He looked at his watch. Only nine thirty, but he knew he wouldn't get back to sleep. He might as well go in.

He stopped for doughnuts and coffee and the second edition. Big headline. HORROR FLICK HORROR. *Blood flowed on the screen and in the aisles last night at the Majestic Theater . . .* Great copy, he thought, great murder for the papers. Stupid murder in a stupid place. Not robbery. Not a hit, not on some salesman from upstate Georgia. Tasco would say somebody boozed, whacked, dusted. Corley didn't think so. This one was weird. There was something going on here, something interesting, a new level, maybe, something new. He sat for a long time thinking.

It was going on eleven by the time he dropped the paper on his desk.

"My kids love those things," said Tasco.

"What things?"

Tasco pointed to the headline. "Horror flicks."

Corley looked at the paper. The story was covered in green felt tip pen with questions about the case, with ideas, with an almost unrecognizable sketch of the scene. Corley didn't remember doodling.

There was a tapping of knuckle on glass. Captain Hupmann motioned them into his office.

"Finally," said Tasco.

"How long you been waiting?" said Corley.

"Too long."

"Sorry." He knew the captain had been waiting on him, had made Tasco wait on him, too.

"Just go easy, okay?" Tasco said.

The captain shut the door and turned to Corley. "So where are we on this one?"

Tasco looked at Corley. Corley shrugged.

The captain started to snap something but Tasco flipped open his notebook. "Family notified," he said. "Victim in town for sales convention, goes to same convention every year, never takes wife. Concession girl remembers him because he talked funny, had an accent she meant, and he made her put extra butter on his popcorn twice and called her ma'am. Nobody else remembers him. Staying at the Plaza, single room, no roommate. They don't take roll at the meetings, so we don't know if he's been to any or if he's been seeing the sights." Tasco looked up, popping his gum, then looked at Corley.

"I think we've got a nut," said Corley. "Random. Maybe a one-shot, maybe a serial."

The captain raised his eyebrows in mock surprise. "Are we taking an interest in our work again?"

Corley shifted his weight.

"A nut," said the captain. "Ray?"

Tasco shrugged. "Seems reasonable, but we're not married to it. Might be a user flipped out by the flick."

The captain turned back to Corley. "Why did he pick Bussey?"

Corley could picture Bussey at the convention, anonymous in the city and the crowd, free to cuss and stay out late if he wanted, hit the bars and the ladies, drink too much and smoke big cigars. But Mr. Bussey hadn't gone that far. He'd just gone to a movie he wouldn't be caught dead in at home.

"He sat in the wrong place," said Corley. "He was on the aisle. Quick exit."

"What quick exit? This is a theater, for chrissakes. This is public. You don't do a random in public." The captain drew his lips together. "Where do you want to go with this?" he asked finally, looking more at Tasco than Corley.

Corley looked at Tasco before answering. He hadn't told Tasco anything. "We want to talk to the pickpocket again, the employees again. We've got some names from the audience, the paper had some more. We want them to see the tapes, see if they recognize somebody coming out of the other theaters. Ray wants to do more with Mr. Bussey's movements, see it there's some connection we don't know about."

"Okay," said the captain "You've both got plenty of other work, but you can keep this one warm for a couple of days. Check the gangs. Maybe something there, initiation ritual, something. If it's some kind of hit, or if it's a user, it won't go far."

"I think it's a serial," said Corley.

"You mean you hope it's a serial," said the captain. "Otherwise you're not going to get him. That it?"

"Yessir," said Tasco.

"Oh, and Corley," the captain said as Corley was halfway through the door, "welcome back. Back to stay?"

They followed up with the employees and what members of the audience they could find, asked if they'd known anybody else in the theater, seen anything unusual, remembered someone walking around near the end of the movie. They showed them pictures of the pickpocket and Mr. Bussey's driver's license, the tapes of the other audiences, asked if anyone looked familiar.

Corley tried to make himself ask the questions as if they were new, as if he'd never even thought of them before. Same questions, same answers, and if you didn't listen because it all seemed the same, you missed something. Tasco always asked the questions right and was somehow not dulled by the routine, by the everlasting sameness. Tasco hunkered down and did his job, could see the waste and the stupidity of it all, say, "Jeez, why do they do that, we got to get the SOB that did this, aren't people horrible." Tasco's saving grace was that he didn't think about it. Corley didn't mean that in a mean way. It was a quality he envied, maybe even admired. Welcome back, back to stay? Sometimes he wondered why he didn't just walk away from it all.

They got Maggie to draw a seating chart and they put little pins in the squares, red for Mr. Bussey, yellow for the people they questioned, blue in seats that yellows remembered being occupied. The media played the story and boosted ratings and circulation, and more people from the audience came forward, and others who claimed to have been there but who Tasco said were probably on Mars at the time. The number of pins increased, but that was all.

"They sat all around him," said Corley, "and they didn't see anything."

"So who in this city ever sees anything?"

"Yeah, well, they should have seen something. Maybe they were watching the movie. Maybe we should see it."

They used their shields to get into the seven o'clock show. The ticket girl told them that the crowd was down, especially in *Deathdancer.* Tasco bought a big tub of popcorn and two cokes, and they sat in the middle about halfway to the screen.

The horror flicks that had scared Corley as a kid played with the dark, the uncertain, the unknown, where you might not even see the killer clearly, where you were never sure if the clicking in the night outside was the antenna wire slapping in the wind or the sound of the giant crabs moving. One thing might be another, and there was no way to tell, and you never really knew if you were safe.

But this wasn't the same. Here the only unknowns were when the next kid was going to get it and how gross it would be. A series of bright red brutalities, each more bizarre than the last, more grotesque, more unreal. Corley couldn't take it seriously. But maybe the audience could. Unless they were cops or medics, maybe this was what it was like. Corley started watching them.

They were mostly under forty, sat in couples or groups, boys close to the screen or all the way to the wall and the corners, girls in the middle, turning their heads away and looking sideways; dates close, touching, copping feels; marrieds a married distance apart. They all talked and laughed too loud. On the screen the killer stalked the victim and the audience got quiet and focused on the movie. Corley could feel muscles stiffen, tension build as the sequence drew the moment out, the moment you knew would come, was coming, came, and they screamed at the killing, and after the killing sank back spent, then started laughing nervously, talking, wisecracking at the screen, at each other. Corley watched three boys sneak up behind a row of girls and grab at their throats, the girls shrieking, leaping, the boys collapsing in laughter. A girl chanted, "Esther wet her panties," and the whole audience broke up. On the screen, the killer started stalking his next victim and the cycle began again.

"What do you think?" asked Corley, lighting a cigarette as soon as they hit the lobby. People in line for the next show stared at their faces as if trying to see if they would be scared or bored or disgusted. Corley thought they all looked hopeful somehow.

Tasco shrugged, placid as ever. "It was a horror flick."

"Was it any good?"

"Who can tell? You'll have to ask my kids."

The summer wind was warm and filled with exhaust fumes.

"You wanta come up for a beer or something?" Corley asked.

Tasco looked at his watch. "Nah, better get back. Evelyn. See you tomorrow."

Corley thought about rephrasing it, asking if he wanted to stop in for a beer somewhere, but Tasco had already made his excuse. Used to be they'd have a beer once or twice a week before Tasco started his thirty minute drive back to Evelyn and the kids and the postage stamp yard he was so proud of but that was before Corley had moved across town, out of his decent apartment, with the courtyard and the pool, into what he lived in now. Tasco had been to the new place once only. He'd looked around and popped his gum and looked surprised and amused and inhaled his beer and left. Corley was relieved that Tasco hadn't asked him why he'd moved. He asked himself the same thing.

After he fed the cat, Corley put on the tape of the audience leaving the other screens. At first they ignored the camera, looked away, pretended not to see it, nudged a companion, pointed discreetly. Some made faces and more people saw it, and more made faces or shot birds or mouthed, "Hi, Mom," or walked straight at the camera so that their faces filled the pictures, stuck hands or popcorn boxes in front of the lens, waved, mugged, danced, pretended to strip, to moon the camera, to kiss Corley through the TV screen.

They had taped three audiences. They acted about the same.

Before he went to bed, Corley posted the newspaper articles and Franks' pictures on the cork wall, with a shot of Mr. Bussey in the center.

The heat woke him. He lay sweating, disoriented, fingers knotted in sheets. The night light threw a yellow oval on the wall opposite, gave the room a focus, showed him right where he was. He hated the panic that came from not being sure. He took three or four deep, slow breaths.

He hadn't always had the night light. He hadn't always strapped an extra gun to his leg or carried two speedloaders in his coat pockets every time he went out. He hadn't always spent so much time in his apartment, in front of the TV, asleep in front of the TV, in bed. He tried not to think about it. He tried not to think.

It was too early to be up, too late to go back to sleep, too hot to stay in the apartment. He could make coffee and go to the roof before the sun hit the tar, could catch the breeze off the river, let the cat stalk pigeons.

While the coffee dripped he sat on the couch and looked at the pictures on the wall. In the central picture Mr. Bussey sat with head up and eyes open, like he was watching the movie, the wound like a big smile. Death in black and white. Not like the deaths in the movie. Real was more . . . something. Casual. Anticlimactic. Prosaic. Unaccompanied by soundtrack. Maybe Bussey wasn't really dead. Maybe it was just special effects. In the picture his hands held Mr. Bussey's head just above the ears. He wiped his palms on his shorts.

Mr. Gianelli's peephole darkened as Corley shut his door and the cat slid up the stairs. He was halfway to the landing when the door opened the width of the chain and Gianelli's face pressed into the crack, cheeks bulging around the wood. Over his shoulder a room was lit by a television's multi-colored glow.

"I know what you're doing, young man," Gianelli called in a rasping voice.

"Sorry if I woke you," Corley said, kept climbing, smiled. Maybe thirty-eight seemed young to Gianelli.

"You leave my antenna alone," Gianelli said. "The one on the chimney. I been seventeen years in this building. I got rights. You hear me, young man? Next time my picture goes I'm calling a cop." He slammed his door and it echoed in the stairwell like a gunshot.

Corley beat Tasco to work.

"Whoa," said Franks on his way to the coffee pot. "On time and everything. You must have figured it out."

"Figured what out?" said Corley.

Franks smiled. "That you won't get fired for being late. You want out, you got to quit."

"So who wants out?"

"Who doesn't?"

Tasco had never said anything about Corley's being late. When Tasco came in, he didn't say anything about Corley's being early.

Another homicide came in and they spent the morning and most of the afternoon down by the river and the warehouses Tasco and Corley and Maggie and Joe and the smells of creosote and fish and gasoline. Some punk had taken a twelve-gauge to the gut, sawed-off, Maggie said, because of the spread and the powder burns, another drug hit as the new champions of free enterprise tried to corner the market. It wasn't going to get solved unless somebody rolled over. A crowd gathered at the yellow police line ribbons. Lopez and Greengills came in for crowd control. The paramedics bitched about hauling corpses. Greengills didn't seem to be bothered by the body.

It was late when they got back to the station.

"I'm going to the movie," said Corley. "I'm going to take our pickpocket. Want to come?"

"What for?"

"Like you said, maybe something in the movie freaked this guy. Maybe we can find something."

"I don't think we're going to get anywhere on this one."

"So you want to come, or not?" Tasco said no.

The pickpocket didn't want to go either. "My treat," Corley told him, not smiling.

Corley sat in Mr. Bussey's seat and told the pickpocket to reconstruct exactly what he had done, when he had done it. He got popcorn and grape soda like Bussey, put the empties into the next seat like Bussey, concentrated on the movie, tried not to see the pickpocket in the corner of his eye, tried to ignore the feeling that his back was to the door, tried to control his breathing. He hated this, hated the dark, the people around him, the long empty aisle on his left, he felt full of energy demanding use, fought to sit still. Finally on the screen the killer reached for the last survivor and the background music shrieked, and

Corley slumped left and lowered his head and sat, and on the screen the girl fought off the killer, and they rescued her just in time, and they killed the killer and comforted the girl, and they discovered that the killer wasn't dead and had escaped, and then Corley felt the pickpocket fall across him, heard his "Sorry," felt the wallet slide out of his coat only because he was waiting for it. He sat slumped over while the audience filed out, giggling or groaning or silent. He sat until a nervous usher shook him and asked him to wake up.

He found the pickpocket throwing up in the men's room.

"We're just going to leave this open for a while," said the captain. "Put the river thing on warm."

Tasco nodded, popping his gum. Corley said nothing.

"Problem, Devin?"

"I'd like to stay on this a while."

"Got something to sell? New leads? Anything?"

Corley shook his head. "Not really."

"Okay, then."

They went back to their desks.

"Learn anything last night?" asked Tasco.

Corley shrugged, remembering the dark, palpable and pressing; the icy air pushing into his lungs as he sat and waited, the effort to exhale; trying to concentrate on the movie, on what might have snapped somebody; and after, trying to help the pickpocket out of the stall, embarrassed for him now, and sorry, and the pickpocket twisting his elbow out of Corley's grip and tearing in half the twenty that Corley had stuffed into his shirt pocket, bloody money maybe, something, he wouldn't have it. "Not much," he said. "Bussey must have gotten it in that last sequence, like we thought."

"Funny, isn't it, all that stuff up there on the screen, and out in the audience some dude flicks out a blade and that's that."

"Yeah," said Corley. "That's that."

Corley found himself at a movie again that night, a horror flick near the university. He sat on the aisle, last row, back to the wall. The movie looked the same as the other, felt the same, same rhythms, same victims, same bright gore. The audience was younger, more the age of the characters on the screen, and louder, maybe, but still much the same as the others, shouting at the screen, groaning, cracking jokes, laughing in the wrong places, trying to scare each other, strange responses, inappropriate somehow. They had come for the audience as much as the movie. They had come to be in a group.

He found himself the next night in another movie, on the aisle, last row, back to the wall, fingering the speedloader in his pocket, trying to remember why he was wasting his time there.

Near the end of the show, he saw a silhouette down front rise and edge toward the aisle, stop, and his guts iced as he saw it reach out its left hand and pull back someone's head, heard a scream, saw it slash across the throat with its right hand and turn and run up the aisle for the exit, coming right for him, too perfect. He braced, tightening his grips on the armrests, fought to sit, sit, as the silhouette ran toward him, then he stuck out a leg and the man went down hard and Corley was on him with his knee in the back and his gun behind the right ear. He yelled for an ambulance, ordered the man to open his fist. The man was slow. Corley brought a gun butt down on the back of his hand. The fingers opened, and something bright rolled onto the carpet. Corley stared at it for a few seconds before he saw it was a tube of lipstick.

"It's only a game, man," said a voice above him, quavering. Corley looked up. The owner of the voice was pointing with a shaking finger to the bright red lipstick slash along his throat. "Only a game."

Corley cuffed them to each other and took them in. He was not gentle with them.

The papers had fun with the story. "Off-duty Detective Nabs Lipstick Slasher," said one headline. Corley posted the stories on the corkboard.

They gave him a hard time when he got to work, asked if he'd been wounded, if the stain would come out, warned him about the chapstick chopper. He didn't let it get to him.

What got to him was how much fun the slasher and his victim had. He tried to tell Tasco about it. He'd almost lost it, he said. He'd been shaking with rage, wanted to push them around, run them in hard, give them a dose of the fear of God but it didn't sink in. They just kept replaying it all the way into the station.

"You really didn't know for sure, did you?" the slasher had asked.

"Thought I was *gone,*" said the victim. "For a second there I thought this was it." He laid his head back on the seat, his face suddenly blue fading to black as the unit passed under a street light. "Oh, wow," he said.

"Shut up," Corley had snarled. "Just shut the hell up." They had gone silent, then looked at each other and giggled.

"Drugs," said Tasco.

"They weren't looped. It was like they were, but they weren't. This guy, the victim — for all he knew it was the killer. He was scared shitless, Ray, and he loved it."

Tasco shrugged. "It's a cheap high. Love that rush, maybe. Or maybe it's like they're in the flick. Makes 'em movie stars. Everybody wants to be a movie star. Put a Walkman on your head and your *life's* a fucking movie."

"I just wish I knew what the hell was going on." Corley rocked back in his chair. "I'm going to a movie tonight. Want to come?"

Tasco stared at Corley for a second or two. "This on your own time?"

"You want to come, or not?"

"The river's on warm, remember? We're not going to get this one. It was a one shot." He paused a second. "You okay?"

Corley rocked forward. "What the hell is that supposed to mean?"

"It's not supposed to mean anything. I only wanted . . ."

"All I did was ask if you wanted to go to a flick."

"Keep your voice down. Jesus. For six months you've been a walking burnout. I've been like partnered with a zombie . . ."

"I do my job, nobody can say I don't do my job."

". . . now suddenly you're doing overtime. I'm your partner. I just want to know if you're okay, that's all."

"I'm fine," Corley snapped.

"Okay, great. I'm just asking."

Corley got up and crossed the squad room and refilled his coffee cup and sat back down. He took a sip, burned his tongue. "Yeah, well," he said, "thanks for asking. You want to come?"

Tasco shook his head. "It's going to be a long day without that."

It was a long day, but Corley made the nine o'clock at the Majestic. The ticket girl let him in on his shield again, said the numbers were up, really up. The lobby was crowded, people two deep at the candy counter, clumped around video games, whooping over electronic explosions as someone blasted something on the screen. There were no seats left at the back or on the aisle, and Corley had to sit between two people. He kept his elbows off the armrests. During the movie the audience seemed more tense, everybody wide-eyed and alert, but he caught himself with knotted muscles more than once and thought the tension maybe was in him.

The lipstick game spread like bad news, and every night Corley ran in one or two slashers for questioning, and for anger, because it wasn't a game when he saw a head snap back or heard a scream, wasn't a game when the man moving down his row or running up the aisle might have a razor tucked in his fist. The games got elaborate, became contests with teams, slashers and victims alternating roles and tallying points in the lobby between shows. Sometimes someone would slash a stranger, and Corley broke up the fights at first, but later didn't bother, didn't waste time or risk injury for a pair of idiots. He went to movies every night that week, and every night he saw more people than the night before, and felt more alert and tense, and left more exhausted. His ulcer flared like sulfur; he was smoking again.

On Friday night near the end of the movie his beeper went off and half the audience screamed and jumped and clutched in their seats, then sank back as a wave of relief swept over them and they gave themselves to laughter and curses and groans and chatter, ignoring the movie.

Corley phoned in from the lobby. They had found a body after the last show at the Astro. He had been slashed.

Corley was strangely pleased.

Could be some frigging copycat," said Tasco the next day, yawning.

Corley wasn't sleepy. "No way," he said. "Exactly the same."

"The paper had the details."

"It's the same guy, Ray."

"Okay, okay," said Tasco, palms up. "Same guy."

The routine began again, interviews, hunting up the audience, blue and yellow pins, lack of a good witness. Tasco asked where they'd sat, what they'd seen, who they'd known. Corley asked them why they'd gone, whether they'd liked it, if they went to horror flicks often, if they'd played the assassin games. They didn't know how to answer him. He made them uncomfortable, sometimes angry, and they addressed their answers to Tasco, who looked amused and popped his gum and wrote it all down.

Corley posted the new pictures on the corkboard, and the articles and the editorials, and the movie ads. Various groups blasted the lipstick game, called for theaters to quit showing horror movies, called for theaters to close completely. Corley's theater owner wrote a guest editorial calling on readers not to be made prisoners by one maniac, not to give in to the creatures of the night. The Moviola ads promised armed guards; the Majestic dared people to come to the late show. The corkboard was covered by the end of the week, a vast montage filling the wall behind the blank television.

Tasco went with him to the movies now. There were lines at every ticket window, longer lines every night. The Moviola's security guards roamed the lobby and aisles; the Majestic installed airport metal detectors at the door; the Astro frisked its patrons, who laughed nervously, or cracked wise like Cagney or Bogart, and the guards made a big production when they found tubes of lipstick, asked if they had a license, were told it was for protection only or that they were collectors or with the FBI. They were all having a great time. The ticket girl said they gave her the creeps.

"That's two of us," Corley said.

Corley and Tasco sat on opposite sides of the theater, on the aisle, backs to the wall, linked with lapel mikes and earphones. Fewer and fewer played the lipstick game, but the audiences seemed electric and intense; Corley felt sharp and coiled, felt he could see everything, felt he was waiting for something.

After the movies, when he came home drained and sagged down on the couch, Corley found himself staring at the wall, at the picture of T. O. Bussey looking out at him from the aisle seat, his hands holding up the head, and he felt like he didn't know anything at all.

Corley turned off his electric razor and turned up the radio. An early morning DJ was interviewing a psychiatrist about the slasher. Corley knew he'd give the standard whacko profile, a quiet, polite, boy-next-door type who repressed sex and hated daddy, and that everybody who knew him would be surprised and say what a nice guy he was and how they could hardly believe it. He got his notebook to write it down so he could quote it to Tasco. "Said he was 'quiet, withdrawn, suffers repressed sexuality and sexual expression, experiences intense emotional build-up and achieves orgasm at climax of movie and murder, cycle of build-up and release, release of life, fluids, satisfaction.'" He flipped the notebook shut.

"Jeez, I hate that," said Tasco. "I hate the hell out of that. That doesn't mean squat. That's just words. Who is he, gets paid to say crap like that? He doesn't know anything."

"I want to talk to this guy," said Corley. "I just want to sit down and talk to him, you know? I just want to buy him a drink or something and ask him what the hell is going on."

"You mean the shrink?" Tasco was squinting.

"Our guy," said Corley. "The slasher."

Tasco didn't say anything.

"He knows something," said Corley.

Tasco looked angry again. "He doesn't know anything. What are you talking about?"

Corley tried to say what he meant, couldn't find it, couldn't make it concrete. Why was it so important to get this guy, see him, find out what he looked like, why he did it, not why, exactly, but how, maybe, how in the sense of giving people a chance to maybe have their throats cut, and having them line up like it was a raffle? What would that tell him about what was driving him off the street, what kept drawing him back down, why he was carrying an extra piece, what kept him in that lousy apartment in the middle of all of this tar and pavement when he could just walk away? What did he want?

"He knows something about people," Corley said finally.

Tasco waved his hand like he was fanning flies. "What could he know? He's just a sicko . . ."

"Come on, Ray, we've seen sickoes. They don't slash in public, not like this."

Anger was in both voices now.

"Maybe they do. Maybe he just wanted to see if he could. Ever think of that? Maybe it's the thrill of offing somebody in front of a live audience. Maybe that's all."

"Yeah, that's all, and all those people out there know he's out there, too, and they can't stay away. Why can't they stay away, Tasco?"

"We can't just keep going to movies, Devin. We got lives, you know."

"We're not going get him unless we get him in the act."

"That's just stupid. That won't happen. That's a stupid thing to say."

"Watch it, sergeant."

"Oh, kiss it, Corley. Jesus."

They were silent again, avoiding each other's eyes.

"I just want to bust this guy," said Corley.

"Yeah, well," said Tasco looking out of the window, "what I want is to go home, see my wife and kids, maybe watch a ball game." He looked back to Corley. "So, we going out again tonight or what?"

They went again that night and the next night and the next. They always sat on the aisle at opposite ends of the last row so that they could cover both rear exits. Tasco would sit through only one show; Corley sat through both. He felt better when Tasco was at the other end, when he could hear him clear his throat, or mutter something to himself, or even snore when he nodded off as he sometimes did, which amazed Corley. Corley stayed braced in his seat.

When Tasco left, Corley felt naked on the aisle, so he'd move in one seat and drape a raincoat across the aisle seat so it looked occupied, so no one would sit there. The nine o'clock show was usually a sellout, the audience filling every seat and pressing in on him, a single vague mass in the dark at a horror flick, hiding a man with a razor, maybe even inviting him, desiring him, seeking him. After five nights Corley was ragged and jumpy.

"I'm going to sit in the projection booth," he told Tasco. "Better view."

Tasco shrugged. "End of the week and that's it, okay?"

"We'll see."

"That's got to be it, Devin."

The booth gave Corley a broader view, and gave him distance, height, a thick glass wall. At first he felt conspicuous whenever a pale face lifted his way as the audience waited for the movie to start. The manager showed him how to override the automatics and turn up the house lights, otherwise hands off. The projector looked like a giant Tommy gun sighted on the screen through a little rectangle outlined on the glass in masking tape. He had expected something more sophisticated.

Tasco was just out of sight below him, left aisle, last row, back to the wall. Through his earphone, Corley could hear the audience from Tasco's lapel mike, a general murmur, a burst of high-pitched laughter, the crying of a baby who shouldn't even be there. Corley wiped his glasses on his tie. Hundreds of people out there, could be any one of them, and what the hell were the rest of them doing out there, and what the hell was he doing up here?

The lights dimmed and the projector lit up, commercials, previews, the main feature. A little out-of-focus movie danced in the rectangle on the glass, blobs of color and movement bleeding out onto the masking tape; the soundtrack was thin and tinny from the booth speaker and just half a beat behind in the earphone, disconcerting. Beyond the glass, on exhibition, the audience stirred and rippled; beyond them the huge and distorted images filled the screen. He watched, and when someone stood and moved toward the aisle, he warned Tasco and felt adrenaline heat arms and legs and the figure reached the aisle and turned and walked toward restroom or candy counter, and Corley tried to relax again. It was easier to relax up here, above it all.

The movie dragged on. Corley found by staring at a central point in the audience and unfocusing his eyes, he could see all movement instantly, and everybody was moving, scratching ears and noses and scalps, lifting hands to mouths to cover coughs or to feed, rocking, putting arms around dates, leaning forward, leaning back, covering eyes with fingers. Again he saw the patterns emerge around the on-screen killings, movements ebbing as the killing neared, freezing at the death itself, melting after, and flowing across the audience again, strong and choppy, then quieter and smooth. He had to concentrate, breathe slowly and carefully, to keep himself from narrowing his vision, focusing on one person. He didn't see the movie.

A flicker in the corner of his eye, flick of light on steel. He swung eyes right, locked on movement, saw the head pulled back, the blade flicker again, realized it was happening, that he hadn't seen the killer move down the row because he was sitting right behind his victim, it was happening now, all the way across the theater from Tasco. He radioed Tasco as he turned for the stairs and punched the lights, heard Tasco yell for the man to stop, knew they were too late for the victim, but they had him now, they had him now, they had him now. He took the stairs three at a time, slipped, skidded down arms flailing, wrenched his shoulder as he tried to break the fall, then on his feet and bursting through the door behind the concession stand, drawing his pistol as he ran, putting out his left arm and vaulting over the counter, popcorn and patron flying. He stopped in front of the double doors, pistol leveled, waiting for the maniac to run into his arms.

Nobody came. Corley crouched, frozen, pistol extended in two hands, and in his left ear the theater, voices and screams and music, and Tasco maybe, Tasco shouting something, and still nobody came. He moved forward, gun still extended, and jerked open a door with his left hand.

Lights still brightening, movie running, and the screams and shouts and music in the earphone echoed, echoed in his right ear and for an instant he lost where he was. Then he heard Tasco calling him in his earphone and saw him trying to hammer his way into a knot of people below the screen, the rest of the audience in their seats, watching the movie or those down front attacking the slasher.

Corley ran down the aisle, yelling for Tasco. The earphone went dead and Tasco was gone. Corley reached the mass, started pulling people out of his way, stepping on them, pushing. Some pushed back and turned on him, and he knocked one down and another man grabbed him, and he hit the man in the face, and backed toward the wall, gun leveled. The man changed his mind, backed away. Corley called Tasco, heard nothing through the earphone. He tried to elbow his way in the crowd, started clubbing with both hands around the pistol, fighting the urge to just start pulling the trigger and have done with it. A huge man turned and started to swing; Corley watched the fist come around in slow motion, easily deflected the blow, put a knee in the solar plexus, watched the man fall like a great tree, cuffed him across the jaw as he went down, felt that he could count the pores in the potato nose. They were right beneath the speakers, the music pounding his bones. He reached for the next one in his way.

He heard a shot, saw Tasco cornered by four or five, his gun pointed toward the ceiling but lowering. The next one wouldn't be a warning shot and those guys knew it and they weren't backing off. Corley tried to shout above the music, raised his pistol and fired toward the ceiling, fired again, heard Tasco's gun answer, fired a third time, and the crowd started breaking at the edges, some hurt, some bloody. Corley tried to hold them back, grabbed at one who twisted away, and they pushed past, ignoring him, laughing or shouting, and the others were leaving their seats now, mixing with them, and some in their seats were applauding and cheering.

There were people lying all around them, some groaning, some bleeding. The slasher's victim sprawled across an aisle seat, throat opened to the stars painted on the ceiling. "Help me, Jesus," someone was saying over and over. "Jesus, help me." He heard someone calling his name, saying something. It was Tasco.

"I couldn't stop them," Tasco was saying. Corley looked down. They had used the slasher's blade, and whatever else was handy. The slasher's features were unrecognizable, the head almost severed from the body. A sudden fury flashed through Corley, and he kicked the person lying nearest to him. "Couldn't stop them," Tasco repeated, his voice trembling.

"Is this him, do you think?" asked Corley.

Tasco didn't say anything.

"Maybe Maggie can tell us," said Corley. "Maybe the M.E." He could hear the desperation in his voice.

"It could be anybody," said Tasco.

When he used the phone in the ticket office to call it all in, he heard people demanding a refund because they hadn't gotten to see the end of the movie.

Corley didn't get home until late the next afternoon. He'd made it through the last eighteen hours by thinking about the crummy little apartment high above the street, with the couch and the double locks and the television. He heard the cat yowling before he even put the key in the first lock.

He fed the cat and opened a beer, and turned on his television, but the pictures were wrong, fuzzy, filled with snow. He tried to fix the image, but nothing worked, and he grew angry. Finally he checked the roof and found his antenna bent over.

"Gianelli," he shouted, pounding, standing to one side of the door, seeing an image of Gianelli spinning in slow motion toward pavement four floors down. "Come out of there, Gianelli." No answer. He spread the name out, kicking on the door once for each syllable. *"Gia-nel-li!"*

"You go away now," came a voice from inside. "You go away. I'm calling the cops."

"I *am* a cop," Corley shouted, dragging out his shield and holding it to the peephole.

"You go away now," Gianelli said after a moment of silence.

Corley gave the door one last kick.

He tried to salvage the antenna, but Gianelli had done a job on it, twisting the crosspieces, cutting the wires into a dozen pieces.

Before he went to sleep, he took down the pictures and clippings about Mr. Bussey, and he dug around until he found the pictures of the previous occupant, and he pinned them all up. He crossed the room and sat on the couch to look at them. They were all black and white, blonde and pale eyes, and he wondered if she had walked away from whatever brought her here. He thought she was very beautiful. But who could tell from pictures?

He locked the doors and cut on the night light.

Dan Fortune and the Hollywood Caper
by Michael Colins

"**S**omeone tried to shoot me," Isabelle Kucera said. "Isn't it wonderful?"

Isabelle is a file clerk in a midtown office where everyone sits in front of a CRT screen all day and feeds a computer. She works nine to five and half a day on Saturday. This was Saturday, we were in my one room loft overlooking Eighth Avenue, and she had come to hire me.

"No one ever tried to *shoot* me before!" she said happily. "I know it's Grace Kelly, Danny. Grace Kelly never lets John Ireland go."

Isabelle is also a thousand old movies walking around. Like a lot of slum kids left alone in a six flight walk-up while her mother worked, Isabelle grew up in front of a television set. Later she branched out into the rerun movie houses in Chelsea and the Village. Only she doesn't leave the movies inside the TV set or the rerun house. She lives them.

"He's a hired killer, like Alan Ladd," Isabelle said, her eyes shining. "Grace Kelly hired him to kill me, and you can track him down, Danny, just like Elliot Gould."

Once, after a movie in which Ingrid Bergman was a noble nun in China, Isabelle tried to join a missionary order. The nuns were nice about it. When she was thirteen, the city sent her to summer camp. She had to be dragged to her seat on the bus. She was Bonita Granville being sent off to a Nazi concentration camp. Now that she's twenty-six, blonde, and beautiful, she's the woman who ruins John Ireland.

"This time I know it's going to work out, Danny!" she glowed. "Pauli really is John Ireland!"

She doesn't mean the real John Ireland, she means the roles he plays. Not in the big movies like *Red River* or *All the King's Men*, where Ireland was as good an actor as anyone who ever stood in front of a camera, but the smaller ones. The movies where Ireland is the ex-Air Force officer who joins a gang of bank robbers to get money for *her;* the hitchhiker *she* picks up and seduces into murdering her husband; the ex-con going straight who is dragged back into crime so *she* can have what she wants; the gas station attendant *she* needs to drive the getaway car.

"Who," I said, "is Pauli?"

"You know," she pouted. "Paul Bambara. The manager down at the Discount Bookstore on Sixth Avenue? He's a dream!"

"Tall?" I remembered. "Kind of skinny? Dark hair? Looks like he needs sleep?"

"That's him. So pale and gaunt, Danny. He suffers so much. We're going to run off to Mexico. Pauli's going to do what he really wants, make things with his hands. Statues and everything. He's just bursting to be free, Danny. The wife never lets Ireland be free."

The woman who ruins John Ireland, destroys him in the end, is Gloria Grahame. For Ireland to run into Grahame in a movie is to be ruined every time. She also ruins Dick Powell the honest private eye, Robert Mitchum the dedicated young doctor, and Broderick Crawford the husband desperate to hold her.

"How long has this been going on, Isabelle?"

"Almost a whole month! He's so sensitive, Danny. He's so unhappy in that store, so unhappy with his wife. I'm going to give him a whole new life!"

Because, of course, Isabelle *is* Gloria Grahame. When Grahame died tragically young some years ago, Isabelle found her best role. She looks enough like Grahame, adds the rest in as fine an acting job as the real GG ever gave. She has the wet pout, the narrow shoulders hunched as if always cold, the thin hand curved to fit the stem of a martini glass. The sleepy eyes that are naked and hooded at the same time. The limp, pipe-stem wrists and dangling cigarette. The slender body and lazy drawl that hides the tiger.

Isabelle lives the role from her clothes to her manner and her men, hanging around with half the gamblers, drug dealers and con men in

Little Italy and the Village. Only they're not important to her. They can't be John Irelands.

"I know it's the real thing this time!" Isabelle said, glowing. "Especially now."

A headache was beginning at the back of my eyes. Isabelle's fantasies have a way of causing headaches.

"Did you happen to see who shot at you, Isabelle?"

"Well, I'm not sure, but there was this big guy in a raincoat and hat and with a kind of limp, just like Robert Ryan."

I felt as if my brain were floating in some late-late show haze. With Isabelle, your reality can begin to blur.

"Grace Kelly got to have hired Ryan, Danny," Isabelle said.

"You mean Paul Bambara's wife, Isabelle?" I had a strong urge to toss a silver dollar in my hand where I sat behind my desk, just like George Raft.

"Of course, silly," Isabelle beamed, and then frowned. "Unless maybe it was Eddie. You know, jealous and drinking because I jilted him. Out to get me."

Eddie Bauer had been last year's John Ireland. A taxi driver whose wife had thrown him out after he got mixed up with Isabelle and lost his job. Isabelle had ditched him for a short fling with a muscular type with dazzling teeth — Burt Lancaster.

"You sure any of this really happened, Isabelle?"

For a moment I felt like Jack Nicholson, feet on my desk, hat tilted down over my eyes. Except that I wasn't wearing a hat. Isabelle will do that to you.

"Dan Fortune! You know I never lie! Does this look like I made it up?"

She held out a handbag about the size of a feedbag for a Clydesdale. There was a neat hole through both sides of the bag. Big holes, about .357 Magnum. Real holes.

"Okay, Isabelle, I'll look around. In the meantime, be careful, and maybe stay away from this Paul Bambara."

She was on her feet, the indignant Gloria Grahame. "Pauli needs me! We're going to go places, do things, be someone! We have to make plans. We're going to *do* something, Danny!"

I sighed. "Okay, pay me some cash before you go."

"Well," she rummaged in that expensive feed bag, came out with a crumpled twenty. "I'm a little short this week, but I'll pay your regular price. Me and Pauli are going to get rich."

"Swell," I said, and resisted a nasty Robert Montgomery laugh.

2

Opening credits voiceover: Who would want to shoot Isabelle? Why? A romantic and an innocent. A dreamer who only wanted to find her John Ireland and ruin him. Ruin him in the eyes of his normal world, that is, the dull everyday world he really hated. Ruined and free to run away to a better life. The better life of doing what he really wanted to do, being what he really wanted to be, even if he fell on his face and ended up drinking alone in some forgotten Mexican village.

For Isabelle, the losers are the winners. She's seen all the movies about all the losers and there's so much life in their misery that compared to our dull lives their suffering becomes happiness. A romantic fantasy, but where was a motive for murder?

I got my beret and duffel coat and went out. In the thin November rain I walked down to the Discount Bookstore on Sixth Avenue. Paul Bambara was out at some warehouse, they didn't know when he'd be back. I got his home address.

It turned out to be a good brownstone on 9th Street near Fifth.

An expensive address and he had the expensive apartment: second floor front, the parlor floor. It wasn't what I would have expected for the manager of a Sixth Avenue bookstore. I rang the mailbox bell and got buzzed in. A woman waited for me in the open doorway of the second floor front.

"What can I do for you?"

"Mrs. Paul Bambara?"

She eyed me coldly. A short, stocky woman with jet black hair and shadowed Mediterranean eyes.

"If you want Paul, he ain't home."

"Can I talk to you?"

"Me?" Suspicion was sharp in her voice. She didn't invite me in. Maybe that was just her natural brand of hospitality.

"Do you know an Isabelle Kucera, Mrs. Bambara?"

Her manner changed abruptly. The cool eyes stared hard at me, but there was a shakiness in her voice. "What about her?"

"Someone tried to shoot her."

"Shoot? You a cop?"

"Private," I said. "Working for Miss Kucera. Can I ask where you were this morning?"

"Right here. I got three witnesses. You want me to get them?"

"Maybe later." She would have the witnesses, real or faked. "Can you think of anyone who would want Miss Kucera dead?"

"A woman like that? Listen, Mr. —?"

"Fortune. Dan Fortune."

"Listen, Mr. Fortune, I know all about that woman and her men. All the other women's husbands." She was hugging her breasts now, looking me straight in the eye. Her full lips were sad, even trembling, and her voice had a dark throb. Not Grace Kelly, no. Ingrid Bergman. Isabelle's fantasies are insidious. "I know her, but I won't fight her. Not that way. Paul is a good man, a good husband. This is his home. He'll come back to me, Mr. Fortune. He'll find he belongs here."

"I hope he does, Mrs. Bambara," I said, which was partly true; Isabelle deserved better. "You're sure you can't think of anyone who would shoot at her?"

"No, and I'd say look into her past, Mr. Fortune."

It seemed like good advice, so I went back to my office and put out some feelers on Eddie Bauer. It was late afternoon before I located him in a flea-trap on the West Side. He was at home with a bottle for company. A long, lean type with two days' growth of beard and a haunted expression. He sneered at me.

"I don't know you, chum."

Dan Duryea down on his luck, or maybe it was my imagination. Maybe just a long day with Isabelle's shadow script, my brain going soft. My own voice lisping an answer.

"I know you, friend. I'm coming in."

Humphrey Bogart. He backed off warily, his hands dangling. I hung a cigarette from my lip, snapped a match on my thumbnail.

"All right, Lou . . . Bauer," I said, "read me the song and dance of where you were this morning, and make it good."

"What's it to you, chum?" Bauer/Duryea sneered.

I told him about Isabelle and the shooting.

"Dead?" he grinned.

"You'd like that, would you?"

"I wouldn't cry too hard, chummy, only you can't hang this one on me. I was here all morning, and I can prove it."

This time I made him prove it. He did. With five poker players from the building, one an off-duty cop. By then it was way past time for a beer and even some dinner so I knocked off.

I wasn't sure I was even hearing what people were really saying by then. Maybe I was just imagining the dialogue according to Isabelle's shooting script. Maybe the holes in her handbag weren't bullet holes. Maybe if I forgot about it, it would all do a quick dissolve.

3

Jump cut: To Isabelle's apartment down on Spring Street. Monday evening. The apartment is early Warner Brothers Greenwich Village just like in *Reds* — orange crates, a covered bathtub for a table, brick and board bookcases. Except for all the photos on the walls. You could have cast a hundred Hollywood epics with the actors and actresses on Isabelle's walls.

In the apartment, just home from work, Isabelle's eyes are shining like Judy Garland seeing Oz for the first time.

"They searched the apartment while I was at work!"

The place is a mess, right enough.

"What's missing?"

"I don't know. I don't keep any money around." Then she almost squealed. "Maybe my diary! That man with the limp is a private eye just like you. Grace Kelly hired him to steal my diary so she could confront John Ireland!"

"Let's take a look." I was trying hard to keep what grip I had on reality. With Isabelle, it has a way of sliding away.

The diary was where she had left it, all its pages intact. I went over the small apartment inch by inch with her, and she found nothing missing for a long time. Then she gave a cry.

"My new makeup case!"

"What makeup case?"

"It's like a little suitcase, you know? It's leather, and it's got all these plastic bottles and jars inside. Pauli only gave it to me a couple of days ago for my acting classes."

"Bambara gave it to you?"

"I said so, didn't I?"

"Let's go find him," I said.

We took a cab to the Discount Bookstore on Sixth, and Isabelle got Paul Bambara to take a coffee break and meet us in the Vesuvius Coffee Shop on Waverly. A pale, scrawny man in his thirties, he was wearing Levi cords, a rugby shirt, and a tweed jacket with fake leather elbow patches from some cutrate men's store up on 14th Street. Isabelle introduced us. He gave me a hard grip and tried to look tough and restless as John Ireland should.

Isabelle told him about the search and the makeup case.

"The case I gave you? Why would anyone want that?"

"Maybe," Isabelle said eagerly, "your wife wants my fingerprints! I remember one time when Ireland's wife got Gloria Grahame's fingerprints so she could check her criminal past."

I said, "Leather doesn't take prints, neither does plastic."

"And you don't have a record," Bambara said. I didn't think he would last. Realism wasn't Isabelle's forte.

"Maybe," Isabelle chewed a fingernail, "she wanted something I'd *touched*, something from my body! Some hair, maybe. Like in that voodoo movie where Agnes Moorehead makes a doll of Gloria Grahame and sticks pins in it to make her die."

"You feel sick?" I asked.

"Not yet, silly. She's only had it half a day."

"Isabelle," I kept a tight grip on my psyche, "this is New York, not Haiti. That stuff only works if you believe it."

"Well," she pouted heavily, almost Shirley Temple, "maybe she just wants evidence for a divorce. I mean, it was a present from Pauli."

"Angela don't believe in divorce," Bambara said, gloomy.

I said, "Where'd you buy the case, Bambara?"

"I didn't, I got it from Angela," Bambara said. "She sells them, you know? She and her brother got a cosmetic and makeup business. Door-to-door like the Avon lady. They make a bundle."

"That's how you can afford that apartment? Her money?"

"We sure couldn't afford it on mine."

"You bought the makeup case from her?"

"Hell no! I mean, she'd want to know why I needed a woman's makeup case, right? I swiped it when she was out. She's got so many, she never even missed it."

There was something in that. Why would Angela Bambara want her own makeup case back? One of perhaps hundreds she had for sale? If she had wanted it back. If someone else hadn't taken it from the apartment.

"Is there anyone who could be after you, Bambara?" I asked. "Someone from your past?"

"I don't have a past," Bambara said. John Ireland all the way. "A lot of crummy jobs like the one I got. Never been out of New York. Never done anything."

"You will," Isabelle said fervently. "There's got to be some kick to life, Pauli. We're going after it even if we can't hold it. Maybe we'll fall on our faces, rot in Mexico, end up hating each other, but we'll have grabbed for the big ring!"

"She's right, ain't she, Fortune?" He gripped my arm like a vulture clawing a tree branch. "Mexico, work with my hands, live if it kills us in the end!"

He had that feverish pipedream in his voice John Ireland always got around Gloria Grahame. Maybe he would last.

"You're sure you don't know why someone would steal that case, Bambara?" I said.

"Not a clue, Fortune."

I left them cooing at each other over their beers, seeing Mexican sunsets in the suds. I walked up Sixth Avenue and across to Eighth and my office. Why steal a simple makeup case? Or take a shot at an innocent like Isabelle? An internal Humphrey Bogart lisped in my ear, "Something funny going on for sure, pal," and I decided to do a stakeout — on Isabelle.

Stock shots: A one-armed man shivering in the November shadows as he watches a bright young couple have a wonderful time. The one-armed man is not having a wonderful time. The one-armed man follows the young couple. The one-armed man is cold. It becomes dark, and the one-armed man becomes aware of a short, stocky man in a black raincoat. Camera angle over the one-armed man's shoulder. The short man is also watching the young couple. Jackpot!

There is a procession. John Ireland and Gloria Grahame hand in hand. The small man, Peter Lorre, casually behind them. The one-armed man, me, behind Peter Lorre. Until Isabelle and Paul Bambara finally reach Isabelle's apartment and go up. Peter Lorre looks up until the light goes on in Isabelle's apartment, then turns away. Fortune/Bogart lisps mentally, "Stick to this character, pal, he'll lead you to the big boy."

Six blocks later I lost him. Quick into an alley, out the other end, and gone. I didn't need a director to tell me I'd been spotted. It looked like Isabelle and Bambara were in for the night. I had nothing to do but go home. I went home.

Did you ever feel that you were sinking into quicksand? Floating away on some swirling cloud of thick fog? The quicksand of Isabelle's imagination. The fog of her fantasies.

My one room office/apartment had been torn apart.

It took me an hour to find out that nothing was missing. But my files had been rifled, the flour poured into the sink, my toothpaste tube cut open, the sugar dumped, all my chairs upended. I felt as if I were on a rollercoaster and all I could do was ride it out. What had Isabelle's make-believe gotten her into? Gotten me into?

My telephone rang.

"Danny!" Isabelle's voice cried. "Pauli's killed someone!"

4

Montage sequence: A one-armed detective running through dark city streets. A thin-faced blonde with a strand of perfectly arranged hair hanging over one eye, a cigarette dangling, and alarm registered on the thin, drooping mouth as if painted. A man in his thirties wearing a cheap tweed jacket and a shocked expression, and holding a smoking Luger.

"Who the hell is he?" I said.

The body lay on the floor of Isabelle's apartment. The short, stocky Peter Lorre who'd been following them. Paul Bambara still held the Luger, sat on the couch staring at the body.

"Joe Ciaccio," Bambara said. "My brother-in-law. He . . . he tried to kill me!"

Bambara told the whole story. He had been alone in the apartment waiting for Isabelle to return with their pizza for dinner — mushrooms, anchovies, pepperoni, the works. When he heard a knock on the door he thought Isabelle had forgotten her keys again. He opened the door. His wife's brother, Joe Ciaccio, pushed him back into the room and started to shout violently.

"Shouting what?" I said.

"It didn't make any sense, you know? All about how I was a dead man! How dumb did we think he and Angela were? A big romance, and she was just a clerk in a crummy office, sure! Mexico! John Ireland! Gloria Grahame! Did I think they were stupid? A hot young kid and a middle-aged bum like me? Then Fortune nosing all around! Just a small-time private eye. Sure he was!"

Bambara stared up at us. "Then . . . then he pulled out this gun. He came up close, yelled right in my face. I was scared. I mean, he was crazy, he was going to shoot me! So I jumped on him. The gun got knocked to the floor. We both grabbed for it, and I knocked him down. I got the gun, he grabbed a brass lamp. He came at me again, still yelling and cursing. I . . . I shot. I had to. He was going to kill me!"

In the silence of the apartment we all looked down at the dead man.

"But," Isabelle said at last, "if he didn't think me and Pauli was in love, what did he think?"

It was the same question I was asking myself. And heard a faint answer somewhere in the back of my mind.

"Isabelle, how are you going to get to Mexico? What are you going to live on while Bambara finds himself?"

"Well, we're going to sell everything we can, and Pauli's going to sort of 'borrow' some of the money his wife makes on her business." Her eyes gleamed with cleverness. "When we get to Mexico, we'll buy a lot of pot and cocaine and sell it up here for a big profit! I know all kinds of guys will buy it."

"Guys?" I said.

"You know, silly. Gangsters and drug dealers. I know lots of them. I gave Pauli a list and he was going to talk to them, but after I got shot at we decided to wait."

"A list?" I said. "Of narcotics pushers? Where is it now?"

"I've got it," Bambara said. He produced a dogeared sheet of typewriter paper. "We never did use it."

"You never contacted any drug dealers?"

"No," Bambara said. Isabelle shook her head.

"But you carried it around? Took it home? Maybe left it out on your bureau when you went to bed, or left it in your jacket pocket?"

"I guess so, yeh."

"And you were going to 'borrow' some of your wife's money?" I said. "Did you check out her account? Find out how much she had in it? Take a look at her records?"

"Sure did," Bambara said. "Even checked with her bank."

I suppose I must have looked like Paul Newman who has just figured out how it all went wrong for him and Sundance.

"Dan?" Isabelle said. "You know what's going on?"

"Maybe," I said. "I think so."

I called Lieutenant Marx then, reported the shooting. Marx is head of the local precinct detective squad. He arrived with his team in under ten minutes. His men went to work on the body and the apartment while Marx listened to me. His eyes glazed as I told him Isabelle and Bambara's story and my glimmer of an answer.

"Can you prove any of that, Fortune?" Marx said, his voice a little stunned.

"Piece of cake, sweetheart," I lisped.

Marx waited until the M.E. had taken the body, told his men to take Bambara and the gun to the station house, warned Isabelle to stay in town, and nodded to me.

"Okay, Fortune, show me."

As we left, Isabelle sat staring at her wall with a faraway look in her eyes. It made me nervous.

5

At the second floor front of the good brownstone on 9th Street near Fifth, Angela Bambara herself opened the door. She stared at me, and then at Lieutenant Marx. She knew Marx, covered her mouth with her hand.

"Mr. Fortune, lieutenant! Something's happened to Paul!"

Maybe just knowing Isabelle does it. She was Ingrid Bergman even to the head twitching slightly sideways, the big eyes not quite looking at you.

"Mrs. Bambara," Marx took charge, "can you tell us where your brother is?"

"My . . . my brother?"

Marx looked at his notebook as if everything was down in damning black and white. We all play games. "Joseph Ciaccio?"

"I . . . I don't know, lieutenant. I mean, I haven't seen Joe for weeks. I mean . . . why are the police interested in Joe?"

"Because he's dead," Marx said. "Shot to death an hour ago by your husband."

"Because he tried to shoot your Paul," I said. "Now why do you suppose he wanted to do that, Mrs. Bambara?"

"Dead?" She blinked at Marx, at me. "Tried to kill Paul? No! I don't believe you! Either of you! I don't believe a word of it. No!"

Bergman down to the fine quiver of the lower lip, the eyes that looked everywhere like trapped birds in a small room. Isabelle was an infection. Play it again, Ingrid. There was no way I could resist.

"You're good," I said, "you're awful good. Only it won't play, not any more. You sent brother Joe to kill your husband. You and Joe were in the whole deal together. That's where all the money comes from for this apartment. You sell all right, only it's not cosmetics or makeup kits. It's the happy stuff, the trips to shiny places. You sell drugs, sweetheart, you and poor Joe. You sell it in those makeup kits, that's why you had to get that one back from Isabelle. It was loaded with H or C or whatever you're pushing.

"You found out Paul was checking your bank accounts. You spotted that list of dope dealers, and Isabelle talked about Mexico, and you got scared. You tried to shoot Isabelle, had your brother tail her, searched my place after I appeared, and tonight you sent Joe to kill Isabelle and Paul. Only Isabelle was out, Paul got the gun away from Joe, Joe's dead, and you're cooked!"

That was when Robert Ryan came out of the bedroom. A tall man in a raincoat, with a limp and a .357 Magnum. Angela Bambara had a 9-mm Luger in both hands, pointed straight at us.

"I told you, Mario!" Angela snarled. "Narcotics agents! That damned blonde and the peeper. Cosying up to Paul, getting the makeup case, checking my bank accounts, giving Paul that list of pushers. I told you the whole crazy run-off-to-Mexico-for-love stuff was a big act!"

"Narks," Ryan/Mario agreed, "both of them. Now we got the cop, too. All three got to be blown away."

Marx said, "Freelancing, De Stefano? The Don doesn't like free-lancing."

"The Don ain't gonna know about it."

I knew the name. Mario De Stefano, a Mafia *cappo.*

"The girl, too," Angela Bambara said. "And Paul."

She was a beaut. Faye Dunaway ready to blast. I tried to smile, Burt Lancaster doing a death scene. It didn't work. I was going over like a two-bit extra.

But I'd reckoned without Gloria Grahame.

She came in through the outside door we'd left ajar. In a battered old trenchcoat fitted to her slim figure like skin. Hands in the pockets, hatless, her blonde hair loose, the wet pout on her lips, the cigarette dangling.

"I just had to talk to you, make you understand. Pauli needs me. Pauli has to be free. I know I'm no good, but —"

Angela Bambara whirled, stumbled into an armchair, shot wildly into the ceiling. Mario De Stefano jumped, tripped over a low hassock, shot hell out of a lamp and a mirror. I fell on Angela Bambara. Marx clobbered De Stefano. His men, staked outside, pounded up the stairs and finished them off.

Isabelle pouted. We had ruined her big confrontation scene. Angela Bambara glared at her before Marx's people hauled her and De Stefano off.

"She didn't fool me! Running off to Mexico with a wimp like Paul? A new life? Who did she think she was fooling? I knew she was a narcotics agent right from the start!"

Isabelle raised her thin nose defiantly, let the cigarette smoke close her left eye, curled her wet GG lip at Angela Bambara. I didn't have the heart to tell Angela or De Stefano the real truth.

At the precinct we gave our statements. The powder in the makeup case turned out to be PCP — angel dust. The late Joe Ciaccio, Angela Bambara, and De Stefano had been making it in a back room of the elegant apartment, selling it under the cover of Angela Bambara's cosmetic business.

Later, I sat with Isabelle in 0. Henry's.

"A real *mafioso*, Danny! Just like Marlon Brando!"

I sighed.

"They really thought I was a narcotics agent!" Her eyes glowed in ecstasy. "Just like —"

I'd had enough. Her fantasies had killed one man, and next time they could kill her. Or me.

"Stop it!" I said. "You're not Gloria Grahame. Bambara's not John Ireland. De Stefano's a two-bit punk, not Marlon Brando!"

She didn't even hear me. "Pauli's going back to Angela. In the end, when Gloria Grahame leaves him, John Ireland always goes back to his wife."

I gave up. Isabelle would always be Isabelle.

"Will she go to prison for long, Danny?" she said. "Angela, I mean?"

"A long time, sweetheart," I said. "When she comes out, Pauli'll be waiting for her, just like Steve McQueen."

Isabelle smiled, her bright eyes seeing all the way to Hollywood.

If Christmas Comes —

by Steve Fisher

THERE ARE A LOT OF THINGS we like about Hollywood that the people outside don't know about, could not know about, because they are just the small everyday things of living. They are things bigger than glamor and glory and money, that never make the publicity columns, and yet are the things that bring flesh and blood and breath to us who are idolized, symbolized, fictionized, and looked upon as immortal beings. In the days when I had to struggle to keep body and soul together, I used to think that money and fame would make a difference, but I know now that it doesn't; it makes it easier, but that is all. There is never anything different. So the little things, the elements around us that we see day in and day out are the things that make us laugh and weep.

Things like the sunshine, and the careless freedom of Hollywood Boulevard, and the parade of girls in slacks, and the blondes who wait on corners and aren't afraid to be picked up if you wear a white sweater and have a Packard roadster. The little barbecue stands where you drive in, after a show, and have food brought to your car, and sit there and eat it and laugh far into the night. Like the beaches which are ordinary beaches but can be gone to either winter or summer. Like the mountains and resorts, and places to dance like the Grove, and places to eat like Musso-Franks where even Garbo will sit at the counter to eat her dinner. Things like open air markets that spray floodlights across heaven to advertise oranges ten cents a dozen; or the little movie house that has a surprise preview picture given to them an hour before the second show goes on.

Little things like those, intangibles all, count up, and mean something, and make Hollywood the best place to live and earn your bread in the whole world. The sentiment and the laughter, things too small to mention, things I cannot even remember — and then the very best of all these things. The day that makes the whole year worth living. Christmas Day in Hollywood.

If you ever went away, Tony, could you *ever* forget Christmas? There is no snow. There is only California grass and trees and flowers and the weather at its worst, but when you walk along Hollywood Boulevard you see Christmas different from that you ever saw before. In the first place it isn't Hollywood Boulevard then, it is Santa Claus Lane. All of the street signs are changed to that (remember?) and on each electric lamp for the entire length of the boulevard there is a color picture of a different star. You *are* a star when your picture is in the gallery along Santa Claus Lane because you're with the best this town ever turned out. You're with Marie Dressler and Jean Harlow and Rudolph Valentino and Lillian Tashman — all of those great ones of today too. Mickey Mouse and Lionel Barrymore and Mae West and Clark Gable and Luise Rainer and all the others. You can see them all on Santa Claus Lane and you can see the ones who aren't posted and who are big. The producers and writers and directors and screen editors. You can see them in open roadsters. In the lobbies of hotels. In the doorways of apartments. Sitting in Henri's, or standing at the Brass Rail, or looking in at the Vine Street Derby for turkey like they never get at home. You can see success and failure and people drinking whiskey which a director said was the "curse of a nation."

It was like that when I came on the boulevard at seven o'clock, which may be early in New York but isn't in Hollywood. You had called me, remember? I left the hotel as soon as I could get dressed. The drugstore from where you had called was on the corner of Highland, but I thought I would walk. I would walk because it was Christmas and I wanted to see the shops dressed up, and the people who were also walking, but for a different reason than I. They were trying to walk off a hangover.

I remember now that I thought it was queer that you should call me because I thought of you only as an agent. A pretty good motion picture agent, I will admit, but no more than that. It was not until later when you started the investigation that I learned your agency was just a blind and that in reality you were a special studio detective. Rather, that your job was to put a heavy foot on the Hollywood crime wave in picture circles; and that made you the world's highest paid detective.

I came into the drug store and you were standing there over the corpse. You were wearing flannels and white shoes, a white sweater and a black coat which is, I guess, the way you always dress, except that your patent leather hair wasn't so patent leather as usual, and I thought I saw trouble in your green eyes, or on your smooth-skinned face.

"Hello, Ben," you said. "Merry Christmas."

"Hello, Tony," I answered. "Merry Christmas to you."

"And Merry Christmas to a corpse," someone said, and I looked up and saw that it was Betty Gale who said that. Betty, your pretty platinum blonde secretary who has curves in the right places. "Hi, Ben," she went on, "how is Hollywood's most prolific scenario writer?"

"I am fine," I said, "who is dead?"

And then we all concentrated our attention on the corpse. It was that of a man, a little man whose hair was sandy and whose blue eyes — which were still open — stared glassily up and past us at some Christmas tinsel on the ceiling. I noticed he was lying there doubled up, and I said:

"How did he get it?"

"Poison," you told me. "He came here for an antidote."

"Yeah," said Betty Gale. "The poor dope was only about half conscious. Must have been whacky drunk. You know. When the store opened he wobbled in and asked the clerk how you could tell when you've been poisoned. He wanted to know how you could tell whether it was poison or appendicitis or indigestion"

"Then he dropped where you see him now," you said, "and he hasn't moved since. The druggist tried to work with him but couldn't. There'll be a wagon pretty soon to take him away."

I nodded, still trying to figure out why all of this should interest you and why you had called me. I saw a bantam-weight guy with gray hair wandering around the store and you introduced him as Mickey Ryan of the Homicide Squad, but that wasn't until later.

"I suppose you wonder why we sent for you?" you said, and I noticed you were looking at your fingernails.

"Yeah," I said, "I *am* a little curious. Just a little though. It's a nice morning to be out."

"Don't you know the corpse?" you asked. I didn't like the sharp edge in your tone.

"No I don't, Tony."

Betty Gale shrugged. "Well, you can't always be right, Tony, my lover. You said Ben Thompson would know the stiff and he doesn't. So what? Do we pay his walking expenses back to the hotel?"

You looked at Betty and said to me: "Isn't it a shame? She's so pretty when she's quiet, too. You would never think she was crazy to look at her, would you?" You lit a cigarette. "Ben," you went on, "I did think you might know the guy, but that wasn't the real reason I asked to see you. Though Betty may claim that it was. The real reason is that I know you are sweet on a girl named Stella Matthews. That's right. You are sweet on her, aren't you?"

"Sure," I said, "plenty."

"Well," you replied, and I noticed a flicker in your green eyes, "it may surprise you to know this, but that guy on the floor was her husband."

I opened and closed my mouth, I was struck dumb with what you had told me. I honestly hadn't known a thing about it until you said it then. I stared down at the corpse and I still couldn't believe it. Stella was so young and naive; so sweet and — oh hell — you know all the words, and I know them, I've written them into enough movies to know them by rote.

You went on: "Yeah, he was an assistant film cutter at Parmet, that's all. I got his name from his wallet. William Blake. Betty scooted back to my office and looked up the data on him. She's a good girl in ways like that." Then as though you had let something out, you added: "We have a file something like they have at Central Casting Bureau, only we list every studio job, not just the actors. We have the registered history of everybody here. Sometimes it comes in handy." You didn't say why it came in handy, and I thought at the time it was to help you place talent in the right places, which, as an agent, you were supposed to do.

"So Blake was her — her —"

"Her husband," you said. "I want you to tell us all you can about her."

"There isn't much to tell," I replied, "if you know what love is."

Betty said: "Tony Key never knows what love is at this time in the morning."

"I met Stella at the studio," I continued, as you arched one eyebrow at Betty. "She was just a little extra kid. I'm sure she was straight. If she had been married to Blake it must have been off with them, because I took her home once. She lived in a little twenty-five-dollar-a-month apartment on Kingsley Drive. One of those places that has a nice front, and inside, a fold-in-the-wall bed. Sometimes she didn't have enough to eat and I'd help her out. Gradually, as time went on, I fell in love with her. I don't know why or how. A writer who has been earning close to two thousand a week in Hollywood for five years has a pretty wide choice of women. But there was something about the kid that seemed straight and honest to me and . . ."

"And the but bit you," said Betty.

"Precisely," I agreed.

You yawned and said: "Betty's right, this is one sweet time of the morning to be talking about love. You turned to the bantamweight Homicide detective. "See you in court, funny face," you said. "I'm going to walk around town a little on this case this morning, then I'm going to bed. Don't glut yourself on Christmas turkey."

You and Betty and I left the drugstore.

We drove over to Kingsley Drive. Stella was in red pajamas when she opened the door and I will say she looked neat. She had been in bed so that she hadn't a chance to wash her face, but it was the prettiest face for that time of morning I have ever seen. Her hair was gold on her shoulder and her eyes were as big as quarters, and bluer than the kind of sky they talk about in western pictures. She was a beautiful little tike. And I was very much in love with her.

"Ben," she said, looking at me in amazement. "what is this? It's not Xmas Eve anymore, and anyhow, I'm *not* having a party."

"Honey," I told her, "this is Tony Key. He has something to talk to you about. Tony is a big agent and if you treat him right you can't tell what he might do for you."

"No," Betty Gale came in, "you certainly can't. You can't *ever* tell about Tony."

There wasn't much more Stella could say and we all came into the apartment. It was a mess, all right, with the bed covers all wrinkled, and a man's pipe on the divan, a bottle of whiskey — half empty — on the kitchen table. She had a little half-pint Christmas tree in the window and there were a couple of presents tied up in red paper and green ribbons lying underneath it.

Stella stood looking at us, and you told her right away: "William Blake is dead. Poison."

She went dead-white. Her hand went to her throat. "He — he —"

"Don't know," you said, "maybe he drank it accidentally, maybe it was suicide. He was pretty drunk when the end came. But from the way he was talking I think it was murder."

"Murder?" she echoed.

"That's right," chirped Betty. "Something they hang people for in this state."

You asked her: "You were married to him, Stella."

"Yes," she answered frankly, "but — but we had separated. We didn't see each other any more. It was something in the past that I thought I could bury and forget." I noticed there were tears in her eyes.

You moved across the room like a cat then, Tony, in your flannels, your coat, that sweater. I could tell that you had gotten an idea when she said that. You picked up the two presents from under the little tree. "For Bill," you read, then the other: "For Ben."

"For me?" I asked, and I gulped down a lump of pain that was in my throat. I didn't know that she was going to buy me anything, and it affected me quite a lot.

"Yeah, for you," you said, and handed me the package which turned out to be a green smoking jacket. I kissed Stella for it right there because she was already so nervous that she was sitting on the bed crying.

"Look," you went on, talking to her. "You've got to answer some questions."

That was when I interrupted and told you she had had enough for one morning. I asked you who you thought you were to take such authority. I guess I got tough with you. But you told me. You told me off then, and Betty added you were not only a detective, but the world's highest paid one. After that you went on with the questions.

"This present marked 'For Bill', Stella. For Bill Blake, isn't it? William Blake?"

"I — ah —"

"It is," you said, "I know it is. Why did you tell me you never saw him any more?"

"Well — on Christmas."

You were nasty: "I catch. You don't see each other all year, but on Christmas you exchange presents."

"Well — yes."

"Tripe," you said, "plain tripe." Then you turned and picked up the pipe from the divan.

"Pipe," said Betty Gale, "plain pipe." Then to Stella: "Honey, he's going to ask you to whom the plain pipe belongs. Have a good answer ready or he'll catch you up."

"It belongs to Roger West," Stella whispered, "his initials are on the bowl of it."

I guess we all looked up then; Roger West, like Clark Gable, was one of the really big stars. I thought she must have stolen it from the studio for its sentimental value, but she went on:

"I don't want to lie to you about anything, Mr. Key. Roger West was here last night. We had a few drinks together."

You put the pipe in your pocket, and said: "You get around, don't you, Stella?"

I was so shocked that I couldn't speak. She had never spoken of knowing West and though there was really no reason that she should have, I felt as though I had been cheated. I felt in my pockets for a cigarette. I knew Stella didn't smoke and finally bummed one from Betty. You were in the kitchen sniffing at the whiskey bottle. It sat among a lot of dirty dishes and wet cigarette butts that had turned brown, the color of the tobacco.

"Well," you said at last, "it's a cinch somebody poisoned Blake, and when we have the autopsy report we'll know what kind of poison. Meanwhile, Betty, my sweet, it looks as though we spend Christmas Day barking in blind alleys. Let's go visit Roger West." You looked at me. "Want to go, Ben? Or do you want to stay here with Stella?"

"I'll go with you," I said. "Stella's in no condition for company."

I just said that in front of her, but when I got outside I told you: "Listen, finding out what I have about Stella has made me pretty sick." This was the truest thing I ever said. "I want to walk it off or something. You don't mind, do you? The murder doesn't mean anything to me, but Stella does — or did. I'm all in a turmoil about her."

You patted my shoulder. "Okay, Ben, but if you want to go, don't think you'll be in the way."

"It isn't that," I said. "It's that I'm tired, and all confused. I want to walk — walk a lot. Then go home and take a cold shower and drink coffee. You know, when you called I rushed out without even changing my shirt — and well, I guess I'm pretty filthy. But I'd appreciate it though, on account of Stella, if you'd drop by and let me know how things turn out. Or Betty could phone me."

"Nah," you said, "we'll come over. Just have a good Christmas drink ready is all."

I wandered around for awhile, just as I told you I was going to, then I went back to my hotel. I was pretty blue. I wished that none of it had happened. I had been happy with Stella and now, knowing what I did, I didn't think I could ever be so much in love with her again. I smoked a lot of cigarettes and paced around. When it came two o'clock I tuned in Bing Crosby and heard him sing *Silent Night*, which he sings every Christmas. It's broadcast from coast to coast and across to England, of course, but that too somehow seems like Hollywood tradition.

I had changed my trousers and was wearing the green smoking robe Stella had given me, when you came in with Betty Gale. You looked pretty glum and flopped down in a chair, crossing your legs, and putting a cigarette in your mouth and lighting it.

"Roger West admits loving Stella," said Betty, "which would be swell copy for Winchell except that Tony is paid to keep down publicity like that as well as to solve murders."

She didn't make me feel any better, saying that, and I phoned down for Tom and Jerrys to be sent up.

You said moodily: "Outside of that, West was a fizzle. Couldn't get anything out of him."

"Yeah," said Betty, "I thought he was a He-Man, even though he's as handsome as seven hundred dollars. But he wears lavendar pajamas, and doesn't smoke or chew, and eats oysters for breakfast."

We sat around, not saying much, then the drinks came up. They warmed us, the foam slopping over a little, and you perked up and said: "You know, Mickey Ryan, that little Homicide detective, has a lead, and I would not be surprised but what he was on the right trail this time. The only trouble is that Mickey can't figure a thing about the murder and doesn't know how to prove what he thinks. Well, we're all in the same boat. But Mickey has another film cutter — Wilt Davis — who every body knows has hated Blake for years. Mickey and the rest of the cops have been questioning Davis. Just a little while ago they let him go."

"Since when," said Betty, "do you go around scavenging discarded police suspects?"

You wriggled your finger at her. "Tush, sweetheart. Cops have discarded killers before."

You got up, walked up and down the room. You stopped at my dresser and stood biting your thumb, though I don't think you saw the mess of junk on the dresser or anything else in the room. You were thinking. At last you turned.

"Well, I can't sit around and drink when there's murder doing. Up and going, Betty. We'll take a look in at this brother film cutter who they say had hatred in his heart that was like rattles on a rattlesnake. He worked right with Blake — Davis did, and — well, come on."

I was nervous and restless, and terribly blue. I thought anything would be better than staying in the room. I asked: "Can I go along?"

"Sure, Ben," you said.

So I put on my coat and shoes and followed along with you and Betty. I was beginning to admire the way you worked and I had taken a liking to Betty.

You remember what Wilt Davis' apartment looked like. It was pretty ritzy for an assistant film cutter, and the pretty brown-haired maid who answered the door didn't seem to fit the surroundings either.

"I'm beginning to see why these guys like their jobs," said Betty. "This is the next thing to elegant. And elegant is a special word with me."

When Davis came out you would have thought he was a producer instead of a film cutter. He was short, and heavy, and I remember how his eyes shone beneath the heavy black brows that were so prominent on his fat face. He was smoking a cigar; and his radio was playing a popular song: *I Get That Old Feeling.*

"Yes, I disliked Bill Blake," he said, "that isn't news."

"Any particular reason ?" you asked.

"Several," said Davis, who was in an ugly mood, "but I see no reason for going into those particular reasons."

"Where were you last night?" you asked.

"Drunk," said Davis. "I was on a round of Christmas Eve parties and I got stinko. I don't remember what I did after midnight."

You went after him for more details, but he stuck to that story, and at last you said we might as well leave. When we were outside walking — the three of us — Betty remarked:

"I can see how the police failed to get anywhere."

You didn't say anything, and we drove in your roadster back to Hollywood Boulevard. You parked in front of the drug store where Blake's corpse had been. We got out and went in. You stepped into the telephone booth for a moment. When you came out you looked at Betty, and told her:

"Cyanide."

"You poor fellow. What you want is a Bromo. Not cyanide. Imagine! So wacky he asks for cyanide!"

"Listen, my stupid platinum assistant," you growled, "cyanide is what they found in Blake's system. I just called the morgue."

"Oh," she said, "oh — that's different."

You lit another cigarette, and then we went out on the boulevard. We walked along without speaking and I was looking at the light posts and the pictures of stars on them and glancing about to see if I could spot any of them in the flesh. Then suddenly I noticed you had stopped. Betty and I hadn't noticed and were a few feet ahead. We stopped and came back. You were in front of a cafeteria.

"Let's go in for coffee."

"Coffee?" echoed Betty. "At this time of day? In *there?*"

"Lamb," you said, speaking to her, "because I give you eighty-five dollars a week and pin money on the side, is no reason you should spurn a perfectly respectable cafeteria."

So we went in, though she didn't feel like coffee and neither did I. This was an all night place, and at four in the afternoon — which it was now — it wasn't in any too good condition. A few sidewalk cowboy extras were having their turkey hash, but outside of that the place was empty. You drank two cups of coffee and kept looking around you, and I saw that same troubled look in your green eyes.

At last you said: "You two excuse me for a moment, please." You walked off.

"I knew two cups of that java would do that to him," Betty told me, and we laughed about it.

We laughed, but we were both nervous because we knew that you were up to something and we didn't know what it was. It must have had something to do with the murder. It seemed to me that you had been acting queerly since leaving Davis' place. Twenty minutes passed before you came back and then if we looked into your face for some sign of expression, we were discouraged because you showed no concern. You sat down. You put a cigarette between your lips and lit it.

"Just take it easy, Ben," you said, "and sit here like nothing has happened, and pretty soon Mickey Ryan is going to come in and get you. I phoned him."

"What do you mean?" I said.

"I mean you brought Bill Blake here under the pretext that you were going to sober him up. You got coffee for him and put cyanide in it. Then, because you didn't want the doorman to see you leave you went into the men's room and out that window. When you come in this place you take a check from an automatic machine. The only time you are seen is when you go out and pay for the stuff they punch on your check. So you went out the window in the men's room figuring Blake would die right then and there and that that would be all there was to it."

"You're crazy," I snapped, "you're just crazy as hell, Tony! You can't prove that!"

"Listen," you said. "When you went out that window you jumped into the dirt down below. There's foot marks that'll fit your shoe."

"But a lot of men wear shoes my size!"

"Sure. But very few men have a check from this cafeteria up on their dresser, like you have. You must have dumped it there when you emptied your pockets to change your pants. If you had paid for your food you would not have had the check because they take them from you. And so you can't steal a check and come in and eat a big meal on a check that's punched for maybe a nickel. They have them marked by the day. A different color for every day. I spotted that on your dresser a little while ago. I took you along with me to Davis' because I wanted to throw the net around you slowly. I didn't want you to be suspicious. I didn't want you to have a chance to get out."

"What net?" I demanded.

"Murder net," you said, "can't you see that I have the set-up right now? You were jealous of Stella's husband and figured you had to get him out of the way. You and he and Stella were at her apartment drinking after Roger West left. West doesn't smoke and neither does Stella, but the kitchen is littered with whiskey-soaked cigarette butts and I put the rest together. The presents under the tree for both you and Blake. It all fits into a perfect picture."

I was gasping, trying to speak.

"I was first suspicious though," you went on, "when you made the break you did after leaving Stella's apartment this morning. I was first suspicious then and that's why Betty and I came back — *not* to drink your Tom and Jerrys. You said you were filthy, that your shirt was dirty because you hadn't had time to *change* it. You meant to say put on a clean one. But your tongue slipped. But the fact was clear: when I called you you had just gotten in from the street and were still dressed. You were dressed, because an hour previous to that you had put the cyanide in Blake's coffee and had jumped out the window of this cafeteria."

Betty Gale was smiling. "And if you don't think that's a murder case, Ben, try getting out of it when they put the noose around your neck."

"It's a murder case," I breathed, "it's that all right. From such clues you trace my movements which covered hours. Oh, you've got something there. There's no getting around that." I straightened up and I guess my face was pretty pale, but I said: "Can't we go out and have a drink on it? One last good Christmas drink before that Homicide man gets here?"

So I'm here in San Quentin now, writing this, Tony. Writing this and watching the hours tick past me. They say it'll never come, that they all hope the same thing, but I'm hoping for a reprieve. Hour after hour I keep waiting for it.

I have written this because it was on my mind and I had to write it, and because also it may be the last writing I will ever do. I was paid two thousand dollars a week for writing, and I guess the habit was too great to break. So maybe it was that. Maybe it was the writer in me that made me put this down on paper, although when I started out, I remember I had something to tell you. It was something I thought you should know, though it really makes no difference.

It was — oh yes — it was that a certain song I heard only once has been buzzing through my mind. The only words I know are those in the title, but they keep coming back. The title is *The Lady Is a Tramp*, and that's what I wanted to tell you. I didn't know Stella was really married to Bill Blake. She told me only that he was someone who had something on her and she hinted that she could never be happy until he had "gone away somewhere." It wasn't until I got up here that I saw the truth. I was obsessed with my love for her, and as Blake seemed to have some mysterious power over her that could make her do what he wanted, and because she cried about this, and because I thought he stood in the way of my love, I killed him. I didn't tell her I was going to, so she is no way an accomplice, but I knew that that was what she wanted me to do.

It wasn't until I went around with you that I saw what it was. She was married to him and they were operating a little blackmail game of their own. He would do the dirty work and she would make up to big-money people like Roger West and myself and they would share the proceeds. But she was getting tired of splitting the money and tired of Blake, and seeing how nuts I was about her she worked on me to kill him. Subtly, of course. You couldn't pin anything on her in a million years. But she wanted Blake out of the way and that was her method. I was the sap. The fall guy. I did it for her. I killed him. But she was the instrument behind me.

I did that because I loved her, Tony, but she hasn't been around to see me, she hasn't even sent me a card; and I keep thinking of how sweet she was, then that song comes into my head. It keeps coming back all the time. That song: *The Lady Is a Tramp* . . .

Well, Tony, I guess that's all — only I keep thinking of Hollywood, and the little things that made life there, like the Barbecue stands and

Musso-Franks and the markets that spray the heaven with lights to advertise oranges at ten cents a dozen — and of Christmas. It's so lonely here. Maybe I'll get pardoned. Maybe they won't hang me. But, Tony, if — if Christmas comes to Hollywood again and I'm not there . . . If I'm not there, take a walk down Santa Claus Lane for me, will you?

And the Winner Is —

by Ron Goulart

HE SHOULDN'T HAVE CONfessed in front of all those people. But when he saw the man he'd murdered starting to come up on the stage to share the award, it unsettled him.

Everybody, since the awards banquet was televised live from Hollywood, knows what Oscar Kornfield did next. Some are even aware of what Joe Tackery was up to and what exactly his last words meant. Hardly anyone, though, knows about the trunkful of money.

I'm probably the only living person, besides perhaps Jana, who has the knowledge that there was $400,000 in cash involved in this business. As to where the trunk is now, I have no idea. Jana doesn't either, so far as I can determine without openly discussing it with her. Which I never will, since I don't want to get entangled any further. Let the money stay lost; there's very likely a curse on it anyway, a jinx.

Joe Tackery and I had lunch the day Kornfield fired him. We met at the Vegetarian Dragon, the health-food Chinese place in Westwood. A few of the tan and healthy-looking patrons gasped, a couple shrieked, even one of the usually unmovable waiters let out a frightened sigh when Joe came strolling in out of the smoggy yellow midday toward my booth.

"See, and he claims I'm unbelievable," Tackery said as he dropped down opposite me. Lowering the dragon-shaped menu, I told him, "Coming to lunch in your makeup is —"

"Gauche, yeah, I know. Thing is, I didn't have time to remove it and still get over here on time. Because of the fist fight."

"You were in a fight? A real fight?"

"With Kornfield, after he fired me. Ha." When he laughed some of the scar tissue on his face cracked. Tackery poked at it, then toyed with his dangling left eyeball. "Should have seen what I did to him." He inspected his fingertip. "Huh, there's some *real* blood. I didn't think that turkey hit me hard enough to —"

"Why were you trading punches with the head of Magnum-Opus Productions? No, thanks."

Our waiter had brought a hot towel and a finger bowl for Tackery to use on his seemingly ruined face.

Tackery grinned up at him, flashing blackened fangs. "All make-believe. Illusion," he said and the waiter went away, leaving the scented towel behind. "You saw me in *Dr. Dementia.* Now, forgetting the story line, you have to admit I was convincing in that film."

"Best bloodbeast I've ever seen."

"Hell, even John Simon on *New York* called me completely disgusting and nauseating, and you know how few things he praises." He hit the table angrily with a bloody fist, causing the hand towel to give out a slippery, squishing sound. "I was even better in *Love Finds Dr. Dementia.* Right? I've been in *movies.* Ever since I had the title role in *Horrifying Slime* I've been considered one of the best horror men in this halfwitted town. Sure, doing my own makeup annoys certain people, but the hell with them. Didn't I almost get an Oscar for *Marylou's Demented Offspring?*"

"What's bothering Kornfield then?"

"He claims I'm no good, that my characterizations aren't believable. 'Wouldn't fool a cockeyed six-year-old,' is how he deftly phrased it. That, however is not the real reason. The real reason is, that toad is consumed by jealousy," explained Tackery. "See, I was supposed to, even though my halfwit agent didn't get it on paper yet, play a running character in this new *Ghost Doctor* TV series Kornfield's producing. Hell, I was doing them a favor to play television at all. By agreeing to be the accident-victim zombie I —"

"Sounds like a difficult character to keep working into stories. Maybe that's why —"

"Naw, Kornfield gave me the ax because of Jana."

"Jana? I thought you were embroiled with a girl named Pam."

"Kim was her name and that's been over since she didn't come right back from the location shooting on *Rapist of the Range*." Absently he started removing the warts and moles from his face. "Don't you know who Jana Dayside is?"

"Sure, my oldest boy has that poster of her hidden under his bed. We used her in a toothpaste commercial couple of years back. Before she hit with *Robots Three* on TV."

"She is, without doubt, the hottest property in Hollywood at the moment."

"You dating her?"

"I am, a real love match," he said, lowering his voice. Trouble is, I strongly suspect Kornfield is, too."

"Kornfield just married the redhaired girl who used to be part of that rock group called Advanced Stages. Item was in the *National Intruder* only —"

"You've lived in this goofy town all your life and you never heard of a producer cheating on his wife?"

"Not so soon after the wedding. According to the *Intruder* he just gifted this redhead with a diamond-studded —"

"Oy, for a man who's slaved ten years in the advertising game, you have a very feeble idea of how the world works."

"Fifteen years actually," I corrected. "Be sixteen next —"

"It's me Jana *loves*, but I think Kornfield forces her to see him. After all, Magnum-Opus is producing *Robots Three*."

"She ought to have enough clout now to be able to say no to Kornfield. The show's been Number One in the ratings for the last month." The waiter was hovering and I picked up my menu again. "We better order. The sweet-sour parsnips are —"

"See, I'm not absolutely certain she is going out with that lecherous grunion, but I *suspect* she is."

"Ask her."

"You don't simply *ask* the hottest property in town if she's two-timing you."

"Two-timing? There's a quaint old phrase —"

"My father used to say that, and when I get angry —"

"We have very nice kelp chow mein," offered our waiter cautiously, while trying not to look at Tackery.

"Come back in a few minutes," he said.

"If you're sure Kornfield fired you for personal reasons you ought to have the Guild look —"

"Ha," laughed Tackery, causing one of his horrible eyebrows to fall off. "I don't need the guild to fix Kornfield's wagon. Once I determine what's what, I'll settle the whole thing myself."

The day after our lunch I had to fly to Florida unexpectedly to untangle some problems they were having with one of our shark-repellent commercials. While the repellent was repelling sharks, it attracted hordes of ugly little blue and orange fish who kept spoiling most of our expensive underwater footage. Since I was head account man, the client expected me to come up with some way of shooing all the ugly little fish away. The first thing I worked out, with the help of a very high-priced marine biologist got rid of the ugly fish but dyed our actor a pale lavender. What with one thing and another, including a mild case of sunstroke, I was three weeks in Florida.

By the time I returned to Los Angeles, Joe Tackery was already at work on his plan to undermine Kornfield while finding out what the producer and Jana Dayside were up to. He took to hanging around the Magnum-Opus studios out in Burbank and around Kornfield's Beverly Hills home wearing various disguises. Once he got himself up as the mutilated vampire he'd played in *Stultified.* Excessive in my opinion, but it seemed to fool Kornfield. Tackery was able to trail him all across Southern California without the producer's being aware of it.

The third day of his vigil Tackery followed Kornfield directly to Jana Dayside's new peach-colored mansion in Bel Air, thus confirming his worst fears. After that he determined to get something on his rival, something damaging enough to put him out of competition.

When he outlined all this to me over lunch at the Frozen Goatherd, that yogurt-on-a-stick place in Santa Monica, I told him it would be much simpler to abandon Jana than to trail Kornfield hither and yon.

"You forget," Tackery said, himself this particular afternoon except for a false mustache, "that Kornfield fired me off the *Ghost Doctor* show. He says I'm not good at makeup and disguise, but what I'm doing proves otherwise. You also forget he's been squiring my lady around town in a most sneaky way."

"With her compliance."

"Who would willingly date a toad like him? She's obviously being coerced. She's a very sensitive, introspective girl and a heavy like —"

"On *Robots Three* I saw her lift up a full garbage truck and heave it through —"

"Trick stuff, as you well know," he said, scowling. "I'm most certainly going to revenge myself on Kornfield. I'm pretty sure, by the way, he's trying to get me blacklisted with some of the other producers in town.

He won't get away with that either."

Right at this point in time I left for the Nyanya Film Festival, where one of our dandruff-fighter commercials was up for a Special Award. Unfortunately the Nyanya rebels picked the week of the festival to stage a terror raid on the capital. Along with nearly 200 other invited guests, I was held hostage in the Royal Palace of Cinema for four and a half days. We had to get along on what food there was in the lobby, mostly popcorn and chocolate-covered raisins.

The diet and the constant threats of violence from our surly captors made my stay in Nyanya less than pleasant. Possibly you didn't see anything about the incident in the papers or on the news — Nyanya doesn't seem able to get much publicity in the outside world. Which is one of the things the rebels were grousing about.

Recuperating from the trip consumed another two weeks, so I wasn't back in the agency until the tail end of summer. My lovely secretary informed me that several strange people had been dropping in asking after me — a one-legged sailor, a very ill-looking Balkan count, a man who appeared to have suffered a severe accident, and a shaggy fellow in a bloodstained overcoat.

"Joe Tackery," I decided.

My secretary screamed just then, gesturing at the opening elevator.

A sinister-looking Oriental was shuffling into the reception area on my floor. "Do you have a moment, most celestial sir?"

"Come on into my office, Joe."

"Shall I alert the authorities?" whispered my secretary.

"Only an actor," I assured her.

"I'm still not used to this town, it's not at all like East Moline."

"Ha, ha!" remarked Tackery when we were closed in my large sun-bright office.

"Is that a cackle of triumph?"

"First, how are you feeling?"

"Not bad, I seem to have —"

"Good, good." He hunkered down in the chair most of the clients prefer. "Let me fill you in on what I've unearthed."

"Don't get yellow all over the chair."

"This is smear-proof Oriental makeup," Tackery said. "I have them now, have them by the proverbial short hairs."

"Who?"

"Kornfield and that little twit of a business partner of his, Tuck Bensen."

"Bensen's about your size. He's not exactly little or —"

"Spiritually he's a shrimp, morally he's a midget. That offensive little —"

"How'd Bensen get into this? Is he going around with Jana too?"

"No, she isn't *that* goofy." He hunched lower in the chair rubbing his gnarled taloned hands together. "I've got them on Murder One."

I blinked, dropping the soy margarine carton I'd been toying with. "Murder?"

He nodded. "Ever hear of a guy known as Mojave McWilliams?"

"Old coot who lives out in the desert, old-time prospector? Struck it rich years ago and built himself some kind of castle out there. Rumored to be fantastically wealthy."

"The rumors are true," he said. "Old Mojave had a steamer trunk chockful of cash money. $400,000 worth to be exact." From out of his robe sleeve he produced a fat wad of bills. "Money like this."

"You mean you stole the old man's life savings?"

"Life savings? Mojave was much more than a prospector — he made his dough in sundry shady enterprises. Besides which, I didn't swipe the loot. Kornfield and Bensen did."

"Then how come you —"

"They don't as yet know I have the trunk or where I hid it." He leaned back and laughed, first as himself and then as the sinister Oriental. "There's an old folksong that advises you to put your money down in your shoe before coming into a town like this, otherwise they're going to take it away from you. Mojave thought he had his cash safely stashed, but he was wrong."

"I don't quite under —"

"Let me explain."

What had been happening was this. After Tackery, in his varied disguises, had been trailing Kornfield for a few weeks he discovered the producer was making several trips out to the desert. Accompanied usually by his partner, Tuck Bensen, he visited the mammoth adobe fortress Mojave McWilliams had erected for himself when he retired from his sundry shady enterprises. McWilliams, who shunned people, had one weakness. Well, more than one actually, but one which Kornfield and Bensen could exploit. He was vain. When they approached him with the notion of Magnum-Opus doing an hour television documentary on his colorful life, the old desert rat admitted them into his fortress and invited them to return whenever they wished.

What Kornfield and his partner were really after was the trunkful of money the old man was rumored to have hidden on the premises.

Despite their apparent success and frequent mentions in such publications as the *National Intruder*, both Oscar Kornfield and Tuck Bensen were on the edge of bankruptcy. Kornfield's cash had flowed out to his earlier wives — there'd been six prior to the redhaired girl from Advanced Stages. Bensen's money had been lost at two places, Las Vegas and the track. $400,000 would be a big help.

So they went after Mojave. One night, long after he'd come to trust them completely, Bensen suddenly jabbed him in the arm with a hypodermic. This knocked the old prospector out, and a different shot caused him to speak the absolute truth. Unfortunately, right after McWilliams told them where the trunk was hidden, he died. Giving unexpected injections to old men sometimes has that effect.

Tackery witnessed all this from a ledge outside the castle living room. Besides being expert at makeup, he was a pretty fair stuntman. He managed to watch as Kornfield and Bensen hid Mojave's body in the cellar room where the trunk had been hidden. Since Mojave was a recluse they didn't expect anyone to find him for a long while. He had no servants, and kept a year's supply of simple foods on hand.

The producer and his partner, with Tackery discreetly following, next drove to a piece of land that Kornfield still owned in one of the undeveloped stretches of canyon beyond Los Angeles. Working all night the two men buried the trunkful of money, intending to let it sit a week or two before making use of it. By that time they'd know if they'd got away clear.

Tackery waited until they drove off, then dug up the loot. After helping himself to enough cash to finance his campaign for a month or more, he took the trunk and hid it at a new and different location.

"Doesn't that make you an accessory to the murder?" I asked when he'd finished the account.

"No, it makes me a light-hearted Robin Hood."

"You witnessed a murder. It's your duty to —"

"Yeah, eventually I'll blow the whistle on the two of them," Tackery promised, grinning inscrutably. "Right now, however, I am going to have some fun."

"Fun?"

"Did you know Kornfield has taken to carrying a gun?"

"No, it wasn't in the *Intruder*."

"While little Bensen is consulting Madame Olga down in Manhattan Beach to get some tips on life on the other side of the veil." Tackery was bouncing in the chair, hugging himself, trying to control his amusement and elation.

"You've been making up like Mojave McWilliams," I accused. "Yes, that must be it. You've been getting yourself up like that old prospector and haunting Kornfield and Bensen."

"Merely giving them little flashes," he said. "You know, at a premiere I'll be at the edge of the crowd where they can only catch a glimpse. Or I might stroll across one of their lawns during a cocktail party. A cinchy impersonation — all you need is lots of whiskers."

"Listen, you're going to —"

"Wait now. I couldn't possibly fool them. Right? Because Kornfield is on record as saying how bad I am at makeup and character work. I'm no good, so I couldn't make anyone believe I was Mojave."

I wasn't happy about all he'd told me. I felt, somehow, as though I were also an accomplice. "How does what you're doing help you with Jana Dayside?"

"Once I've toppled Kornfield, turned him into a quivering wreck, he'll leave her alone. Since I started this game I haven't had much time for her, but that'll soon change."

"If he and Bensen go under, that could ruin Magnum-Opus and probably spell the end of *Robots Three*."

"Naw, they can be replaced. Anyway, M-O is secretly owned by a syndicate of Arabs. They aren't about to let a hot show like Jana's fold."

"Seems to me there are moral issues involved —"

"Come on, don't start laying that kind of talk on me. I confide in you because I know you're above morality."

"Even so —"

"Even so, you get ready to see that toad Kornfield go right down the chute."

Maybe, since I'd made the mistake of mentioning moral issues, Tackery began to feel differently about confiding in me. I know I saw him much less from then on, though it may only be because I got heavily involved in refilming six of our dog-food commercials. The client didn't feel the original canines were lively enough. While attempting to reshoot with livelier dogs I was attacked by one of the German shepherds, and a St. Bernard tried to eat part of one of the cameras. It was a hectic period, causing me to forget about Joe Tackery and his situation.

As it turned out, that meeting in my office, when he was in his Oriental getup, was to be my last encounter with him. I saw him once more, as millions of others all across America did, on the Lulu Awards

Show. Except, I guess, most of those who saw him didn't realize it was Joe Tackery. They thought they were seeing Tuck Bensen.

None of what follows I am absolutely certain of. Some of it I didn't even find out about until weeks after the telecast. This is, however, what I believe must have happened. Tackery continued to follow Kornfield, now and then giving him a glimpse of himself as Mojave McWilliams. Kornfield grew increasingly nervous and finally drove out to the desert. A hot wind was roaring on the night he let himself into the fortress. He ventured into the cellar and found the body of the dead prospector exactly where they'd left it. Tackery couldn't quite see the producer's expression from his vantage point, flat out on the stones of the courtyard yet he sensed it must be an exquisite one. Here was Mojave dead so who had he been seeing? Was it a ghost? Or was he crazy?

The next thing the worried producer did was hurry to the spot where he and Bensen had buried the loot. This time, hidden behind scruffy brush and thin trees, Tackery did see Kornfield's face. It was indeed an exquisite expression which touched the producer's features when he discovered the trunkful of money was gone.

Kornfield went to the home of his partner. Tuck Bensen denied moving the money, which was perfectly true. Kornfield didn't believe him. They quarreled and Kornfield strangled the smaller man to death. He was unhappy on realizing what he'd done. Now, so far as he knew, he'd never find the $400,000. His only piece of good luck was that, since Bensen was in such terrible financial shape, there were no servants in his big Moorish home. Kornfield searched it thoroughly, twice, and found not a trace of the missing money.

Lugging the body of his defunct partner to his car, Kornfield re turned to his empty lot and deposited him in the hole where the trunk once had been. He covered him with earth and announced, on returning to Magnum-Opus the next morning, that his partner was off on a well-deserved vacation in South America. This way he'd have a few days to figure out his next move.

Kornfield still hadn't worked out much in the way of a plan by the night of the Lulu Awards banquet for the best television shows of the year. He and Bensen were up for a golden statuette as co-producers in the Best Detective Series category. Accompanied by his newest wife and attired in a sky-blue dinner jacket which concealed the revolver he always carried now, Kornfield attended. If you noticed him at his table you wouldn't have realized he was nervous or distraught. He was smiling, gracious, attentive to his guests.

The Award ceremonies ran smoothly, except when they were giving out the Best Animal Actor award. During that the German shepherd candidate chased the presenter, that platinum-blond guy who's in *City Morgue*, around the dais while nipping at his tux. It was the same nasty dog who'd tried to destroy me when we refilmed our dog-food spots. I was pleased to see, watching at home over TV, that the dog could be mean with other people. The client hinted there was something about me which had agitated a usually amiable animal.

Jana Dayside was the one who was to present the Lulu for Best Detective series and she looked completely stunning.

"Stunning," I said.

"Obvious," said my wife.

Jana read the nominees in that husky voice of hers, tossed her abundant blonde hair and very sensually opened the envelope.

"And the winner is *City Morgue* Magnum-Opus Productions," she read. "Mr. Oscar Kornfield will accept."

In a very stately, for him, manner Kornfield made his way up to the dais Jana gave him a quick hug before handing over the Lulu.

Kornfield leaned into the arc of microphones. "I'm very pleased, as well as honored, to accept this award," he began. "Obviously this honor wouldn't have been possible without the help and support of a great many people. Chief among them is my devoted partner, Tuck Bensen, who unfortunately can't be here since he's enjoying a much deserved vacation —"

"But I'm not on vacation, Oscar."

What Kornfield saw was his dead partner, miraculously alive again, moving toward him into the limelight. "You can't be here!" Kornfield shouted. "I killed and buried you." With an angry grunt he yanked out the pistol from his shoulder holster. "And I'll do it again!"

He fired four shots into Joe Tackery's chest.

Before Tackery died he managed to say something. It was picked up by the microphones. "I told you I was good," he said.

Class
Act

by Jay Speyerer

MALCOLM DORN SAT IN HIS
dirty green Maverick and listened to the rain hammer the roof. He lit
his third cigarette, sucking the orange glow from the dashboard lighter.
He sipped cold, fast-food coffee from a styrofoam cup. It tasted wretched
and left a cottony coating on his tongue, but it was coffee.

He stared through the smoke and the windshield across the parking lot at the main gate of the Terminal Island Federal Correctional
Institution. Seen through the streaming glass, the black bars were
rain-warped and looked deceptively passable. But Dorn's research
showed that these bars had held Michael Leonard Vosler for thirty-
seven years.

Dorn checked his watch. Quarter to one. According to his information, Vosler was to have been released at noon on this first day of
March. He was running his usual rosary of curses at bureaucracy and
rainy Mondays when he noticed blurred activity at the gate. He turned
the ignition key a notch, getting juice from the battery, and turned on
the wipers.

Two figures stood at the open gate, a uniformed guard and a tall,
thin man in a topcoat and snap-brim hat. Dorn watched as they faced
each other for a moment and then shook hands in an abrupt up-and-
down motion. Then the thin man bent and picked up a small gym bag,
and moved slowly down the walk toward the street.

He seemed oblivious to the steady rain, not even looking up to inspect his freedom. He kept his eyes on the pavement six feet ahead until he reached the shelter of the bus stop. Dorn watched him sit down on the bench, placing his gym bag beside him.

Dorn turned off the ignition and pocketed the keys. Then he took a final drag on his cigarette, opened the door, and got out, flipping the butt away. He raised the collar of his jean jacket and hunched his shoulders against the downpour as he hurried across the lot to the shelter.

The old man did not move as Dorn entered the shelter. He continued to lean forward on the bench, his forearms resting on his knees. His hat and topcoat were mottled dark in patches from the rain. From his high angle, Dorn could not see the other man's eyes, and so could not tell if he had received a glance of acknowledgment. Dorn took a deep breath, held it a beat, then let it out. Feeling his heart thudding, he spoke loudly enough to be heard over the drumming of the rain. "Mr. Vosler," he said.

The other man looked up, brown eyes hooded and wary. His face was pale and freckled, and the wrinkles seemed set in stone, immobile. A long moment, then, "Yeah?"

"I'm Malcolm Dorn."

Vosler remained unmoving at first, but then Dorn saw the awareness grow, a tectonic shift in the planes of his face, glacially slow but certain. His eyes still pinning Dorn, the old man's right hand moved to the brim of his hat and pushed it back off his forehead. Dorn followed the movement, unable to look away from the hand and the empty space where the little finger should have been. Finally Vosler spoke, his voice a sere whisper, molten anger bubbling below. "You malign the dead. I have nothing to say to you, scribbler."

"Every word I wrote was true."

Vosler turned his head away, looking down the street for the bus.

"It wasn't easy. In fact, it was the hardest story I ever wrote. Lane Broderick was my hero when I was little. I wanted to be a cowboy just like him when I grew up." Dorn stuck his hands in the pockets of his jeans. "I'm too young to have seen those cliffhangers in a theater, but I saw them on TV in the fifties. Saturday mornings. The Lone Ranger, the Cisco Kid, Roy Rogers, and the Phantom Rider."

Still looking away, Vosler said, "Fine way to treat a hero, scribbler."

"Mr. Vosler, I wrote that story because the only thing most people remember about that trial is that Vera Justine was going to have Lane Broderick's child. They've forgotten the unanswered questions."

"Picked a rotten rag to publish it in," the old man muttered.

"The *Tattler* was last on my list, if that means anything."

"It doesn't."

Dorn stood with his hands in his pockets, feeling the rainwater drip from his hair and run down his neck. "I wanted to be a cowboy when I was six," he said. "When I was sixteen, I wanted to be a stuntman."

Vosler gave him a sideways look. "What would a sixteen-year-old know about stuntmen?"

"I knew that Yakima Canutt staged the chariot race in *Ben Hur.* Dave Sharpe did the stunts in *Captain Marvel.* Tom Steele, Jock Mahoney. They're all legends."

Dorn wiped water from his forehead. "I also knew that even legends have idols. That if Buddy Vosler walked away from a stunt because he thought it was too dangerous, no one else would touch it."

After several moments, the old man spoke. "We were friends, Brod an' me. Probably doesn't mean much these days, but it did then. We broke into the movies together. Walk-ons, bit parts. He gradually got bigger speaking parts and I fell into stunt work. Then Monolith hired us both in '38." He paused for a beat, then said, "That's where he met Vera."

Vosler looked up, the fierce glint still in his eyes. "Brod was a good man. Generous. He did charity work, USO shows, visited sick kids in hospitals. He was a class act."

"I wrote that, too."

Vosler grunted in grudging acknowledgement. "I suppose you did." He shook his head. "He stayed a class act till the day he died. He was always a pro, always knew his lines. Even reduced to taking bit parts on 'Fantasy Island' and 'Love Boat' and spots on 'Hollywood Squares.'"

"Fine way to treat a hero, huh, Mr. Vosler?"

Vosler gave him a long look, then nodded. "You ever see Brod's last ride? *Phantom Train?*"

"Many times."

"Real tricky gag, a horse-to-train transfer. He knew it was his last movie, the last serial Monolith was gonna make. He wanted to go out in style, so he did the stunt himself." He looked off again, down the street at the bus that was now approaching. "Didn't even want me on the set."

Dorn leaned forward, trying to see the other man's face. "Shame you didn't do that stunt. Considering it happened at the same time Vera Justine was being killed."

The bus pulled up to the stop and the doors sighed open. Vosler stood and picked up his bag.

"Where are you going?" Dorn said. "I'll drive you."

The old man stepped over to the doors, then stopped and looked back. Dorn had to strain to hear him over the driving rain. "Let it go. Vera's dead and I did my time. Now Brod's dead and I just want to be left alone." He stepped onto the bus and glanced back at Dorn. "And I don't want anything from anyone, especially you."

Malcolm Dorn stared up at him. "Not even an alibi?"

The bus closed its doors and pulled away in a cloud of exhaust. Dorn dashed across the parking lot to his car. He fired up the engine, pulled out into traffic to a chorus of angry horns, and followed the bus. Of all the emotions Dorn had expected to see in Buddy Vosler's face, the last one he would have bet on was fear.

Following the bus into Long Beach was a no-brainer, so Dorn's mind filled again with the fragments of facts that made up Vera Justine's last day.

Lane Broderick's celebrated horse-to-train transfer was the final shot of *The Phantom Train*. Ten o'clock on a Tuesday morning in May, 1954. After reminding William Paige, the director, that he had practiced the stunt repeatedly, Broderick donned his black hat and mask, took the horse from the wrangler, and rode off out of sight behind a low hill.

After some last-minute camera adjustments and final instructions to the crew, Paige gave the start-up signal to the train engineer, who stayed hidden on the floor of the cab, giving the illusion that the train was a runaway. When the train reached a predetermined point, horse and rider emerged from their hiding place and gave chase. After leaping to the train and bringing it to a halt, the Phantom Rider remounted his horse and raced off out of sight behind another hill just as a posse of extras entered the scene.

The director yelled "cut," the extras dismounted, and everyone stood around congratulating each other on a perfect take for the final scene. A couple of minutes later, someone noticed that the star had not returned. One of the extras rode over and found Broderick's horse grazing at the top of a shallow ravine and a dazed Lane Broderick sitting at the bottom. The actor was covered with minor cuts and bruises, and, he said later, the bump behind his right ear where his head had hit the ground had rendered him unconscious for a few moments.

When the two men got back to the location, the first-aid man examined the star and suggested that a doctor take a look at him. As crew members were helping Broderick into a truck for the ride to the infirmary, word arrived of the murder of Vera Justine. According to the testimony of several who were there, Lane Broderick, upon hearing the news, immediately looked around and said, "Where's Vosler?"

The body of Monolith's star foreign import was found by the wardrobe mistress in her trailer two and three-tenths miles away where she was shooting another picture on location. The actress had broken her neck falling against a table. There were other signs of a struggle. And Buddy Vosler had cuts and bruises on his face and could not account for his whereabouts.

The headlines weren't as lurid as they could have been: SWISS FILM BEAUTY SLAIN. STUNTMAN CHARGED.

The rain had slacked off, so Dorn turned off his windshield wipers. On Ocean Boulevard, a few blocks past the Queen Mary, the bus let off two teenage boys and the old man. The boys hurried off down the street while Vosler stood there in the drizzle, looking around and trying to get his bearings.

Dorn pulled up to the curb, leaned across, and rolled down the passenger window. "Where are you going, Mr. Vosler?"

The man leaned down to look in the window. He stared at Dorn for half a dozen heartbeats, and then shrugged. "YMCA, I guess."

"Closest one's about six blocks away. I'll drive you."

A few more beats passed, then Vosler opened the door and eased himself into the seat. Dorn put the car in gear and merged with the line of traffic.

After several blocks of silence, Vosler shifted in his seat and said, "Taking a long time to go six blocks."

"We're taking a little side trip," Dorn said, keeping his eyes on the traffic.

The old man sat still, but Dorn heard the change in his breathing and the thinly disguised tension in his voice. "Where?"

"My place."

"What for?" Vosler said, turning his head to look at Dorn.

"Have some coffee. Talk." Dorn took his eyes from the road long enough to meet the other man's gaze. "Watch a movie." He returned his eyes to the street.

Dorn felt the stuntman's stare for another half block until Vosler turned away and looked out his side window. They drove for another thirty minutes in silence, as the houses grew farther apart and the trees closer together. Just past Garden Grove, Dorn turned onto a side road, finally pulling in to the Sighing Palms Trailer Court. They parked, and Dorn watched Buddy Vosler as he peered warily out the window at the small blue motor home with the canvas awning over the door.

"You live here?"

"It's not much, but the rent's free."

"Why's that?"

"I manage the place for the owner. Collect the rent, make repairs, like that." Dorn opened his door. "Come on in. Mind the step."

Inside, Dorn draped their coats over the back of a kitchen chair and said, "Want coffee?"

Vosler nodded. His thin neck sprouted from the collar of a blue flannel shirt a size too large for him. The cuffs of his khaki trousers stopped an inch above round-toed black shoes. While Dorn busied himself with the coffee maker, the old man inspected the rest of the trailer. He glanced at the tiny writing area jammed with computer and reference books; the living room with the big-screen TV and VCR; the bedroom and bath.

From around the corner of the hall, Vosler said, "Use your bathroom?"

"Help yourself."

Dorn was setting two mugs of coffee on the scarred formica table when the other man came out of the bathroom.

"Like pissing in a phone booth," he said, sitting down at the table.

"Cream or sugar?"

Vosler shook his head. "Life's too short." He blew across the coffee to cool it. Nodding toward the living area, he said, "Don't believe I've ever seen a television bigger than a bathroom. You must do all right."

"It's rented by the week."

"Uh-huh." The old man sipped his coffee. Abruptly, he said, "What magazines you write for?"

"Tabloids mostly."

Vosler frowned. "That where I'm gonna show up?"

"No. I pitched the idea of an article about you to *Screen Years,* and they liked the idea enough to have me do it on spec."

Vosler looked up from his coffee. "How's that?"

"No guarantee they'll buy it."

"That the usual way of doing things?"

"It is when you haven't made your bones with the big-paying markets." Dorn paused, then said, "So. Who starts?"

"You're the one dropped the bomb about an alibi." He sipped his coffee. "You must write fiction too, eh, scribbler?"

Dorn smiled. "Sometimes. How about I tell you a story, and you tell me if it would make a good movie of the week."

Vosler merely sipped his coffee, saying nothing.

Staring at the stump where the man's little finger should have been, Dorn said, "It has all the elements. Sex. Intrigue. Sacrifice. Unrequited love. Tear-jerker and nail-biter all in one package."

"Get to it," Vosler snapped.

Dorn leaned back, rocking his chair onto its back legs. "Okay, here it is. Straight-arrow cowboy actor and virginal Swiss musical star are having a secret, torrid affair. The studio doesn't like it, so they have his stuntman double for him in the public romance scenes. Nightclubs, movie premieres, like that. But they don't count on, or maybe don't care about, the stand-in falling for the leading lady.

"And what the studio and the stand-in don't know is that our cowboy hero has gotten fair lady in the family way. So he's feeling proprietary and protective and doesn't care for the attention the mother of his child is getting from the poor stuntman. Who incidentally has so many stars in his eyes he doesn't know which way the wind is blowing, pardon the mixed metaphor. So our cowboy makes our stuntman the fall guy. Literally."

Dorn lit a cigarette and blew smoke at the ceiling. "Mid-morning. Final shot of the star's last cliffhanger. Not the last scene of the movie of course, since they shoot out of sequence. Anyway, train's ready to go, camera's in position. Our hero takes the horse and rides off out of sight to wait for the signal. But the stuntman's waiting there, and they switch places. And then . . . Something wrong?"

Vosler was leaning back in his chair, smiling and shaking his head. "Far-fetched. Too many people on a movie set to hide a switch like that. Could never happen."

Dorn nodded. "Mm-hm. I see." He drained the last of his coffee and set the mug on the table. Stubbing out his cigarette, he stood up and said, "How about we watch that movie now?"

The old man's smile faltered an instant, then he shrugged and got up. They moved to the living area and sat on the sofa.

Dorn picked up the remote control from the end table and turned on the monitor and the VCR. "We're not going to watch the whole movie, just one scene. Tape's already cued up."

The monitor's screen blinked awake:

A clear sky canopies an endless prairie. The rolling terrain is broken in the middle distance by a knife edge of railroad track. Suddenly a train explodes into the frame, screen right. A churning gout of black smoke pours from the stack of the steam engine and streams straight back over the tender and the half-dozen passenger cars. The music reaches a crescendo. The camera follows the engine, keeping pace. The engine cab is empty.

Still abreast of the runaway train, the camera pans to the right, past the cars toward the caboose. The pounding music takes on a sinister tone as, at the crest of a hill behind the caboose, a horseman appears, dressed in black. After barely a moment, the Phantom Rider spurs his horse down the hill in pursuit of the speeding train.

Trailing a wake of dust, the horse leaps the tracks. Now on the same side of the engine as the camera, horse and rider seem as one straining to pull abreast of the tender. The camera pulls in now, slightly, and the masked rider leans forward and reaches for the ladder at the rear of the coal car. His black-gloved right hand hovers there, fingers outstretched, a foot away from the ladder.

Then he leaps, and his right hand clasps the upright of the ladder. His left hand follows barely a second later, and in a flash he climbs to the top of the car. He crosses the rocky terrain, his boots seeking purchase on the lumps of coal as the car rocks from side to side. Finally, the black rider reaches the front of the car, crouches, grabs the rear of the engine cab's roof, and swings down into the cab. The background music slows as the train chuffs to a halt, the rising steam carried off by the wind.

The rider leaps from the cab to his waiting horse and speeds away from the camera, disappearing behind a hill just as a posse of riders enters the frame from the right.

"Amazing," Dorn said. "Now let's look at it more closely." He thumbed the remote, resulting in a reverse, high-speed replay. Then he froze the frame just as the rider was gripping the ladder of the coal car. "There."

Vosler leaned forward and squinted at the screen. His lips parted, and Dorn could hear his raspy breathing.

Dorn hesitated, then spoke. "I must have run this scene a hundred times. Something about it kept bothering me, but I couldn't nail it down. Then one night I saw it. It's only on screen for two video frames, a fifteenth of a second. Look at the right hand. It's grainy and hard to see against the dark coal-car. See it?"

The old man stared at the frozen image from the past. The right hand in the black glove gripped the upright of the ladder, and, inches below it, the blurred left hand was moving up. But it did not quite obscure the right hand's little finger, extended and rigid.

"A fraction of a second faster with the left hand, and the right one would have been covered. No one would ever have known. That's your hand, Mr. Vosler, with a prosthesis in the glove. You did the stunt while Lane Broderick rode the two and three-tenths miles and killed Vera Justine." He leaned forward, resting his elbows on his knees, looking at the old man. Vosler's eyes were still on the screen, but Dorn knew he was looking farther away. "Why, Buddy? Why have you been acting the part of a murderer for thirty-seven years?"

The old man sat back, seeming to sink into the sofa. With shaking hands, he dry-washed his face, then turned to Dorn. "Acting," he said. "Who was acting? I did kill her, sure as if I'd snapped her neck with my own hands."

Dorn's heart was thudding. He lit a cigarette just to give his hands something to do.

"When Brod and I set up the switch, all he told me was that he didn't want to do the stunt. But he didn't want to back out, on account of it had already been noised around the lot. So I agreed. Why not? I believed him." He shuddered a sigh. "I had no idea he was going to see Vera.

"He musta thought he was living a movie. He was going over to her trailer and sweep her up in his arms and elope. He'd shot the last scene of his movie, and running off with Vera would have set her picture behind schedule, but he didn't think of things like that." Vosler glanced at Dorn. "Brod was the one had stars in his eyes. Fairy tale endings, that's what he always thought life should have. But, the way I figure it, when he got over there, she told him about the baby. And he snapped."

"That's what I don't get," Dorn said. "So what if she was pregnant? The public would have forgiven them. They forgave Ingrid Bergman and Roberto Rosselini. Why not Vera Justine and Lane Broderick?"

"There's a lot you don't get, scribbler. Lane Broderick was sterile. That was my baby she was gonna have."

After a stunned silence, Dorn's mind began sorting and sifting and questioning. "Why didn't the train engineer recognize you?"

"He wasn't in a good position to see me, and I was wearing a mask. Besides, he was expecting to see Lane Broderick, so that's who he saw."

"Where did the marks on your face come from?"

"Broderick. After I did the gag and rode behind the hill, I wondered where he'd gone off to. Then all of a sudden, he comes charging in and jumps me from his horse. We fall down the ravine and throw a few punches and we both get marked up some. Finally I pin him to the ground and he tells me what happened."

Vosler leaned forward and rested his elbows on his knees, hands hanging limply. "I didn't know whether to kill him or cry like a baby. I suppose I was in shock. I only remember hightailing it out of there when we heard somebody coming."

"How could he have had time to ride all that distance and kill her? The scene only lasts four minutes."

"Thing you do most on a movie set is wait. Everybody does his job, just not at the same time. After Brod took his horse and rode off to wait for the train, they had to do something to the camera mount and the reflectors on the truck. Then there were last-minute instructions to the engineer. That took a good twenty minutes. Add that to the fifteen minutes after the stunt before they came to check on Brod." He stared at the floor and shook his head. When he spoke, his voice was a dry whisper. "Plenty of time."

"You let him frame you."

"No. He was my friend. I should have told him — about the baby, about Vera and me. Hell, it was an accident anyway. Way he told it, she was cussing and throwing things at him. That's how she was. He just defended himself too hard."

Dorn looked off into space, thinking. "And he let everyone believe it was his baby because he had an image of virility to maintain. Or because if the police found out the baby was yours, his motive for murder would have stuck out like a — well, it would have been irresistible." He lit another cigarette. "You're a piece of work, you know that? Doing time because you thought you deserved it. Why'd you let him off? What kind of friend was he to do that to you?"

"Wasn't his fault. What good would it have done, anyway? Just be one less hero for your generation." He pushed his hands against his knees, leaned forward, and stood up slowly. "Gonna write about this, scribbler?"

"The last stunt of your career?" Dorn stood and faced Buddy Vosler. "I have to. I'm just sorry I found out all this too late to do you any good. Besides, I've written too much sleaze in my life. It's time I wrote about a real class act."

The old man gave him a long look, then shrugged and said, "Don't suppose I can stop you." After an awkward pause, he said, "Well, I really should get that room at the Y."

Dorn nodded. "I'll drive you."

Buddy Vosler almost smiled. "We really going there this time?"

"Promise. Uh . . . We'll need to talk again. More details."

"Such as?" he asked, shrugging into his topcoat.

"Well, it's a small point, but . . ." He gestured to Vosler's right hand. "I was wondering how you lost your finger."

Buttoning his coat, Vosler said, "Happened when I was ten years old. I used to go down by the railroad tracks and watch the older boys hop the freights. One day they dared me to do it. First time I ever tried anything like that. Well, I didn't quite make it." He picked up his hat with his right hand and put it on. "Lost my grip and fell. Train ran over it."

The Curtain

by
Raymond Chandler

THE FIRST TIME I EVER SAW
Larry Batzel he was drunk outside Sardi's in a second-hand Rolls-
Royce. There was a tall blonde with him who had eyes you wouldn't
forget. I helped her argue him out from under the wheel so that she
could drive.

The second time I saw him he didn't have any Rolls-Royce or any
blonde or any job in pictures. All he had was the jitters and a suit that
needed pressing. He remembered me. He was that kind of drunk.

I bought him enough drinks to do him some good and gave him half
my cigarettes. I used to see him from time to time "between pictures."
I got to lending him money. I don't know just why. He was a big handsome brute with eyes like a cow and something innocent and honest
in them. Something I don't get much of in my business.

The funny part was he had been a liquor runner for a pretty hard
mob before Repeal. He never got anywhere in pictures, and after a
while I didn't see him around any more.

Then one day out of the clear blue I got a check for all he owed me
and a note that he was working on the tables — gambling not dining
— at the Dardanella Club, and to come out and look him up. So I knew
he was back in the rackets.

I didn't go to see him, but I found out somehow or other that Joe
Mesarvey owned the place, and that Joe Mesarvey was married to the

blonde with the eyes, the one Larry Batzel had been with in the Rolls that time. I still didn't go out there.

Then very early one morning there was a dim figure standing by my bed, between me and the windows. The blinds had been pulled down. That must have been what wakened me. The figure was large and had a gun.

I rolled over and rubbed my eyes.

"Okay," I said sourly. "There's twelve bucks in my pants and my wrist watch cost twenty-seven fifty. You couldn't get anything on that."

The figure went over to the window and pulled a blind aside an inch and looked down at the street. When he turned again, I saw that it was Larry Batzel.

His face was drawn and tired and he needed a shave. He had dinner clothes on still and a dark double-breasted overcoat with a dwarf rose drooping in the lapel.

He sat down and held the gun on his knee for a moment before he put it away, with a puzzled frown, as if he didn't know how it got into his hand.

"You're going to drive me to Berdoo," he said. "I've got to get out of town. They've put the pencil on me."

"Okay," I said. "Tell me about it."

I sat up and felt the carpet with my toes and lit a cigarette. It was a little after five thirty.

"I jimmied your lock with a piece of celluloid," he said. "You ought to use your night latch once in a while. I wasn't sure which was your flop and I didn't want to rouse the house."

"Try the mailboxes next time," I said. "But go ahead. You're not drunk, are you?"

"I'd like to be, but I've got to get away first. I'm just rattled. I'm not so tough as I used to be. You read about the O'Mara disappearance of course."

"Yeah."

"Listen, anyway. If I keep talking I won't blow up. I don't think I'm spotted here."

"One drink won't hurt either of us," I said. "The Scotch is on the table there."

He poured a couple of drinks quickly and handed me one. I put on a bathrobe and slippers. The glass rattled against his teeth when he drank.

He put his empty glass down and held his hands tight together.

"I used to know Dud O'Mara pretty well. We used to run stuff together down from Hueneme Point. We even carried the torch for the same girl. She's married to Joe Mesarvey now. Dud married five million dollars. He married General Dade Winslow's rickety-rackety divorcee daughter."

"I know all that," I said.

"Yeah. Just listen: She picked him out of a speak, just like I'd pick up a cafeteria tray. But he didn't like the life. I guess he used to see Mona. He got wise. Joe Mesarvey and Lash Yeager had a hot can racket on the side. They knocked him off."

"The hell they did," I said. "Have another drink."

"No. Just listen. There's just two points. The night O'Mara pulled d down the curtain — no, the night the papers got it — Mona Mesarvey disappeared too. Only she didn't. They hid her out in a shack a couple of miles beyond Realito in the orange belt. Next door to a garage run by a heel named Art Huck, a hot car drop. I found out. I trailed Joe there."

"What made it your business?" I asked.

"I'm still soft on her. I'm telling you this because you were pretty swell to me once. You can make something of it after I blow. They hid her out there so it would look as if Dud had blown with her. Naturally the cops were not too dumb to see Joe after the disappearance. But they didn't find Mona. They have a system on disappearances and they play the system."

He got up and went over to the window again, looking through the side of the blind.

"There's a blue sedan down there I think I've seen before," he said. "But maybe not. There's a lot like it."

He sat down again. I didn't speak.

"This place beyond Realito is on the first side road north from the Foothill Boulevard. You can't miss it. It stands all alone, the garage and the house next door. There's an old cyanide plant up above there. I'm telling you this —"

"That's point one," I said. "What was the second point?"

"The punk that used to drive for Lash Yeager lit out a couple of weeks back and went East. I lent him fifty bucks. He was broke. He told me Yeager was out to the Winslow estate the night Dud O'Mara disappeared."

I stared at him. "It's interesting, Larry. But not enough to break eggs over. After all, we do have a police department."

"Yeah. Add this. I got drunk last night and told Yeager what I knew. Then I quit the job at the Dardanella. So somebody shot at me outside where I live when I got home. I've been on the dodge ever since. Now, will you drive me to Berdoo?"

I stood up. It was May but I felt cold. Larry Batzel looked cold, even with his overcoat on.

"Absolutely," I said. "But take it easy. Later will be much safer than now. Have another drink. You don't *know* they knocked O'Mara off."

"If he found out about the hot car racket, with Mona married to Joe Mesarvey, they'd have to knock him off. He was that kind of guy."

I stood up and went toward the bathroom. Larry went over to the window again.

"It's still there," he said over his shoulder. "You might get shot at riding with me."

"I'd hate that," I said.

"You're a good sort of heel, Carmady. It's going to rain. I'd hate like hell to be buried in the rain, wouldn't you?"

"You talk too damn much," I said, and went into the bathroom.

It was the last time I ever spoke to him.

I heard him moving around while I was shaving, but not after I got under the shower, of course. When I came out he was gone. I padded over and looked into the kitchenette. He wasn't in there. I grabbed a bathrobe and peeked out into the hall. It was empty except for a milkman starting down the back stairs with his wiry tray of bottles, and the fresh folded papers leaning against the shut doors.

"Hey," I called out to the milkman, "did a guy just come out of here and go by you?"

He looked back at me from the corner of the wall and opened his mouth to answer. He was a nice looking boy with fine large white teeth. I remember his teeth well, because I was looking at them when I heard the shots.

They were not very near or very far. Out back of the apartment house, by the garages, or in the alley, I thought. There were two quick, hard shots and then the riveting machine. A burst of five or six, all a good chopper should ever need. Then the roar of the car going away.

The milkman shut his mouth as if a winch controlled it. His eyes were huge and empty looking at me. Then he very carefully set his bottles down on the top step and leaned against the wall.

"That sounded like shots," he said.

All this took a couple of seconds and felt like half an hour. I went back into my place and threw clothes on, grabbed odds and ends off the bureau, barged out into the hall. It was still empty, even of the milkman. A siren was dying somewhere near. A bald head with a hangover under it poked out of a door and made a snuffling noise.

I went down the back stairs.

There were two or three people out in the lower hall. I went out back. The garages were in two rows facing each other across a cement space, then two more at the end, leaving a space to go out to the alley. A couple of kids were coming over a fence three houses away.

Larry Batzel lay on his face, with his hat a yard away from his head, and one hand flung out to within a foot of a big black automatic. His ankles were crossed, as if he had spun as he fell. Blood was thick on the side of his face, on his blond hair, especially on his neck. It was also thick on the cement yard.

Two radio cops and the milk driver and a man in a brown sweater and bibless overalls were bending over him. The man in overalls was our janitor.

I went up to them, about the same time the two kids from over the fence hit the yard. The milk driver looked at me with a queer, strained expression. One of the cops straightened up and said, "Either of you guys know him? He's still got half his face."

He wasn't talking to me. The milk driver shook his head and kept on looking at me from the corner of his eyes. The janitor said, "He ain't a tenant here. He might of been a visitor. Kind of early for visitors, though, ain't it?"

"He's got party clothes on. You know your flophouse better'n I do," the cop said heavily. He got out a notebook.

The other cop straightened up too and shook his head and went toward the house, with the janitor trotting beside him.

The cop with the notebook jerked a thumb at me and said harshly, "You was here first after these two guys. Anything from you?"

I looked at the milkman. Larry Batzel wouldn't care, and a man has a living to earn. It wasn't a story for a prowl car anyway.

"I just heard the shots and came running," I said.

The cop took that for an answer. The milk driver looked up at the lowering gray sky and said nothing.

After a while I got back into my apartment and finished my dressing. When I picked my hat up off the window table by the Scotch bottle there was a small rosebud lying on a piece of scrawled paper.

The note said: "You're a good guy, but I think I'll go it alone. Give the rose to Mona, if you ever should get a chance. Larry."

I put those things in my wallet, and braced myself with a drink.

About three o'clock that afternoon I stood in the main hallway of the Winslow place and waited for the butler to come back. I had spent most of the day not going near my office or apartment, and not meeting any homicide men. It was only a question of time until I had to come through, but I wanted to see General Dade Winslow first. He was hard to see.

Oil paintings hung all around me, mostly portraits. There were a couple of statues and several suits of time-darkened armor on pedestals of dark wood. High over the huge marble fireplace hung two bullet-torn — or moth-eaten — cavalry pennants crossed in a glass case, and below them the painted likeness of a thin, spry-looking man with a black beard and mustachios and full regimentals of about the time of the Mexican War. This might be General Dade Winslow's father. The general himself, though pretty ancient, couldn't be quite that old.

Then the butler came back and said General Winslow was in the orchid house and would I follow him, please.

We went out of the French doors at the back and across the lawns to a big glass pavilion well beyond the garages. The butler opened the door into a sort of vestibule and shut it when I was inside, and it was already hot. Then he opened the inner door and it was really hot.

The air steamed. The walls and ceiling of the greenhouse dripped. In the half light enormous tropical plants spread their blooms and branches all over the place, and the smell of them was almost as overpowering as the smell of boiling alcohol.

The butler, who was old and thin and very straight and white-haired, held branches of the plants back for me to pass, and we came to an opening in the middle of the place. A large reddish Turkish rug was spread down on the hexagonal flagstones. In the middle of the rug, in a wheel chair, a very old man sat with a traveling rug around his body and watched us come.

Nothing lived in his face but the eyes. Black eyes, deep-set, shining, untouchable. The rest of his face was the leaden mask of death, sunken temples, a sharp nose, outward-turning ear lobes, a mouth that was a thin white slit. He was wrapped partly in a reddish and very shabby bathrobe and partly in the rug. His hands had purple fingernails and were clasped loosely, motionless on the rug.

The butler said, "This is Mr. Carmady, General."

The old man stared at me. After a while a sharp, shrewish voice said, "Place a chair for Mr. Carmady."

The butler dragged a wicker chair out and I sat down. I put my hat on the floor. The butler picked it up.

"Brandy," the general said. "How do you like your brandy, sir?"

"Anyway at all," I said.

He snorted. The butler went away. The general stared at me with his unblinking eyes. He snorted again.

"I always take champagne with mine," he said. "A third of a glass of brandy under the champagne, and the champagne as cold as Valley Forge. Colder, if you can get it colder."

A noise that might have been a chuckle came out of him.

"Not that I was at Valley Forge," he said. "Not quite that bad. You may smoke, sir."

I thanked him and said I was tired of smoking for a while. I got a handkerchief out and mopped my face.

"Take your coat off, sir. Dud always did. Orchids require heat, Mr. Carmady — like sick old men."

I took my coat off, a raincoat I had brought along. It looked like rain. Larry Batzel had said it was going to rain.

"Dud is my son-in-law. Dudley O'Mara. I believe you had something to tell me about him."

"Just hearsay," I said. "I wouldn't want to go into it, unless I had your okay, General Winslow."

The basilisk eyes stared at me. "You are a private detective. You want to be paid, I suppose."

"I'm in that line of business," I said. "But that doesn't mean I have to be paid for every breath I draw. It's just something I heard. You might like to pass it on yourself to the Missing Persons Bureau."

"I see," he said quietly. "A scandal of some sort."

The butler came back before I could answer. He wheeled a tea wagon in through the jungle, set it at my elbow, and mixed me a brandy and soda. He went away.

I sipped the drink. "It seems there was a girl," I said. "He knew her before he knew your daughter. She's married to a racketeer now. It seems —"

"I've heard all that," he said. "I don't give a damn. What I want to know is where he is and if he's all right. If he's happy."

I stared at him popeyed. After a moment I said weakly, "Maybe I could find the girl, or the boys downtown could, with what I could tell them."

He plucked at the edge of his rug and moved his head about an inch. I think he was nodding. Then he said very slowly, "Probably I'm talking too much for my health, but I want to make something clear. I'm a cripple. I have two ruined legs and half my lower belly. I don't eat much or sleep much. I'm a bore to myself and a damn nuisance to everybody else. So I miss Dud. He used to spend a lot of time with me. Why, God only knows."

"Well —" I began.

"Shut up. You're a young man to me, so I can be rude to you. Dud left without saying good-bye to me. That wasn't like him. He drove his car away one evening and nobody has heard from him since. If he got tired of my fool daughter and her brat, if he wanted some other woman, that's all right. He got a brainstorm and left without saying good-bye to me, and now he's sorry. That's why I don't hear from him. Find him and tell him I understand. That's all — unless he needs money. If he does, he can have all he wants."

His leaden cheeks almost had a pink tinge now. His black eyes were brighter, if possible. He leaned back very slowly and closed his eyes.

I drank a lot of my drink in one long swallow. I said, "Suppose he's in a jam. Say, on account of the girl's husband. This Joe Mesarvey."

He opened his eyes and winked. "Not an O'Mara," he said. "It's the other fellow would be in a jam."

"Okay. Shall I just pass on to the Bureau where I heard the girl was?"

"Certainly not. They've done nothing. Let them go on doing it. Find him yourself. I'll pay you a thousand dollars — even if you only have to walk across the street. Tell him everything is all right here. The old man's doing fine and sends his love. That's all."

I couldn't tell him. Suddenly I couldn't tell him anything Larry Batzel had told me, or what had happened to Larry, or anything about it.

I finished my drink and stood up and put my coat back on. I said, "That's too much money for the job, General Winslow. We can talk about that later. Have I authority to represent you in my own way?"

He pressed a bell on his wheel chair. "Just tell him," he said. "I want to know he's all right and I want him to know I'm all right. That's all — unless he needs money. Now you'll have to excuse me. I'm tired."

He closed his eyes. I went back through the jungle and the butler met me at the door with my hat.

I breathed in some cool air and said, "The general wants me to see Mrs. O'Mara."

This room had a white carpet from wall to wall. Ivory drapes of immense height lay tumbled casually on the white carpet inside the many windows. The windows stared toward the dark foothills, and the air beyond the glass was dark too. It hadn't started to rain yet, but there was a feeling of pressure in the atmosphere.

Mrs. O'Mara was stretched out on a white chaise lounge with both her slippers off and her feet in the net stockings they don't wear any more. She was tall and dark, with a sulky mouth. Handsome, but this side of beautiful.

She said, "What in the world can *I* do for you? It is all known. Too damn known. Except that I don't know you, do I?"

"Well, hardly," I said. "I'm just a private copper in a small way of business."

She reached for a glass I hadn't noticed but would have looked for in a moment, on account of her way of talking and the fact she had her slippers off. She drank languidly, flashing a ring.

"I met him in a speakeasy," she said with a sharp laugh. "A very handsome bootlegger, with thick curly hair and an Irish grin. So I married him. Out of boredom. As for him, the bootlegging business was even then uncertain — if there were no other attractions."

She waited for me to say there were, but not as if she cared a lot whether I came through. I just said, "You didn't see him leave on the day he disappeared?"

"No. I seldom saw him leave, or come back. It was like that." She drank some more of her drink.

"Huh," I grunted. "But, of course, you didn't quarrel." They never do.

"There are so many ways of quarreling, Mr. Carmady."

"Yeah. I like your saying that. Of course you knew about the girl."

"I'm glad I'm being properly frank to an old family detective. Yes, I knew about the girl." She curled a tendril of inky hair behind her ear.

"Did you know about her before he disappeared?" I asked politely.

"Certainly."

"How?"

"You're pretty direct, aren't you? Connections, as they say. I'm an old speak fancier. Or didn't you know that?"

"Did you know the bunch at the Dardanella?"

"I've been there." She didn't look startled, or even surprised. "In fact, I practically lived there for a week. That's where I met Dudley O'Mara."

"Yeah. Your father married pretty late in life, didn't he?"

I watched color fade in her cheeks. I wanted her mad, but there was nothing doing. She smiled and the color came back and she rang a push bell on a cord down in the swansdown cushions of the chaise lounge.

"Very late," she said, "if it's any of your business."

"It's not," I said.

A coy-looking maid came in and mixed a couple of drinks at a side table. She gave one to Mrs. O'Mara, put one down beside me. She went away again, showing a nice pair of legs under a short skirt.

Mrs. O'Mara watched the door shut and then said, "The whole thing has got Father into a mood. I wish Dud would wire or write or something."

I said slowly, "He's an old, old man, crippled, half buried already. One thin thread of interest held him to life. The thread snapped and nobody gives a damn. He tries to act as if he didn't give a damn himself. I don't call that a mood. I call that a pretty swell display of intestinal fortitude."

"Gallant," she said, and her eyes were daggers. "But you haven't touched your drink."

"I have to go," I said. "Thanks all the same."

She held a slim, tinted hand out and I went over and touched it. The thunder burst suddenly behind the hills and she jumped. A gust of air shook the windows.

I went down a tiled staircase to the hallway and the butler appeared out of a shadow and opened the door for me.

I looked down a succession of terraces decorated with flowerbeds and imported trees. At the bottom a high metal railing with gilded spearheads and a six-foot hedge inside. A sunken driveway crawled down to the main gates and a lodge inside them.

Beyond the estate the hill sloped down to the city and the old oil wells of La Brea, now partly a park, partly a deserted stretch of fenced-in wild land. Some of the wooden derricks still stood. These had made the wealth of the Winslow family and then the family had run away from them up the hill, far enough to get away from the smell of the sumps, not too far for them to look out of the front windows and see what made them rich.

I walked down brick steps between the terraced lawns. On one of them a dark-haired, pale-faced kid of ten or eleven was throwing darts at a target hung on a tree. I went along near him.

"You young O'Mara?" I asked.

He leaned against a stone bench with four darts in his hand and looked at me with cold, slaty eyes, old eyes.

"I'm Dade Winslow Trevillyan," he said grimly.

"Oh, then Dudley O'Mara's not your dad."

"Of course not." His voice was full of scorn. "Who are you?"

"I'm a detective. I'm going to find your — I mean, Mr. O'Mara."

That didn't bring us any closer. Detectives were nothing to him. The thunder was tumbling about in the hills like a bunch of elephants playing tag. I had another idea.

"Bet you can't put four out of five into the gold at thirty feet."

He livened up. "With these?"

"Uh-huh."

"How much you bet?" he snapped.

"Oh, a dollar."

He ran to the target and cleaned darts off it, came back, and took a stance by the bench.

"That's not thirty feet," I said.

He gave me a sour look and went a few feet behind the bench. I grinned, then I stopped grinning.

His small hand darted so swiftly I could hardly follow it. Live darts hung in the gold center of the target in less than that many seconds. He stared at me triumphantly.

"Gosh, you're pretty good, Master Trevillyan," I grunted, and got my dollar out.

His small hand snapped at it like a trout taking the fly. He had it out of sight like a flash.

"That's nothing," he chuckled. "You ought to see me on our target range back of the garages. Want to go over there and bet some more?"

I looked back up the hill and saw part of a low white building backed up to a bank.

"Well, not today," I said. "Next time I visit here maybe. So Dud O'Mara is not your dad. If I find him anyway, will it be all right with you?"

He shrugged his thin, sharp shoulders in a maroon sweater "Sure. But what can you do the police can't do?"

"It's a thought," I said, and left him.

I went on down the brick walk to the bottom of the lawns and along inside the hedge toward the gatehouse. I could see glimpses of the street through the hedge. When I was halfway to the lodge I saw the blue sedan outside. It was a small neat car, low-slung, very clean, lighter than a police car, but about the same size. Over beyond it I could see my roadster waiting under the pepper tree.

I stood looking at the sedan through the hedge. I could see the drift of somebody's cigarette smoke against the windshield inside the car. I turned my back to the lodge and looked up the hill. The Trevillyan kid had gone somewhere out of sight, to salt his dollar down maybe, though a dollar shouldn't have meant much to him.

I bent over and unsheathed the 7.65 Luger I was wearing that day and stuck it nose-down inside my left sock, inside my shoe. I could walk that way, if I didn't walk too fast. I went on to the gates.

They kept them locked and nobody got in without identification from the house. The lodgekeeper, a big husky with a gun under his arm, came out and let me through a small postern at the side of the gates. I stood talking to him through the bars for a minute, watching the sedan.

It looked all right. There seemed to be two men in it. It was about a hundred feet alone in the shadow of the high wall on the other side. It was a very narrow street, without sidewalks. I didn't have far to go to my roadster.

I walked a little stiffly across the dark pavement and got in, grabbed quickly down into a small compartment in the front part of the seat where I kept a spare gun. It was a police Colt. I slid it inside my under-arm holster and started the car.

I eased the brake off and pulled away. Suddenly the rain let go in big splashing drops and the sky was as black as Carrie Nation's bonnet. Not so black but that I saw the sedan wheel away from the curb behind me.

I started the windshield wiper and built up to forty miles an hour in a hurry. I had gone about eight blocks when they gave me the siren. That fooled me. It was a quiet street, deadly quiet. I slowed down and pulled over to the curb. The sedan slid up beside me and I was looking at the black snout of a submachine gun over the sill of the rear door.

Behind it a narrow face with reddened eyes, a fixed mouth. A voice above the sound of the rain and the windshield wiper and the noise of the two motors said, "Get in here with us. Be nice, if you know what I mean."

They were not cops. It didn't matter now. I shut off the ignition, dropped my car keys on the floor, and got out. The man behind the wheel of the sedan didn't look at me. The one behind kicked a door open and slid away along the seat, holding the tommygun nicely.

I got into the sedan.

"Okay, Louis. The frisk."

The driver came out from under his wheel and got behind me. He got the Colt from under my arm, tapped my hips and pockets, my belt line.

"Clean," he said, and got back into the front of the car.

The man with the tommy reached forward with his left hand and took my Colt from the driver, then lowered the tommy to the floor of the car and draped a brown rug over it. He leaned back in the corner again, smooth and relaxed, holding the Colt on his knee.

"Okay, Louie. Now let's ride."

We rode — idly, gently, the rain drumming on the roof and streaming down the windows on one side. We wound along curving hill streets, among estates that covered acres, whose houses were distant clusters of wet gables beyond blurred trees.

A tang of cigarette smoke floated under my nose and the red-eyed man said, "What did he tell you?"

"Little enough," I said, "That Mona blew town the night the papers got it. Old Winslow knew it already."

"He wouldn't have to dig very deep for that," Red-eyes said. "The buttons didn't. What else?"

"He said he's been shot at. He wanted me to ride him out of town. At the last moment he ran off alone. I don't know why."

"Loosen up, peeper," Red-eyes said dryly. "It's your only way out."

"That's all there is," I said, and looked out of the window at the driving rain.

"You on the case for the old guy?"

"No. He's tight."

Red-eyes laughed. The gun in my shoe felt heavy and unsteady, and very far away. I said, "That might be all there is to know about O'Mara."

The man in the front seat turned his head a little and growled, "Where the hell did you say that street was?"

"Top of Beverly Glen, stupid. Mulholland Drive."

"Oh, that. Jeeze, that ain't paved worth a damn."

"We'll pave it with the peeper," Red-eyes said.

The estates thinned out and scrub oak took possession of the hillsides.

"You ain't a bad guy," Red-eyes said. "You're just tight, like the old man. Don't you get the idea? We want to know *everything* he said, so we'll know whether we got to blot you or no."

"Go to hell," I said. "You wouldn't believe me anyway."

"Try us. This is just a job to us. We just do it and pass on."

"It must be nice work," I said. "While it lasts."

"You'll crack wise once too often, guy."

"I did — long ago, while you were still in Reform School. I'm still getting myself disliked."

Red-eyes laughed again. There seemed to be very little bluster about him.

"Far as we know you're clean with the law. Didn't make no cracks this morning. That right?"

"If I say yes, you can blot me right now. Okay."

"How about a grand pin money and forget the whole thing?"

"You wouldn't believe that either."

"Yeah, we would. Here's the idea. We do the job and pass on. We're an organization. But you live here, you got good will and a business. You'd play ball."

"Sure," I said. "I'd play ball."

"We don't," Red-eyes said softly, "never knock off a legit. Bad for the trade."

He leaned back in the corner, the gun on his right knee, and reached into an inner pocket. He spread a large tan wallet on his knee and fished two bills out of it, slid them folded along the seat. The wallet went back into his pocket.

"Yours," he said gravely. "You won't last twenty-four hours if you slip your cable."

I picked the bills up. Two five hundreds. I tucked them in my vest. "Right," I said. "I wouldn't be a legit any more then, would I?"

"Think that over dick."

We grinned at each other, a couple of nice lads getting along in a harsh, unfriendly world. Then Red-eyes turned his head sharply.

"Okay, Louie. Forget the Mulholland stuff. Pull up."

The car was halfway up a long bleak twist of hill. The rains drove in gray curtains down the slope. There was no ceiling, no horizon. I could see a quarter of a mile and I could see nothing outside our car that lived.

The driver edged over to the side of the bank and shut his motor off. He lit a cigarette and draped an arm on the back seat.

He smiled at me. He had a nice smile — like an alligator.

"We'll have a drink on it," Red-eyes said. "I wish I could make me a grand that easy. Just tyin' my nose to my chin."

"You ain't got no chin," Louie said, and went on smiling.

Red-eyes put the Colt down on the seat and drew a flat half-pint out of his side pocket. It looked like good stuff, green stamp, bottled in bond. He unscrewed the top with his teeth, sniffed at the liquor, and smacked his lips.

"No Crow McGee in this," he said. "This is the company spread. Tilt her."

He reached along the seat and gave me the bottle. I could have had his wrist, but there was Louie, and I was too far from my ankle.

I breathed shallowly from the top of my lungs and held the bottle near my lips, sniffed carefully. Behind the charred smell of the bourbon there was something else, very faint, a fruity odor that would have meant nothing to me in another place.

Suddenly and for no reason at all I remembered something Larry Batzel had said, something like: "East of Realito, towards the mountains, near the old cyanide plant." Cyanide. That was the word.

There was a swift tightness in my temples as I put the bottle to my mouth. I could feel my skin crawling, and the air was suddenly cold on it. I held the bottle high up around the liquor level and took a long gurgling drag at it. Very hearty and relaxing. About half a teaspoonful went into my mouth and none of that stayed there.

I coughed sharply and lurched forward gagging. Red-eyes laughed. "Don't say you're sick from just one drink, pal."

I dropped the bottle and sagged far down in the seat, gagging violently. My legs slid way to the left, the left one underneath. I sprawled down on top of them, my arms limp. I had the gun.

I shot him under my left arm, almost without looking. He never touched the Colt except to knock it off the seat. The one shot was enough. I heard him lurch. I snapped a shot upward toward where Louie would be.

Louie wasn't there. He was down behind the front seat. He was silent. The whole car, the whole landscape was silent. Even the rain seemed for a moment to be utterly silent rain.

I still didn't have time to look at Red-eyes, but he wasn't doing anything. I dropped the Luger and yanked the tommygun out from under the rug, got my left hand on the front grip, got it set against my shoulder low down. Louie hadn't made a sound.

"Listen, Louie," I said softly, "I've got the stutter gun. How's about it?"

A shot came through the seat, a shot that Louie knew wasn't going to do any good. It starred a frame of unbreakable glass. There was more silence.

Then Louie said thickly, "I got a pineapple here. Want it?"

"Pull the pin and hold it," I said. "It will take care of both of us."

"Hell" Louie said violently. "Is he croaked? I ain't got no pineapple."

I looked at Red-eyes then. He looked very comfortable in the corner of the seat, leaning back. He seemed to have three eyes, one of them redder even than the other two. For underarm shooting that was something to be almost bashful about. It was too good.

"Yeah, Louie, he's croaked," I said. "How do we get together?"

I could hear his hard breathing now, and the rain had stopped being silent.

"Get out of the heap," he growled. "I'll blow."

"You get out, Louie. I'll blow."

"Jeeze, I can't walk home from here, pal."

"You won't have to, Louie. I'll send a car for you."

"Jeeze, I ain't done nothing. All I done was drive."

"Then reckless driving will be the charge, Louie. You can fix that — you and your organization. Get out before I uncork this popgun."

A door latch clicked and feet thumped on the roadway. I straightened up suddenly with the chopper. Louie was in the road in the rain, his hands empty and the alligator smile still on his face.

I got out past the dead man's neatly shod feet, got my Colt and the Luger off the floor, laid the heavy twelve-pound tommygun back on the car floor. I got handcuffs off my hip, motioned to Louie. He turned around sulkily and put his hands behind him.

"You got nothing on me," he complained. "I got protection."

I clicked the cuffs on him and went over him for guns, much more carefully than he had gone over me. He had one besides the one he had left in the car.

I dragged Red-eyes out of the car and let him arrange himself on the wet roadway. He began to bleed again, but he was quite dead.

Louie eyed him bitterly. "He was a smart guy," he said. "Different. He liked tricks. Hello, smart guy."

I got my handcuff key out and unlocked one cuff, dragged it down, and locked it to the dead man's lifted wrist.

Louie's eyes got round and horrified and at last his smile went away.

"Jeeze," he whined. "Holy — ! Jeeze. You ain't going to leave me like this, pal?"

"Good-bye, Louie," I said. "That was a friend of mine you cut down this morning."

"Holy — !" Louie whined.

I got into the sedan and started it, drove on to a place where I could turn, drove back down the hill past him. He stood stiffly as a scorched tree, his face as white as snow, with the dead man at his feet, one linked hand reaching up to Louie's hand. There was the horror of a thousand nightmares in his eyes.

I left him there in the rain.

It was getting dark early. I left the sedan a couple of blocks from my own car and locked it up, put the keys in the oil strainer. I walked back to my roadster and drove downtown.

I called the homicide detail from a phone booth, asked for a man named Grinnell, told him quickly what had happened and where to find Louie and the sedan. I told him I thought they were the thugs that machine-gunned Larry Batzel. I didn't tell him anything about Dud O'Mara.

"Nice work" Grinnell said in a queer voice. "But you better come in fast. There's a tag out for you, account of what some milk driver phoned in an hour ago."

"I'm all in," I said. "I've got to eat. Keep me off the air and I'll come in after a while."

"You better come in, boy. I'm sorry, but you better."

"Well, okay," I said.

I hung up and left the neighborhood without hanging around. I had to break it now. I had to, or get broken myself.

I had a meal down near the Plaza and started for Realito.

At about eight o'clock two yellow vapor lamps glowed high up in the rain and a dim stencil sign strung across the highway read: *Welcome to Realito*.

Frame houses on the main street, a sudden knot of stores, the lights of the corner drug store behind fogged glass, a flying-cluster of cars in front of a tiny movie palace, and a dark bank on another corner with a knot of men standing in front of it in the rain.

That was Realito. I went on. Empty fields closed in again.

This was past the orange country; nothing but the empty fields and the crouched foothills, and the rain.

It was a smart mile, more like three, before I spotted a side road and a faint light on it, as if from behind drawn blinds in a house. Just at that moment my left front tire let go with an angry hiss. That was cute. Then the right rear let go the same way.

I stopped almost exactly at the intersection. Very cute indeed. I got out, turned my raincoat up a little higher, unshipped a flash, and looked at a flock of heavy galvanized tacks with heads as big as dimes. The flat shiny butt of one of them blinked at me from my tire.

Two flats and one spare. I tucked my chin down and started toward the faint light up the side road.

It was the place all right. The light came from the tilted skylight on the garage roof. Big double doors in front were shut tight, but light showed at the cracks, strong white light. I tossed the beam of the flash up and read: *Art Huck — Auto Repairs and Refinishing*.

Beyond the garage a house sat back from the muddy road behind a thin clump of trees. That had light too. I saw a small buttoned-up coupe in front of the wooden porch.

The first thing was the tires, if it could be worked, and they didn't know me. It was a wet night for walking.

I snapped the flash out and rapped on the doors with it. The light inside went out. I stood there licking rain off my upper lip, the flash in my left hand, my right inside my coat. I had the Luger back under my arm again.

A voice spoke through the door, and didn't sound pleased.

"What you want? Who are you?"

"Open up," I said. "I've got two flat tires on the highway and only one spare. I need help."

"We're closed up, mister. Realito's a mile west of here."

I started to kick the door. There was swearing inside, then another, much softer voice.

"A wise guy, huh? Open up, Art."

A bolt squealed and half of the door sagged inward. I snapped the flash again and it hit a gaunt face. Then an arm swept and knocked it out of my hand. A gun had just peeked at me from the flailing hand.

I dropped low, felt around for the flash, and was still. I just didn't pull a gun.

"Kill the spot, mister. Guys get hurt that way."

The flash was burning down in the mud. I snapped it off, stood up with it. Light went on inside the garage, outlined a tall man in coveralls. He backed inward and his gun held on me.

"Come on in and shut the door."

I did that. "Tacks all over the end of your street," I said. "I thought you wanted the business."

"Ain't you got any sense? A bank job was pulled at Realito this afternoon."

"I'm a stranger here," I said, remembering the knot of men in front of the bank in the rain.

"Okay, okay. Well, there was and the punks are hid out somewhere in the hills, they say. You stepped on their tacks, huh?"

"So it seems." I looked at the other man in the garage:

He was short, heavy-set, with a cool brown face and cool brown eyes. He wore a belted raincoat of brown leather. His brown hat had the usual rakish tilt and was dry. His hands were in his pockets and he looked bored.

There was a hot sweetish smell of pyroxylin paint on the air. A big sedan over in the corner had a paint gun lying on its fender. It was a Buick, almost new. It didn't need the paint it was getting.

The man in coveralls tucked his gun out of sight through a flap in the side of his clothes. He looked at the brown man. The brown man looked at me and said gently, "Where you from, stranger?"

"Seattle," I said.

"Going west — to the big city?" He had a soft voice, soft and dry, like the rustle of well-worn leather.

"Yes. How far is it?"

"About forty miles. Seems farther in this weather. Come the long way, didn't you? By Tahoe and Lone Pine?"

"Not Tahoe," I said. "Reno and Carson City."

"Still the long way." A fleeting smile touched the brown lips.

"Take a jack and get his flats, Art."

"Now, listen, Lash —" the man in the coveralls growled, and stopped as though his throat had been cut from ear to ear.

I could have sworn that he shivered. There was dead silence. The brown man didn't move a muscle. Something looked out of his eyes, and then his eyes lowered, almost shyly. His voice was the same soft, dry rustle of sound.

"Take two jacks, Art. He's got two flats."

The gaunt man swallowed. Then he went over to a corner and put a coat on, and a cap. He grabbed up a socket wrench and a handjack and wheeled a dolly jack over to the doors.

"Back on the highway, is it?" he asked me almost tenderly.

"Yeah. You can use the spare for one spot, if you're busy," I said.

"He's not busy," the brown man said and looked at his fingernails.

Art went out with his tools. The door shut again. I looked at the Buick. I didn't look at Lash Yeager. I knew it was Lash Yeager. There wouldn't be two men called Lash that came to that garage. I didn't look at him because I would be looking across the sprawled body of Larry Batzel, and it would show in my face. For a moment, anyway.

He glanced toward the Buick himself. "Just a panel job to start with," he drawled. "But the guy that owns it has dough and his driver needed a few bucks. You know the racket."

"Sure," I said.

The minutes passed on tiptoe. Long, sluggish minutes. Then feet crunched outside and the door was pushed open. The light hit pencils of rain and made silver wires of them.

Art trundled two muddy flats in sulkily, kicked the door shut, let one of the flats fall on its side. The rain and fresh air had given him his nerve back. He looked at me savagely.

"Seattle," he snarled. "Seattle, my eye!"

The brown man lit a cigarette as if he hadn't heard. Art peeled his coat off and yanked my tire up on a rim spreader, tore it loose viciously, had the tube out and cold-patched in nothing flat. He strode scowling over to the wall near me and grabbed an air hose, let enough air into the tube to give it body, and hefted it in both hands to dip it in a washtub of water.

I was a sap, but their teamwork was very good. Neither had looked at the other since Art came back with my tires.

Art tossed the air-stiffened tube up casually, caught it with both hands wide, looked it over sourly beside the washtub of water, took one short easy step, and slammed it down over my head and shoulders.

He jumped behind me in a flash, leaned his weight down on the rubber, dragged it tight against my chest and arms. I could move my hands, but I couldn't get near my gun.

The brown man brought his right hand out of his pocket and tossed a wrapped cylinder of nickels up and down on his palm as he stepped lithely across the floor.

I heaved back hard, then suddenly threw all my weight forward. Just as suddenly Art let go of the tube, and kneed me from behind.

I sprawled, but I never knew when I reached the floor. The fist with the weighted tube of nickels met me in mid-flight. Perfectly timed, perfectly weighted, and with my own weight to help it out.

I went out like a puff of dust in a draft.

It seemed there was a woman and she was sitting beside a lamp. Light shone on my face, so I shut my eyes again and tried to look at her through my eyelashes. She was so platinumed that her head shone like a silver fruit bowl.

She wore a green traveling dress with a mannish cut to it and a broad white collar falling over the lapels. A sharp-angled glossy bag stood at her feet. She was smoking, and a drink was tall and pale at her elbow.

I opened my eyes wider and said, "Hello there."

Her eyes were the eyes I remembered, outside Sardi's in a second-hand Rolls-Royce. Very blue eyes, very soft and lovely. Not the eyes of a hustler around the fast money boys.

"How do you feel?" Her voice was soft and lovely too.

"Great," I said. "Except somebody built a filling station on my jaw."

"What did you expect, Mr. Carmady? Orchids?"

"So you know my name."

"You slept well. They had plenty of time to go through your pockets. They did everything but embalm you."

"Right," I said.

I could move a little, not very much. My wrists were behind my back, handcuffed. There was a little poetic justice in that. From the cuffs a cord ran to my ankles, and tied them, and then dropped down out of sight over the end of the davenport and was tied somewhere else. I was almost as helpless as if I had been screwed up in a coffin.

"What time is it?"

She looked sideways down at her wrist, beyond the spiral of her cigarette smoke.

"Ten seventeen. Got a date?"

"Is this the house next the garage? Where are the boys — digging a grave?"

"You wouldn't care, Carmady. They'll be back."

"Unless you have the key to these bracelets you might spare me a little of that drink."

She rose all in one piece and came over to me, with the tall amber glass in her hand. She bent over me. Her breath was delicate. I gulped from the glass craning my neck up.

"I hope they don't hurt you," she said distantly, stepping back. "I hate killing."

"And you Joe Mesarvey's wife. Shame on you. Gimme some more of the hooch."

She gave me some more. Blood began to move in my stiffened body.

"I kind of like you," she said. "Even if your face does look like a collision mat."

"Make the most of it," I said. "It won't last long even this good."

She looked around swiftly and seemed to listen. One of the two doors was ajar. She looked toward that. Her face seemed pale. But the sounds were only the rain.

She sat down by the lamp again.

"Why did you come here and stick your neck out?" she asked slowly, looking at the floor.

The carpet was made of red and tan squares. There were bright green pine trees on the wallpaper and the curtains were blue. The furniture, what I could see of it. Looked as if it came from one of those places that advertise on bus benches.

"I had a rose for you," I said. "From Larry Batzel."

She lifted something off the table and twirled it slowly, the dwarf rose he had left for her.

"I got it," she said quietly. "There was a note, but they didn't show me that. Was it for me?"

"No, for me. He left it on my table before he went out and got shot."

Her face fell apart like something you see in a nightmare. Her mouth and eyes were black hollows. She didn't make a sound. And after a moment her face settled back into the same calmly beautiful lines.

"They didn't tell me that either," she said softly.

"He got shot," I said carefully, "because he found out what Joe and Lash Yeager did to Dud O'Mara. Bumped him off."

That one didn't faze her at all. "Joe didn't do anything to Dud O'Mara," she said quietly. "I haven't seen Dud in two years. That was just newspaper hooey, about me seeing him."

"It wasn't in the papers," I said.

"Well, it was hooey wherever it was. Joe is in Chicago. He went yesterday by plane to sell out. If the deal goes through, Lash and I are to follow him. Joe is no killer."

I stared at her.

Her eyes got haunted again. "Is Larry — is he —?"

"He's dead," I said. "It was a professional job, with a tommygun. I didn't mean they did it personally."

She took hold of her lip and held it for a moment tight between her teeth. I could hear her slow, hard breathing. She jammed her cigarette in an ashtray and stood up.

"Joe didn't do it!" she stormed. "I know damn well he didn't. He —"

She stopped cold, glared at me, touched her hair, then suddenly yanked it off. It was a wig. Underneath, her own hair was short like a boy's, and streaked yellow and whitish brown, with darker tints at the roots. It couldn't make her ugly.

I managed a sort of laugh. "You just came out here to molt, didn't you, Silver-Wig? And I thought they were hiding you out — so it would look as if you had skipped with Dud O'Mara."

She kept on staring at me. As if she hadn't heard a word I said. Then she strode over to a wall mirror and put the wig back on, straightened it, turned and faced me.

"Joe didn't kill anybody," she said again, in a low, tight voice. "He's a heel — but not that kind of heel. He doesn't know anything more about where Dud O'Mara went than I do. And I don't know anything."

"He just got tired of the rich lady and scrammed," I said dully.

She stood near me now, her white fingers at her sides, shining in the lamplight. Her head above me was almost in shadow. The rain drummed and my jaw felt large and hot and the nerve along the jawbone ached, ached.

"Lash has the only car that was here," she said softly. "Can you walk to Realito, if I cut the ropes?"

"Sure. Then what?"

"I've never been mixed up in a murder. I won't now. I won't ever."

She went out of the room very quickly, and came back with a long kitchen knife and sawed the cord that tied my ankles, pulled it off, cut the place where it was tied to the handcuffs. She stopped once to listen, but it was just the rain again.

I rolled up to a sitting position and stood up. My feet were numb, but that would pass. I could walk. I could run, if I had to.

"Lash has the key to the cuffs," she said dully.

"Let's go," I said. "Got a gun?"

"No. I'm not going. You beat it. He may be back any minute. They were just moving stuff out of the garage."

I went over close to her. "You're going to stay here after turning me loose? Wait for that killer? You're nuts. Come on, Silver-Wig, you're going with me."

"No."

"Suppose," I said, "he did kill O'Mara? Then he also killed Larry. It's got to be that way."

"Joe never killed anybody," she almost snarled at me.

"Well, suppose Yeager did."

"You're lying, Carmady. Just to scare me. Get out. I'm not afraid of Lash Yeager. I'm his boss's wife."

"Joe Mesarvey is a handful of mush," I snarled back. "The only time a girl like you goes for a wrong gee is when he's a handful of mush. Let's drift."

"Get out!" she said hoarsely.

"Okay." I turned away from her and went through the door.

She almost ran past me into the hallway and opened the front door, looked out into the black wetness. She motioned me forward.

"Good-bye," she whispered. "I hope you find Dud. I hope you find who killed Larry. But it wasn't Joe."

I stepped close to her, almost pushed her against the wall with my body.

"You're still crazy, Silver-Wig. Good-bye."

She raised her hands quickly and put them on my face. Cold hands, icy cold. She kissed me swiftly on the mouth with cold lips.

"Beat it, strong guy. I'll be seeing you some more. Maybe in heaven."

I went through the door and down the dark slithery wooden steps of the porch, across gravel to the round grass plot and the clump of thin trees. I came past them to the roadway, went back along it toward

Foothill Boulevard. The rain touched my face with fingers of ice that were no colder than her fingers.

The curtained roadster stood just where I had left it, leaned over, the left front axle on the tarred shoulder of the highway. My spare and one stripped rim were thrown in the ditch.

They had probably searched it, but I still hoped. I crawled in backward and banged my head on the steering post and rolled over to get the manacled hands into my little secret gun pocket. They touched the barrel. It was still there.

I got it out, got myself out of the car, got hold of the gun by the right end and looked it over.

I held it tight against my back to protect it a little from the rain and started back toward the house.

I was halfway there when he came back. His lights turning quickly off the highway almost caught me. I flopped into the ditch and put my nose in the mud and prayed.

The car hummed past. I heard the wet rasp of its tires shouldering the gravel in front of the house. The motor died and lights went off. The door slammed. I didn't hear the house door shut, but I caught a feeble fringe of light through the trees as it opened.

I got up on my feet and went on. I came up beside the car, a small coupe, rather old. The gun was down at my side, pulled around my hip as far as the cuffs would let it come.

The coupe was empty. Water gurgled in the radiator. I listened and heard nothing from the house. No loud voices, no quarrel. Only the heavy bong-bong-bong of the raindrops hitting the elbows at the bottom of rain gutters.

Yeager was in the house. She had let me go and Yeager was in there with her. Probably she wouldn't tell him anything. She would just stand and look at him. She was his boss's wife. That would scare Yeager to death.

He wouldn't stay long, but he wouldn't leave her behind, alive or dead. He would be on his way and take her with him. What happened to her later on was something else.

All I had to do was wait for him to come out. I didn't do it.

I shifted the gun into my left hand and leaned down to scoop up some gravel. I threw it against the front window. It was a weak effort. Very little even reached the glass.

I ran back behind the coupe and got its door open and saw the keys in the ignition lock. I crouched down, holding on to the door post.

The house had already gone dark, but that was all. There wasn't any sound from it. No soap. Yeager was too cagey.

I reached in with my foot and found the starter, then strained back with one hand and turned the ignition key. The warm motor caught at once, throbbed gently against the pounding rain.

I got back to the ground and slid along to the rear of the car, crouched down.

The sound of the motor got him. He couldn't be left there without a car.

A darkened window slid up an inch, only some shifting of light on the glass showing it moved. Flame spouted from it, the racket of three quick shots. Glass broke in the coupe.

I screamed and let the scream die into a gurgling groan. I was getting good at that sort of thing. I let the groan die in a choked gasp. I was through, finished. He had got me. Nice shooting, Yeager.

Inside the house a man laughed. Then silence again, except for the rain and the quietly throbbing motor of the coupe.

Then the house door inched open. A figure showed in it. She came out on the porch, stiffly, the white showing at her collar, the wig showing a little but not so much. She came down the steps like a wooden woman. I saw Yeager behind her.

She started across the gravel. Her voice said slowly, without any tone at all, "I can't see a thing, Lash. The windows are all misted."

She jerked a little, as if a gun had prodded her, and came on. Yeager didn't speak. I could see him now past her shoulder, his hat, part of his face. But no kind of a shot for a man with cuffs on his wrists.

She stopped again, and her voice was suddenly horrified.

"He's behind the wheel!" she yelled. "Slumped over!"

He fell for it. He knocked her to one side and started to blast again. More glass jumped around. A bullet hit a tree on my side of the car. A cricket whined somewhere. The motor kept right on humming.

He was low, crouched against the black, his face a grayness without form that seemed to come back; very slowly after the glare of the shots. His own fire had blinded him too — for a second. That was enough.

I shot him four times, straining the pulsing Colt against my ribs.

He tried to turn and the gun slipped away from his hand. He half snatched for it in the air, before both his hands suddenly went against his stomach and stayed there. He sat down on the wet gravel and his harsh panting dominated every other sound of the wet night.

I watched him lie down on his side, very slowly, without taking his hands away from his stomach. The panting stopped.

It seemed like an age before Silver-Wig called out to me. Then she was beside me, grabbing my arm.

"Shut the motor off!" I yelled at her. "And get the key of these damn irons out of his pocket."

"You d-darn fool," she babbled. "W-what did you come back for?"

Captain Al Roof of the Missing Persons Bureau swung in his chair and looked at the sunny window. This was another day, and the rain had stopped long since.

He said gruffly, "You're making a lot of mistakes, brother. Dud O'Mara just pulled down the curtain. None of those people knocked him off. The Batzel killing had nothing to do with it. They've got Mesarvey in Chicago and he looks clean. The lug you anchored to the dead guy don't even know who they were pulling the job for. Our boys asked him enough to be sure of that."

"I'll bet they did," I said. "I've been in the same bucket all night and I couldn't tell them much either."

He looked at me slowly, with large, bleak, tired eyes. "Killing Yeager was all right, I guess. And the chopper. In the circumstances. Besides, I'm not homicide. I couldn't link any of that to O'Mara — unless you could."

I could, but I hadn't. Not yet. "No," I said. "I guess not."

I stuffed and lit my pipe. After a sleepless night it tasted better.

"That's all that's worrying you?"

"I wondered why you didn't find the girl, at Realito. It couldn't have been very hard — for you."

"We just didn't. We should have. I admit it. We didn't. Anything else?"

I blew smoke across his desk. "I'm looking for O'Mara because the general told me to. It wasn't any use my telling him you would do everything that could be done. He could afford a man with all his time on it. I suppose you resent that."

He wasn't amused. "Not at all, if he wants to waste money. The people that resent you are behind a door marked Homicide Bureau."

He planted his feet with a slap and elbowed his desk.

"O'Mara had fifteen grand in his clothes. That's a lot of jack, but O'Mara would be the boy to have it. So he could take it out and have his old pals see him with it. Only they wouldn't think it was fifteen grand of real dough. His wife says it was. Now with any other guy but an ex-legger in the gravy that might indicate an intention to disappear. But not O'Mara. He packed it all the time."

He bit a cigar and put a match to it. He waved a large finger, "See?"

I said I saw.

"Okay. O'Mara had fifteen grand, and a guy that pulls down the curtain can keep it down only so long as his wad lasts. Fifteen grand is a good wad. I might disappear myself, if I had that much. But after it's gone we get him. He cashes a check, lays down a marker, hits a hotel or store for credit, gives a reference, writes a letter or gets one. He's in a new town and he's got a new name, but he's got the same old appetite. He has to get back into the fiscal system one way or another. A guy can't have friends everywhere, and if he had, they wouldn't all stay clammed forever. Would they?"

"No, they wouldn't," I said.

"He went far," Roof said. "But the fifteen grand was all the preparation he made. No baggage, no boat or rail or plane reservation, no taxi or private rental hack to a point out of town. That's all checked. His own car was found a dozen blocks from where he lived. But that means nothing. He knew people who would ferry him several hundred miles and keep quiet about it, even in the face of a reward. Here, but not everywhere. Not new friends."

"But you'll get him," I said.

"When he gets hungry."

"That could take a year or two. General Winslow may not live a year. That is a matter of sentiment, not whether you have an open file when you retire."

"You attend to the sentiment, brother." His eyes moved and bushy reddish eyebrows moved with them. He didn't like me. Nobody did, in the police department, that day.

"I'd like to," I said and stood up. "Maybe I'd go pretty far to attend to that sentiment."

"Sure," Roof said, suddenly thoughtful. "Well, Winslow is a big man. Anything I can do let me know."

"You could find out who had Larry Batzel gunned," I said. "Even if there isn't any connection."

"We'll do that. Glad to," he guffawed and flicked ash over his desk. "You just knock off the guys who can talk and we'll do the rest. We like to work that way."

"It was self-defense," I growled. "I couldn't help myself."

"Sure. Take the air, brother. I'm busy."

But his large bleak eyes twinkled at me as I went out.

The morning was all blue and gold and the birds in the ornamental trees of the Winslow estate were crazy with song after the rain.

The gatekeeper let me in through the postern and I walked up the driveway and along the top terrace to the huge carved Italian front door. Before I rang the bell I looked down the hill and saw the Trevill-yan kid sitting on his stone bench with his head cupped in his hands, staring at nothing.

I went down the brick path to him. "No darts today, son?"

He looked up at me with his lean, slaty, sunken eyes.

"No. Did you find him?"

"Your dad? No, sonny, not yet."

He jerked his head. His nostrils flared angrily. "He's not my dad I told you. And don't talk to me as if I were four years old. My dad he's — he's in Florida or somewhere."

"Well, I haven't found him yet, whoever's dad he is," I said.

"Who smacked your jaw?" he asked, staring at me.

"Oh, a fellow with a roll of nickels in his hand."

"Nickels?"

"Yeah. That's as good as brass knuckles. Try it sometime, but not on me." I grinned.

"You won't find him," he said bitterly, staring at my jaw. "Him, I mean. My mother's husband."

"I bet I do."

"How much you bet?"

"More money than even you've got in your pants."

He kicked viciously at the edge of a red brick in the walk. His voice was still sulky, but more smooth. His eyes speculated.

"Want to bet on something else? C'mon over to the range. I bet you a dollar I can knock down eight out of ten pipes in ten shots."

I looked back toward the house. Nobody seemed impatient to receive me.

"Well," I said, "we'll have to make it snappy. Let's go."

We went along the side of the house under the windows. The orchid greenhouse showed over the tops of some bushy trees far back. A man in neat whipcord was polishing the chromium on a big car in front of the garages. We went past there to the low white building against the bank.

The boy took a key out and unlocked the door and we went into close air that still held traces of cordite fumes. The boy clicked a spring lock on the door.

"Me first," he snapped.

The place looked something like a small beach shooting gallery.

There was a counter with a .22 repeating rifle on it and a long, slim target pistol. Both well oiled but dusty. About thirty feet beyond the counter was a waist-high, solid-looking partition across the building, and behind that a simple layout of clay pipes and ducks and two round white targets marked off with black; rings and stained by lead bullets.

The clay pipes ran in an even line across the middle, and there was a big skylight, and a row of hooded overhead lights.

The boy pulled a cord on the wall and a thick canvas blind slid across the skylight. He turned on the hooded lights and then the place really looked like a beach shooting gallery.

He picked up the .22 rifle and loaded it quickly from a cardboard box of shells, .22 shorts.

"A dollar I get eight out of ten pipes?"

"Blast away," I said, and put my money on the counter.

He took aim almost casually, fired too fast, showing off. He missed three pipes. It was pretty fancy shooting at that. He threw the rifle down on the counter.

"Gee, go set up some more. Let's not count that one. I wasn't set."

"You don't aim to lose any money, do you, son? Go set 'em up yourself. It's your range."

His narrow face got angry and his voice got shrill. "You do it! I've got to relax, see. I've got to relax."

I shrugged at him, lifted a flap in the counter, and went along the whitewashed side wall, squeezed past the end of the low partition. The boy clicked his reloaded rifle shut behind me.

"Put that down," I growled back at him. "Never touch a gun when there's anyone in front of you."

He put it down, looking hurt.

I bent down and grabbed a handful of clay pipes out of the sawdust in a big wooden box on the floor. I shook the yellow grains of wood off them and started to straighten up.

I stopped with my hat above the barrier, just the top of my hat. I never knew why I stopped. Blind instinct.

The .22 cracked and the lead bullet bonged into the target in front of my head. My hat stirred lazily on my head, as though a blackbird had swooped at it during the nesting season.

A nice kid. He was full of tricks, like Red-eyes. I dropped the pipes and took hold of my hat by the brim, lifted it straight up off my head a few inches. The gun cracked again. Another metallic bong on the target.

I let myself fall heavily to the wooden flooring, among the clay pipes.

A door opened and shut. That was all. Nothing else. The hard glare from the hooded lights beat down on me. The sun peeked in at the edges of the skylight blind. There were two bright new splashes on the nearest target, and there were four small round holes in my hat, two and two, on each side.

I crawled to the end of the barrier and peeked around it. The boy was gone. I could see the small muzzles of the two guns on the counter.

I stood up and went back along the wall, switched the lights off, turned the knob of the spring lock; and went out. The Winslow chauffeur whistled at his polish job around in front of the garages.

I crushed my hat in my hand and went back along the side of the house, looking for the kid. I didn't see him. I rang the front doorbell.

I asked for Mrs. O'Mara. I didn't let the butler take my hat.

She was in an oyster-white something, with white fur at the cuffs and collar and around the bottom. A breakfast table on wheels was pushed to one side of her chair and she was flicking ashes among the silver.

The coy-looking maid with the nice legs came and took the table out and shut the tall white door. I sat down.

Mrs. O'Mara leaned her head back against a cushion and looked tired. The line of her throat was distant, cold. She stared at me with a cool, hard look, in which there was plenty of dislike.

"You seemed rather human yesterday," she said. "But I see you are just a brute like the rest of them. Just a brutal cop."

"I came to ask you about Lash Yeager," I said.

She didn't even pretend to be amused. "And why should you think of asking me?"

"Well — if you lived a week at the Dardanella Club —" I waved my crunched-together hat.

She looked at her cigarette fixedly. "Well, I did meet him, I believe. I remember the rather unusual name."

"They all have names like that, those animals," I said. "It seems that Larry Batzel — I guess you read in your paper about him too — was a friend of Dud O'Mara's once. I didn't tell you about him yesterday. Maybe that was a mistake."

A pulse began to throb in her throat. She said softly, "I have a suspicion you are about to become very insolent, that I may even have to have you thrown out."

"Not before I've said my piece," I said. "It seems that Mr. Yeager's driver — they have drivers as well as unusual names, those animals — told Larry Batzel that Mr. Yeager was out this way the night O'Mara disappeared ."

The old army blood had to be good for something in her. She didn't move a muscle. She just froze solid.

I got up and took the cigarette from between her frozen fingers and killed it in a white jade ashtray. I laid my hat carefully on her white satin knee. I sat down again.

Her eyes moved after a while. They moved down and looked at the hat. Her face flushed very slowly, in two vivid patches over the cheekbones. She fought around with her tongue and lips.

"I know," I said. "It's not much of a hat. I'm not making you a present of it. But just look at the bullet holes in it once."

Her hands became alive and snatched at the hat. Her eyes became flames.

She spread the crown out, looked at the holes, and shuddered.

"Yeager?" she asked, very faintly. It was a wisp of a voice, an old voice.

I said very slowly, "Yeager wouldn't use a .22 target rifle, Mrs. O'Mara."

The flame died in her eyes. They were pools of darkness, much emptier than darkness.

"You're his mother," I said. "What do you want to do about it?"

"Merciful God! Dade! He . . . shot at you!"

"Twice," I said.

"But why? . . . Oh, why?"

"You think I'm a wise guy, Mrs. O'Mara. Just another hard-eyed boy from the other side of the tracks. It would be easy in this spot, if I was. But I'm not that at all, really. Do I have to tell why he shot at me!"

She didn't speak. She nodded slowly. Her face was a mask now.

"I'd say he probably can't help it," I said. "He didn't want me to find his stepfather, for one thing. Then he's a little lad that likes money. That seems small, but it's part of the picture. He almost lost a dollar on me on his shooting. It seems small, but he lives in a small world. Most of all, of course, he's a crazy little sadist with an itchy trigger finger."

"How dare you!" she flared. It didn't mean anything. She forgot it herself instantly.

"How dare I? I do dare. Let's not bother figuring why he shot at *me*. I'm not the first, am I? You wouldn't have known what I was talking about, you wouldn't have assumed he did it on purpose."

She didn't move or speak. I took a deep breath.

"So let's talk about why he shot Dud O'Mara," I said.

If I thought she would yell even this time, I fooled myself. The old man in the orchid house had put more into her than her tallness and her dark hair and her reckless eyes.

She pulled her lips back and tried to lick them, and it made her look like a scared little girl, for a second. The lines of her cheeks sharpened and her hand went up like an artificial hand moved by wires and took hold of the white fur at her throat and pulled it tight and squeezed it until her knuckles looked like bleached bone.

Then she just stared at me.

My hat slid off her knee onto the floor, without her moving. The sound it made falling was one of the loudest sounds I had ever heard.

"Money," she said in a dry croak. "Of course you want money."

"How much money do I want?"

"Fifteen thousand dollars."

I nodded, stiff-necked as a floor-walker trying to see with his back.

"That would be about right. That would be the established retainer. That would be about what he had in his pockets and what Yeager got for getting rid of him."

"You're too — damned smart," she said horribly. "I could kill you myself and like it."

I tried to grin. "That's right. Smart and without a feeling in the world. It happened something like this. The boy got O'Mara where he got me, by the same simple ruse. I don't think it was a plan. He hated his stepfather, but he wouldn't exactly plan to kill him."

"He hated him," she said.

"So they're in the little shooting gallery and O'Mara is dead on the floor, behind the barrier, out of sight. The shots, of course, meant nothing there. And very little blood, with a head shot, small caliber. So the boy goes out and locks the door and hides. But after a while he has to tell somebody. He has to. He tells you. You're his mother. You're the one to tell."

"Yes," she breathed. "He did just that." Her eyes had stopped hating me.

"You think about calling it an accident, which is okay, except for one thing. The boy's not a normal boy, and you know it. The general knows it, the servants know. There must be other people that know it. And the law, dumb as you think they are, are pretty smart with subnormal types. They get to handle so many of them. And I think he would have talked. I think, after a while, he would even have bragged."

"Go on," she said.

"You wouldn't risk that," I said. "Not for your son and not for the sick old man in the orchid house. You'd do any awful criminal callous thing rather than risk that. You did it. You knew Yeager and you hired him to get rid of the body. That's all — except that hiding the girl, Mona Mesarvey, helped to make it look like a deliberate disappearance."

"He took him away after dark, in Dud's own car," she said hollowly.

I reached down and picked my hat off the floor. "How about the servants?"

"Norris knows. The butler. He'd die on the rack before he told."

"Yeah. Now you know why Larry Batzel was knocked off and why I was taken for a ride, don't you?"

"Blackmail," she said. "It hadn't come yet, but I was waiting for it. I would have paid anything, and he would know that."

"Bit by bit, year by year, there was a quarter of a million in it for him, easy. I don't think Joe Mesarvey was in it at all. I know the girl wasn't."

She didn't say anything. She just kept her eyes on my face.

"Why in hell," I groaned, "didn't you take the guns away from him?"

"He's worse than you think. That would have started something worse. I'm — I'm almost afraid of him myself."

"Take him away," I said. "From here. From the old man. He's young enough to be cured, by the right handling. Take him to Europe. Far away. Take him now. It would kill the general to know his blood was in that."

She got up draggingly and dragged herself across to the windows. She stood motionless, almost blending into the heavy white drapes. Her hands hung at her sides, very motionless also.

After a while she turned and walked past me. When she was behind me she caught her breath and sobbed just once.

"It was very vile. It was the vilest thing I ever heard of. Yet I would do it again. Father would not have done it. He would have spoken right out. It would, as you say, have killed him."

"Take him away," I pounded on. "He's hiding out there now. He thinks he got me. He's hiding somewhere like an animal. Get him. He can't help it."

"I offered you money," she said, still behind me. "That's nasty. I wasn't in love with Dudley O'Mara. That's nasty too. I can't thank you. I don't know what to say."

"Forget it," I said. "I'm just an old workhorse. Put your work on the boy."

"I promise. Good-bye, Mr. Carmady."

We didn't shake hands. I went back down the stairs and the butler was at the front door as usual. Nothing in his face but politeness.

"You will not want to see the general today, sir?"

"Not today, Norris."

I didn't see the boy outside. I went through the postern and got into my rented Ford and drove on down the hill, past where the old oil wells were.

Around some of them, not visible from the street, there were still sumps in which waste water lay and festered with a scum of oil on top.

They would be ten or twelve feet deep, maybe more. There would be dark things in them. Perhaps in one of them —

I was glad I had killed Yeager.

On the way back downtown I stopped at a bar and had a couple of drinks. They didn't do me any good.

All they did was make me think of Silver-Wig, and I never saw her again.

One Big Happy Family

by Lionel Booker

"**I**T'S THE PEOPLE, NOT THE premise."

Leonard Farrell leaned back in his chair and smiled expansively at the actor seated across from his desk. He indicated a bronze plaque hanging on the wall. "The network gave us that award when we passed our third year. So far we've picked up six Emmys, and this year the ratings have been better than ever before."

Dugan Murray gazed dutifully at the plaque. It was no secret that *Make Room for Me* was one of the hottest sitcoms on television. In this era of fast-disappearing half-hour shows, it was consistently holding its own in the Top Twenty week after week since its debut four seasons ago.

"You can't tell me," Farrell went on complacently, "that *The Mary Tyler Moore Show* made it because it was set in a newsroom in Minneapolis or that *M.A.S.H.* became a classic because it dealt with the Korean War. It just happened that they brought together a group of people who clicked, who had that special chemistry that made audiences tune them in every week. They could see the genuine affection the actors felt for each other."

He leaned forward and picked up a red-covered script, waving it like a victory flag.

"So what have we got here? A basic, run-of-the-mill family comedy, with the usual bumbling father, loving mother, and two cute kids. Why did it hit so big?" He tossed the script on the desk and tapped it significantly, slowing his voice down for emphasis. "Because Tod Thurman played the father, Elaine Brubaker is the mother, and Sue Grandville and Jimmy Lovel are the kids. Each one has done shows before — films, guest spots, commercials — but this is the first time they've worked together. Together they're — they're a real family."

Dugan looked back at the walls. All around him were photographs of the cast of *Make Room for Me*. Some were magazine covers, some were publicity shots, some were surrounded with texts from articles and newspaper clippings, the titles reading: "The Hawkins Don't Stop Caring When the Cameras Turn Off," "What Sue Grandville Learned from Her Make-Believe Parents," and "Tod Thurman's Favorite Date Is His Favorite TV Wife." All depicted the four actors with broad smiles and in warm, intimate poses.

His eyes rested for a long while on Tod Thurman's face. Farrell must have sensed his slight pang of guilt because he spoke in a sympathetic voice.

"It was a tragic accident, but these things happen. You didn't ask for this opportunity. The important thing is the show."

It was early that season when Thurman was playing a scene about plastering the ceiling of the living room. Clad in coveralls, he had to mount a high scaffold about twelve feet off the ground. The structure gave way during the taping before a live audience, plummeting him to the hard sound-stage floor. The audience, thinking it was a planned bit, howled with laughter until Farrell sped across the set and bent over the unconscious actor. He then informed everyone that the taping had to be discontinued while Thurman was rushed to the hospital for emergency treatment.

The next morning the country felt it had lost a dear friend when it woke to the news that Thurman had passed away in the hospital due to unexpected complications. What had been diagnosed as a broken arm and mild concussion, plus external bleeding, had suddenly become more serious during treatment as inexplicable physical reactions proved fatal.

Thurman was a double-divorcé who had no children, and there wasn't even a next-of-kin listed in his wallet when he was brought into the hospital. His main mourners at the funeral were the shattered cast members and the production executives, who saw his death as the end of a long and lucrative enterprise. Farrell was alone in his belief that a successor could be found. Hundreds of actors were auditioned before Dugan Murray was selected. He not only resembled Thurman, but Farrell was sure he would project the same charm and appeal.

"We're very grateful you're with us, Dugan," the producer assured him, having risen and placed a hand on the actor's shoulder. His voice was filled with enthusiasm. "We've got it all worked out. You'll be Thurman's brother, who rushes to the family's side after his death. By incorporating real events and emotions into the plot, we have a whole new line of possibilities. We can use the uncertainty of it all. You want to help, but you're an outsider. The kids try to accept you but also want to stay loyal to their father's memory. Elaine has been devastated by Tod's passing. They were quite close in real life and she'll have a hard time adjusting. We'll show that in her TV character. Above all, we've got to stay honest."

The next day Dugan reported to the sound stage for the first reading of the new episode — the episode that would introduce his character. He could feel the tension as he walked to the long table where the cast sat studying their scripts.

Elaine Brubaker, an ash-blonde woman in her thirties with a beautiful face, was the first to look up at him — with eyes that looked as if she had been crying a good deal lately. For a moment she and Dugan stared at one another, and then she forced a welcoming smile and held out her hand. "Hello," she said. "This is going to be difficult for you, I know, but we'll do everything we can to help."

Sue and Jimmy were also staring at him now. They had more trouble masking their apprehension, but they managed to nod and say hello.

"Thank you," Dugan said, sitting down next to them. "Thank you for knowing I'm just as frightened as you are."

At the other end of the table, the writers exchanged glances and made notes.

Dugan's words became the first line his character uttered in the show that week.

The ratings of *Make Room for Me* remained respectable as viewers tuned in out of curiosity, but the true test came a few weeks later when the novelty of the new setup wore off. To everyone's delight, the show began a steady climb, which eventually put it back into the Top Twenty. Then it climbed further. By mid-season it was consistently in fifth or sixth place — and four months after Dugan Murray's first appearance, the show became Number One throughout the country.

To Dugan it was a new lease on life. Not long ago, his wife had died, leaving him alone after fifteen wonderful years. Acting parts had been scarce as he moved out of the leading man category into character roles. There had seemed to be little future for him in his profession, and the loneliness of his personal life was becoming unbearable. But now he was considered a star. Every minute of every day was spent in rehearsals, performance, or promotion. He was photographed wherever he went and most of his time off the set was spent at premieres, charity functions, supermarket openings, and award ceremonies.

Jimmy and Sue had finally accepted him openly and treated him almost as if he was their real father. The older, Jimmy, reminded him of himself in his early twenties. Like him, the young man yearned to be a big name and was impatient with anything that interfered with that ambition. Dugan could sympathize with that and gave him understanding when others criticized him as insensitive — even ruthless.

Sue's loneliness reflected his own. There was a rule against family and friends visiting during working hours, so that they wouldn't distract from the performers' family relationship, and the girl's parents were content to keep away from her and not endanger her paychecks. Dugan was happy to fill this void in her life as best he could.

Best of all, there was Elaine. Since the first day, he had been attracted to this kind, lovely woman who had made things so easy for him. She brought back the tenderness he had known with his wife, and they would often dine together — a fact not unnoticed or unwelcomed by the production executives.

"Here's to our twentieth anniversary," Elaine said as she raised her glass. Dugan clinked his against it and gazed at her through the candlelight on the restaurant table. "Twenty weeks ago you joined us."

She had never married, he learned. She said she never found anyone who could tolerate her. She had started out as a fiercely ambitious ingenue in New York, where she had done a few Broadway plays before she was brought to California for her first film — a dismal failure at the box-office that did much to weaken her self-confidence. Four more unremarkable movies led her into television, but the big break never came and she had become known as a serviceable leading lady until she was cast as the mother in *Make Room for Me*.

"You've been good for us, Dugan," she said, drinking champagne. "Everybody's so happy with the way things are working out."

"It's been wonderful for me, too, Elaine," he answered, taking her hand. "But I keep thinking about Tod. I know how close you both were, and if it hadn't been for that accident he'd be sitting here instead of me."

Her face clouded. "Don't think that way. Poor Tod. It was so sad watching him suffer toward the end."

"Suffer?"

"He wasn't as happy as the rest of us. Something was bothering him. Something that was growing worse every day. Leonard tried to talk to him, but it didn't do any good. In a way, it was almost as if he wanted to die."

Two weeks later, Dugan reported to the studio to rehearse the last show of the season, which involved the family getting ready to go on vacation. He had spent the weekend in Palm Springs with the rest of the cast, posing for stills to be used as publicity during the summer hiatus.

In reality the actors had all received offers for feature-film work now that they were free for a spell to pursue outside jobs. The only restriction was that Farrell had to approve the roles and pictures before they could accept them, to make sure they wouldn't damage their image in the series.

Dugan was glad to see the end of the season because he had to admit he was getting a bit weary of spending all his time with the same people and under such heavy restrictions.

When he entered the sound stage, he was surprised to see the living-room set gone. He knew the plot was going to take place in travel agencies and they needed the space for the new scenes, but it was still strange to see the old familiar set missing from the spot where it had stood for four years, long before he came. The floor had become discolored in the areas where the wall sections had been.

Dominick, the prop man, came up to him and handed him a small cardboard box. "I found all this stuff when they struck the set. Check them out, will you, and ask the cast if any of it is theirs?"

Dugan nodded and took it over to the long reading table where Sue Grandville sat alone with her script, staring at the blank space before them.

"It's like seeing your own home torn down, isn't it, Princess?" Dugan said. She returned his smile. He sat down and showed her the box, telling her what the contents were. Together they examined a collection of pens, keys, coins, pieces of paper, and a small metal bracelet that attracted Dugan's eye. He picked it up and wiped some of the dust and grime off. It was an oval attached at each end to a thin, broken chain.

Dugan turned it over and over in his hand, looking at it closely.

"What's that?" asked Sue.

"It's a medical bracelet," he told her. "My wife used to wear one because she had diabetes. People with certain physical problems use them as a precaution in case they need medical attention and can't speak for themselves — if they'd been knocked unconscious in an accident or had an epileptic seizure, say. Doctors are trained to look for them. They're wonderful. My wife was never without hers."

"You know," Sue said, "Tod wore one like that. I always meant to ask him what it was."

"Was he diabetic?"

"I don't know." She looked up as Jimmy came toward the table. "Jimmy, you know that thing Tod wore on his wrist? Dugan says it was a medical bracelet. The prop man just found one when they struck the set —"

She broke off abruptly. A strange look had come on the young man's face. At first Dugan thought it was fear but then decided he was angry, so angry the blood was rushing to his cheeks. "Wardrobe's been looking for you," Jimmy snapped at the bewildered girl. "You have a fitting session."

"But —"

"Never mind, just come on. I was sent to find you." He almost yanked her to her feet. Dugan watched them disappear in wonder. He had never seen Jimmy act like this before. He was still puzzling over it when he returned the box to Dominick . . .

Later, during a break, he saw Sue sitting alone in the audience section. He started toward her to ask her about the incident, but when she saw him coming she got up and moved away. It appeared to Dugan as if she was avoiding him and he didn't pursue her.

Toward the end of the day, after the run-through for the production staff, he noticed Jimmy in a heated conversation with Farrell. The boy pointed to his own wrist and waved his head in Dugan's direction. When he walked off, Farrell came over to Dugan with a smile on his face.

"Did you hear they found my medical bracelet today?"

"One of the crew showed it to me. It's yours, then? I thought —"

"Well, not mine," Farrell cut in amiably, "it's my wife's. She has high blood pressure. I was going to have it repaired when I lost it last week. We were just about to have another one made."

In the parking lot, Dugan saw Dominick getting into his car and couldn't resist asking him where he'd found the bracelet.

"Oh, that? It was wedged between the base of the living-room wall and the floor. It had been jammed in there so tight we couldn't see it until we took the set down. — Mr. Farrell? No, he never claimed it was his. I haven't seen him all day."

"Why are you making such a big thing about it?" Elaine asked him as they drove home that night from a charity ball, where they had been named honorary chairpersons. She had seen his troubled expression when he arrived and got him to tell her the whole affair.

"I wouldn't have," he answered testily, "if everyone hadn't acted so strangely." They were both tired and had an early call in the morning. "Jimmy sounded mad at Sue for telling me about Tod's bracelet and she looked damned scared when I tried to talk to her later. And why did Leonard lie about it?"

"Lie?"

"He said it was his wife's bracelet. For one thing, Dominick said he never stopped by for it, and for another it was too dusty to be lost last week. And I read what it said before I put it back, and there was nothing about high blood-pressure."

Elaine began to look worried.

"Dugan, you're very tired right now and you shouldn't trouble yourself about this."

He sighed. "I suppose you're right, but there's something I can't get out of my head. Tell me, was Tod wearing his medical bracelet at the time of the accident?"

"I imagine so. I wasn't there when he fell. I was backstage. When I got there, Leonard wouldn't let me see him. He was afraid I'd go to pieces. But I did go to the hospital after they took him there. He was wearing a pair of coveralls with no pockets and I took his personal things to him. There was no bracelet with them, so he must have had it on."

They drove in silence for a moment.

"I read about it in the papers," Dugan said. "Tod was unconscious, but his injuries weren't that serious. It was during treatment that he died. Since he was bleeding, they probably gave him antibiotics." His voice grew soft. "Elaine, that bracelet that was found today. It said 'Allergic to penicillin.' "

He heard her gasp. "Oh, Dugan," she whispered in a horrified tone. "You mean that's what killed him? His bracelet had broken off and he couldn't tell them — how awful!"

"Yes," he answered quietly. "It *was* awful." But, he thought, it still doesn't explain what happened today.

In the morning he tried to forget the whole thing. The entire cast was going to be presenters at an awards ceremony that night and they had a full day of rehearsal before them.

The scene called for him to enter with a vacation poster in his hands, but when he called for Dominick to bring him the prop a stranger appeared. "Where's Dom?" he asked.

"He's not with us any more, Mr. Murray. They transferred him to another show today. Don't worry, I've got the poster here."

Dugan took it woodenly, feeling a cold chill in the pit of his stomach. He leaned against the flat, the apprehensions of the previous day flooding back. They had to repeat his cue three times before he responded.

"Are you feeling all right?" Farrell asked him that afternoon as Dugan lay stretched out on the couch in his dressing room. "They tell me you've been behaving a little strange on the set today."

"I'm just tired, Leonard," Dugan said evasively. "I wonder if it would be okay if I missed the awards ceremony tonight."

Farrell's eyes narrowed. "We've already told everyone you'd be there, Dugan." There was a coldness in his tone Dugan hadn't heard before. "If you're sick, we'll have a doctor look at you, but if it's only because you're tired — well, we all have our obligations to the show. I know you don't want to neglect yours and hurt everyone else. After all, we're one big happy family here."

Dugan swallowed. There was a look of suppressed rage on the producer's face as he stared down at him. "Of course, Leonard," he said quickly. "I'll be there."

At nine o'clock he and Elaine sat alone in the green room of the TV studio, waiting to go on and present their award, she in a blue evening gown, he in a tuxedo. They silently watched the monitor showing what was happening onstage for a while and then he said "Elaine, tell me about Tod."

"Tell you what?"

"You said he was suffering toward the end. Was it because of the show? Was he unhappy spending all his time living this make-believe existence without a chance to relax, to be himself? They don't even want us to have outside friends. They watch every move we make — as if they owned us."

She frowned. "He did resent it. I know how he felt. We all get tired of it sometimes."

"Did he threaten to do anything about it?"

"What could he do? He had a contract."

"No one can contract a life. Agreements can always be broken if a man is willing to pay the price. He'd just lose the income, maybe go through a lawsuit. Was Tod so sick of this that he was prepared to pay that price?"

"I don't know," she answered uneasily. Her eyes were on the television screen but she began to twist her hands in her lap. "He and Leonard had some arguments. He never told me what they were about, but I know they were angry with each other. He'd sometimes shout at the kids, too. Jimmy especially."

"I reread a newspaper account of his death. Leonard was the first one to reach him after the fall, wasn't he?" She didn't answer. Dugan lowered the volume on the monitor. "Elaine, if Tod left the show under such circumstances, it would have ruined the family image that's kept it going. Everyone would learn things weren't as blissful as they'd been led to believe. This is a multi-million-dollar project and it would all be lost. Especially for Leonard. A TV series doesn't make any money for the producer until it goes into syndication. Right now only the networks are making a profit — Leonard's just getting a salary. But when the rights of the show revert back to him after its first run, he can make a fortune from the reruns. If the show is discredited now, if it's taken off the air and loses its appeal, or alienates the audience, he'll lose everything."

"Dugan, I can't listen to any more of this. Do you realize what you're saying? You're suggesting Leonard killed Tod."

"Elaine —"

"That's unthinkable! More than that, it's impossible! That scaffold was checked to see why it gave way. A safety board proved it was a worn-out rope that hadn't been tampered with. How could Leonard know it would break when Tod got on it? How could he plan the kind of injuries he'd receive and then rush up to him before anybody else, rip off his medical bracelet, and send him off to the hospital knowing they'd give him penicillin?"

"That's not what I'm saying," Dugan cut in sharply. "I know it didn't happen that way. Leonard couldn't rip off a metal bracelet, and even if he could he would have put it in his pocket, not dropped it on the floor. No, it must have caught on something when Tod fell. That could even have been what broke his arm. It was a one-chance-in-a-million accident, but a lucky one for Leonard. When he reached Tod, he could have seen the bracelet lying on the floor, knowing what it meant. We all had to take complete physical examinations when we were hired, and those reports were sent to the producer. He knew the bracelet would help Tod. He saw he was bleeding and there was a possibility they might give him penicillin. His hatred for him, the man who was going to ruin everything for him, could have been so great that he kicked the bracelet out of sight and waited to see what happened."

"He might have *accidentally* done that! Or someone else did!"

"Yes, but then why did he lie about it? Why was Dominick, who found it and told me about it, sent away? And what about Jimmy? Sue didn't know what the bracelet was for and you were backstage and didn't know it had come off. In fact, Leonard kept you away so you couldn't have known. But Jimmy could have mentioned it when they took Tod away."

"He forgot! Or he didn't notice it was gone! Dugan, what's happening to you?"

"He was furious at Sue when she told me about it. He scared her away from me and talked to Leonard just before Leonard lied to me. Jimmy's an ambitious kid. He wants to succeed more than anything else and this show is helping him do it. Tod was as much a threat to him as he was to Leonard."

Tears were streaming from Elaine's eyes. "Dear God, Dugan. If you're right, what are we going to do? Go to the police?"

He shook his head, trying to get hold of himself. "No. You're right that there's no proof they did it deliberately. I'd give anything to believe this is all my imagination. But don't you see? Until we can know that for sure, we could both be in danger. If we complain or refuse to show complete cooperation, if they suspect we might want to bow out at any cost, we could be next."

At that point they heard their names announced on the monitor and realized they were being introduced. For a moment, they froze, and then they got up and rushed to the door, not daring to be late.

Friday was taping day and the actors didn't have to be at the studio until early afternoon. Dugan decided to use this rare moment of freedom to look for the proof he needed, and he went to the hospital where Tod died. He debated asking Elaine to come with him but remembered how haggard she looked when he took her home on Tuesday night. She had been shaken by Dugan's suspicions, and he decided he wouldn't talk to her further about them until after he'd spoken to the doctor who had attended Tod. Perhaps he'd have good news to tell her, news that would show that his worries were groundless.

Doctor Shigunta was a heavy-set Japanese-American with a friendly, open manner. He was puzzled by Dugan's visit and at first reluctant to discuss the case with him, but he was also a fan of the show and couldn't help looking on the actor in the role he had seen him play so often — that of the deceased's brother.

"We did a post-mortem on Mr. Thurman," he said, "and the official cause of death was the reaction to the antibiotic."

"There was no indication that he was allergic to penicillin?"

"Of course not," Dr. Shigunta said emphatically. "If there had been, we certainly wouldn't have administered it."

"I'm told Tod wore a medical bracelet to that effect and that it was broken off during the fall."

Dr. Shigunta shook his head. "I'm sure you must be mistaken about that."

"Why?"

"Well, people who wear such warnings don't rely exclusively on them. There is another precaution. They also carry a card on their person, issued by the company, that says the same thing as the bracelet. It even gives the name of their doctor and a telephone number we can call twenty-four hours a day."

Dugan gripped the chair arm. Of course. His wife had carried the card in her purse. She was never without it. He had forgotten about that.

"Did you look through his wallet?" he asked the doctor.

"Yes. We took everything out of it. He hadn't been carrying the wallet, but we got it from his wife — excuse me, I mean the woman who plays his wife on TV. She had all his personal effects and handed them to me here in the hospital. We found no card."

As usual they did two tapings of the show, one in the afternoon by themselves and one before an audience that night. During both performances, he marveled at how good Elaine was. She was a wonderful actress and it was too bad she hadn't received the acclaim she deserved during her younger days. But at least she had it now, if she could hold onto it.

Another thought struck him as he lay in bed that night, hoping for a few hours' sleep to escape from the growing certainty of his fears. He had never told Leonard Farrell who had found the bracelet — he had just said it was one of the crew. But he had mentioned Dominick's name to Elaine when he related their conversation in the parking lot.

The film Dugan made during the summer hiatus never found a distributor and was finally shelved. The projects the other cast members had accepted didn't do much better. It seemed the only hold they had on success was the sitcom they did together, and each one reported back to work in the fall, grateful for the money, security, and fame it brought them in an extremely precarious business.

Dugan never mentioned Tod Thurman again, nor did he consider going to the police. In fact, he went out of his way to appear completely contented with his lot. When the seven-year contracts expired for the original cast members, he was quick to assure everyone — especially Leonard Farrell, Jimmy Lovel, and Elaine Brubaker — that he intended to sign up for another seven years as willingly as they no doubt did.

There was a rumor that Sue Grandville, now of age and no longer legally controlled by her parents, was going to get out of show business, but it proved to be unsubstantiated.

"Why would Sue want to leave us?" Leonard Farrell asked the reporter who had brought up the rumor. He had his arm around the quiet girl, whose broad smile belied what looked like a sparkle of terror in her eyes. "After all, we're just one big happy family."

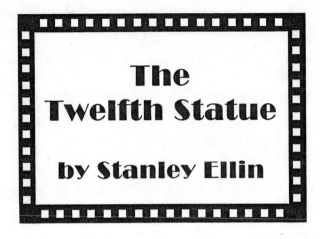

The Twelfth Statue

by Stanley Ellin

ONE FINE MIDSUMMER EVE-
ning, in the environs of the ancient city of Rome, an American motion
picture producer named Alexander File walked out of the door of his
office and vanished from the face of the earth as utterly and completely
as if the devil had snatched him down to hell by the heels.

However, when it comes to the mysterious disappearance of
American citizens, the Italian police are inclined to shrug off the devil
and his works and look elsewhere for clues. There had been four people
remaining in the office after File had slammed its door behind him
and apparently stepped off into limbo. One of the people had been Mel
Gordon. So Mel was not surprised to find the note in his letter box at
the hotel politely requesting him to meet with *Commissario* Odoardo
Ucci at Police Headquarters to discuss *l'affaire* File.

He handed the note to his wife at the breakfast table.

"A Commissioner, no less," Betty said gloomily after she had
skimmed through it. "What are you going to tell him?"

"I guess the best policy is to answer everything with a simple yes or
no and keep my private thoughts private." The mere sight of the coffee
and roll before him made Mel's stomach churn. "You'd better drive me
over there. I don't think I'm up to handling the car in this swinging
Roman traffic, the way I feel right now."

His first look at Commissioner Ucci's office didn't make him feel any better. It was as bleak and uninviting as the operating room of a rundown hospital, its walls faced with grimy white tile from floor to ceiling, and, in a corner, among a tangle of steam and water pipes, there was a faucet which dripped with a slow, hesitant tinkle into the wash basin below it.

The Commissioner seemed to fit these surroundings. Bald, fat, sleepy-eyed, his clothing rumpled, his tie askew, he asked his questions in precise, almost uninflected English, and painstakingly recorded the answers with a pencil scarred by toothmarks. Sublimation, thought Mel. He can't chew up witnesses, so he chews up pencils. But don't let those sleepy-looking eyes fool you, son. There might be a shrewd brain behind them. So stay close to the facts and try to keep the little white lies to a minimum.

"Signor File was a cinema producer exclusively? He had no other business interests?"

"That's right, Commissioner."

And so it was. File might have manufactured only the cheapest quickies of them all, the sleaziest kind of gladiator-and-slave-girl junk, but he was nonetheless a movie producer. And his other interests had nothing to do with business, but with dewy and nubile maidens, unripe lovelies all the more enticing to him because they were unripe. He loved them, did File, with a mouth-watering, hard-breathing, popeyed love. Loved them, in fact, almost as much as he loved his money.

"There were two other people besides yourself and your wife who were the last to see the missing man Signor Gordon. One of them, Cyrus Goldsmith, was the director of the picture you were making?"

"Yes he was."

And a sad case, too, was Cy Goldsmith. Started as a stunt man in horse operas, got to be a Second Unit Director for DeMille — one of those guys who handled chariot races and cavalry charges for the Maestro — and by the time he became a full director of his own, of low-budget quickies, he had absorbed too much DeMille into his system for his own good.

The trouble was that, whatever else DeMille's pictures might be, as spectacles they are the best. They are demonstrations of tender loving care for technical perfection, of craftsmanship exercised on every detail, and hang the expense. Quickies, on the other hand, have to be belted out fast and cheap. So Cy made them fast and cheap, but each time he did it he was putting an overdeveloped conscience on the rack, he was betraying all those standards of careful movie-making that had become ingrained in him. And, as the psychology experts would have it, a compulsive perfectionist forced to do sloppy work is like someone with claustrophobia trapped in an elevator between floors. And to be trapped the rest of your lifetime this way — !

That's what happened to Cy, that's why he hit the bottle harder and harder until he was marked unreliable, on the skids, all washed up, so that finally the only producer who would give him work was good old Alexander File who paid him as little as possible to turn out those awful five-and-dime spectaculars of his. This is no reflection on others who might have been as charitable to Cy. The sad truth is that Signor File was the only producer on record who, as time went on, could keep Cy sober enough for a few weeks at a stretch to get a picture out of him, although, unless you like watching a sadistic animal trainer put a weary old lion through its paces, it wasn't nice to watch the way he did it. A razor-edged tongue can be a cruel instrument when wielded by a character like File.

And, of course, since he was as small and skinny as Cy was big and brawny it must have given him a rich satisfaction to abuse a defenseless victim who towered over him. It might have been as much the reason for his taking a chance on Cy, picture after picture, as the fact that Cy always delivered the best that could be made of the picture, and at the lowest possible price.

"Regarding this Cyrus Goldsmith Signor Gordon —"

"Yes?"

"Was he on bad terms with the missing man?"

"Well — no."

Commissioner Ucci rubbed a stubby forefinger up and down his nose. A drop of water tinkled into the wash basin approximately every five seconds. Very significant, that nose rubbing. Or was it simply that the Commissioner's nose itched?

"And this other man who was with you that evening, this Henry MacAaron. What was his function?"

"He was director of photography for the picture, in charge of all the cameramen. Is, I should say. We still intend to finish the picture."

"Even without Signor File?"

"Yes."

"Ah. And this MacAaron and Goldsmith are longtime associates of each other, are they not?"

"Yes."

Very longtime, Commissioner. From as far back as the DeMille days, in fact, when Cy gave MacAaron his first chance behind a camera. Since then, like Mary and her lamb, where Cy is, there is MacAaron, although he's a pretty morose and hardbitten lamb. And, incidentally, one hell of a good cameraman. He could have done just fine for himself if he hadn't made it his life's work to worshipfully tag after Cy and nurse him through his binges.

"*And you yourself, Signor Gordon, are the author who wrote this cinema work for Signor File?*"

"*Yes.*"

Yes, because it's not worth explaining to this dough-faced cop the difference between an author and a rewrite man. When it comes to that, who's to say which is the real creator of any script — the author of the inept original or the long-suffering expert who has to make a mountain out of its molehill of inspiration?

Commissioner Ucci rubbed his nose again, slowly and thoughtfully.

"*When all of you were with Signor File in the office that evening, was there a quarrel? A violent disagreement?*"

"*No.*"

"*No. Then is it possible that immediately after he left he had a quarrel with someone else working on the picture?*"

"*Well, as to that Commissioner —*"

An hour later, Mel escaped at last to the blessed sunlight of the courtyard where Betty was waiting in the rented Fiat.

"Head for the hills," he said as he climbed in beside her. "They're after us."

"Very funny. How did it go?"

"All right, I guess." He was dripping with sweat, and when he lit a cigarette he found that his hands were trembling uncontrollably. "He wasn't very friendly though."

Betty maneuvered the car through the traffic jamming the entrance to the bridge across the Tiber. When they were on the other side of the river she said, "You know, I can understand how the police feel about it because it's driving me crazy, too. A man just can't disappear the way Alex did. He just can't, Mel. It's impossible."

"Sure it is. All the same he *has* disappeared."

"But where? Where is he? What happened to him?"

"I don't know. That's the truth, baby. You can believe every word of it."

"I do," Betty sighed. "But, my God, if Alex had only not mailed you that script —"

That was when it had all started, of course, when File air-mailed that script the long distance from Rome to Los Angeles. It had been a surprise, getting the script, because a few years before, Mel had thought he was done with File forever and had told him so right there on the job. And File had shrugged it off to indicate he couldn't care less.

The decision that day to kiss off File and the deals he sometimes offered hadn't been an act of bravado. A TV series Mel had been doctoring was, according to the latest ratings, showing a vast improvement in health, and with a successful series to his credit he envisioned a nice secure future for a long time to come. It worked out that way, too.

The series had a good run, and when it folded, the reruns started paying off, which meant there was no reason for ever working for File again or even of thinking of working for him.

Now File suddenly wanted him again, although it was hard to tell why since it was obvious that a Mel Gordon with those residuals rolling in would be higher-priced than the old Mel Gordon who took what he could get. In the end they compromised, with File, as usual, getting the better of the deal. The trouble was that he knew Mel's weakness for tinkering with defective scripts, knew that once Mel had gone through the unbelievably defective script of *Emperor of Lust* he might be hooked by the problems it presented, and if hooked he could be reeled in without too much trouble.

That was how it worked out. File's Hollywood lawyer — a Big Name who openly despised File and so, inevitably, was the one man in the world File trusted — saw to the signing of the contract, and before the ink was dry on it, Mel, his wife at his side, and the script of *Emperor of Lust* under his arm, was on his way to a reunion with File.

They held the reunion at a sidewalk *café* on the Via Veneto, the tables around crowded by characters out of Fellini gracefully displaying their ennui in the June sunlight and by tourists ungracefully gaping at the Fellini characters.

There were four at their table besides Mel and Betty. File, of course, as small and pale and hard-featured as ever, his hair, iron-gray when Mel had last seen it, now completely white; and Cy Goldsmith, gaunt and craggy and bleary-eyed with hangover; and the dour MacAaron with that perpetual squint as if he were always sizing up camera angles; and a newcomer on the scene, a big, breasty, road-company version of Loren named Wanda Pericola who, it turned out, was going to get a leading role in the picture and who really had the tourists all agape.

Six of them at the table altogether. Four Camparis, a double Scotch for Cy, a cup of tea for File. File, although living most of each year abroad, distrusted all foreign food and drink.

The reunion was short and to the point. File impatiently allowed the necessary time to renew old acquaintance and for an introduction to Wanda who spoke just enough English to say hello, and then he said abruptly to Mel, "How much have you done on the script?"

"On the script? Alex, we just got in this morning."

"What's that got to do with it? You used to take one look at a script and start popping with ideas like a real old-fashioned corn popper. You mean making out big on the idiot box has gone and ruined that gorgeous talent?"

Once, when payments on house, car, and grocer's bills depended on the inflections of File's voice, Mel had been meek as a lamb. Now, braced by the thought of those residuals pouring out of the TV cornucopia, he found he could be brave as a lion.

"You want to know something, Alex?" he said. "If my gorgeous talent is ruined you're in real bad trouble, because that script is a disaster."

"So you say. All it needs is a couple of touches here and there."

"It needs a whole new script, that's what it needs, before we make sense out of all that crummy wordage. After I read it I looked up the life of the emperor Tiberius in the history books —"

"Well, thanks for that much anyhow."

"— and I can tell you everything has to build up the way he's corrupted by power and suspicion and lust until he goes mad, holed up in that palace on Capri where they have the daily orgies. And the key scene is where he goes off his rocker."

"So what? That's in the script right now, isn't it?"

"It's all wrong right now, with this Jekyll into Hyde treatment. All that raving and rug chewing makes the whole thing low comedy. But suppose no one around him can see that Tiberius has gone mad — if only the audience realizes it —"

"Yeah?" File was warily interested now. "And how do you show that?"

"This way. In that corridor outside Tiberius' bedroom in the palace we want a row of life-sized marble statues. Let's say six of them, a round half dozen. Statues of some great Romans, all calmly looking down at this man who's supposed to be carrying on their traditions. We establish in advance his respect for those marble images, the way he squares his shoulders with dignity when he passes them. Then the big moment arrives when he cracks wide open.

"How do we punch it across? We leave the bedroom with him, truck with him past those statues, see them as *he* sees them — and what we see is all his madness engraved on *their* faces! Get it, Alex? The faces of those statues Tiberius is staring at are now distorted, terrifying reflections of the madman he himself has finally become. That's it. A few feet of film and we're home free."

"Home free," echoed Cy Goldsmith. He gingerly pivoted his head toward MacAaron. "What do you think, Mac?" and MacAaron grunted "It'll do" — which from him was a great deal of conversation, as well as the stamp of high approval.

"Do?" Wanda said anxiously. *"Che succede?"* — because, as Mel knew sympathetically, what she wanted to hear was her name being bandied about by these people in charge of her destiny; so it was only natural when Betty explained to her in her San Francisco Italian what had been said that Wand a should look disappointed.

But it was File's reaction that mattered, and Mel was braced for it.

'Statues," File finally said with open distaste.

"Twelve of them, Alex," Mel said flatly. "Six sanes and six mads. Six befores and six afters. This is the key scene, the big scene. Don't short-change it."

"You know what artwork like that costs, sonny boy? You look at our budget —"

"Ah, the hell with the budget on this shot," Cy protested. "This scene can make all the difference, Alex. The way I see it —"

"You?" File turned to him open-mouthed, as if thunderstruck by this interruption. And File's voice was penetrating enough to be heard over all the racket of the traffic behind him. "Why, you're so loaded right now you can't see your hand in front of your face, you miserable lush. And with the picture almost ready to shoot, too. Now go on and try to sober up before next week. You heard me. Get going."

The others at the table — and this, Mel saw, included even Wanda who must have got the music if not the words — sat rigid with embarrassment while Cy clenched his empty glass in his fist as if to crush it into splinters, then lurched to his feet and set off down the street full-tilt, ricocheting into bypassers as he went. When MacAaron promptly rose to follow him File said, "Where are you going? I didn't say I was done with you yet, did I?"

"Didn't you?" said MacAaron, and then was gone, too.

File shrugged off this act of mutiny.

"A great team," he observed. "A rummy has-been and his nurse-maid. A fine thing to be stuck with." He picked up his cup of tea and sipped it, studying Mel through drooping eyelids. "Anyhow, the statues are out."

"They're in, Alex. All twelve of them. Otherwise, it might take me a long, long time to get going on the script."

This was the point where, in the past, File would slap his hand down on the table to end all argument. But now, Mel saw as File digested his tea, there was no slapping of the table.

"If I say okay," said File, "you should be able to give me a synopsis of the whole story tomorrow, shouldn't you?"

You give me my synopsis and I'll give you your statues. It was File's way of bargaining, because File never gave something for nothing. And even though it meant a long night's work ahead, Mel said, with a sharp sense of triumph, "I'll have it for you tomorrow." For once — for the first time in all his dealings with File — he hadn't knuckled under at the mention of that sacred word Budget.

When he and Betty departed, not even the thought of the ugly scene with Cy could dim his pleasure in knowing he had browbeaten File into allotting the picture a few thousand dollars more than his precious budget provided. After all, Mel told himself, Cy hardly needed others to comfort him in his sad plight when he had MacAaron to do that for him on a full-time basis.

Back in the hotel room, Mel stretched out on the bed with the script of *Emperor of Lust* — a title, he was sure, that had to be File's inspiration — while Betty readied herself at her portable typewriter, waiting for her husband to uncork the creative flow. Fifteen years before, she had been the secretary assigned him on his first movie job; they were married the second week on the job, and ever since then she had admirably combined the dual careers of amanuensis and wife. Married this long and completely, it was hard for them to surprise each other with anything said or done, but still Mel was surprised when Betty, who had been sitting in abstracted silence, said out of a clear sky, "She isn't the one."

"What?"

"Wanda, I mean, she's not Alex's playmate-of-the-month. She's not the one he's going to bed with."

"I'd say that's their problem. Anyhow, what makes you so sure about it?"

"For one thing, she's too old."

"She must be a fast twenty or twenty-one."

"That's still past the schoolgirl age. And she's just too much woman for him, no matter how you look at it. I think Alex is afraid of real women, the way he always goes for the Alice in Wonderland type."

"So?"

"So you know what I'm getting at. We've been through it before with him. Sooner or later he'll turn up with some wide-eyed little Alice, and it makes me sick when that happens. I don't care if it does sound terribly quaint, but I think a man of sixty parading down the Via Veneto with a kid in her first high heels is really obscene. And sitting at the table with us, playing footsie with her. And showing her what a big man he is by putting down someone like Cy —"

"Oh?" said Mel. "And which one is really on your mind? The Alice type or Cy?"

"I pity both of them. Mel, you said last time you'd never work for Alex again. Why did you take this job anyhow?"

"So that I could put him down, the way I did about those statues. I needed that for the good of my soul, sweetheart; it was long overdue. Also because the New York *Times* said that the last one I did for Alex was surprisingly literate, and maybe I can get them to say it again."

"Still and all —"

"Still and all, it'll be a hectic enough summer without worrying about Cy and Alice in Movieland and all the rest of it. Right now we've got to put together some kind of story synopsis, so tomorrow we'll run over to Cinecitta to see what sets we'll have to work with, and after that we'll be so busy manufacturing stirring dialogue that there won't be time to think of other people's troubles."

"Unless they're shoved down your throat," said Betty. "Poor Cy. The day he kills Alex, I want to be there to see it."

Cinecitta is the Italian-style Hollywood outside Rome where most of File's pictures were shot. But when Mel phoned him about meeting him there, he was told to forget it; this one would be made in a lot a few miles south of the city right past Forte Appia on the Via Appia Antiqua, the old Appian Way.

This arrangement, as File described it, was typical of his manipulations. Pan-Italia Productions had built its sets on that lot for an elaborate picture about Saint Paul, and when the picture was completed File had rented the lot, sets and all, dirt-cheap, on condition that he clear away everything when he left. The fact that the sets might be useless in terms of the script File had bought — also dirt-cheap — didn't bother him any. They were out of Roman history and that was good enough for him.

In a way, it was this kind of thing which often made working for File as intriguing to Mel as it was infuriating. The script he was handed and the sets and properties File provided usually had as much relationship to each other as the traditional square peg and round hole, and there was a fascination in trying to fit them together. When it came to an Alexander File Production, Mel sometimes reflected, necessity was without doubt the mother of improvisation.

The next day he and Betty rented a car and drove out to the lot to see what Pan-Italia had left him to improvise with. They went by way of the Porta San Sebastiano, past the catacombs, and along the narrow ancient Roman road through green countryside until they arrived at what looked like a restoration of Caesar's forum rising out of a meadow half a mile off the road. Beyond it was the production's working quarters, a huddle of buildings surrounding a structure the size of a small airplane hangar which was undoubtedly the sound stage.

There was a ten-foot-high wire fence running around the entire lot, and the guard at its gate, a tough-looking character with a pistol strapped to his hip, made a big project out of checking them through. Once inside, it wasn't hard to find File's headquarters, which was the building nearest the gate and had a few cars parked before it, among them File's big Cadillac convertible. The only sign of activity in the area was a hollow sound of hammering from inside the sound stage nearby.

File was waiting in his office along with Cy, MacAaron, and a couple of Italian technicians whom Mel remembered from the last picture, a Second Unit Director and a lighting man. Neither of them was much good at his job, Cy had once told him — DeMille wouldn't have let them sweep up for him — but they came cheap and understood English, which was all File wanted of them.

Mel found that the procedure of starting work for File hadn't varied over the years.

"All right, all right, let's see it," File said to him without preliminary, and when the story synopsis was handed across the desk to him he read it through laboriously, then said, "I guess it'll have to do. When can you have some stuff to start shooting?"

"In about a week."

"That's what you think. This is Friday. Monday morning, Wanda and the other leads are showing up bright and early along with a flock of extras for mob scenes. So eight o'clock Monday morning you'll be here with enough for Goldsmith to work on for a couple of days. And you'll have some interior scenes ready, too, in case it rains. Then everybody won't be sitting around on the payroll doing nothing."

"Look, Alex, let's get one thing straight right now —"

"Let's, sonny boy. And what we'll get straight is that it don't matter how big you made it on TV, when you work for me you produce like you always did. You are not Ernie Hemingway, understand? You are a hack, a shoemaker, and all you want to do is get some nails into the shoes before the customer gets sore. And no use looking daggers about it, because if you got any ideas of making trouble or walking out on this contract, I'll tie you up so tight in court you'll never write another script for anybody for the next fifty years. What do you think of that?"

Mel felt his collar grow chokingly tight, knew his face must be scarlet with helpless, apoplectic rage. The worst of it, as far as he was concerned, was that everyone else in the room was embarrassedly trying to avoid his eye the way those at the table the day before had tried to avoid Cy's when File had put him in his place. Only Betty aimed an outraged forefinger at File and said, "Listen, Alex — !"

"Stay out of this," File said evenly. "You're married to him, so maybe you like it when he makes like a genius. I don't."

Before Betty could fire back, Mel shook his head warningly at her. After all, the contract had been signed, sealed, and delivered. There was no way out of it now.

"All right, Alex," he said, hating to say it, "Monday, I'll have some nails in your shoes."

"I figured you would. Now let's go take a look at the layout."

They all trooped out into the blazing sunshine, File leading the way, Mel lagging behind with Betty's hand clutching his in consolation. As insurance against mud and dust, Pan-Italia had laid down a tarmac, a hard-surfaced shell, on this section of the lot, and although it was hardly noon Mel could feel it already softening underfoot in the heat. Most of Rome closed up shop and took a siesta during the worst of the midday heat in summer, but there were no siestas on an Alexander File Production.

Cy Goldsmith fell in step beside Mel. The heat seemed to weigh heavily on Cy; yesterday's ruddiness was gone from his face leaving it jaundiced and mottled, and his lips with an unhealthy blueish tinge. But his eyes were bright and sharp, the bleariness cleared from them, which meant that he was, temporarily at least, off the bottle.

"What the hell," he said. "It figured Alex would want to slip the knife into you because of those statues, didn't it?"

"Did it? Well, if it wasn't for the contract I'm stuck with he could shove his whole picture. And if he thinks I'm going to really put out for him —"

"Don't talk like that, Mel. Look, for once we've got everything going for us — a good story, first-class sets, even some actors who know what it's all about. I signed them on myself."

"Like Wanda, our great big beautiful leading lady? Who are you kidding, Cy? What kind of performance can you get out of someone whose lines have to be written in phonetic English?"

"I'll get a good performance out of her. Just don't let Alex sour you on this job, Mel. You never dogged it on the job yet. This is no time to start doing it."

The pleading note in his voice sickened Mel. Bad enough this big hulk should have taken what File dished out over the years. Now, God help him, he seemed to be gratefully licking File's hand for it.

The tarmac came to an end beyond the huge structure housing the sound stage, and another high wire fence here bisected the property and barred the way to the backlot and the replica of the forum on it. The guard at the backlot gate, like his counterpart at the front gate, wore a pistol on his hip.

When they had passed through the fence and caught up to File he jerked a thumb in the direction of the guard.

"That's how the money goes," he said. "You need a guy like that on duty twenty-four hours a day around here. Otherwise, these ginzos would pick the place clean."

"Well, thanks," said Betty, whose maiden name happened to be Capoletta. *"Mille grazie, padrone."*

"Don't be so touchy," File said. "I'm not talking about any Italians from Fisherman's Wharf, I'm talking strictly about the local talent"; and Mel observed that the pair of technicians who must have understood every word of this looked as politely expressionless as if they didn't. After all, a job was a job.

The tour of the sets on the backlot indicated that File had got himself a real bargain. Pan-Italia had built not only the replica of the forum for its Saint Paul picture, but also a beautifully detailed full-scale model of an ancient Roman street complete with shops and houses, and a magnificent porticoed villa which stood on a height overlooking the rest.

This last, said File, would serve as Tiberius' palace in Capri, although its interiors would be done on the sound stage. MacAaron and a couple of the camera crew had already been to Capri the week before and taken some footage of the scenery there to make establishing shots look authentic. A Cy Goldsmith brainstorm, that Capri footage, he added irritably, because what difference could it make to the slobs in the audience —

To get away from File, Mel climbed alone to the portico of the villa. Standing there, looking out over the forum and the umbrella pines and cypresses lining the Appian Way, he could see the time-worn curves of the Alban Hills on the horizon and had the feeling that all this might well be ancient Rome come to life again. Only a dazzle of sunlight reflected from a passing car in the distance intruded on that feeling, but even that flash of light might have been from the burnished armor of some Roman warrior heading south to Ostia in his chariot.

Then Cy was there beside him, looking at him quizzically.

"How do you like it?" he asked.

"I like it."

"And everything fits in with the Tiberius period. Now do you get what I meant about making an honest-to-God picture this time out? I mean, with everything done right. It's all here waiting to be made."

"Not by us. Why don't you quit pushing so hard, Cy? It takes rewrites and retakes and rehearsals to make the kind of picture you're talking about. The three R's. And you know how Alex feels about them."

"I know. But we can fight it out with Alex right down the line."

"Sure we can."

"Mel, I'm on the level. Would you believe me if I told you this was the last picture I'll ever work on?"

"You're kidding."

Cy smiled crookedly. "Not from what the doctors had to say. This is strictly between you and me and Mac — Betty, too, if you want to let her know — but I'm all gone inside." He patted his sagging belly. "It'll be a big deal if the machinery in here holds out for this picture, let alone another next year."

So that was it, Mel thought wonderingly, and just how corny can a man wind up being after a long hard lifetime? That explained everything. Cy Goldsmith was a dying man close to the end of his string, and this picture was to be his swan song. A good one, the best he was capable of, no matter how Alexander File felt about it.

"Look, Cy, doctors can make mistakes. If you went back to the States right now and saw a specialist there — maybe tried the Mayo Clinic —"

"That's where they gave me the word, Mel, at Mayo. Straight from the shoulder. You want to know how straight? Well, the first thing I did before flying out here on this job was to hop back to L.A. and make all the arrangements to be put away in Elysian Park when the time comes. A big mausoleum, a nice box, everything. The funny part was that I felt a hell of a lot better when I signed those papers. It gave me a good idea why those old Romans and Egyptians wanted to make sure everything was all set for the big day. It makes you look the facts in

SILVER SCREAMS: MURDER GOES HOLLYWOOD

the face. After that, you can live with them."

At least, Mel thought, until this picture was made the way you wanted it made. And, in the light of that, Cy had paid him the handsomest tribute he could. Everything depended on the script, and it was Mel Gordon who had been called a long way to work on it.

"Tell me one thing, Cy," he said. "It was your idea to get me out here on this script, wasn't it? Not Alex's."

"That's right. Doesn't that prove I can win a battle with Alex when I have to?"

"I guess it does," said Mel. "Now all we have to do is win the war."

And it was war, even without shot and shell being fired. Once File had the first draft of the complete script in his hands and had drawn up a shooting schedule from it, he quickly caught on to the fact that something strange was going on. After that, life became merry hell for everyone involved in the making of *Emperor* of *Lust*.

Including, as Mel pointed out to Betty with satisfaction, File himself. For the first time in File's career one of his pictures lagged steadily behind its schedule as Cy grimly ordered retake after retake until he got what he wanted of a scene, doubled in brass as his own Second Unit Director, drilling Roman legions and barbarian hordes in the fields outside the lot until they threatened open rebellion, bullied Mel into endlessly rewriting one scene after another until the dialogue suited the limited capabilities of the cast without losing any of its color or sense.

For that matter, all the conspirators doubled in brass. Mel found himself directing two-shots between his writing chores. MacAaron took over lighting and sound mixing despite roars of protest from outraged union delegates. Even Betty, toiling without pay, spent hours drilling Wanda Pericola in the pronunciation of her lines until the two of them hated the sight of each other.

Long days, long nights for all of them, culminated usually in the projection room where they wearily gathered to see the latest rushes while File sat apart from them in a cold fury delivering scathing comment on what he viewed on the screen and what it was costing him. The most grotesque part of it, Mel saw, was that File never understood what they were trying to do and flatly refused to believe the explanation of it that Betty gave him in a loud and frustrating private conference. As far as File was concerned, they were deliberately and maliciously goldbricking on the job, sabotaging him, driving him to ruin, and he let them know it at every turn.

In the long run it was his own cheapness that kept him from doing more than that. As Cy noted, he could have fired them all, but contracts cut ice both ways. Firing them would mean paying them off in full for having done only part of the picture, and replacing them would mean paying others in full for doing the other part, and this for File was unthinkable.

"I know," Mel said. "All the same, I wish there was some way of keeping him off our backs for five minutes at a time. Now if he'd only find himself some nice little distraction —"

It wasn't the wish that made it so, of course. But for better or worse, early the next morning along came the distraction.

She arrived riding pillion on a noisy motorbike — a small slender girl with one arm around the waist of the bearded young man who drove the motorbike and the other arm clutching to her a bulky parcel done up in wrapping paper. A northerner, Mel surmised, taking in the fair skin, the honey-colored hair, the neatly chiseled, slightly upturned Tuscan nose. A skinny, underfed kid, really, but pretty as they come.

They were standing in front of File's headquarters when the bike pulled up — Mel and Betty, Cy, MacAaron, and File — having the usual morning squabble about the day's shooting schedule. As the girl dismounted, now gingerly holding the parcel in both hands as if it were made of fine glass, her skirt rode up over her thighs, and Mel saw File do almost a comic double-take, the man's eyes fixing on the whiteness of exposed thigh, then narrowing with interest as they moved up to take in the whole girl.

What made it worse, Mel thought, was the quality of flagrant innocence about her, of country freshness. He glanced at Betty. From her expression he knew the same word must have flashed through her mind as his at that instant. *Alice.*

The bearded driver of the motorbike came up to them, the girl following in his shadow as if trying to keep out of sight. Close up, Mel saw that the driver's straggling reddish beard was a hopeless attempt to add years and dignity to a guileless and youthful face.

"Signor File, I am here as you requested."

"Yeah," File grunted. He turned sourly to Mel. "You wanted statues? He's the guy who'll take care of them for you."

"Paolo Varese," said the youth. "And this is my sister, Claudia." He reached a hand behind him to draw her forward. "What are you afraid of, you stupid girl?" he asked her teasingly. "You must forgive her," he said to the others. "She is only a month from Campofriddo, and all this is new to her. It impresses her very much."

"Where's Campofriddo?" asked Betty.

"Near Lucca, in the hills there." Paolo laughed deprecatingly. "You know. Twenty people, forty goats. That kind of place. So Papa and Mama let Claudia come to live with me in Rome where she could get good schooling, because she did well in school at home."

He put an arm around the girl's narrow shoulders and gave her a brotherly hug which made her blush bright red. "But you know how girls are about the cinema. When she heard I was to work here where you are photographing one —"

"Sure," Cy said impatiently, "but about those statues —"

"Yes, yes, of course." Paolo took the parcel from his sister, tore open its wrappings, and held up before them a statuette of a robed figure. It was beautifully carved out of what looked like polished white marble, and, Mel saw with foreboding, it was not quite two feet tall.

"The statues were supposed to be life-sized," he said, bracing himself for another bout with File. "This one —"

"But this is only the — the —" Paolo struck his knuckles to his forehead, groping for the word "— the sample. They will be life-sized. Twelve of them, all life-sized." He held out the sample at arm's length and regarded it with admiration. "This is Augustus. The others will be Sulla, Marius, Pompey, Caesar, and Tiberius himself, all copies of the pieces in the Museo Capitoline, all life-sized."

Mel took the figurine and found it surprisingly light. "It's not marble?"

"How could it be?" Paolo said. "Marble would take months to work, perhaps more. No, no, this is a trick. A device of my own. If you will show me where I am to work, I can demonstrate it for you."

His sister anxiously tugged at his arm. *Che cosa devo fare, Paolo?* she asked, then whispered to him in more rapid Italian.

"Oh yes." Paolo nodded apologetically at File. "Claudia has a little time before she must go along to school, and she would like to look around here and see how a cinema is made. She would he very careful."

"Look around, hey?" File considered this frowningly, his eyes on the girl. "Well, why not? I'll even show her around myself," and from the way Claudia's face lit up, Mel saw she knew at least enough English to understand this. "And I have to go back to town in a little while," said File, "so I can drop her off at her school on the way."

Paolo seemed simultaneously alarmed and delighted by this kindness. "But, Signor File, to take such trouble —"

"It's all right, it's all right." File curtly waved aside the stammered gratitude. "You just get on the job and do what you're being paid for.

Goldsmith here'll show you the shop."

Watching File motion the girl to follow him and then briskly stride off with her in his wake, Mel felt an angry admiration for the way the man handled these little situations. You had to know him to know the score. Otherwise, what you were seeing was a small white-haired grandfatherly type, concealing a heart of gold beneath a crusty exterior.

A sculptor's studio had been partitioned off in the carpenters' shop near the entrance to the sound stage, and it was already crowded with the materials and equipment for the making of the statues. The sculptoring process itself, as Paolo described it in rapt detail, was intriguing. A pipework armature, the size of the subject, was set up, its crosspiece at shoulder height. From the crosspiece, wire screening was then unspooled around and around down to the base where it was firmly attached, the whole thing making a cylinder of screening in roughly human proportions. To this was applied a thin layer of clay which was etched into the flowing lines of a Roman toga. As for the head —

Paolo took the statuette, and, despite Betty's wail of protest, ruthlessly chipped away its features with a knifeblade.

"It would take a long time to model the head in clay," he said, "but this way it can be done very quickly."

He brushed away marble-colored flakes, revealing beneath them what appeared to be a skull, although its eye and nose sockets were filled in. He tapped it with a fingernail. "Hollow, you see. *Papier maché* such as masks are made of. One merely soaks it in this stuff — *colla* — you know?"

"Glue," said Betty.

"Yes, yes. Then it can be quickly shaped into a whole head. It dries almost at once. Then clay goes over it for the fine work, and here is our Roman."

"How do you get it to look like marble?" Cy asked.

"Enamel paint is sprayed on, white and ivory mixed. That, too, dries while you wait."

"But the clay under it is still wet, isn't it?"

"Oh, no. Before the paint goes on, one uses the torch — the blow-torch, that is — up and down and back and forth for a few hours. But with all this it takes only one day. So there will be twelve statues in twelve days, as I have promised Signor File."

"Do you have the designs for the other statues with you?" Cy asked, and when they were produced, much crumpled and stained, from Paolo's pocket, it was clear that File had once again made himself an excellent deal.

Standing at the open door of the shop ready to take their departure, they saw File heave into sight with Claudia, direct her into the Cadillac, and climb behind the wheel.

"Beautiful," breathed Paolo, his eyes on the car rather than his sister. Then as the car headed for the gate, he reminded himself of something. *"La bicicletta! La bicicletta!"* he shouted after the girl, waving toward the motorbike propped on the ground before File's office, but she only made a small gesture of helplessness, and then the car was out of range.

Paolo shrugged in resignation.

"The autobus out here is very irregular, so she is supposed to bring me here on the bicycle each morning and then use it herself to go to school. That means I must take the autobus home at night, but today it looks as if I will be able to drive myself home without any trouble."

"There's a piece of luck," Betty said drily. "You know, Paolo, Claudia is a very pretty girl."

"But how well I know." Paolo raised his eyes to heaven in despair. "That was one reason I had so much trouble with Mama and Papa about permitting her to live with me here, where she could improve herself, become educated, perhaps become a teacher at school, not the wife of some stupid peasant. They are good people, Mama and Papa, but they hear stories, you know? So they think all the men in Rome want to do is eat the pretty little girls. They forget Claudia is with me, and that I —"

"Paolo," Betty cut in, "sometimes she is not with you. And while I don't know about all the other men in Rome, I know about Signor File. Signor File likes to eat pretty little girls."

The boy looked taken aback.

"He? Really, *signora,* he does not seem like someone who —"

"Faccia atttenzione, signore," said Betty in a hard voice. *"Il padrone é un libertino. Capisco?"*

Paolo nodded gravely.

"Capisce signora. Thank you. I will tell Claudia. She is already sixteen, not a child. She will understand."

But, Mel observed, there were days after that when File, contrary to his custom, left the lot in mid-afternoon and returned only late in the evening, if at all.

Betty observed this as well.

"And you know where he goes, don't you?" she said to her husband.

"I don't know. I suspect. That's different from knowing."

"Look, dear, let's not split hairs. He's with that child, and you darn well know it."

"So what? For one thing, Mother of the Gracchi, sixteen, going on seventeen, is not a child in these parts, as her brother himself remarked. For another thing, you've done all you could about it — angels could do no more. As far as I'm concerned —"

"Oh, sure. As far as you're concerned — and Cy and Mac, too — you're just glad Alex isn't around all the time, no matter what."

There was no denying that. It was a godsend not having File always underfoot, and they weren't going to question whatever reason he had for staying away from them. Their nerves were ragged with overwork and tension, but the picture was near completion, and all they needed was enough stamina to finish it in style. Considering the drain that File was on their stamina — complaining, threatening, countermanding orders — the sight of that Cadillac convertible pulling out of the gate in the afternoon was like a shot in the arm.

For that matter, Mel wasn't sure that even if Paolo suspected what might be going on he would be so anxious to rock the boat himself. The commission to do the statues, he had confided to Mel, meant enough money to see him through a difficult time. It was lucky Signor File had asked the Art Institute to recommend someone who would handle the commission at the lowest possible rate, because as one of their prize graduates the year before, he, Paolo, had got the recommendation. Very lucky. Money was hard to come by for a young sculptor without a patron; the family at home had no money to spare, so it was a case of always scratching for a few lire, taking odd jobs, doing anything to get up enough for the next rent day. But now — !

So from early morning to late at night, stripped to the waist and pouring sweat, Paolo toiled happily at the statues, and one by one they were carted away to the sound stage and mounted in place on the set there. The first six, faces in stern repose, looked good in the establishing shots; the ones that followed, faces distorted with madness, looked even better. The last to be done, and, Mel thought, the most elective of all according to the sketches of those agonized features, would be Tiberius in his madness.

When this was in its place along with the other five in the corridor of the palace, and MacAaron had made his trucking shots and close-ups, the picture was all but finished. Finished, that is, except for Cy's editing — the delicate job of cutting, rearranging, finding the proper rhythm for each scene, and finally resplicing the whole thing into what would be shown on the screen. In the last analysis, everything depended on the editing, but this would be Cy's baby alone.

With the end in sight none of them wanted to rock the boat. And then, one stormy night, it came close to capsizing.

The storm had begun in the late afternoon, one of those drought-breaking Roman downpours that went on hour after hour, turning the meadows around them into a quagmire and covering even the tarmac with an inch of water. At midnight, when Mel and Betty splashed their way to the car, they saw Paolo standing hopelessly in the doorway of the carpenter's shop looking out into the deluge, and so they stopped to pick him up.

He was profusely grateful as he scrambled past Betty into the back seat. He lived in Trastevere, but if they dropped him anywhere in the city he could easily find his way home from there.

"No, it won't be any trouble taking you right to the door," Mel lied. "You just show me the way."

The way, as Paolo pointed it out, lay across the Ponte Publicio and to the Piazza Matrai, in the heart of a shabby, working-class district. The apartment he and his sister occupied was in a tenement that looked centuries old and stood in an alleyway leading off from the piazza. And parked in solitary grandeur at the head of the alley was a big Cadillac convertible.

Mel's foot came down involuntarily on the brake when he saw it, and the little Fiat lurched to a stop halfway across the piazza. At the same moment he heard Paolo make a hissing sound between his teeth, felt the pressure of the boy's body against the back of the driver's seat as he leaned forward and stared through the rain-spattered windshield.

And then, as if timing his approach to settle all doubts, File came into view down the alley, heading for the Cadillac at a fast trot, head down and shoulders hunched against the rain. He had almost reached it before Paolo suddenly roused himself from his paralysis of horror.

He pushed frantically at the back of Betty's seat. "*Signora*, let me out!"

Betty stubbornly remained unmoving. "Why? So you can commit murder and wind up in jail for the rest of your life? What good will that do Claudia now?"

"That is my affair. Let me out. I insist!"

From his tone Mel had the feeling there would be murder committed if Betty yielded. Then File was out of reach. The Cadillac's taillights blinked on, started to move away, then disappeared down the Via della Luce. Paolo hammered his fist on his knee.

"You had no right!" he gasped. "Why should you protect him?"

Mel thought of the next morning when this half-hysterical boy would have a chance to catch up to File on the lot.

"Now look," he said reasonably, although it struck him that under the circumstances reason was the height of futility. "Nobody knows exactly what happened up in that apartment, so if you keep your head and talk to Claudia —"

"Yes," Paolo said savagely, "and when I do — !"

"But I'll talk to her first," Betty announced. "I know," she said as Paolo started to blurt out an angry protest. "It's not my affair, I have no right to interfere, but I'm going to do it just the same. And you'll wait here with Signor Gordon until I'm back."

It was a tedious, nerve-racking wait, and the ceaseless drumming of the rain on the roof of the car made it that much more nerve-racking. The trouble was, Mel glumly reflected, that not having children of her own, Betty was always ready to adopt any waif or stray in sight and recklessly try to solve his problems for him. Only in this case, nothing she could say or do would mean anything. The boy sitting in deadly silence behind him had too much of a score to settle. The one practical way of forestalling serious trouble was to warn File about it and hope he had sense enough to take the warning to heart. If he didn't —

At last Betty emerged from the building and ducked into the car.

"Well," said Paolo coldly, "you have talked to her?"

"Yes."

"And she told you how much she was paid to — to —?"

"Yes."

Paolo had not expected this. "She would never tell you that," he said incredulously. "She would lie, try to deceive you the way she did with me. She —"

"First let me tell you what she said. She said your agreement with Signor File was that you would get a small payment for the statues in advance and the rest of the money when the work was done. Is that the truth?"

"Yes. But what does that have to do with it?"

"A great deal. Everything, in fact. Because Signor File told her that if she wasn't nice to him, you would never get the rest of the money. He would say your work was no good, and, more than that, he would let everyone know this so that you'd never get a chance at such commissions again. So what your sister thought she was sacrificing herself for, *signore,* was the money and the reputation she was sure you would otherwise be cheated out of."

Paolo clapped a hand to his forehead.

"But how could she think this?" he said wildly. "She knows there was a paper signed before the lawyers. How could she believe such lies?"

"Because she is only a child, no matter what your opinion is of that, and she had no one to tell her better. Now when you go upstairs, you must let her know you understand that. Will you?"

"*Signora* —"

"Will you?"

"Yes, yes, I will. But as for that man — ?"

"Paolo, listen to me. I know how you feel about it, but anything you do to him can only mean a scandal that will hurt Claudia. Whatever happens will be in all the newspapers. After that, can the girl go back to school? Can she ever go back home to Campofriddo without everyone staring at her and whispering about her? Even if you take him to court —"

"Even that," Paolo said bitterly. He placed a hand on the latch of the door. "But I must not keep you any longer with my affairs." And when Betty reluctantly leaned forward so that he could climb past her out of the car, he added, "You do not understand these things, *signora*, but I will think over what you have said. *Ciaou.*"

Mel watched him disappear into the tenement, and then started the car.

"It doesn't sound very promising," he said. "I guess I'll have to slip Alex a word of warning tomorrow, much as I'd like to see him get what's coming to him."

"I know." Betty shook her head despairingly. "My God, you ought to see the way those kids are living. A room like a rathole with a curtain across the middle so they can each have a little privacy. And rain seeping right through the walls. And the furniture all orange crates. And a stinking, leaky toilet out in the hall. You wouldn't believe that in this day and age —"

"Oh, sure, but *la vie Boheme is* hardly ever as fancy as *la dolce vita.* Anyhow, whatever Alex is paying for this commission means some improvement in those living standards when he settles up."

"Does it? Mel, how much do you think Alex is paying?"

"How would I know? Why? Did Claudia tell you how much?"

"She did. Now take a guess. Please."

Mel did some swift mental arithmetic.

"Well," he said, "since the statues are all Paolo's work from the original designs up to the finished product, they ought to be worth between five and ten thousand bucks. But I'll bet the kid never got more than two thousand from Alex."

"Mel, he got five hundred. One hundred down, and the rest on completion. Five hundred dollars altogether!"

You couldn't beat File, Mel thought almost with awe as they recrossed the bridge over the swollen and murky Tiber. A lousy $500 for all twelve statues. And with Claudia Varese thrown in for good measure.

Mel had it out with File the next morning, glad that Cy and MacAaron were there in the office with them to get an earful about what had been going on.

Physically, File was not the bravest man in the world. He was plainly alarmed by the outlook.

"What the hell," he blustered, "you know these girls around here. If it wasn't me yesterday, it would be somebody else today. But if this brother of hers got any ideas about sticking a shiv in my back, maybe I can—"

"I didn't say that," Mel pointed out. "All I said was you'd be smart to steer clear of him. He'll be done with his job tomorrow. You might find something to do in town until he's gone."

"You mean, let this ginzo kid run me off my own property?"

"You started the whole thing, didn't you? Your bad luck you just happened to pick the wrong kind of girl this time."

"All right, all right! But I'll be back in the evening to see that last set of rushes, and we've got an important meeting in the office here right afterward. All of us, you understand? So you all be here."

That had an ominous sound, they agreed after File left, but it didn't bother them. There were only a couple of scenes left to be shot, about a week's work editing the picture, and that was it. File had done his worst, but it hadn't stopped them from doing their best. Whatever card he now had up his sleeve — and File could always produce some kind of nasty surprise at those meetings — it was too late for him to play it. That was all that mattered.

They were wrong. File returned late in the evening to view the rushes with them, and when they gathered in his office afterward, he pulled from his sleeve, not a card, but a bombshell.

"I want to clear up one little point," he said, "and then the meeting's over. One little point is all. Goldsmith, I got an idea you're finally supposed to be done with the photography this week. Is that a fact?"

"By Friday," Cy said.

"Then it's settled. So Friday night when you all walk out of here it'll be for the last time. Get the point? Once you're on the other side of that gate you're staying there. And don't try to con the guard into anything, because he'll have special instructions about keeping you there."

"Sure," said Cy, "except that you overlooked one little detail, Alex. The picture has to be edited. You'll have to wait another week before you tell the guard to pull his gun on me."

"Oh?" said File with elaborate interest. "Another week?" His face hardened. "No, thanks, Goldsmith. We're already carrying a guy on the payroll as film editor, so you just wave goodbye Friday and forget you ever knew me."

"Alex, you're not serious about Gariglia doing the editing. But he's completely useless. If I'm not there to tell him what to do —"

"So from now on I'll tell him what to do."

"You?"

"That's right. Me." File angrily jabbed a forefinger into his chest. "Me. Alex File who was making pictures when you were still jumping ponies over a cliff for Monogram at ten bucks a jump."

"You never made a picture like this in your life."

"You bet I didn't." File's voice started to rise. "A month over schedule. Twenty per cent over budget. Twenty per cent, you hear?"

Cy's face was bloodless now, his breath coming hard.

"Alex, I won't let you or anybody else butcher this picture. If you try to bar me from the lot before the editing is done —"

"If I try to?" File smashed his fist down on the desk. "I'm not trying to, Goldsmith, I'm doing it! And this meeting is finished, do you hear? It's all over. And there won't be any more meetings, because I'm staying away from here until Saturday. All I got from this picture so far is ulcers, but Saturday the cure begins!"

This was no feigned fury, Mel saw. The man was blind with rage, literally shaking with it. The gods he worshipped were Budget and Schedule, and he had seen them spat on and overthrown. Now, like a high priest fleeing a place of sacrilege, he strode to the door bristling with outrage.

Cy's pleading voice stopped him there, hand on the knob.

"Look, Alex, we've known each other too long for this kind of nonsense. If we —"

"If we what?" File wheeled around, hand still on the knob. "If we sit and talk about it all night, maybe I'll change my mind? After what's been going on here all summer? Well, get this straight, you lousy double-crosser, I wouldn't!"

The door was flung open. It slammed shut. File was gone.

The four of them stood there staring at each other. It was so silent in the room that Mel heard every sound from outside as if it were being amplified — the highpitched piping of a train whistle in the distance, the creaking of the light globe outside the building swinging back and forth on its chain in the warm nighttime breeze, the sharp rapping of File's footsteps as he walked toward his car.

It was Betty who broke the silence in the room.

"Dear God," she whispered, and it sounded as if she didn't know whether to laugh or cry, "he meant it. He'll ruin the picture and not even know he's ruining it."

"Wait a second," Mel said. "If Cy's contract provides him with the right to edit the picture —"

"Only it don't," said MacAaron. He was watching Cy closely. "How do you feel?" he asked.

Cy grimaced.

"Great. It only hurts when I laugh."

"You look lousy. If I thought you'd settle for one little drink —"

"I'll settle for it. Let's just get the hell out of here, that's all."

They went outside. The moon, low on the horizon, was only a wafer-thin crescent, but the stars were so thickly clustered overhead that they seemed to light the way to the parked cars with a pale phosphorescence.

Then Mel noticed that File's Cadillac was still standing there, headlights not on, but door to the driver's seat swung open. And File was not in the car

Mel looked around at the dark expanse of the lot. Strange, he thought, File was a creature of rigid habit who got into his car when the day's work was done and headed right out of the gate. He had never before been known to go wandering around the deserted lot after working hours, and what reason he might have for doing it now —

Cy and MacAaron had been walking ahead, and Mel saw Cy suddenly pull up short. He walked back to Mel with MacAaron at his heels.

"I could have sworn I heard that little punk going this way when we were inside," he said "He doesn't have another car stashed around here, does he?"

Mel shook his head "Just the Caddie. The door is open, too, so it looks as if he was getting in when he changed his mind about it. Where do you figure he went?"

"I don't know," said Cy "All I know is that it's not like him to make any tour of inspection this time of night."

They all stood and looked vaguely around the emptiness of the lot. There was a dim light suspended over the office door, another light over the gate, half revealing the gatekeeper's house which was the size of a telephone booth, and that was all there was to be seen by way of illumination. The rest was the uncertain shadowy forms of buildings against pitch blackness, the outline of the sound stage towering over all the others.

"Well, what are we waiting for?" MacAaron said at last. "If something happened to him, we can always send poison ivy to the funeral. Come on, let's get going."

It would have been better if he hadn't said it, Mel thought resentfully. Then they could have shrugged off the mystery and left. Now the spoken suggestion that something might be wrong seemed to impose on them the burden of doing something about it, no matter how they felt about File.

It appeared that Cy shared this thought.

"You know," he said to Mel, "Mac is right. There's no need for you and Betty to hang around."

"What about you?"

"I'll wait it out a while. He'll probably show up in a few minutes."

"Then we can wait with you," Mel said, closing his ears to Betty's muttered comment on File.

The minutes dragged by. Then, at the sound of approaching footsteps, they all came to attention. But it wasn't File who showed up out of the darkness, it was the projectionist who had screened the rushes for them. He had been rewinding the film, he explained in answer to Cy's questions, and no, he had not seen Signor File since the screening. *Buona nota, signora, signori* — and off he went on his scooter amid a noisome belching of gasoline fumes.

They watched the guard emerge from his booth to open the gate for him, the scooter disappear through the gate, and then all was silence again.

"Hell," Cy said abruptly, "we should have thought of it right off. That guard might have seen Alex." And he shambled off to engage the guard in brisk conversation.

When he returned, shaking his head, he said, "No dice. The guard heard the office door slam, but he was reading his paper in the booth so he didn't see anything. And he says the only ones he hasn't signed out yet are Alex and us — and Paolo Varese."

That was it, Mel thought. If they all felt about it the way he did, that was the ominous possibility they had all been trying to close their eyes to. It was the real reason for this sense of disaster in the air. File and Paolo Varese. The boy hidden out of sight in back of the car, File opening the door, seating himself behind the wheel, the knife or gun suddenly menacing him, the two figures, one prodding the other out of the car, moving off into the darkness so that the job could be finished in some safe corner.

Or was there a skull-crushing blow delivered right there on the spot with one of those iron bars used in assembling the armatures for the statues, then the body hoisted to a muscular shoulder and borne away into that all-enveloping darkness? But the evidence would remain. Spatters of blood. Worse, perhaps.

The temptation to look into the car, see what there was to be seen on its leather upholstery, rose in Mel along with a violent nausea. He weakly gestured toward the car.

"Maybe we ought to —"

"It's all right," Cy said, clearly taking pity on him, "I'll do it."

Mel gratefully watched him walk to the car and lean inside it. Then the small glow of the light on the instrument panel could be seen behind the windshield.

"The keys are in the lock," Cy called in a muffled voice, "but there's no sign of any trouble here."

The dashboard light went off, and he withdrew from the car. Keys in hand, he went around behind it, opened the trunk lid, and peered inside. He closed the lid and returned to them.

"Nothing," he said. "All we know is that Alex got into the car and then got out again."

"So?" Betty said.

"So I'm going to look in at the carpenters' shop and see if Varese is there in that studio of his. Meanwhile, Mac can take a look through the sound stage. But there's no need for you and Mel —"

"Don't worry about that," Betty said. "It's still the shank of the evening."

"All right, then you two take your car and run over to the backlot gate and check with the guard there. On the way back here cruise around and look over as much of the grounds as you can. Take your time and keep the headlights on full."

They followed instructions to the letter, and when they rejoined Cy and MacAaron in front of the office twenty minutes later, Mel was relieved to see that both still reflected only puzzlement.

"Mac tells me the sound stage is all clear," Cy said. "As for the kid, he's in the shop working on that last statue, and he swears on his mother's life he hasn't been out of there since dinner. I believe him, too, not that he made any secret about how happy he'd be if Alex broke his neck. The fact is, if he really intended to jump Alex, he'd never do it out here in the open until that guard only fifty feet away and with us likely to walk out of the office any minute. So unless you can picture a chickenheart like Alex walking into that studio all by himself and looking for trouble —"

"Not a chance," said Mel.

"That's how I feel about it. What did the guard at the backlot have to say?"

"Nothing, except that he locked up the gate at quitting time and hasn't seen a soul around there since then. We covered the lot, too, and all we turned up was a couple of stray cats. Now where does that leave us?"

Cy shook his head. "With a ten-foot fence all around and no way out for Alex unless he learned how to fly with his hands and feet. He's sure as hell around here somewhere, but I can't think where. The only thing left to do is comb through every building and see what turns up. Mac will help me with that. You get Betty back to the hotel. She looks dead on her feet."

She did, Mel saw. And he could well imagine what she was thinking. As long as Paolo was in the clear —

"Well, if you can get along without us," he said.

"We'll manage. Oh, yeah, on your way out, find some excuse to have the guard look into your car trunk. Make sure he gets a good look. And don't worry about what he'll find there, because I already checked it. You don't mind, do you?"

"No," said Mel, "not as long as Alex wasn't in it."

He was wakened early the next morning by a phone call from Cy at the lot reporting that he and MacAaron — and Paolo Varese, too, when he had finished the twelfth statue — had searched every inch of the lot and turned up no trace of File.

"He's gone all right," Cy said tiredly. "I even called his hotel just now on the wild chance he somehow got out of here, but they told me he didn't show up all night and isn't there now. So I figured the best thing to do was call in the police. They'll be here in a little while."

"I'll get out there right away. But wasn't this calling in the police pretty fast, Cy? It's only been a few hours altogether."

"I know, but later on someone might ask why we didn't get the cops in as soon as we smelled something wrong. Anyhow, it's done now, and the only question is what we tell them about that little fracas in the office just before Alex walked out. I'll be honest with you, Mel. I think it would be a mistake to say anything about the film editing or about being barred from the lot after Friday. Betty was there, too, so if they want to start pinning things on us —"

Mel glanced at Betty who was sitting up in bed and regarding him with alarm. "What is it?" she whispered. "What's wrong?"

"Nothing. No," he said in answer to Cy's query, "I was talking to Betty. I'll explain everything to her. She'll understand. I suppose you already talked it over with Mac?"

"Yes. He sees it the way we do."

"And how much do we tell about Paolo?"

"Anything we're asked to tell. Why not?"

"Don't play dumb, Cy. If the cops find out what happened when I drove the kid home in the rain the other night —"

"Let them. As long as he had nothing to do with Alex disappearing, there's nothing they can pin on him. And maybe you didn't notice, but Wanda Pericola was standing right outside that office window when you were giving Alex hell about him and Varese's sister. What'll you bet Wanda spills the beans first chance she gets?"

It was not a fair bet, Mel knew. It was too much of a sure thing.

The police, two men in plainclothes, were already at the lot when he and Betty arrived there, and, as the day passed, Mel saw that in terms of the official attitude it was divided into three distinct periods.

First, there was the cynical period when the two plainclothesmen smilingly indicated that this whole affair was obviously a publicity stunt arranged by File Productions.

Then, persuaded otherwise, they became the sober investigators, ordering everyone to report to the sound stage for a brisk questioning and a show of identification papers.

And finally, now thoroughly baffled and angry, they called headquarters for help and led a squad of uniformed men through a painstaking search of the entire lot.

Close behind the squad of police came reporters and a gang of *paparazzi* — freelance photographers, most of them mounted on battered scooters — and the sight of them gathered before the front gate, aiming their cameras through the wiring, shouting questions at anyone who passed within hailing distance, seemed to annoy Inspector Conti, the senior of the two plainclothesmen, almost as much as his failure to locate the missing Alexander File.

"Nuisances," he said when Cy asked about holding some sort of press conference in the office. "They will stay on the other side of that fence where they belong. There can be no doubt that Signor File, alive or dead, is here inside the perimeter of that fence, and until we find him no one is permitted to enter or leave. It will not take long. Assuming the worst, that a crime has been committed, it is impossible to dispose of the victim beneath the pavement which covers the entire area. And thanks to your foresight, *signore* —" he nodded at Cy who wearily shrugged off the compliment" — this place has been hermetically sealed since immediately after the disappearance. There can be no question about it. Signor File is here. It is only a matter of hours at the most before we find him."

The Inspector was a stubborn man. Not until sunset, after his squad had, to no avail, moved across the lot like a swarm of locusts, not until File's records and correspondence had futilely been examined page by page, did he acknowledge temporary defeat.

"You may leave now," he announced to the company assembled in the sound stage, "but you will make yourselves available for further questioning when called on. Until permission is granted by the authorities, no one will enter here."

By now Cy was groggy with exhaustion, but this brought him angrily to his feet. "Look, we've got a movie to finish, and if you —"

"All in good time, *signore.*" The Inspector's voice was flat with finality. "Those of you who are not citizens will now surrender their passports to me, please. They will be held for you at headquarters."

Outside in the parking space, Mel saw that the door of File's Cadillac had been closed but was discolored by a grayish powder. It took him a moment to realize that this must have been the work of a fingerprint expert, and that realization, more than anything else that had happened during the day, made File's disappearance real and menacing. The questions asked by the police had only scratched the surface so far — there had been no need to mention either Claudia Varese or the editing of the picture; but there was further questioning to come, and next time it was likely to do much more than scratch the surface.

Cy was pursuing a different line of thought.

"First thing," he said, "is to make sure everybody we need for those last scenes stays on call."

"For what?" Mel said. "Without Alex, who takes care of the payroll, the release, the promotion? We can't sign anything for him."

"We won't have to. Look," Cy said urgently, "that big Hollywood lawyer of Alex's is empowered to act for him in his absence. He also happens to have a lot of dough tied up in this picture, and he's damn near as tight as Alex about money. When I get in touch with him and tell him what's going on here he'll see to it we finish the job. I guarantee that."

"Only if Alex is absent," Mel said. "But what if he's dead?"

"Then we're licked. The footage we shot so far is part of his estate, and by the time the Surrogates Court settles the estate we'll all be dead and gone ourselves. But we don't know Alex is dead, do we? Nobody knows if he is or not. So what we do is get his lawyer's okay to finish the picture in return for an agreement to deliver it to him for release."

"Without being allowed back on the lot?" said Betty. "And who knows how long it'll be before we are allowed back? Further questioning, that detective said. It might take weeks before they get around to it. Or months."

"It might," said Cy, "but I have a hunch it won't."

He was right. The very next morning Mel was called to his interview with Commissioner Odoardo Ucci at Police Headquarters and had as unpleasant a time of it as he had anticipated.

The worst of it was when the Commissioner, after much deliberate nose scratching, suddenly introduced the subject of Paolo Varese's hostility toward his employer, and when Mel hedged in his answers, Ucci revealed an astonishing familiarity with the scene played that rainy night on the Piazza Matrai. Which meant, Mel thought hopelessly, that Wanda had indeed spilled the beans at the first opportunity.

Under such conditions, Mel knew, there was no use being evasive about it. So he described the scene in detail and took what consolation he could from the memory of Cy's reminder that since Paolo had nothing to do with File's disappearance, there was nothing that could be pinned on him.

Ucci's reaction jolted him.

"If you had given this vital information to Inspector Conti at once —" he said.

"Vital?" Mel said. "Listen, Commissioner, we walked out of that of office a minute or two after Mr. File. If Varese had tried to do anything to him out there —"

"But the possibility did enter your mind, *signore,* that he might have tried?"

"Yes, and I found out very quickly that I was wrong about it."

"I think I will soon prove otherwise, *signore.* Before the day is over, in fact. So you and Signora Gordon will please remain *incommunicado* in your hotel until then. As a favor to yourself, no telephone calls and no visitors, please."

It was Ucci himself who picked them up in a chauffeured car late in the afternoon.

"Where are we going?" Betty asked him as the car swung away from the curb.

"To the location of your cinema company, *signora*, to demonstrate that the mystery of Signor File's disappearance was never a mystery at all."

"Then you found him? But where? What happened to him?"

"Patience, *signora*, patience." The Commissioner's manner was almost playful. "You will shortly see the answer for yourself. If," he added grimly, "you have the stomach for it."

A *carabiniere* bearing a Tommy gun admitted them through the gate of the lot; another came to attention at the door of the carpenters' shop as they entered it. In the sculptor's studio behind the partition at the rear of the shop was a small gathering waiting for them.

Cy and MacAaron stood at one side of the room; and Paolo Varese, tight-lipped and smoldering, stood at the other side between Inspector Conti and the subordinate plainclothesman. And in the center of the room, towering over them all on its pedestal, was a life-sized statue.

Tiberius mad, Mel thought, and then recoiled as understanding exploded in him. There was a distinct resemblance between this statue and the one of Tiberius sane which had already been photographed and stored away in the prop room; but there was an even greater resemblance between these distorted features and the face of Alexander File in a paroxysm of rage.

"Oh, no," Betty whispered in anguish, "it looks like —"

"Yes?" prompted Ucci, and when Betty mutely shook her head he said, "I am sorry, *signora,* but I wanted you to observe for yourself why the mystery never was a mystery. Once I had compared this statue with photographs of Signor File, the solution was clear. Wet *papier maché* molded to the face seems to reproduce it so that even a layer of clay over the mask, skillfully worked as it may be, does not conceal the true image underneath.

"However —" he nodded toward Inspector Conti — "it was my assistant who unearthed the most important clue. A series of these statues had been made before the disappearance. Only one — this one — was completed *after* the disappearance, and the use it was put to is obvious. Also, *signora,* highly unpleasant. So if you wish to leave the room now while we produce the evidence of the crime —"

When she left, moving as if she were sleepwalking through a nightmare, Mel knew guiltily that he should have gone with her; but he found himself helplessly rooted to the spot, transfixed by the sight of the Commissioner picking up a mallet and chisel and approaching the statue.

That sight stirred Paolo Varese to violent action. He suddenly flung himself at Ucci, almost overthrowing him in the effort to wrest the tools from his hands. When the two plainclothesmen locked their arms through his and dragged him back he struggled furiously to free himself from their grasp, then subsided, gasping.

"You can't!" he shouted at Ucci. "That is a work of art!"

"And a clever one," said Ucci coldly. "Almost brilliant, in fact. A work of art that can be removed from here at your leisure and sent anywhere in the world without a single person knowing its contents. A fine business, young man, to use such a talent as yours for the purpose of concealing a murder. Do you at least confess to that murder now?"

"No! Whatever you find in my statue, I will never confess to any murder!"

"Ah? Then perhaps this will change your mind?"

The Commissioner placed the edge of the chisel into a fold of the toga draping the figure and struck it a careful blow. Then another and another.

As shards of white-enameled clay fell to the floor Mel closed his eyes, but that couldn't keep him from hearing the sound of those remorseless blows, the thudding on the floor of chunks of clay.

Then there was a different sound — the striking of metal against metal.

And finally a wrathful exclamation by Ucci.

Mel opened his eyes. What he saw at first glance was Ucci's broad face, almost ludicrous in its open-mouthed incredulity. Cy, MacAaron, the two plainclothesmen, all wore the same expression; all stared unbelievingly at the exposed interior of the statue which revealed the rods of an armature, a cylinder of wire screening — and nothing more.

"Impossible," Ucci muttered. "But this is impossible."

As if venting his frustration on the statue, he swung the mallet flush against its head. The head bounded to the floor and lay there, an empty mask of *papier mâché,* patches of whitened clay still adhering to it.

Paolo pulled himself free of the plainclothesmen's grasp. He picked up the mask and tenderly ran his fingers over the damage in it made by the mallet.

"Barbarian," he said to Ucci. "Vandal. Did you really think I was a murderer? Did you have to destroy my work to learn better?"

233

Ucci shook his head dazedly.

"Young man, I tell you that everything, all the evidence —"

"What evidence? Do I look like some peasant from the south who lives by the vendetta?" The boy thrust out the mask toward Ucci who recoiled as if afraid it would bite him. "This was my revenge — to shape this so that the whole world would know what an animal that man was. And it was all the revenge I asked, because I am an artist, you understand, not a butcher. Now you can try to put the pieces of my statue together, because I am finished here." He looked at Cy. "As soon as I have packed my tools, *signore*, I will go."

"But we'll be back tomorrow," Cy pleaded. He turned to Ucci. "You can't have any objections to that now, can you?"

"Objections?" The Commissioner still seemed lost in a daze. "No, no, *signore.* The premises have been fully investigated, so you are free to use them. But it is impossible — I cannot understand —"

"You see?" Cy said to Paolo. "And all I ask is one more day's work. Just one more day."

"No, *signore.* I have done the work I agreed to do. I am finished here."

As Mel started out of the studio, Cy followed him with lagging steps.

"Damn," he said. "I hate to do that scene one statue short."

"You can shoot around it. Hell, I'm glad it turned out like this, statue or not. For a minute, that cop had me convinced —"

"You? He had us all convinced. When Betty walked out of here she looked like she was ready to cave in. You want my advice, Mel, you'll book the first flight home tomorrow and get her away from here as quick as you can. The picture's just about done anyhow, and Betty's the one you have to worry about, not Alex."

The *carbiniere* on guard at the door motioned around the building, and they found Betty waiting for them there, her eyes red and swollen, the traces of tears shiny on her cheeks.

"What happened?" she asked, as if dreading to ask it. "Did they —?"

"No," said Mel, "they didn't. Paolo is out of it." And then as she stood there, helplessly shaking her head from side to side — looking, in fact, as if she were ready to cave in — Mel put his arms tight around her.

"It's all right, baby," he said, "it's all right. We're going home tomorrow."

Cy Goldsmith died the first day of winter that year, a few weeks after the picture was released; so at least, as Betty put it, he knew before he went that the critics thought the picture was good. Not an Oscar winner, of course, but plausible, dramatic, beautifully directed. It wasn't a bad send-off for a man on his deathbed.

The mystery of File's disappearance didn't hurt at the box office either. The press had a field day when the story first broke, and even when interest had died down somewhat it didn't take much to revive it. Every week or so Alexander File would be reported seen in some other corner of the world, a victim of amnesia, of drug addiction, of a Red plot, and the tabloids would once more heat up the embers of public interest. Then there was the release of the picture and Cy's death soon afterward to keep the embers burning.

Mel and Betty were in San Francisco getting ready to spend the Christmas week with her family when they saw the news in the paper — Cyrus Goldsmith died in Cedars of Lebanon Hospital after a long illness and would be buried at Elysian Park Cemetery — and it was the unpleasant thought of the reporters and photographers flocking around again that made Mel decide not to attend the funeral, but to settle instead for an extravagant wreath.

Reading that mention of Elysian Park reminded him also of the time when he and Cy had stood on the portico of the make-believe palace in the backlot, looking down on the Appian Way, and Cy had confided to him how comforting it had been to arrange for the mausoleum he would soon be occupying. He had been like a relic of antiquity, had Cyrus Goldsmith. A devout believer in the idea that a chamber of granite with one's name on it somehow meant a happier afterlife than a six-foot hole in the ground.

Mel shook his head at the thought. Cy had no family to mourn him, the only person in the world close to him had been MacAaron so MacAaron must have been in charge of the funeral arrangements. Too bad Mac wasn't the kind of man to do things up in real-imaginative style. Seen to it, perhaps, that, just as the pharoahs had been buried with the full equipage for a happy existence in heaven, Cy should have been provided with his idea of the necessities for a pleasant eternity — a supply of Scotch, a print of *Emperor of Lust,* even a handsomely mounted picture of a futilely snarling Alexander File on the mausoleum wall to keep fresh that taste of the final victory.

A few days later — the day after Christmas when the household was still trying to recover from the festivities — Mel and Betty slipped away and drove downtown to see the picture for the first time. Mel had long ago given up attending public showings of anything he had worked on because watching the audience around him fail to appreciate his lines was too much like sitting in a dentist's chair and having a tooth needlessly drilled; but this time Betty insisted.

"After all, we didn't go to the funeral," she argued with a woman's logic, "so this is the least we can do for Cy."

"Darling, no disrespect intended, but where Cy is now, he couldn't care less what we do for him."

"Then I'll go see it by myself. Don't be like that, Mel. You know this one is different."

And so it was, he saw. Different and shocking in a way that no one else in the audience could appreciate. At his suggestion, and to Betty's pleased bewilderment, they sat through it a second time. Then, while Betty was in the theater lounge, he raced to a phone in the lobby and put through a call to MacAaron's home in North Hollywood.

"Mac, this is Mel Gordon."

"Sure. Say, I'm sorry you couldn't make it to the funeral, but those flowers you sent —"

"Never mind that. Mac, I just saw the picture, and there's one shot in it — well, I have to get together with you about it as soon as possible."

There was a long silence at the other end of the line.

"Then you know," MacAaron said at last.

"That's right. I see you do, too."

"For a long time. And Betty?"

"I'm sure she doesn't."

"Good," said MacAaron with obvious relief. "Look, where are you right now?"

"With my in-laws, in San Francisco. But I can be at your place first thing tomorrow."

"Well, first thing tomorrow I have to go over to Elysian Park and settle Cy's account for him. He put me in charge of it. You ever see the way he's fixed up there?"

"No."

"Then this'll give you a chance to. You can meet me there at ten. The man at the gate will show you where Cy is."

Punctuality was a fetish with MacAaron. When Mel arrived for the meeting a few minutes after ten, Mac was already there, seated on a bench close by a mausoleum with the name GOLDSMITH inscribed over its massive bronze door. The structure was made of roughhewn granite blocks without ornamentation or windows, and it stood on a grassy mount overlooking a somewhat unkempt greensward thickly strewn with grave markers. Unlike the fashionable new cemeteries around

Los Angeles, Elysian Park looked distinctly like a burial ground.

MacAaron moved to make room for Mel on the bench.

"How many times did you see the picture?" he asked without preliminary.

"Twice around."

"That all? You caught on quick."

"It was simple arithmetic," Mel said, wondering why he felt impelled to make it almost an apology. "Six statues already used and locked up in the prop room, six more in that long shot of the corridor — and the one in the studio that the police smashed up. Thirteen statues. Not twelve. Thirteen."

"I know. I caught wise the day we shot the last scenes with those statues, and I counted six of them standing there, not five. That's when I backed Cy into a corner and made him tell me everything, much as he didn't want to. After he did, I had sense enough to cut away from that sixth statue before the camera could get it; but I never did notice that one long shot of the whole corridor showing all six of those damn things until the night of the big premiere, and then it was too late to do anything about it. So there they were, just waiting for you to turn up and start counting them." He shook his head dolefully.

"As long as the police didn't start counting them," Mel said. "Anyhow, all it proves is that Paolo Varese was a lot smarter than we gave him credit for. The statue in his studio was just a dummy, a red herring. All that time we were watching the Commissioner chop it apart, Alex was sealed up in the sixth one in the corridor. Right there on that set in the sound stage, with everyone walking back and forth past him."

"He was. But do you really think it was Varese who had the brains to handle the deal? He was as green as he looked, that kid. Him and his little sister both. A real pair of babes in the woods."

"You mean it was Cy who killed Alex?"

"Hell, no. The last thing Cy wanted was Alex dead, because then the picture would be tied up in Surrogates Court. No, the kid did it, all right, but it was Cy — look, maybe the best way to tell it is right from the beginning."

"Maybe it is," said Mel.

"Then first of all, you remember what Cy had us do after we saw the Caddie standing there that night with the door open and Alex nowhere around?"

"Yes. He had you go through the sound stage hunting for Alex, and Betty and me look around the grounds."

"Because he wanted all three of us out of the way for the time being. He had an idea Alex had gone to see the kid and that something might have happened. So he —"

"Hold on," Mel said. "We all agreed right there that Alex would never have the guts to face the kid."

"That's the track Cy put us on, but in the back of his mind he figured Alex might have one good reason for getting together with Varese. Just one. Alex was yellow right down to the bottom of the backbone, right? But he also had to do business in Rome every year, and that's where the kid lived. Who knew when they'd bump into each other, or when the kid would get all steamed up after a few drinks and come looking for him?

"So what does a guy like Alex do about it? He goes to the kid waving a white flag and tries to buy him off. Cheap, of course, but the way things are with Varese and the sister he feels a few hundred bucks should settle the case very nicely. About three hundred bucks, in fact. Twenty thousand lire. Cy knew how much it was because when he walked into the studio there was the money all over the floor, and Alex lying there dead with his face all black, and the kid standing there not knowing what had happened. Cy says it took him five minutes just to bring him out of shock.

"Anyhow, he finally got the kid to making sense, and it turned out that Alex had walked into the studio, waving the money in his hand, a big smile on that mean little face of his, and he let the kid know that, what the hell, the girl wasn't really hurt in any way, but if it would make her feel better to buy something nice for herself —"

"But how stupid could he be? To misjudge anyone that way!"

"Yeah, that's about the size of it." MacAaron nodded somberly. "Anyhow, it sure lit the kid's fuse. He didn't even know what happened next. All he knew was that he got his hands around that skinny throat, and when he let go it was too late."

"Even so," Mel said unhappily, "it was still murder."

"It was," agreed MacAaron. "And a long stretch in jail, and the papers full of how the little sister had gone wrong. It sure looked hopeless, all right. And you know the weirdest part of it?"

"What?"

"That the only thing on Varese's mind was the way he'd let his folks down, his Mama and his Papa. Going to jail didn't seem to bother him one bit as much as that he had argued his people into letting the girl go to Rome and then he had let her become a pigeon for Alex. It never struck him anything could be done about Alex being dead. As far as he was concerned, it was just a case of calling in the cops now and getting it over with.

"But, naturally, the last thing Cy wanted was for anyone to know Alex was dead, because then the picture was really washed up. And looking at that Tiberius statue which was almost finished, he got the idea that maybe something *could* be done. The hitch was that you and me and Betty were right there on the spot, but once he got you two off the lot and then had me hunting for Alex like a fool through all those buildings and shops, he had room to move in.

"First off, he had the kid rush through a whole new Tiberius statue. That was the thirteenth statue, the one they stuck Alex inside of, and Cy said it was all he and the kid could do to keep their dinner down while they were at it. It took almost all night, too, and when it was done they trucked it over to the sound stage and set it up there and brought the other one back to the studio."

"But he told me he had Paolo helping you and him look for Alex most of the night. If I had asked you about it —"

"Oh, that." The ghost of a smile showed on MacAaron's hardbitten face. "He wasn't taking any chance with that story, because he had the kid go by me a couple of times looking around the lot with a flashlight in his hand. If I had any doubts about him up to then, that settled them. When Inspector Conti questioned me next day I didn't even mention the kid, I was so sure he was in the clear about Alex."

"You didn't have to mention him. Wanda was only waiting to."

"Wanda?" MacAaron said with genuine surprise. "What would she know? Hell, it was Cy who told the Inspector about what happened when you took the kid home that night. But the right way, you understand, sort of letting it be dragged out of him. And sort of steered him around to the studio so he could get a good look at that statue after seeing some photos of Alex.

"It was Cy all the way. Once he made sure the Inspector and the Commissioner knew those other statues in the prop room and on the sound stage had absolutely been there before Alex disappeared, Cy wanted that showdown in the studio. He wanted everything pinned on the kid and then cleared up once and for all. The only question was whether the kid could hold up under pressure in the big scene, and you saw for yourself how he did.

"Now do you get the whole setup? Make the lot look like it was sealed up airtight, make it look like the kid was the only possible suspect, and then clear him completely. If I could swear on the Bible that the kid was helping us hunt for Alex that night, and if Alex isn't in that statue — what's left?"

"A statue with a body in it," Mel said. "A murder."

"Yeah, I understand," MacAaron said sympathetically. "Now you're sorry you know the whole thing. But I'm not, Mel. And I don't mean because it's been so hard keeping it to myself. What's been eating me is that up to now nobody else in the world knew how Cy proved the kind of man he was."

"Proved what?" Mel said harshly. "It wasn't hard for him to be that kind of man, feeling the way he did about the picture and knowing he had only a little while to live. How much was he really risking under those conditions? If things went wrong, he'd be dead before they could bring him to trial, and the kid would take the whole rap."

"You still don't get it. You don't get it at all. How could you if you weren't even there at the finish? Well, I was."

To Mel's horror, MacAaron, the imperturbable, the stoic, looked as if he were fighting back tears, his face wrinkling monkeylike in his effort to restrain them. "Mel, it went on forever in that hospital. Week after week, and every day of it the pain got worse. It was like knives being run into him. But all that time he would never let them give him a needle to kill the pain. They wanted to, but he wouldn't let them. He told them it was all right, he wouldn't make any fuss about how it hurt, and he didn't. Just lay there twisting around in that bed, chewing on a handkerchief he kept stuffed in his mouth, and sweat, the size of marbles, dripping down his face. But no needles. Not until right near the end after he didn't know what was going on any more."

"So what? If he was afraid of a lousy needle —"

"But don't you see why?" MacAaron said despairingly. "Don't you get it? He was scared that if he had any dope in him he might talk about Alex and the kid without even knowing it. He might give the whole thing away and send the kid to jail after all. That was the one big thing on his mind. That was the kind of man he was. So however you want to fault him —"

He stared at Mel, searching for a response, and was evidently satisfied with what he saw.

"It'll be tough keeping this to ourselves," he said. "I know that, Mel. But we have to. If we didn't, it would mean wasting everything Cy went through."

"And how long do you think we'll get away with it? There's still that statue with Alex rotting away inside of it, wherever it is. Sooner or later —"

"Not sooner," MacAaron said. "Maybe a long time later. A couple of lifetimes later." He got us stiffly, walked over to the mausoleum and inserted a key into the lock of the bronze door. "Take a look," he said. "This is the only key, so now's your chance."

An unseen force lifted Mel to his feet and propelled him toward that open door. He knew he didn't want to go, didn't want to see what was to be seen, but there was no resisting that force.

Sunlight through the doorway flooded the chill depths of the granite chamber and spilled over an immense casket on a shelf against its far wall. And standing at its foot, facing it with features twisted into an eternal, impotent fury, was the statue of Tiberius mad.

Unreasonable Facsimile

by George Baxt

ANDREW SOMERS CAREFULLY
piloted his Mercedes Benz up the winding driveway that led to the
fabled palace of Naomi Lawes. He drove slowly, marshaling his
thoughts. How does one deal with a legend? he wondered — as he had
been wondering ever since she had consented to see him. Naomi Lawes,
as famous a legend as Garbo, Dietrich, and Rae Dawn Chong. In the
early Nineteen Forties, Naomi accomplished a coup that made
Hollywood history. She succeeded in winning the heart of the so-called
"boy wonder" of films, Erwin Lawes.

In his early twenties, Erwin had been appointed head of the faltering
Majestic Films and filmdom scoffed and laughed and circulated
scurrilous jokes about the slender, fragile young man from Jersey City.
"Jersey City!" exclaimed Joan Crawford in the powder room of the
Mocambo nightclub. "You'd think he'd have the class to claim someplace ritzy for his birthplace. But Jersey City!" Miss Crawford had long
ago developed amnesia as to her own lowly origins.

But Erwin Lawes had the last laugh. Within two years of his shrewd
guidance and management, Majestic Films ground out box-office
smash after box-office smash, and a few were in good taste. He took
talentless nobodies and seemingly overnight developed them into
talentless somebodies. He found Naomi Gribble in an amateur
production of *Rain*, John Colton's adaptation of W. Somerset

Maugham's short story, "Miss Thompson," in a tiny theater off Sunset Boulevard. Within a year, Naomi rose from bits and walk-ons to featured roles in "A" productions interspersed with leads in a number of low-budgeted "B"s. Naomi didn't have to know how to act — it was enough that the camera loved her. She photographed magnificently. She was also great in bed. So Erwin married her.

To no one's surprise, she changed Naomi Gribble to Naomi Lawes, and under her husband's careful and relentless supervision she starred and triumphed in a series of films that secured her position in the pantheon of film greats. Naomi as Camille, Naomi as Carmen, Naomi as Joan of Arc, Naomi as Madame DuBarry, Naomi as Mary Magdalene, Naomi as any character she wished to play.

Then the tragedy that brought about the ruination of Majestic Films and the permanent retirement of Naomi Lawes. One February night, an intruder broke into the Lawes palace (Erwin had imported it brick by brick from Italy as a wedding present for his bride) and brutally stabbed Erwin to death while his beloved wife slept in her suite across the hall from his. The coroner counted twenty-eight knife wounds and clucked his tongue each time he repeated the number. Naomi suffered a nervous breakdown and was sequestered in a sanitarium for over three months. When she recovered her senses, she found herself to be an incredibly wealthy widow.

The film industry was amazed she made no attempt to resume her career. In one of her rare interviews (given to Louella Parsons or else) she said, "Without Erwin, I'm nothing. Without his love and reassurance and brilliant guidance, there is no future for me in films any more. Yes, I did just receive an offer but I'll be damned if I'll play Rita Hayworth's mother."

The murderer was never apprehended and the case remained open in the annals of the Los Angeles Police Department. After the sanitarium, Naomi went into seclusion for more than a year, taking up knitting, crossword puzzles, chinese checkers, and vodka daiquiris. Eventually and gradually, Naomi emerged from her self-imposed exile and allowed herself a few romantic flings — with a used-car salesman, a tennis instructor (she was crazy about his underhand), a chauffeur, and a Seventh Day Adventist. And so the years went by. Her wealth accumulated, thanks to shrewd management by her brokers and lawyers. Time treated her face and her body kindly.

Andrew Somers couldn't believe that this gorgeous creature mixing the vodka martinis was sixty years of age, give or take a few minutes.

He couldn't believe the Tintoretto, the Gauguin, the Van Gogh, and the other masters in the room were authentic — but she reassured him. "They're about the only things in this town that aren't fakes." She poured the drinks, handing him one and taking one for herself, and then draped herself artistically on a sofa without spilling a drop of her martini.

"I've seen some of your films, Mr. Somers."

"Andrew," he suggested.

"No no no no, let's not get too familiar too soon." He blushed and she found it charming. "As I was saying, I've seen your films and they're quite good. I think Erwin, God rest his soul, were he alive today and in a projection room, would also approve of them."

"You're very kind."

"Not always." She sipped her drink. "This film you'd like to do about my husband, it's not based on any of those awful books written about him, is it?"

"No, it's based on my own research — close to three years of it."

"Why are you so obsessed with my husband?"

"I'm obsessed with his story."

"And I suppose you, too, have a theory as to who murdered him?"

"Hollywood murdered him."

She arched an eyebrow cynically. "You think the entire community should be put on trial for murdering Erwin?"

"I think it was someone envious of his success and vaunted position who killed him."

She placed her drink on the coffee table that separated them and commented melodically, "What an interesting theory. You know, you just might be right. David O. Selznick hated his guts. Likewise Darryl Zanuck."

"I'm sure it was some other psychopath."

Naomi toyed with a diamond-and-emerald bracelet. "Who do you have in mind to play Erwin? DeNiro? Beatty? Costner? — Mick Jagger?"

"I want an unknown."

She looked over his head at nothing in particular. "An unknown. That's what I was when Erwin discovered me and molded me into a legendary superstar." She nailed him with her eyes. "Do you have a script?"

"A very sketchy one. It needs to be fleshed out." He paused dramatically. "I desperately need your cooperation."

"And if I don't give it, you'll go right ahead with some cock-and-bull fiction you'll concoct to please the prurient. You can do anything you want with Erwin's life — it's in the public domain, I can't stop you — but you can't use Naomi Lawes without the consent of Naomi Lawes." He didn't know what to make of the strange smile on her face. Then she said abruptly, "Michelle Pfeiffer will have to play me. She's one of the few female names around today who has the right to call herself a star."

She didn't hear Andrew's heart singing. "I repeat, Mr. Somers, I admire your work. And sooner or later, in my time or after, some hotshot will do the story and it will be shabby, distorted, synthetic, and a pack of perverted lies. I've discussed you with my lawyers. They agree that you're probably the only hyphenate in this town we could possibly trust with the project." Andrew was a producer-director — hence the term "hyphenate."

"Subject to certain conditions."

The smile froze. "What are the conditions?"

She stood up and paced the room, which was slightly smaller than a Roman amphitheater. "I want reasonable script control." Before he could remonstrate, she added: "I can assure you I'll be reasonable. I always have been, even when I had the power not to be."

Andrew had it on good authority that she had rarely pulled rank when she was the queen of the Majestic lot. "I'll understand when you have to add icing to the cake," she said. "But two things I positively demand."

Andrew foresaw what was coming and was prepared for it.

"I want approval of the actress who plays me, and I want to select the unknown who plays Erwin. And once we find him —" she was seated again for a refreshing sip of her martini "— I want to work with him before he goes before the camera. I want to help him recreate Erwin, Erwin as I knew him, Erwin as no one else knew him, not even his dominating ogre of a mother or his mistresses."

Andrew coughed.

"I'm sure you've heard of his mistresses, real and apocryphal. It will mean this actor will have to come and live here with me. But I can assure you, Mr. Somers, that when I hand over the finished product to you you'll see a performance that will be nothing less than earth-shattering. He will also win an Academy Award." She swallowed more of the martini. "I'm sure you'd like some time to think this over."

"I don't have to," Somers told her. "I foresaw your conditions. I agree to them."

She laughed. "So few producer-directors are prescient. If they were, they'd invest their money wisely. Now then, who's this young unknown you have in mind to play Erwin?"

"What?" He was blushing again.

"You were so firm about an unknown playing Erwin, it was patently obvious you had someone in mind." She tossed her head impatiently. "Come, come, who is this young man and where did you find him?"

Somers exhaled and said, "I found him waiting table at Orso's. And Miss Lawes, the resemblance to your husband is uncanny. Truly uncanny."

"How old is he?"

"Twenty-three."

"Just the age Erwin was when he took over control of Majestic. How tall is he?"

"Five feet eight inches."

"He's also the right height. What's his name?"

"Murray Carewe. He's appearing weekends in Inglewood in a revival of *Outward Bound*. He plays John, the young would-be suicide.

"Take me to see him on Friday night. But don't tell him I'll be in the audience."

"It's a very small theater. Only ninety-nine seats. He might catch a glimpse of you and recognize you. I've shown him photographs of you and your husband."

"An actor who sneaks a look at his audience is not a very professional actor," she commented imperiously. "I trust your Murray Carewe is above such unprofessional behavior — Andrew."

"I'm sure he is."

"Good. If I like him, we'll take him to supper after the performance . . ."

It had been years since Naomi Lawes was astonished, but when Murray Carewe made his entrance in the play Somers heard her sudden intake of breath. Naomi clutched her handbag tightly. When Murray spoke, it wasn't the voice of Erwin Lawes but it had that soft, romantic, vulnerable quality that had drawn her to Erwin. Carewe's looks were very plain and ordinary, but his personality was as overpowering as that of the late Erwin Lawes, whose looks had also been very plain and ordinary. Somers heard her whisper, "Oh, my God."

Naomi couldn't resist suggesting Orso's for supper. She knew it would delight the young man to be the envy of the other waiters and waitresses, most of whom would go through life waiting for *that* job interview or *that* call back or that invitation to dine with the celebrated Andrew Somers and the legendary film star of yesteryear, Naomi Lawes.

When the drinks had been served, Naomi said to the nervous young actor, "Your resemblance to my late husband is quite remarkable. I'm wondering if he might have had an affair with your mother."

"Only if he's ever been to Hammond, Indiana."

Naomi laughed. "I'm positive he'd never been there."

"And I'm positive my mother's never been West."

The evening went swimmingly. Murray, much to the surprise of the restaurant staff who knew his passion for gin and bitters, kept his intake of spirits wisely to two glasses of wine. He didn't protest when told he'd be expected to take up residence with the actress while she trained him.

Naomi said, "There will be gossip, of course, but gossip is the backbone of the film industry and it can only help whet interest in the film. I'm sure Andrew agrees."

Andrew agreed.

"Murray," Naomi went on, "I think you should move in as quickly as possible while Andrew sets to work fleshing out the script."

She said to Murray, "It's going to be very strange reliving this part of my life. Not everyone is given a chance to relive a part of their life. But then, I've always been more or less privileged."

The Sunday of that weekend, Murray arrived at the palace in his slightly under-the-weather M.G. He was awestruck at the magnificence of the vast estate and could hardly wait to write his beloved mother in Hammond, Indiana, who would of course see only the worst in the situation.

Naomi had left Erwin's suite in its original state through the decades following his murder, except to have all traces of the blood and the blood-stained mattress removed. The housekeeper had aired the rooms and replenished them with fresh linens and towels. The bar was stocked with a variety of liquors and there were expensive cigars again in residence in the humidors. Murray was overwhelmed when Naomi led him into the suite, instructing him to call her by her first name as Erwin did and reminding him that she and she alone dealt with the servants. She had instructed him to bring no luggage and no personal belongings, not even anything of sentimental value. In other words, he was to leave every trace of Murray Carewe behind in the loft in West Hollywood he shared with three other aspiring actors.

Within an hour of Murray's arrival, there descended on the suite a tailor and six assistants, in addition to personnel from the best and most expensive male haberdashers in Beverly Hills, who brought with them carloads of shirts, ties, pajamas, hose, dressing gowns, handkerchiefs (which would be suitably monogrammed), etc., from which Naomi selected what she knew would have suited Erwin's tastes. Murray didn't know it then, but he would never again wear a T-shirt or blue jeans torn at the knees.

Once the scene in the suite had been played and Naomi had been reassured by the tailor that he would miraculously whip up Murray's new wardrobe overnight, Naomi began the young man's training in earnest. Before lunch, over a Bloody Mary, Erwin's favorite drink before lunch (but only one), Naomi instructed Murray in Erwin's food preferences.

"Believe it or not, he didn't like anything fancy or gussied up by some imported maniacal chef programmed to run amok in the kitchen. Erwin liked his food either broiled or roasted, never boiled, and God forbid never fried." There go potato chips, thought Murray mournfully. "His fish was always broiled or baked."

"I hate fish."

Naomi stabbed him with her eyes. "You are Erwin Lawes. You love fish. Repeat after me, 'I love fish.'"

Murray mumbled, "I love fish." He prayed it wouldn't be on the menu too often.

"In the morning he liked three-minute eggs with a slice of rye toast and two cups of coffee. He ate a lot of fruit and a lot of vegetables and he had a connoisseur's taste for wine." Murray smiled. Maybe he'd like being Erwin Lawes after all. "He worked six days a week, from eight to fifteen hours a day." She found his look of chagrin charming. "Since you're not producing or directing this picture, I'll trust to your talent as an actor to do justice to that side of Erwin." Murray looked suitably grateful. "Shall we go in to lunch?" Naomi said.

When seated, she taught him the correct use of the silverware. Twice she told him he wasn't eating fast enough. It seems the late Erwin was a vacuum cleaner where food was concerned. "Slop your food."

"What?"

"Let some drip on your shirt. Erwin was a slob."

"Oh."

"No need to look embarrassed. That's what this is all about, turning Murray Carewe into Erwin Lawes. Slop some of that soup over yourself, cream of mushroom slops beautifully."

Murray did as he was told and felt a fool. Then he remembered to ask her, "Do I call you Miss Lawes or do I call you Naomi?"

She said sternly, "Naomi, of course! I'm your wife!"

Later, while Naomi took a nap, Murray reported to Andrew Somers. "Listen, Andrew, I'm not so sure this is going to work."

"From what you've told me and from what she's told me —"

"You spoke to her?"

"Briefly, but she'll be in constant touch. Whatever she teaches you, I need for the script." He laughed. "She says so far you're an excellent student."

"Listen, Andrew. This is not the Erwin Lawes I read up on. I mean, this guy is a mean-mannered, bad-tempered slob of a son of a bitch! Although he dressed beautifully."

Andrew couldn't retain his excitement. "That's what's going to make this one hell of a picture and get you an Academy nomination. Don't you feel it, too?"

"Yeah, sure — sure I do. Listen, keep in constant touch, okay?"

"Of course I will. I'll be dropping by frequently."

The week flew by for Naomi. It crawled for Murray. Naomi was molding him into an Erwin Lawes who was more Jekyll and Hyde than an urbane Hollywood genius. Murray found himself smoking cigars (which he loathed), insulting the servants (which came easily because they were snobbish and overbearing), and where Murray Carewe was unusually neat and hygienic, Murray as Erwin Lawes left his suite in a mess and had to be pleaded with to bathe.

One afternoon Murray managed to sneak away and meet Andrew in a nearby coffee shop. Murray was at the beginning of his third week of rigorous training and feeling on the verge of a nervous breakdown. Somers came right to the point. "What about sex?" Murray stirred his coffee and said nothing. "Didn't they have a sex life?" persisted Somers. "I mean, no sex life, I got no movie. There's got to be sex."

Murray, when he finally spoke, spoke softly: "Sado-masochism."

Somers eyes widened with prurient joy. "He beat her up?"

Murray's eyes teared. "No. She beat the hell out of him." Somers gasped. "She's got all kinds of whips in one of her bedroom closets. Sometimes she tells me I'm an Alaskan husky and when she yells 'Mush!' my back is lacerated! Please, Andrew — please let me out of this. Get Dustin Hoffman. He likes realism."

"No way. By God, this is really terrific. This is Cannes Film Festival stuff. Murray, you're going to make film history."

"If I live that long."

When he returned to the palace, Naomi came hurtling out of the library wearing a voluminous housecoat designed for her years ago by Jean Louis. Her face was an ugly contortion of rage and hatred. "You've been to see that woman again!"

Murray backed away from her toward the staircase leading to the second story. "What woman? I haven't seen any woman!"

"That blonde bitch in Sherman Oaks!"

"I don't know any blonde bitch in Sherman Oaks. I used to know one in Encino, but I haven't seen her in a couple of years." He was racing up the stairs with Naomi in amazingly nimble pursuit.

"Lies, lies, lies! Nothing but lies! No wonder I have to beat you with whips! You're a bad little boy! A bad, bad, bad, bad, bad little boy! I'm tired of you cheating on me! You won't let me have children because you say you're impotent! But that's a lie, too! That blonde bitch has had two abortions and they were yours, both of them were yours!"

"Please, Naomi, control yourself!" he shouted, wishing a servant would appear and interrupt the sordid scene. He ran into his suite, hoping to barricade the door, but she was too quick for him. "For crying out loud, Naomi, this is getting out of hand! I quit! I'm going back to Orso's! I don't want to be Erwin Lawes! You can have him back! *I don't want to be Erwin Lawes!*"

"That's what you always say, you puling little runt! You always wanted to be Clark Gable! Well, wishing won't make it so!"

Andrew Somers had arrived and the butler told him there seemed to be a bit of a domestic difficulty being enacted in the master's suite. Andrew hurried upstairs, realizing that his hunch to come by had been psychic.

"You don't want to be Erwin Lawes?" he heard Naomi screaming. "Very well, Erwin, your wish shall be granted!" From under the folds of the housecoat, she produced a steak knife. "I'm freeing you, Erwin, the way you would never free me. No divorce ever! No children ever! Play parts I never wanted to play! Debase and degrade me into disgusting sado-masochism, robbing me of my identity!" All the time she spoke, she plunged the knife repeatedly into Murray's chest, he having tripped and fallen back on the bed. "You're free, Erwin! You're free!"

Andrew Somers was horrified by the sight of Naomi repeatedly stabbing the young actor. "Stop that! Stop it! You're killing Murray!" He wrestled with the maniacal woman, attempting to force her to drop the knife.

"I'm killing *Erwin!* I'm killing Erwin Lawes!"

The knife dropped from her hand to the floor and she stepped back away from the bed, away from the dead young man, away from Andrew Somers. She said in an ugly voice, "I'm tired of being told what to do. I killed Erwin." She turned to Somers with a sly smile. "I should know what I'm doing —" the madness danced in her eyes "— after all, I've killed Erwin Lawes before!"

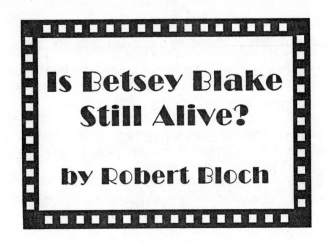

Is Betsey Blake Still Alive?

by Robert Bloch

IN APRIL, STEVE RENTED A LIT-
tle cottage down at the beach. Strictly speaking, it wasn't "down" at
all; it stood right on the edge of a steep cliff, and you had to walk
almost a quarter of a mile until you got to the nearest steps. But Steve
didn't care. He hadn't come to the beach to go swimming.

He'd holed up here for a dual purpose. He wanted to lick his wounds
and he wanted to write. Things hadn't gone too well for Steve during
the past year — six weeks as a junior writer at one of the major studios,
but no contract, and two originals picked up by small independent
producers on option, only both options had lapsed without anybody
getting excited. So Steve had broken with his agent after one of those
standard "To hell with Hollywood!" routines and retreated to the beach.
Sometimes he thought he was going to write the Great American Novel.
At other times, when the fog rolled in, he'd stand at the window and
gaze down at the water, thinking how easy it would be to jump.

Then he met Jimmy Powers, and things got worse.

Jimmy Powers had a cottage right down the line from the one Steve
had rented. He came rolling up four or five nights a week in a big new
Buick convertible. He had a nice collection of Italian silk suits, but
when he was at the beach he preferred to lounge around in matching
shorts-and-shirts outfits, all of which had his initials monogrammed
on the pockets. Often he came for the weekend, hauling a case of

champagne in the trunk of the car. On such occasions Jimmy was usually accompanied by a stock-contract girl from the studio where he was employed as a public relations man.

The thing that got Steve down was the fact that Jimmy Powers (Buick, silk suits, monogrammed shirts, champagne and starlets) was only twenty-three.

"How does he do it?" Steve asked himself over and over. "The guy's got nothing on the ball. He can't write for sour apples. He's not even a good front man. It isn't charm, or personality, or good looks, or anything like that. What's his secret?"

But Jimmy Powers never talked about his work at the studio; and whenever Steve brought up the subject, he'll switch to another topic. But one evening, when both of them had half a load on, Steve tried again.

"How long you had this job, Jimmy?"

This time it worked.

"Almost three years."

"You mean you started when you were twenty? Just walked into one of the biggest outfits in the business and snagged a public relations job?"

"That's right."

"No previous experience? And right away they let you do promotion puffs on their top stars?"

"That's the way the ball bounced."

"I don't get it." Steve stared at him. "How does a guy fall into something like that?"

"Oh, it isn't so much, really," Jimmy told him. "Only three bills a week."

"*Only* three bills." Steve grunted. "For a kid like you? I've never come close to a steady three hundred a week, and I've knocked around the Industry for years. What gives, Jimmy? Level with me. Do you know where the body is buried?"

"Something like that," Jimmy answered. He gave Steve a kind of funny look and changed the subject, fast.

After that evening, Jimmy Powers wasn't very friendly any more. There were no further invitations to the handsomely furnished cottage. Then for about three weeks Jimmy stopped coming down to the beach altogether. By this time Steve was actually in production, grinding away at a book.

He was hard at it that evening in June when Jimmy Powers knocked on his door.

"Hi, sweetheart," he said. "Mind if I barge in?"

At first Steve thought Jimmy was drunk, but a double-take convinced him that the guy was just terribly excited. Powers paced up and down, snapping his fingers like a cornball juvenile in an expectant-father routine.

"Still writing the Great American Novel, huh?" Jimmy said. "Come off it, chum. Maybe I can steer you onto some real moola."

"Like three bills a week?" Steve asked.

"Peanuts. I'm talking about big money. The minute I hit this angle I thought of you."

"Very kind, I'm sure. What do I have to do — help you stick up the Bank of America?"

Jimmy ignored the gag. "You know where I just come from? M.P.'s office. That's right — for the last five hours, solid, I've been sitting in Mr. Big's office preaching the Word. Ended up with cart blank to handle the whole deal. Any way I want."

"What deal?"

Jimmy sat down then, and when he spoke again his voice was softer.

"You know what happened to Betsey Blake?" he asked.

Steve nodded. He knew what had happened to Betsey Blake, all right. Every man, woman, and child in the United States had been bombarded for the past two weeks with news reports about the Betsey Blake tragedy.

It had been one of those freak accidents. Betsey Blake, the Screen's Blonde Baby, the one and only Miss Mystery, was piloting her speedboat just outside Catalina Channel around twilight on the evening of June 2nd. According to the reports, she was preparing to enter the annual racing event the following Sunday, to try for her fourth straight win. Nobody knew just what had happened because there were no witnesses, but apparently her speedboat rammed into another boat head-on, killing a Mr. Louis Fryer of Pasadena. And herself.

Both boats had gone down immediately, and divers were still making half-hearted efforts to recover them from the deep water outside the choppy channel when, two days later, Fryer's body was washed up on a lonely beach. The next day Betsey Blake's corpse made a farewell appearance in the same place.

Betsey's identification took another few days to be established definitely enough to satisfy authorities, but there was no doubt about it. The Blonde Baby was no more.

It was a big story, because The Blonde Baby had been up there for a long time. The "Miss Mystery" tag had been pinned on her when she first rose to prominence in pictures, and she'd always lived up to it, taking unusual care to conceal her private life, which rumor had it was just one lurid escapade after another.

So the papers had had a field day digging up her past. They managed to ring in the name of virtually every important male star of the past twenty years. Some of the scandal sheets hinted that they could also mention the names of most of the studio set-dressers, gaffers, and truck-drivers over the same period.

"What happened?" Steve asked Powers. "Did your boss have a heart attack?"

Jimmy nodded. "Just about. Her death puts us on a real spot. The Friday before, she'd just finished her part in *Splendor*. Studio wrapped the picture up, four million bucks' worth of Technicolor, Super-Cinemascope, three top stars — the works. It's all finished, no more retakes, the sets are struck, the film is in the can. And then Betsey kicks off."

"So?"

"So? M.P. is sitting there with a very cold turkey. Sure, if he could push *Splendor* out to the exhibitors right away, maybe he could capitalize on the headlines a little. But this is our biggest picture for the year. We already set it up for late Fall release, around November, to catch the holiday trade and make a bid for the Awards. You begin to see the grief? Comes November, and Betsey Blake will be dead six months. By that time all the excitement is over. Who's going to plunk down a dollar-twenty to see somebody who's putting out free lunch to the worms? M.P. has to gross at least five million to break even. How's he going to do it? So for the past two weeks he's been nursing a real headache. Takes a lot of aspirin to cure a headache like that."

"But where do you come in?"

"With the U.S. Marines," Jimmy said. "Here M.P. and all the big wheels have been batting their brains out trying to come up with an angle — naturally, they had to junk the whole publicity campaign — and all they've got for their pains is sweat. Well, I got busy, and today I walked into M.P.'s office and laid five million potatoes right in his lap — maybe seven or eight."

"You found a solution?" Steve asked.

"Damned right I found a solution! It was sitting there staring them in the face all the time. I say it — right on M.P.'s wall. I walked over and pointed to the picture. That's all, brother."

"Picture on the wall?" Steve said. "Whose picture?"

Jimmy made with the dramatic pause.

"Valentino."

"Come again?"

"Rudolph Valentino. You've heard of him?"

"Sure I've heard of him."

"Yeah. Well, chances are you wouldn't have if some bright boy hadn't pulled the same stunt back in '26."

"What stunt?"

"Valentino went up like a skyrocket, but he was coming down fast. Then, just when he'd finished *The Son of the Sheik* — bingo! he gets appendicitis or something and croaks. So there the studio sits — until a dead star and a dead flicker. That's when some genius pulled a rabbit out of the hat."

Jimmy Powers snapped his fingers again. "They staged the most sensational funeral you ever saw. Poured out the puffs about the passing of the screen's Greatest Lover. Filled the newspapers, jammed the magazines, flooded the country with Valentino. Made out that all the dames who used to flip over him on the screen were soaking their handkerchiefs now that he was gone. By the time his picture was released they had everybody so hot to see it there was no holding them. The picture and the re-releases made so much dough that even the Valentino estate paid its debts and showed a profit. How did they do it? Women weeping at the grave, rumors cropping up that Rudy was still alive — publicity. Publicity — with a capital P."

Jimmy Powers grinned. "Well, I guess you get my angle. M.P. sure latched onto it! And I pointed out to him that we had an even better deal going for us. Because we had this Miss Mystery gimmick to play with, and a real mysterious death. We can even start a story that Betsey Blake is still alive — stuff like that."

"But she was positively identified —"

"I know, I know! So was Booth, and Mata Hari, and this Anasthesia dame, or whatever her name was, over in Russia. But the suckers go for that angle. *Is Betsy Blake Still Alive?* We plant articles in all the rags. Maybe even pony up some loot to get out special one-shots. *The Betsey Blake Magazine.* You know, like they did on this kid Presley, and a lot of others. Hire some kids to start Betsey Blake fan clubs. Get some of the high-priced talent to write sob stuff for the women's magazines. Like how Betsey Blake was a symbol of American girlhood."

"But she wasn't a symbol," Steve objected. "And she wasn't exactly a girl, either."

"Sure, sure, she was past forty. And I happen to know M.P. was going to axe her the minute her contract ran out. But she was well-preserved, you got to admit that, and a lot of the kids still went for her. We can build it up — yes sir, man, we can build it up!"

No doubt about it, Jimmy Powers was very excited. "And think of what we can do with her past! Nobody has dope on her real name, or just how she got started in show biz back in the Thirties. Wait'll we get to work on *The Real Betsey Blake* and *The Betsey Blake Nobody Knows.*"

The excitement was contagious. In spite of himself Steve found himself saying, "Say, that's a possibility, isn't it? You might be able to uncover all sorts of things. Didn't I once hear a rumor that she'd had an illegitimate child by some producer? And that she was once married to —"

Jimmy Powers shook his head.

"No, that isn't the kind of stuff we want at all! You hear that stuff about everybody in the Industry. I'm giving strict orders to lay off any investigation, get me? We'll cook up our own stories. Make any kind of a past we want. Maybe get her mixed up with some of these mystic cults, you know what I mean. Hint foul play, too. Oh, we'll have a ball!"

"We? I thought this was just your baby."

"It is — M.P. gave me the green light all the way. But it's a big job, Steve. That's why I thought of you, sweetheart. You'd be a natural on this kind of promotion — doing some of the high-class stuff — like, say, for those women's rags I mentioned. So how's about it, Stevie-burger? How'd you like to be a great big legend-maker?"

Steve sat there for a moment without opening his mouth. And when finally he did open it, he had no idea what was going to come out.

"You know Betsey Blake when she was alive?" he asked.

"Of course I did. Handled most of her promotion — Stalzbuck was in charge, really, but I did a lot of the work. I thought you knew that."

"I wasn't sure." Steve hesitated. "What kind of person was she, really?"

Jimmy Powers shrugged. "An oddball. What difference does it make?"

"Was she friendly? Would you say she was a kind person?"

"In a way. Yes, she was. So why the District Attorney bit?"

"Because she's dead, Jimmy. Dead and gone, in a tragic accident. And the dead should be allowed to rest in peace. You can't just go and pitch a sideshow over her grave."

"Who says I can't?"

It was Steve's turn to shrug. "All right. I suppose you can. And nothing I say is going to stop you, is it?"

"Damned right it won't!"

Steve nodded. "Then go ahead. But, in the classic phrase, include me out. And thanks all the same. I can't be a ghoul."

Jimmy stared at him. "So I'm a ghoul, huh?" he muttered. "Well, I've got news for you. I'm a ghoul and you're a fool. A damned fool."

"Knock it off, please."

"Okay." Jimmy paused at the door. "You were always asking me what it takes to get along in this racket. Well, Stevie, it takes guts, that's what it takes. Guts to see your big opportunity when it comes along, and guts to follow through. Guts that you haven't got, Stevie-boy."

"Maybe I was brought up differently."

Jimmy laughed harshly. "You can say that again! Brother, if you only knew how differently I got the perfect training for this particular job, believe me. And just you watch how I make good on it."

Then he was gone, and Steve tried to go back to work.

Jimmy stayed away from the beach for a long time — right through the height of the summer season. Steve figured he was working on his promotion, but there was no word from him.

Then the news started trickling in. The trickle became a stream, the stream became a flood.

The Betsey Blake legend burst open the American public during the latter part of August. By September the first magazines hit the stands, carrying their planted stories. By October the specials were out, the fan clubs were formed, and the television people were combing their files for old kinescopes of Betsey Blake's few live shows.

The whole thing was just as Jimmy Powers had outlined it, only more so. *I Was Betsey Blake's Last Date* vied for attention with *The Loves of Betsey*. And there was *The Truth About* —, and *The Real* —, and *What They Don't Dare Print About* —, and a hundred others. The studio, meanwhile, was doing an indefatigable job tying in *Splendor*. Betsey Blake in her last and greatest performance! The greatest actress of the American screen!

On a different level there was the *Betsey Blake — The Woman Nobody Knew* approach. In this series it was possible to learn that Betsey Blake had herself been the daughter of a reigning celebrity of the silent screen, or of royal European blood, or merely a youngster out of Hollywood High School who deliberately set out to fashion a career for herself.

There were as many, and as conflicting, details as to her love life. And there was much speculation about why she had maintained such an air of secrecy concerning her personal affairs. She was a devout churchgoer, she was a free-thinker, she was a secret Satanist, she dabbled in astrology, she attended Voodoo ceremonies in Haiti, she was really an old woman who had discovered the secret of eternal youth. She was secretly an intellectual and her lovers included most of the celebrated literary figures of our generation; she was actually a shy, sensitive person who couldn't face her own image on the screen; she was a devoted student of the drama who had planned to retire from the screen and establish her own repertory theater. She loved children and wanted to adopt half a dozen, she had been jilted as a girl and still cherished the memory of her one real love, she was on the verge of a nervous breakdown and spent all her money on psychiatrists.

All this, and much more, could be learned by any reader during early fall.

But Jimmy Powers had prophesied correctly when he said that the mystery angle would prove to be the most attractive part of the legend. There was the *Betsey Blake Did Not Die!* theory, which played up the "strange circumstances" surrounding the case, the "unexplained disappearance" of the two boats, the "reluctance" of the studio to exhibit the body in a public funeral. This angle fastened on every conceivable circumstance, real or rumored, which could be offered as "proof."

As November approached, the volume and tempo of the articles neared a crescendo. For now the Betsey Blake legend was public property, and the fake fan clubs had given way to real fan clubs. Some of the scandal rags were printing the "inside story" and the "real lowdown" — Betsey Blake had been a tramp, she had been an alcoholic, she had started out posing for "art studies" and worse — but none of these allegations affected the legend. Rather, they served to strengthen it. To her growing army of devotees came the teenagers, and that was the final victory. Everyone from eight to eighty was breathlessly awaiting the advent of *Splendor* on their local screens.

It was early one night in November, as Steve sat typing the second draft of his novel, that Jimmy Powers reappeared.

Once again he hailed Steve from the doorway, and once again Steve thought he might be drunk.

This time, however, he had more grounds for his suspicion, because as Jimmy entered the room he brought an alcoholic aura with him.

"How ya doing, boy?" he shouted.

Steve started to tell him, but Powers wasn't really listening.

"Guess I don't have to tell you how I'm doing," he exclaimed. "We open nation-wide next week. Nation-wide, get me? No previews, no test spots, no New York first run — just solid bookings straight across the board. Every key city, and the highest percentage of the gross we ever sold a picture for! And who did it, Stevie-burger? Me, that's who."

Steve lit a cigarette to avoid having to make any comment.

"And don't think the Industry doesn't know it! Man, are the offers pouring in. Of course, M.P.'s a smart old buzzard — he's not going to let me get away from him. Two grand a week, five years noncancellable, and that's not all. When the pic opens I get a bonus. Fifty Gs under the table. You imagine that? Fifty Gs, cash, that nobody will ever know about. No taxes, nothing. Let me tell you, M.P. knows how to make a gesture. Of course, it's worth it to him. I been sweating blood on this thing, Stevie. Nobody will ever know the throats I had to cut —"

"Don't tell me," Steve said.

"Still playing it simon-pure, huh? Well, that's okay by me, no hard feelings. I just wanted you to know what you missed out on, sweetheart. This was the biggest coup of the century."

"You can say that again."

Both Jimmy Powers and Steve stared at the woman in the doorway. She was short, brown-haired, and plump enough to fill out the rather bedraggled slacks-and-sweater combination she was wearing. Her feet were bare, and she had some difficulty balancing on them, because she was obviously tight as a tick.

"What the hell —?" Jimmy began as she weaved toward him with a smirk.

"Saw you leave your shack just as I came along," she said. "So I just sneaked in there by myself and had a little drinkie. I could hear you talking over here, so I thought why not come over and join the party?"

"Mind telling me who you are?" Steve asked, a premonition growing in him.

The woman grinned and pointed at Jimmy Powers. "Ask him," she said.

Jimmy Powers just stood there, his face going from red to white.

"No," he said. "No, it isn't — it can't be —"

"The hell it isn't," said the woman. "You know better than to try and get away with that."

"But what happened ? Where have you been?"

"Took myself a little trip." The woman giggled. "It's kind of a long sh-story." She turned to Steve. "Got anything to drink?"

Before Steve could answer, Jimmy stepped forward. "You've had enough," he said. "Tell your story and make it fast."

"All right, all right, hold your horses." The woman flopped into an armchair and for a moment stared at the floor.

"I saw the papers, of course," she said. "They got it all wrong."

"Then why didn't you do something?" Jimmy growled.

"Because I was on a trip, remember? I mean I saw them all right, but they were a couple of months old." She paused. "You going to let me tell this my way?"

"Go ahead."

"Sure, I cracked into this other boat, like they said. Damn thing running without a light, motor throttled down so's I never heard a thing. This Louis Fryer was on board, like they said — I knew old Louie from 'way back. What the papers didn't know, of course, is that he wasn't alone. He must have picked up some tramp off the beach, some blonde floozy hanging around the Yacht Club. Anyway, when we hit she got it, too. At least that's the way it figures. She got it and when her body came up they identified her as me."

"And what happened to —?"

"I'm coming to that part. I passed out, I guess. But I had sense enough to hang onto the boat."

"The boat went down. They never found it."

"The boat didn't go down. And the reason they never found it was that it got picked up that night. With me with it. Little Mexican freighter spotted us just outside the channel and hauled us on board. Me and the boat. I was out cold — guess I had a concussion. When I came to, I was on my way to Chile."

"Chile?"

The woman nodded. "Sure, Chile. That's in South America, you know? Valparaiso, Santiago— we went everywhere. Those little wildcat freighters, they take their own good-natured time when they make a trip. Besides, I sold the boat down there for a good price. Made enough to pay my way and plenty left over for tequila. Captain was a good friend of mine. Whole crew, for that matter. You see, they didn't ever catch on to who I was. All they could see was a blonde. At least, after I got another bottle of rinse and touched it up a bit." The woman gestured toward her tousled hair. "You know how they flip for a blonde." She giggled again.

Jimmy Powers stood up. "You mean to tell me you've spent the last five months helling around on a freighter with a bunch of Mex grease-monkeys?" he shouted.

"And why not? First real vacation I've had in years. And believe me, it was one long party. When I found out in Santiago what the score was, I thought the hell with it, let 'em suffer. This was my big chance to get off the hook for a while and live a little. So I lived. But we ran out of cash, the Captain and I, so when we docked at Long Beach today I came ashore. I knew M.P. would blow his stack if I walked in on him cold. I figured I'd see you first. Maybe we can cook up a publicity angle together, so when we hit M.P. he won't go through the roof."

The woman turned to Steve. "You sure you haven't got a drinkie?" she asked. "Jeez, look at my hair. Got to get to a beauty parlor right away. Nobody'd recognize me. Isn't that right, pal? Go ahead, admit it — you didn't recognize me either at first, did you? Gained fifteen pounds, hair grown out. And next week the picture opens —"

"That's right," Jimmy Powers said. "Next week the picture opens."

The woman stood up, swaying. "One thing I got to hand you," she said. "You did a wonderful promotion job. Even in Chile they knew all about it. And when I hit town today, first thing I did was hike over to the magazine racks. There I am, all over the place. A wonderful job."

"Yeah," said Jimmy,

"Well, don't just stand there. Now you gotta do even a more wonderful job. Because I'm back. That's the real topper, isn't it ? Wait until this one hits the good old public!"

"Yeah," said Jimmy.

"Of course, this time I'll be around to help you. I got a line all cooked up. The Captain, he won't do any talking — he's shoving off again for Mexico tomorrow morning. We can handle it any way we like. Hah, I can just see the look on the face of old Louie Fryer's wife when she finds out he had a blonde on board! But it's a wonderful story. It'll be a big needle for the picture."

"Yeah," said Jimmy.

She turned away and faced Steve again. "How about that drinkie, lover-boy?"

"I'll give you a drink," Jimmy Powers said. "Over at my place. Come along now."

"Betcha."

He placed his arm around the woman and guided her toward the door. Then he paused and looked at Steve. "Stick around, will you?" he said. "I want to talk to you later."

Steve nodded.

He saw them disappear into Jimmy's cabin. It was the only other cottage with lights on all along the beach — November is off-season.

He could even have listened and caught some of their conversation. But Steve couldn't concentrate. He was too busy calling himself names.

Was this the woman he'd been too noble to help turn into a legend? Was her reputation worth protecting at the sacrifice of his own future? Jimmy had been right — the trouble with him was he had no guts. His chance had come and he'd muffed it. For what?

Steve was too wrapped up in name calling to notice what time it was Jimmy and the woman left. When he finally glanced across the way he saw that the lights of the cottage had gone out.

Jimmy Powers had said he was coming back. Where was he? Steve started for the door. He was quite sure Jimmy hadn't driven away, because he would have heard the sound of the car.

Just then Jimmy came stumbling up the walk. He seemed to have taken on quite a bit more to drink.

Steve said, "What's the matter? Where's Betsey Blake?"

"Who?" Jimmy staggered in the doorway, then steadied himself against the side of the screen. "You mean the old bat who barged in here? I hope you didn't go for that line of malarkey she tried to hand out."

"But it figures, Jimmy. You can check up on it —"

"I don't have to. When I got her over to my place I started asking a few questions and she broke down. She was just running a bluff — made the whole thing up. She's no more Betsey Blake than you are."

"What!"

Jimmy Powers wiped his forehead. "I think she was figuring on a shakedown. You know — come out with the story just before the picture's set to break, and threaten to queer the works unless the studio pays off." He shook his head. "Anyway, it doesn't matter, now."

"You scared her off?"

"No." Jimmy gulped. "Don't get me wrong, pal. Nobody scared her. She just left of her own free will and under her own steam. You got to get that straight, see? Because I — I think there's been sort of an accident."

"Accident?"

Steve stiffened, and Jimmy went limp.

"I'm not sure yet. That's why I came over. I wanted you to come with me and look —"

"Look at what? Where is she?"

"Well, you must have noticed, she was crocked, wasn't she? I happened to be at the back window after she left, and I saw her stumbling along the edge of the cliff, like. I was all set to holler at her — listen to what I'm telling you, Stevie-boy, you got to get this — I was all set to holler at her when she sort of fell. Bingo, like that, she's gone."

"You mean she . . . But that's a sixty-foot drop!"

Jimmy gulped again. "I know. I haven't looked. I'm afraid to, alone."

"We'd better call the cops," Steve said.

"Yeah, sure. But I wanted to talk to you first. Alone, see? I mean, we call them, right away they'll ask a lot of questions. Who was she, where did she come from, what did she want around here? You know cops."

"Tell them the truth."

"And queer the picture?"

"But you say she wasn't Betsey Blake."

"She wasn't, but the minute they found out she *claimed* to be, the whole campaign is in the soup. Don't you understand, Steve? People will start wondering — was she or wasn't she? I worked my tail off building up a legend, and now it can all tumble down just because some dizzy old bag takes a header off a cliff."

Steve tried to get Jimmy Powers to meet his stare, but the bloodshot eyes kept rolling. "What I mean to say," he was muttering, "is why not just forget the whole thing?"

"But we've got to notify the authorities. Who knows? She may still be alive down there." Steve started for the phone.

"I know, I know. You got to tell them. But she isn't alive, she couldn't be. And all I want is that you don't say anything about her coming here tonight. Or that she said anything. Make believe it never happened. I just looked out the window before I went to bed and I noticed this beach bum stagger over the edge. That's the way it was. No harm done, is there, Steve? I mean, look at all that's at stake."

"I'm looking," Steve said. "And I'll think about it." He went to the phone and dialed. "Hello, get me police headquarters. I want to report an accident . . ."

He didn't waste words. No details — a woman had apparently fallen over the cliff, such-and-such an address; yes, he'd be waiting for them.

When Steve hung up, the publicity man expelled his breath in a deep sigh.

"That's the way to do it," he said. "You handled it just right. I won't forget you, Stevie-boy."

"I'm still thinking," Steve said. "When they get here I'll make up my mind what to say."

"Now, listen —"

"You listen to me. What makes you so sure that woman wasn't who she claimed to be? No, don't give me that blackmail argument again. Nobody gets drunk when they're out to pull a shakedown." He walked over to Jimmy Powers. "Let me ask you another question. Suppose she really was Betsey Blake. Then what? Why couldn't you have made the announcement tomorrow, the way she said? Think of the sensation it would have made, what it would have done for the picture."

Jimmy drew back against the door. "To hell with the picture," he said. "It's me I'm thinking about. Don't you understand that, meathead? This is *my* promotion, mine all the way. I cooked it up. I nursed it. It's my baby, and everybody in this town knows it. The picture's gonna be a smash, and who gets the credit? Me, that's who.

"Figure it your way and see what happens. So she breaks the story, and there's a sensation all right. Maybe even a bigger sensation, a real sockeroo. But it's not going to do the picture any more good — we've got it made already, just the way it is. And so Betsey Blake turns up alive, then what? She's still an old bag — she can't play leads any more, not even if they photograph her through a scrim to take the wrinkles out. Alive, she's just a middle-aged tramp who hits the sauce. Dead, she's a legend. She's right up there with Valentino and Harlow and James Dean. Her old pictures are worth a fortune in re-run rights. I tell you, it adds up!

"Besides, if she breaks the story, what happens to me? I'm the fair-haired boy right now. But if she tops me, then she gets the credit. You heard her say it yourself, how 'we' were gonna figure out an angle together. I know that 'together' line from way back! She'd take all the bows, steal all the scenes. Believe me, Steve, I know! She was always like that, couldn't stand to have anyone else share the spot with her. It was Betsey Blake, first, last, and always. The things she pulled with me personally! I would have rotted in the publicity department the rest of my life if this break hadn't come along. You don't get this kind of a chance often out here, Steve. I took it, and I worked on it, and nobody's gonna grab it away from me at the last minute. I wouldn't let her —"

Steve put his hand on the man's shoulder. "You told me what I wanted to know," he said. "She *was* Betsey Blake, wasn't she?"

"I ain't saying. And you don't have to say anything either, when the cops come. I mean, Steve, have a heart — what good can it do now? You don't know anything about it, that's all you tell 'em. I've got five grand I can bring over here tomorrow morning. Five grand in cash that says you don't know anything. Hell, ten grand. And a job at the studio —"

"So she was Betsey Blake," Steve murmured. "And she just walked out of your place and fell off the cliff."

"Those things happen, you know how it is, a drunk dame and her foot slips. It was an accident, I swear it was! All right, if you must know, I was with her — I didn't want to tell you that part. I was with her, I was going to drive her home, and then she let go of my arm and stumbled off."

"There'll be footprints in the sand," Steve said. "And they'll check anyway, they always do. They'll find out who she really is, and they'll investigate from start to finish. They'll go all the way back —"

Jimmy Powers wilted. Steve had to hold him up.

"I never figured," he said. "Sure, they'll go all the way back."

"You shouldn't have killed her."

"Don't say that, Stevie!"

"It's true, isn't it? You did kill her. You knew she was Betsey Blake, but you killed her anyway, because you thought she'd queer your big deal."

Jimmy didn't answer. Instead he hit out at Steve, and Steve twisted and brought up his arm. Jimmy sagged. Steve held him there, listening for the sound of a siren in the distance.

"Fifty grand," Jimmy whispered. "I told you I had it coming. Fifty grand, all in cash. Nobody'd ever know."

Steve sighed. "When I heard about the money I was ready to kick myself," he said. "I thought I was a sucker because I didn't have your kind of guts. But now I know what it means to have them. It means you don't stop at anything, not even killing."

"You don't understand," Jimmy whimpered. "I wanted to live it up, I wanted my chance to be a big shot. She never give it to me while she was alive, and when she disappeared I thought my big break had finally come. But what's the use now? Like you say, they'll find out sooner or later. I ought to have doped it out. I couldn't get away with it. And now it'll kill the legend, too."

"Never mind the legend," Steve said. "You killed a woman." The sirens were close now; he could hear the tires squealing to a halt. "I guess I don't understand at that," Steve said. "I don't understand your breed of rat at all. Call yourself a big-shot publicity man, do you? Why, you'd murder your own mother for a story."

Jimmy Powers gave him a funny look as the cops came in. "That's right," he whispered. "How'd you guess?"

About the Editors

Cynthia Manson
is Vice President of Subsidiary Rights and Marketing at Dell Magazines. Also known to the mystery field as editor of numerous anthologies, her bestselling works include the popular series *Mystery for Christmas*, *Mystery Cats*, *Murder Most Cozy*, and *Women of Mystery*. Recent books include *Canine Crimes*, *Tales of Obsession*, and *Blood Threat & Fears*. Upcoming new titles are *Murder on Trial*, *Crime a la Carte*, and *Death on the Verandah*. To date she has packaged thirty-five anthologies with a number of different book publishing companies.

Adam Stern
is a former Subsidiary Rights Coordinator at Dell Magazines. He joined the department of Subsidiary Rights in 1992 after graduating from N.Y.U. Adam collaborates in the development of ancillary products for all the Dell Magazine titles including anthologies.

If you enjoyed this Longmeadow Press Edition you may want to add the following titles to your collection:

TEM No.	TITLE	PRICE
)-681-00525-4	New Eves: Science Fiction About the Extraordinary Women of Today and Tomorrow	12.95
)-681-00534-3	365 Science Fiction Short Short Stories	16.95
)-681-00693-5	Bloodlines	17.95
)-681-41598-3	The Book of Webster's	17.95
)-681-45480-6	Justice in Manhattan	17.95
)-681-41819-2	Classic Mysteries of Sherlock Holmes	18.95

Ordering is easy and convenient.
Order by phone with Visa, MasterCard, American Express or Discover:
☎ **1-800-322-2000,** Dept. 706
or send your order to:
Longmeadow Press, Order/Dept. 706,
P.O. Box 305188, Nashville, TN 37230-5188

Name _____

Address _____

City _____ State _____ Zip _____

Item No.	Title	Qty	Total

Check or Money Order enclosed Payable to Longmeadow Press | Subtotal |

Charge: ❑ MasterCard ❑ VISA ❑ American Express ❑ Discover | Tax |

Account Number | Shipping | 2.95

| | | | | | | | | | | | | | | | | | | |

| Total |

Card Expires

| | | | | Signaure _____ Date _____

Please add your applicable sales tax: AK, DE, MT, OR, 0.0%—CO, 3.8%—AL, HI, LA, MI, WY, 4.0%—VA. 4.5%—GA, IA, ID, IN, MA, MD, ME, OH, SC, SD, VT, WI, 5.0%—AR, AZ, 5.5%—MO, 5.725%—KS, 5.9%—CT, DC, FL, KY, NC, ND, NE, NJ, PA, WV, 6.0%—IL, MN, UT, 6.25%—MN, 6.5%—MS, NV, NY, RI, 7.0%—CA, TX, 7.25%—OK, 7.5%—WA. 7.8%—TN, 8.25%